Praise for Miner

"Spencer creates characters ... ger to see Phoebe's sist...

-Publishe

THE BOXING BARONESS

"Swooningly romantic, sizzling sensual…superbly realized."

–*Booklist* STARRED REVIEW

A *Library Journal* Best Book of 2022

A Publishers Marketplace Buzz Books Romance Selection

"Fans of historical romances with strong female characters in non-traditional roles and the men who aren't afraid to love them won't be disappointed by this series starter."

–*Library Journal* STARRED REVIEW

"Spencer (*Notorious*) launches her Wicked Women of Whitechapel Regency series with an outstanding romance based in part on a real historical figure. . . This is sure to wow!"

-*Publishers Weekly* STARRED REVIEW

THE DUELING DUCHESS:

"Another carefully calibrated mix of steamy passion, delectably dry humor, and daringly original characters."

—*Booklist* STARRED REVIEW

VERDICT**:** Readers who enjoyed *The Boxing Baroness* won't want to miss Spencer's sequel.

–*Library Journal* STARRED REVIEW

A *Library Journal* Best Book of 2023

"[A] pitch perfect Regency …. Readers will be hooked." (***THE MUSIC OF LOVE)***

★Publishers Weekly STARRED REVIEW

Praise for Minerva Spencer's *Outcasts* series:

"Minerva Spencer's writing is sophisticated and wickedly witty. Dangerous is a delight from start to finish with swashbuckling action, scorching love scenes, and a coolly arrogant hero to die for. Spencer is my new auto-buy!"

-*NYT Bestselling Author* **Elizabeth Hoyt**

"[**SCANDALOUS** is] A standout...Spencer's brilliant and original tale of the high seas bursts with wonderfully real protagonists, plenty of action, and passionate romance."

★Publishers Weekly STARRED REVIEW

"Fans of Amanda Quick's early historicals will find much to savor." ***★Booklist STARRED REVIEW***

"Sexy, witty, and fiercely entertaining."

★Kirkus STARRED REVIEW

Praise for S.M. LaViolette's Books:

"Lovers of historical romance will be hooked on this twisty story of revenge, redemption, and reversal of fortunes."

★Publishers Weekly STARRED REVIEW

"A remarkably resourceful heroine who can more than hold her own against any character invented by best-selling Bertrice Small, a suavely sophisticated hero with sex appeal to spare, and a cascade of lushly detailed love scenes give Spencer's dazzling debut its deliciously fun retro flavor."

★Booklist STARRED REVIEW

"Readers will love this lusty and unusual marriage of convenience story."

NYT Bestselling Author MADELINE HUNTER

More books by S.M. LaViolette & Minerva Spencer

THE ACADEMY OF LOVE SERIES

The Music of Love
A Figure of Love
A Portrait of Love
The Language of Love
Dancing with Love
A Story of Love
The Etiquette of Love*

THE OUTCASTS SERIES

Dangerous
Barbarous
Scandalous

THE REBELS OF THE *TON*

Notorious
Outrageous
Infamous
Audacious

THE MASQUERADERS

The Footman
The Postilion
The Bastard

THE SEDUCERS

Melissa and The Vicar
Joss and The Countess
Hugo and The Maiden

VICTORIAN DECADENCE

His Harlot
His Valet
His Countess
Her Master
Her Beast
Their Master
Her Villain

THE BELLAMY SISTERS

PHOEBE
HYACINTH
SELINA
AURELIA
A VERY BELLAMY CHRISTMAS
KATHRYN*

<u>THE WILD WOMEN OF WHITECHAPEL</u>

THE BOXING BARONESS
THE DUELING DUCHESS
THE CUTTHROAT COUNTESS

<u>THE HALE FAMILY: AMERICANS IN LONDON</u>

BALTHAZAR: THE SPARE
IO: THE SHREW
ARES: THE RAKE*

This book is dedicated to all those readers who have reached out to me with such kind, supportive, wonderful messages over the years.

Minerva Spencer

writing as S.M. LAVIOLETTE

Crooked Sixpence
CS
P
Press

CROOKED SIXPENCE BOOKS are published by

CROOKED SIXPENCE PRESS

2 State Road 230

El Prado, NM 87529

Copyright © 2024 Shantal M. LaViolette

All rights reserved. No part of this publication may be reproduced, distributed, or transmitted in any form or by any means, including photocopying, recording, or other electronic or mechanical methods, without the prior written permission of the publisher, except in the case of brief quotations embodied in critical reviews and certain other noncommercial uses permitted by copyright law. For permission requests, write to the publisher, addressed "Attention: Permissions Coordinator," at the address above.

To the extent that the image or images on the cover of this book depict a person or persons, such person or persons are merely models, and are not intended to portray any character or characters featured in the book.

If you purchased this book without a cover you should be aware that this book is stolen property. It was reported as "unsold and destroyed" to the Publisher and neither the Author nor the Publisher has received any payment for this "stripped book."

First printing December 2024

10 9 8 7 6 5 4 3 2 1

Any references to historical events, real people, or real places are used fictitiously. Names, characters, and places are products of the author's imagination.

Printed in the United States of America

Chapter 1

London
1816

"I have heard the Lewisham chit is worth close to a quarter of a million pounds," the Earl of Tynedale brayed in a voice loud enough to be heard over the din of the orchestra and three-hundred-and-fifty chattering voices.

"With a face like that I would need at least that much to do my duty to King and country," a different voice retorted, causing the crowd of young bucks to guffaw.

"All cats are grey in the dark, Fulton."

The men laughed uproariously at Tynedale's comment.

Stand Fast Makepeace, Viscount Severn and heir to the Marquess of Grandon, tried to ignore the men's blathering. He would have liked to ignore them entirely, but he couldn't seem to evade the bloody pests.

Fast—as only his friends were allowed to call him—had scarcely been back in England a week when he'd attracted a group of admiring young fools who followed him like a clutch of besotted schoolgirls. The men—or boys, rather—were exhaustingly eager to learn the finer points of raking from a man who'd once been known as the *King of the Rakes*. It didn't seem to matter to the brainless lads that Fast had absolutely no interest in repeating the exploits of his long-ago youth.

He firmly pushed his court of fawning, babbling admirers from his thoughts and stared out over the crowded dance floor. If a person had asked Fast a month ago if he would ever return to England, he would have laughed in their face. And he would have howled with disbelief if anyone had suggested that he would ever attend another *ton* function.

And yet here he was in a ballroom surrounded by the crème-de-la-crème of London society.

If you are so goddamned ashamed of me, I will leave England forever! Those were the last words Fast had flung at his grandfather—the Marquess of Grandon—the night he'd fled the family home. And Fast had adhered to his oath for more than a decade and a half. He had been twenty-three when he'd left behind the only home he'd ever known and plunged into the great unknown. In a few months he would be thirty-nine.

Looking back on his early years he could now accept that even if he'd not been guilty of all his grandfather's accusations, he *had* been a wild, willful, and ungovernable youth.

As much as it pained him to admit it, he'd once been every bit as witless as the young Corinthians now trailing him about London. Fast had been up for all dares and wagers in his younger days, ready to engage in any foolishness no matter how dangerous.

Fast's first years away from England had given him one shock after another. The sort of reckless behavior that he had engaged in with other young aristocrats would get a man killed at sea. He had grown up quickly and his life had been a constant struggle for survival. It had taken years before he had achieved a measure of success—and even a bit of contentment, if not actual happiness.

Fast would never have returned to England if not for the letter he'd received from his grandfather a few months ago. Claiming rapidly failing health, the old man had all but begged him to come home. Fast could hardly ignore his grandfather's pleas, especially when the man had never issued anything except commands in all the years he'd known him.

So, he had hurried home, only to discover that the marquess had lied. He was not ill; he was alive and well, albeit very, very old.

As grateful as he'd been that his grandfather wasn't at death's door, Fast had been furious at the old man's deception. But after his initial anger had faded, he'd felt almost grateful for his grandfather's ruse. Surprisingly, coming home had made him realize how much he'd missed England. It also reminded him of his duty to his family.

The marquess had not apologized for accusing Fast of driving his twin brother—Perseverance, or Percy as his family and friends had always called him—to commit suicide all those years ago, but the old man made it clear by his actions that he regretted his angry words.

Slowly and tentatively Fast and the marquess had spent the last month getting reacquainted. The old man's demands—which had seemed extreme when Fast was three-and-twenty—now appeared not only reasonable, but justifiable. The marquess wanted what he had always wanted: an heir to carry on the family name. He was desperate for Fast to settle down and marry.

At almost forty years of age Fast no longer rebelled against the prospect of marriage. Indeed, for the last few years he'd begun to not just consider a wife and children, but to yearn for both.

It was because of that yearning that Fast had, in a moment of weakness, capitulated to his grandfather's plea that he marry.

But Fast had two requirements of his own.

First, he'd given his word to a friend that he would make one last run on his ship, the *Vixen.* The journey would take nine months. Only when that trip was over would he return to England and marry.

Second, while Fast accepted the value of family connections and good breeding, he refused to marry an aristocratic broodmare. He would choose a wife to suit himself, first and foremost. His wife's social standing would be a secondary concern.

The marquess had unhappily accepted the first condition—he understood the sanctity of a gentleman's word—but he had vigorously opposed the second.

The wily old man had already compiled a list of a dozen appropriate marital prospects and wanted Fast to promise that he would only select one of those women.

Arguments had ensued and tempers had flared. Finally, when matters were on the verge of becoming ugly, Fast had suggested tabling the discussion until he returned, at which time he promised to be guided by his grandfather's wishes. He'd put heavy emphasis on the word *guided.*

Fast wasn't looking forward to resuming that particular discussion, but he *was* looking forward to moving back to England and settling down, even though being home made him miss his long-dead twin fiercely. Indeed, the ache of the ancient wound was sharper than it had been in years. That is what his brother's death had always felt like to Fast: a physical wound that had never completely healed. Clearly avoiding England hadn't healed it; maybe taking up his family duties—responsibilities that Percy had taken very seriously when he had been the heir—might ease the pain.

Fast was pulled from his musing by the sight of the Earl of Avington—whose betrothal ball this was—waltzing with a striking dark-haired woman wearing an ill-fitting blue gown.

His jaw dropped when he recognized her. It was bloody Lorelei Fontenot! What in the name of God was *she* doing at this ball?

It wasn't common knowledge, but Fast knew that Miss Fontenot was an especially sharp-quilled gossip columnist who wrote under the bi-line of *Miss Emily*. He'd seen the blasted woman at dozens of parties and assemblies, but never at a function as exclusive as Avington's betrothal ball.

Fast suspected that *Miss Emily* wasn't the only *nom de plume* she wrote under because she followed him all over London—to places that were decidedly not good *ton*.

Miss Fontenot was just one of the dozens of newspaper journalists who shadowed his every move, harassed the crew of the *Vixen,* and pestered the servants at his grandfather's house on Berkeley Square. The only reason Fast knew her name was because of her gender. As far as he knew, she was the only female scandalmonger in London.

Why in the hell was Avington dancing with her? Did he know who she really was? Fast had always assumed the woman crashed *ton* events. Was it possible that she had actually been *invited* to Avington's betrothal ball?

Forget about the blasted woman. You'll be leaving in less than a week. Besides, the last thing you want to do tonight is cause a stir. There will be plenty written about you in the newspapers tomorrow without you adding to it.

That was true enough. Fast thrust Miss Fontenot from his thoughts; let somebody else deal with the pestilential newspaperwoman.

He turned his back on the dance floor only to be confronted by his youthful group of male admirers, all eagerly waiting to see what Fast might do next.

"Bloody hell," he muttered. He couldn't bear another minute of this idiocy. He'd made an appearance, given his best wishes to Avington—an old friend and the sole reason for coming to this blasted ball—and there really wasn't any need for him to stay.

You could begin looking for your wife-to-be. Several of the women on your grandfather's list are in this very room…

Fast ignored the snide suggestion. Instead, he headed toward the door.

He could not stay on his ship tonight—not with all the excitement planned for later—but he could go to Grandon House—his family home on Berkeley Square—and have an early evening for once.

***

Lorelei Fontenot watched in dismay as Viscount Severn strode toward the door. She'd been waiting for the perfect moment to approach him all night, and now he was leaving!

Lori shoved through the crowd, making liberal use of her elbows and earning more than a few irritated glances in the process. She nudged aside the clutch of young men immediately behind the viscount and tapped him on the shoulder.

He whirled around and stared down at her, his eyes a stunning frosty blue that appeared even lighter close up.

Lori had been spying on him for weeks and knew he was an enormous man, but she had never been so close to him before. Seeing him across a dance floor was one thing; standing six inches away from him was another experience entirely. Although his prominent cheekbones, chiseled jaw, and jutting blade of a nose were far too severe for him to ever be called classically handsome there was no denying that he was ruggedly masculine and attractive.

In addition to his massive person and striking features were his eyes, which were a startlingly pale blue. But it wasn't just their icy color that seized a person's attention, but the keen, predatory intelligence that blazed out of them.

Right now, those cold orbs exhibited a surprising recognition in their frigid depths.

"*You*," he hissed, the single word pulsing with loathing and menace.

Lori tried to step back, but there were bodies all around her. She swallowed and licked her lips, which were sticking to her teeth. "Er, you know who I am?"

"How are you even at this ball?" An unpleasant smile spread across his lips. "I'll wager our hostess would be surprised to learn she's allowed an ink-stained wretch into her house."

Three of the young lords who slavishly tailed after Viscount Severn snickered and murmured encouragement to their idol.

Lori's face heated under his contemptuous gaze. "Perhaps we might go somewhere private to discuss this matter, my lord."

He crossed his arms, the action drawing attention to his large biceps and massive chest. "I like it right here. Go ahead, Miss, er—" he broke off, his pale eyes narrowing. "I'm afraid I don't know your real name as it doesn't appear on the gossipy rubbish your employer—David Parker—publishes in that rag he calls a *news*paper."

His words stung because Lori happened to agree with his assessment—or at least partly. The truth was that many of the stories David, her editor, chose to publish *were* rubbish. And Lori hated that she was reduced to haunting *ton* functions to collect society gossip to print under her *Miss Emily* byline. Unfortunately, she needed to earn a living, just like everyone else. Or at least everyone who wasn't a wealthy peer like the man in front of her.

Lori opened her mouth to tell him as much, but he was not finished.

"Never mind—I don't care what your real name is. I'll just call you *Miss Emily*." He sneered. "Perhaps I should investigate *you,* Miss Emily? Do you just provide brainless drivel for Parker's shameless rag or are you also his doxy?" His eyes glinted with malicious humor at her stunned gasp. "I'll wager I could concoct a truly salacious tale about the two of you and sell it to one of Parker's crack-brained competitors. How would you like that?"

Her foot twitched with the urge to kick him and Lori had to strenuously remind herself that she was a professional journalist. She crossed her arms, her hostile pose a mirror of his. "My name is Miss Fontenot, but I suspect you already know that. I want—"

"I don't give a tinker's damn what you want!" he snarled. "You people hound me day and night wherever I go. My servants say that you have even rooted through my rubbish. And now you have the audacity to follow me to the betrothal ball of one of my friends to trawl for salacious gossip?"

People had begun to gather around them—not just Severn's cadre of young bucks—and were watching their exchange with wide-eyed interest.

"Please, my lord. Can we not step outside?" She glanced meaningfully at their rapidly growing audience.

The nostrils of Severn's fine, high-bridged nose flared, as if Lori was the rankest of vermin. "You must be off your chump if you think I will tell you anything that you can twist and contort and then print in Parker's slimy rag."

The urge to scurry away like the rat he obviously believed her to be was strong. Only the thought of David Parker's displeasure if she did *not* deliver her story kept Lori rooted in place.

"I am going to give you a chance to admit or deny my findings. You should be thanking me for that opportunity rather than insulting me, my lord."

For one long, tension-filled moment she thought he'd tell her to go to the devil.

But then he jerked his chin toward the French doors that led to the terrace. "Outside," he barked. When the group of young bucks prepared to follow, he glared at them. "The rest of you *stay*."

Before Lori could gloat over their shattered expressions Lord Severn snapped his fingers at her. "With me, Miss Fontenot!" He turned and strode toward the doors without waiting to see if she followed.

Lori seethed at his peremptory command but trotted after him like an obedient puppy. Severn didn't have to push and shove through the crowd; they just parted for him as if he were some Biblical prophet of old.

Once they were outside, Severn didn't stop on the terrace but continued down one of the well-lighted paths that led into the garden. When they were quite alone, he abruptly stopped, turned, and once again crossed his arms. "Speak."

His arrogant behavior made her want to tell him to go to the devil, but she controlled herself and said, "I have recently acquired evidence about a smuggling ring that is being operated out of the West Dock. "

His black eyebrows descended. "So what? There are more smugglers in London than there are fleas on a cur, and a great many of them make use of the West Dock. What makes *your* smuggling ring so special?"

"It involves two ships, five London brothels, and an untold number of street procurers who abduct girls and boys and sell them to brothels in Marseilles. My sources confirm that your ship, the *Vixen,* and your brothel—the er, The King's Purse—are both involved."

His lips curved into an unpleasant smile. "How did you come by this information?"

"Three journalists have been tracking your movements." Or so her employer claimed. Lori wasn't sure she believed David, but she'd seen Severn talking to at least three of the procurers herself, so she felt secure in her claim.

"Is that so?" he asked, his voice eerily without any inflection.

"That is so."

"And what have they seen, pray?"

"You speaking to all five of the brothel owners involved in this child prostitution ring."

He didn't speak. Instead, he just stared.

Lori felt as if something invisible was pressing down on her, growing heavier and heavier by the second.

"How interesting," he said after about a century. His voice was mild—far milder than it had been just a moment earlier—but, for some reason, it made the hairs on the back of her neck stand up.

"Did you hear these conversations?"

"Er, no."

"So, just observing conversations is enough for you to believe that I'm involved in selling children?"

She blinked at the question. "No. There is more evidence than just those conversations." Not that David Parker, her editor, had shared any of it with Lori.

"Who provided this information, Miss Fontenot?"

"I can't tell you that. A source's identity is—"

He turned and strode back toward the house.

"Wait!" Lori called after him. "Where are you going?" She had to trot to keep pace with him. "Lord Severn! If you leave now, my editor will print this story, which implicates you as the—"

For a huge man, he moved like a cat and Lori yelped and staggered back when he turned on her. In her haste to get away from him, she tripped over one of the many rock features that bordered the pathway and would have fallen if his huge hands hadn't closed around her upper arms and then jerked her upright.

"Thank you, my lord. Er, you can release me now," she said when he did not let her go.

His hands tightened. "Tell me specifically how I am supposed to be involved, Miss Fontenot?" His jaw flexed and his pale eyes glittered coldly. "Or am I not allowed to know the charges being made against me?"

She swallowed. "You provide the capital to purchase the stolen children and then transport them on your ship. You brought the buyer and seller together. You were the one who—"

"That is all a lie," he growled between clenched teeth.

How had Lori ever thought that Severn was icy and controlled? Right now, the air around him crackled with barely suppressed violence and the air itself was almost too hot to breathe.

"D-do you have any evidence of that?" she stammered.

A look of startlement passed over his starkly handsome features and then he gave a bark of unamused laughter. "I need to provide evidence of something that has never happened? How am I supposed to do that, Miss Fontenot?"

Lori perked up. "If you would allow me to come aboard your ship and—"

"No."

"I would only ask them ab—"

"*No.*"

"It is not a case of your word against one other person's," she warned him. "We have several witnesses willing to attest to what you are doing." Or so David had promised her.

His hands tightened painfully. "I want names."

"I cannot—"

"How *dare* you threaten to wreck my life with lies and innuendo and refuse me the right to face my accusers?"

Lori opened her mouth.

"If you print a story accusing me of engaging in child slavery and prostitution you will be very, very sorry. And so will your weasel of an employer." His arresting eyes lowered to her mouth, and he leaned so close that for one terrifying moment Lori thought he was going to kiss her. But then his gaze snapped back to her eyes. "Heed my warning,

Miss Fontenot: Do not have anything to do with the printing of these lies."

As suddenly as he'd grabbed her, he released her and stormed down the path, disappearing so quickly into the darkness that he might have been just another shadow.

Chapter 2

Lori woke up well past noon the day after the Avington betrothal ball. The weather was sunny and warm, and her employer had given her leave to take the day for herself, so she decided to enjoy a leisurely breakfast on the garden terrace.

She shared the house with Lady Winifred Sedgewick and normally ate her meals with Freddie, but her friend had already gone out by the time Lori woke up, so she nipped down to the kitchen and waited while Una, their cook, assembled a tray for her. Mrs. Brinkley, the housekeeper, disapproved of such casual manners, but there were only four servants, and Lori did not like to pull them from their duties to fetch and carry for her when she'd been the one to miss breakfast.

Armed with a pot of coffee and a plate heaped with bacon, eggs, and toast, she proceeded to the terrace, where her only companions were the resident pet turkeys, Mr. and Mrs. Vickers.

The birds had been scratching beneath the rose bushes when Lori came outside but they immediately and majestically drifted closer when they spied her tray of food.

Lori glanced around to make sure Mrs. Brinkley—who didn't believe in giving fowl treats—wasn't nearby before she tossed several small pieces of toast to the pair.

Mr. Vickers demonstrated his gratitude by fluffing up to three times his size and strutting to-and-fro for Lori's entertainment. While the tom preened his less spectacular but wiser spouse speedily gobbled up the food. The turkeys lived in a large enclosure at the far end of the garden and were fed twice a day but never turned their beaks up at a little extra forage.

Lori poured herself a cup of strong black coffee and settled back in her chair before opening *The Mercury*, which she paid to have delivered every morning.

She had been awake until almost four o'clock helping David Parker, the owner and editor of *The Mercury*, pull the story about Lord Severn together. It was the first time an article of hers had made it to the front page. Not that David had given her any credit.

"This story isn't really the fruit of your investigation, Lori. You only provided some of the fact checking," he'd said when she asked why her name was nowhere to be seen. "*I* will be the one to stitch it all together into a coherent article."

"But I am the one who discovered the smuggling ring and brought it to your attention," Lori pointed out.

"Fortunately, you had the intelligence to give the story to somebody wiser and more experienced. That is how one learns to be a journalist, Lori. It takes time; don't get ahead of yourself and try to run before you can walk." And then he'd smiled in a condescending way that had made her seethe. "Watch me and learn, my dear child. Watch me and learn. Oh, by the by," he'd added once he was satisfied that she had been put in her place. "I am going to dinner with Mr. Merrow on Friday. He is looking for new and exciting work to publish and I shall be sure to mention your manuscript to him."

David knew exactly what sort of hope to dangle in front of Lori to keep her compliant. It had physically pained her to keep her tongue between her teeth, but she'd swallowed her pride and fury, accepted the paltry payment for the story she'd delivered, and resigned herself to getting no credit for it.

As she read through the article today, she recognized more than a few of her sentences, verbatim.

"You thieving turd," she muttered, angrily biting into a piece of toast.

It didn't surprise her that Parker had stolen her work. What *did* surprise her was the liberties he'd taken with some of the information she had provided. Several of his accusations had no foundation in fact. At least not any facts that Lori knew of.

The more she read, the more agitated she became. By the time she reached the last paragraph her breathing was fast and ragged, and her skin prickled with perspiration.

Good Lord! David had taken the information she'd given him and distorted it almost beyond recognition.

Unless he had other information that he'd concealed from her? She couldn't imagine why he would have done that, but surely it had to be the case because he would never dare to make such allegations without proof to support them.

Would he?

"Good morning, Lori."

Lori jolted at the sound of Freddie's voice. "Good morning," she muttered absently, commencing to re-read the story, hoping it wasn't as reckless as it seemed.

"Lori?"

She tore her gaze away from the paper and looked up to find Freddie holding a special edition of *The London Times.*

"What? Why are you—" she broke off with a squawk when the headline—in bold block letters—leapt out at her: *Emory Wayne Arrested as Leader of Child Prostitution Ring!*

"Emory Wayne?" she repeated faintly.

Freddie nodded. "It appears that one of England's most respected religious leaders has been engaging in more than reform." She gestured to the copy of *The Mercury* in Lori's hands. "I read that earlier, before this extra became available. David Parker will be facing a libel suit. And losing it. I hope you didn't have any part in this article, Lori."

Lori wordlessly took the newspaper from Freddie.

"My God!" she gasped a moment later, having read only the first few paragraphs. "This says Lord Severn provided the information that led to Emory Wayne's arrest—along with dozens of others. And this all happened last night!" Lori kept reading, her whimpers of shock turning to groans of despair by the time she reached the end. She flung the paper onto the table, buried her face in her hands, and moaned, "Dear Lord. This is a disaster."

For a moment there was nothing but the distant sound of street traffic. And then Freddie spoke. "Lori?"

Lori dropped her hands and looked up.

"Is this"—Freddie gestured to the newspaper, "why you confronted Viscount Severn at the ball last night?"

Lori grimaced. "Oh, you noticed that?"

"I was not the only one who noticed."

"My name was not on the story." The excuse sounded lame even to her own ears.

"No, but I daresay that is because your Mr. Parker thought to steal all the glory for himself."

"He's not *my* Mr. Parker," Lori retorted, uncomfortably reminded of Lord Severn's accusation. She sighed. "But you're right, Freddie. Only his greed saved me from making a terrible fool of myself."

"I'll be astounded if Severn does not bring suit against Parker."

Lori nodded, too dispirited to speak.

Freddie gestured to the crumpled copy of *The Mercury*. "I cannot believe Lord Severn told you any of those lies."

"He never told me anything." Well, that wasn't true. He *had* told her that she would be *very sorry* if the paper printed the story. And she was sorry, although not as sorry as Parker probably was.

"I know Mr. Parker has promised to help you get your manuscript published, Lori, but surely there must be a better way to go about it?" Freddie gave her a look of pained disapproval. "I did not object to the Miss Emily articles, but this"—Freddie broke off and shook her head. "Well, this sort of journalism is something else, entirely." When Lori didn't answer—because what could she say?—Freddie asked, "Are you sure you know what you are doing?"

"Don't you think I've looked for a better way?" Lori demanded. "I have submitted the story to more than a dozen publishers. I have loitered for more afternoons than I can count at The Temple of the Muses," she said, naming the famous bookstore which everyone said was the best place for a writer to find a publisher. "It was there that I became acquainted with Mr. Keats and Mr. Hazlitt, and they very kindly offered to show the manuscript to George Lackington." At Freddie's puzzled look Lori explained, "He's the publisher who just released that marvelous story—*The Modern Prometheus*."

"You mean that monster story—*Frankenstein*?"

Lori smiled. "It's not really about a monster, Freddie. It's an allegory for—" she broke off, not wanting to get into a literary debate. "Anyhow, Mr. Keats is friends with Mr. and Mrs. Shelley, and he claims that it was Mrs. Shelley who wrote the novel, if you can believe it." The woman was scarcely more than a child! Lori had been both overjoyed to learn a woman had written the magnificent book and demoralized because she feared that she would never write anything even half so good. Or at least she hadn't yet.

Freddie did not look impressed. "The Shelleys have cast themselves so far beyond the pale that they will never be readmitted to decent society."

"I know they are outcasts, Freddie, but in the world of publishing Shelley is a force to be reckoned with. And evidently his wife, who is scarcely eight-and-ten, not only wrote this masterpiece, but she somehow managed to get it published. Lackington is one of the few publishers who will even consider a manuscript written by a female."

"If Mr. Lackington will accept stories written by women, then *why* are you working for Mr. Parker?"

Lori bit back a groan of frustration. "It isn't that simple, Freddie. I need help getting my manuscript in front of Lackington. Until that happens, I need to earn a living."

"I have told you again and again that I would pay you to be my assistant."

"You don't need an assistant, and we both know it. You already don't charge me enough for my room and board—"

"I feel dreadful accepting any money at all when you insist on living in the carriage house!"

"I like it out there."

Freddie sighed but did not argue. Instead, she gestured to the paper in front of Lori, "What are you going—"

The French door opened and Mrs. Brinkley came onto the terrace, scowling at the sight of the turkeys. "Have you been feeding them?"

"No," Lori lied. "Mr. Vickers just came over to cheer me up and Mrs. Vickers followed along to see what he was doing."

Mrs. Brinkley rolled her eyes. Although she'd worked at the house for years—long enough to have seen at least five sets of turkeys come and go—she still considered them nuisances rather than pets.

She held out a small envelope. "This just came for you, Miss Lori."

"Thank you, Mrs. Brinkley." She waited until the housekeeper went back inside before glancing down at the message and groaning at the familiar handwriting.

"Parker?" Freddie asked.

Lori nodded and gingerly unfolded the message, as if a live asp might leap out at her.

The words were worse than a venomous reptile.

I want to see you immediately. This story is your mess, and you will draft a retraction.

After you've done that, we will discuss whether you have a future at my newspaper.

She refolded the paper slowly and looked up to meet Freddie's knowing gaze.

"Did he give you the sack?"

Lori smiled sickly. "Not yet. He has at least one more piece of work for me."

Chapter 3

Eleven Months Later

Lori was perched atop a stack of packing crates outside The King's Purse, peeking in a second-floor window when something small and hard slammed into her back.

"*Aaarrgh*!" Her startled shriek was joined by an ear-splitting *mreeeeoooooooow* as sharp claws embedded themselves into her shoulders.

She scrabbled at the windowsill for purchase, but her thick leather gloves skittered uselessly across the rough windowsill. Time seemed to stand still as the precarious pillar of pallets swayed from side to side.

And then the claws in her back scaled up her neck and Lori screamed again and thrashed her arms, trying to dislodge her tormentor.

Down the tower went, both Lori and her squirming passenger screeching the entire way to the ground.

The journey was short, but still long enough for Lori to be grateful that she'd had the foresight to empty several crates' worth of softwood shavings at the base of her platform. But even with that to break her fall, Lori hit the cobbles hard enough to knock the breath from her lungs.

The cat suffered no such loss of wind thanks to having Lori's body as a cushion. It screeched loudly in her ear, used her back as a mounting block to push off, and disappeared into the moonless night with a final feline yowl.

Panic seized her when she couldn't breathe, but without any air in her lungs, Lori was at least spared the mortification of howling like the cat.

It felt like a lifetime but was probably less than a minute before she could finally inhale. The first thing she did after drawing a thin stream of air into her starved lungs was make sure she could still move her arms and legs.

Her legs felt undamaged, but a sharp pain shot from her right wrist when she tried to rotate it. It didn't hurt enough to be broken, but it was a painful sprain. Lori grimaced. Wonderful; she needed her right hand to write.

Not if you don't get this story.

That was true.

Something fluttered far above her and Lori squinted. "Oh, bother!" she hissed when she recognized her cloak; somehow it had become snagged on the brickwork just beneath the window.

It wasn't just her cloak that was lost; her money was in the hidden pocket of the heavy wool garment.

"Drat, drat, drat," she muttered. If this wasn't the most humiliating night of her life, it was certainly close.

Lori tried to look for a silver lining in the situation. At least she was alone and nobody except the cat had witnes—

"Well, well, well. What have we here?" a deep, cultured voice demanded from the darkness.

Lori uttered a shriek and scrambled to stand. An ominous *riiiiip* accompanied her hasty movement and cool night air whispered along bare skin that should not have felt it. She hastily pulled up her torn bodice and held it closed while she pushed up onto her knees.

Or at least she tried to do so, but her skirt held her back, evidently snagged on something.

Lovely. Just lovely.

"Is this tattered look the new fashion for ladies in London?" the same male voice as before asked. "I would have returned to England decades earlier if I had but known."

Male laughter filled the air and three—no, four—men materialized from the gloom. One of the men was *huge*—even bigger than Lord Severn—and all four of them loomed over her.

"Very droll," she retorted, pleased when her voice didn't shake. At least not much. "I don't suppose one of you *gentlemen* would help me up?"

"Allow me." The owner of the voice came closer. Lori recognized him as one of the men she had seen with Lord Severn in the past. He was garbed in far nicer clothing than his three cohorts—snug buckskins, a neatly tied cravat, and a well-fitted clawhammer coat—and wouldn't have been out of place riding in Hyde Park. He smirked down at her, his sharp featured face devilish in the low light, and held out a hand. "Up you get, miss."

Lori reluctantly set her hand in his, and then yelped as a piece of rough, splintered lumber scraped across her bare bottom when she began to stand.

"*Do* stop yanking on my arm," she demanded, rather unfairly as the man hadn't been pulling at all.

He immediately released her. "Sorry, love," he said, not sounding sorry at all. Certainly not *looking* sorry.

"My skirt is still caught on something," she said, pulling on the fabric, which stubbornly refused to budge. "I need help to get it loose," she added, when the obtuse fool refused to see that she only had one hand available as the other was needed to hold her torn bodice closed.

"By all means use both hands. You needn't bother yourself about modesty. It's nothing we've not seen before."

"I beg to differ, you—you *cad. I* am *very much* something you've never seen before."

The men hooted, causing Lori to feel as if she had her very own Greek chorus.

"That's enough, lads," the leader chided smilingly. He gestured to the mountain of a man. "Help the lady, Barker."

"Aye, Mr. Gregg." The huge man's low voice seemed to vibrate the very cobbles.

Lori's eyes narrowed; ah, so that's who this man was: Piers Amory Gregg, Lord Severn's former first mate. She had seen his name in the newspaper whenever their ship, the *Vixen*, had seized other vessels.

Barker strode behind her, tossed the broken pile of lumber aside as if it were tissue paper, and then jerked on the gray wool.

Lori briefly squeezed her eyes shut at the sound of fabric tearing. "You oaf! If I had wished to rend it to shreds then *I* could have done it myself." Cool air on her bottom told her the rip was substantial. She scowled up at the giant while trying to hold both her bodice *and* her skirt in place.

Gregg chuckled. "She's got the wind up her sails, Barker. You'd best carry her."

Before she could open her mouth to object to both his vulgar assessment and his order, the giant bent low and scooped her up, holding her cradled in arms that felt as huge and hard as the thick wooden piers that secured the docks.

"Put me down immediately!" she ordered, squirming and twisting.

Barker shifted slightly to get a better grip.

Lori slapped away the big paw that brushed against her bosom. "Watch where you put your hand!"

"Sorry, miss."

"Barker, are you getting fresh with the lady?"

"No, Mr. Gregg."

Gregg came close enough for her to see the details of his face. He was lean and tall and reminded her of a knife with his aquiline nose, well-defined chin, and angular cheekbones that looked sharp enough to cut glass. His eyes were heavy lidded and coffee brown, a shade that should have been warm but instead glittered coldly. The combination of brown eyes and ash blond hair was quite rare and striking. She would have thought him attractive if not for the annoying smirk twisting his thin lips.

He was close enough that she could smell a hint of bay rum and see the prickles of his ashy blond night beard. "I take it you wanted to see his lordship?" he asked.

"I don't know who you mean," she said.

The other three found her attempt at innocence laughable.

Gregg's teeth briefly flashed in the dim light. "You didn't need to risk life and limb to see Lord Severn, did she, lads?"

A chorus of *no's* answered him.

"You could have just walked right up to the front door and knocked," Gregg said.

"It is a *brothel* and I am a *female*. I could scarcely just stride right in."

Another smile slid across his sharp face, this one slow and wicked. "Women are allowed inside."

"Not as customers," she retorted, refusing to allow him to cow her into submission just because the subject was salacious.

Her answer made all the men roar with laughter.

Lori glared from Gregg to the sniggering men behind him. She shifted in the giant's arms, sitting up straighter. "I fail to see what is so amusing. No decent woman would step foot in such a place."

"Now, now, miss, I wouldn't be so cocksure about that if I were you."

She felt a prickle of interest at Gregg's words. "What are you saying?"

He just chuckled and shook his head. "His lordship spent time in America and some of those egalitarian notions they have over there rubbed off on him."

Lori's face flamed. Was he saying that Lord Severn's brothel serviced women?

Surely not.

She had spent a great deal of time lurking in the less savory parts of London but had never heard of such a thing.

As much as she wanted to say something to wipe the superior smirk from his face, Lori knew that he was far more knowledgeable when it came to licentiousness than she could even imagine. Discretion truly was the better part of valor in such a situation, so she kept her mouth shut.

He clucked his tongue as his disconcertingly dark eyes wandered over her face and body. "A lady like you shouldn't be out here at this time of night. Let's get you inside."

"If you really wanted to be of help you would go up there and fetch my cloak."

All the men turned to look at the window. The cloak rippled lazily—almost mockingly—in the sluggish, malodorous breeze off the Thames.

"Any of you gents want to climb up to his lordship's window?"

The men glanced at each other in silent communication.

"Naw, Guv," one finally said.

Gregg shrugged his broad shoulders and shook his head at her. "Sorry, love, it looks like that offer has no takers. Now, quit squirming and allow Mr. Barker to carry you. It's for the best," he added, gesturing for Barker to proceed before Lori could argue.

Gregg strode along beside them. "Why have you developed such an obsession with Lord Severn? Didn't that fracas last year about the child slavery ring teach you anything?"

Lori would have scowled at the slyly mocking man, but she was already scowling. "I do *not* have an obsession with him."

Gregg ignored her heated words and said, "I daresay you might have got away with your creeping and spying tonight it if not for Mr. Pouncefoot-Jones."

Lori frowned. "Mr. Pouncefoot-Jones?"

Gregg pointed to the sleek black cat trotting alongside them, just as if it were part of their group.

Lori narrowed her eyes at the beast. "*You*," she hissed.

The big tomcat cut her a haughty look—as if *she* had knocked *him* off his perch instead of the other way round—and then glanced away, evidently deciding that Lori wasn't interesting enough.

"Lord Severn would have invited you inside if you'd just asked nicely," Mr. Gregg said. "You didn't need to scale the building and risk life and limb."

She forced a sweet smile. "If that is the case then why don't you instruct your giant to put me down, loan me your coat, and I shall go knock on the front door as you suggested?"

The men chuckled.

"I believe we'll escort you right to his lordship's door, Miss Fontenot," Gregg demurred. "I must say it is a pleasure to finally meet you face-to-face after all this time." When Lori didn't return the compliment, he said, "I've been keeping an eye on you for some time now."

"What do you mean *keeping an eye*?"

"I will leave his lordship to explain that, miss." He flashed her a grin that showed altogether too many teeth. "He's almost as vexed with you as Old Joe is."

"Who on earth is Old Joe?"

"The rag and bone man who usually works this alleyway. He considers the rubbish bin outside The King's Purse to be his property. He said you've been riffling the bin and stealing all the choicest bits for days, now."

"I have *not* stolen the choicest bits. I have not stolen any bits." But not for lack of trying; she'd simply not found any papers worth taking.

"Is that how you find information for your stories? In a rubbish bin?" He chuckled.

Lori ignored him and seethed in silence.

"I've enjoyed reading your stories—you've got an awe-inspiring imagination. But his lordship"—Gregg broke off and clucked his tongue. "Well…"

"What about his lordship?" Lori asked before she could stop herself.

Gregg stopped in front of an inconspicuous door on the back side of the brothel and slid a key into the lock. Once the door was open, he motioned for Barker to go ahead of him.

"What about his lordship?" Lori repeated, twisting in Barker's arms to stare over the big man's shoulder at Gregg.

"I'm afraid Severn doesn't have my well-developed sense of humor—especially not since he's been the subject of your prying." Gregg's voice floated up behind her as they ascended stairs so narrow and utilitarian that they must be used by servants.

"Prying?" Lori's attempt at sounding innocent failed miserably. "Er, if you mean me digging in his rubbish, I assure you that I found nothing. What else could he be angry about?"

Gregg stopped on the landing and unlocked yet another door. His chuckle echoed eerily in the gloomy stairwell. "You'll find out soon enough what he's angry about, Miss Fontenot."

Chapter 4

A short time earlier...

Fast was getting his knob polished when an ear-piercing scream came from outside his window and almost rendered him a eunuch.

"Bloody hell!" he shouted when the Countess of Mansfield's otherwise velvet mouth deployed some very un-velvet-like teeth on the head of his cock.

The countess jolted at his yelp, mercifully halting the clenching of her jaws before irreparable damage could be done.

Grimacing, Fast carefully extricated his prick from her mouth.

"Oh, Fast! I'm so sorry. Are you hurt?" Lady Margaret Mansfield caught her full lower lip with the same pearly white teeth that had just been clamped around the most vulnerable part of his body.

Fast examined his rod, which had shrunk with alarming, but prudent, speed when faced with an almost full set of ivories. There were distinct indentations, but no blood.

A sharp rap on the door interrupted his examination. Before he could shout *just a moment*, the door opened a crack and Gregg, Fast's closest friend and erstwhile first mate, peered through the gap.

"Sorry to interrupt, my lord, but I heard your shout." Gregg's keen gaze slid from the kneeling peeress to Fast's prick—nothing Gregg hadn't seen in the past as the two men had whored across half the world together—and lifted an eyebrow. "Er, everything still intact?"

Fast was in no mood for Gregg's clever tongue. "Get your arse outside and find out what the hell made that noise."

"Aye, sir."

The door shut with a snap and Fast turned back to Meg, who reached for his softened cock. "I feel dreadful about what I almost did to you! Please let me—"

He laid a staying hand over hers. "Er, thank you, but I believe we are finished for tonight, love." He quickly tucked himself into his breeches and then stood and helped the peeress to her feet.

She pushed out her lower lip and pouted up at him. "Are you angry with me?"

"Of course not." Fast leaned low and claimed her mouth with a deep kiss to demonstrate there were no hard feelings.

When he pulled away, she sighed and gave him a wry look. "You're going to send me home, aren't you, you stubborn, gorgeous man?"

"*Mmm-hmm*," he murmured, kissing her lightly on the nose while sliding his hands beneath the loose robe she wore and cupping her generous breasts. "That I am, love."

She rubbed a hand over his breeches, cupping his cock, which had bedded down for the night. With her other hand she gestured to the messy four-poster bed, where Fast had spent several pleasurable hours making Meg scream—with pleasure rather than pain—earlier in the evening. "It hardly seems fair that you've done all the work tonight and were finally receiving your reward when we were so rudely interrupted."

"Oh, darling, if you think I don't enjoy worshipping your delicious body then I must not be doing it right."

She gave a husky laugh. "If you did it any *righter,* I would not be able to walk at all, Fast."

He grinned, released her breasts, and nudged the robe off her shoulders. "You must get dressed. I'm going to have your carriage brought round."

She grumbled but moved toward the pile of clothing he'd stripped off of her several hours earlier.

While she dressed Fast opened the door that led to a private entrance reserved for this suite of rooms. A maid named Dora dozed in front of the barely glowing fire.

The brothel madam, Mrs. Marlowe, had assured Fast that Dora had been sternly cautioned against gossiping about her master's *secret* visitors.

"Dora?"

She opened her eyes and blinked blearily at him. "Yes, my lord?"

"Go have Mrs. Smith's carriage brought round and then hurry back so you can escort her to it. Quickly now," he added when she stared woozily at him.

She scrambled from the chair. "Of course, my lord."

Fast shut the door and turned back to his guest.

"Help me with this," Meg commanded.

This was her black satin stays, which she'd slipped on over a black silk chemise. Neither of the rather unconventional garments matched the demure gown she'd worn to the brothel, which looked a great deal like the one that Dora wore.

Regardless of the simple gown and cloak, the countess's regal deportment made a mockery of her humble disguise. Anyone with a particle of sense would know she was a peeress and not a housemaid.

"You shouldn't come here, Meg. It's not safe," he chided as he tightened the laces on her corset.

"I would not get to see you if I didn't take the risk, Fast. You're never at your house."

It was because of Meg—and several other *ton* ladies who'd decided that Fast was their entertainment this Season—that he had stopped staying at his family's house on Berkeley Square.

It wasn't that he didn't enjoy indulging in affairs with mature, sensual women who knew what they wanted from a lover and didn't develop any *expectations*, but he had a great deal to do and only a short time in which to do it. It was difficult to get anything done with a constant parade of well-known society matrons lined up outside his bedroom window.

Of course he could hardly say that to her.

Instead, he said, "These newspapermen have been hounding me night and day since I've returned. They are thickest around Grandon House, but there are a goodly number of them sniffing around The King's Purse, too. Your reputation would be ruined if any of them saw you in this part of the city."

That was putting it lightly. Meg might be a wealthy widow, but her brother was the Duke of Margrave and a stern stickler for convention.

If Meg embarrassed His Grace by visiting brothels, Margrave was the sort of man who'd exercise his considerable power as her closest male relative and curtail her liberty, demonstrating just how un-free she was—generous jointure, or no.

"Oh, fiddle," Meg said as Fast helped slip her gown over her head. "You are such a celebrity that having my name linked with yours would likely increase my social credit, Fast."

He took her shoulders and turned her to face him, staring hard at her beautiful, willful face. "Being seen entering or leaving a brothel *will* destroy even your sterling reputation, regardless of whether I'm here or not. Don't come here again, Meg, or you will put me in the unpleasant position of denying you admission."

She pulled a face. "Oh, very well. I won't come here. But only if you promise to attend my house party."

Fast stifled a howl of frustration. This was easily the tenth invitation he'd received to a bloody house party, an activity he had no time for. Even if he did have time, no matter which invitation he accepted, he'd be insulting somebody else if he didn't accept *their* offer, as well.

He forced a smile and lied, "I shall consider it."

"But—"

"Meg."

Her lids lowered and she shivered. "Oh, I *do* love it when you employ such a stern, masterful tone. Perhaps I need a spanking to encourage me to obey?" She gave him a hopeful smile.

Fast snorted. "You must go," he said, draping the plain gray cloak over her shoulders and tying it shut.

He'd just finished when there was a soft knock.

"Yes, come in," he called out.

The door opened a crack and Dora hovered on the threshold. "The carriage is ready, my lord."

He turned back to Meg, drew her hood up until only the tip of her nose was visible, and kissed said nose. "Off you go."

"Think about my party," she urged, and then hurried from the room.

Fast exhaled heavily once the door closed behind her, his thoughts turning back to the scream and crash. What now?

He pulled a shirt over his head, opened the door to the main corridor, and was just about to shout for Gregg when the door to the servant stairwell opened.

Fast gave a rude laugh at he saw who Barker was cradling in his arms. "Why, look who has come to visit! What a delightful surprise," he said in a tone indicating the exact opposite was true.

Miss Fontenot pursed her lips and glared, her face the color of a beet.

Fast shook his head; bloody incredible! The woman wasn't content to savage his tattered reputation in the scandal sheets, her screeching had almost been responsible for the savaging of his cock, as well.

"Where did you find her?" he asked Gregg.

"She'd stacked up enough crates to see in the second-floor window," Gregg said, and then grinned. "Er, *this* room's window, my lord. She'd probably still be out there watching like a hole-and-corner pervert if Mr. Pouncefoot-Jones hadn't interrupted her ogling."

"*Pervert?*" Miss Fontenot struggled to sit up in Barker's arms.

Fast was truly at a loss for words. The utter and complete *gall* of this woman!

Her green eyes blazed at him. "My lord, I demand—"

"You are in no position to demand anything," Fast said icily. "Indeed, you will be fortunate if I don't summon a constable and have you tossed in gaol." He opened the door to the bedchamber wider and pointed toward the red velvet chaise longue. "Put her down over there, Barker."

As annoyed as he was with Miss Nosy Fontenot, he couldn't help enjoying the sight of the disheveled woman in the middle of the whorish room. She was dressed like a nun and the juxtaposition between all the red and gold and her prim, high-necked gown made his cock—which he'd believed too terrified by its recent brush with mutilation—stir.

Lorelei Fontenot might be the human equivalent of a burr in Fast's arse, but the woman was a beauty. She was a strapping dark-haired, green-eyed lass who possessed the sort of dangerous curves that could lure a man to his doom.

Too bad she was such a prying, lying, relentless harpy.

She clasped her torn bodice closed with one hand and tugged at her tattered skirt with the other. Both gestures were largely ineffectual as he could see the strap of her chemise and more leg than a woman of her class typically exhibited. A remarkably shapely leg it was, too, sheathed in white cotton, the sort of stocking he'd not seen in…

Hell. Fast couldn't recall when he'd last seen something so demure. His women of choice—generally older, more experienced females—

wore undergarments that reflected their sexual sophistication. Frilly, silky things with lots of lace, much like Meg had hidden beneath her maid's outfit.

Fast hadn't realized that plain white cotton could be so damned erotic.

"May I *please* have something to cover myself," she demanded through gritted teeth.

"No."

Her plump lips parted in an unwittingly suggestive way that made him harden. While he was grateful to discover that his equipment still functioned, he was annoyed by the source of the stimulation. But then his cock never had possessed any judgement when it came to amorous matters.

"You can go," he said to Barker and Gregg, both of whom looked ready to settle down and enjoy the entertainment. "Oh, and see that Mr. Pouncefoot-Jones is amply rewarded for his vigilance after you find out why none of my *human* guards noticed a newspaperwoman scaling the building."

"Aye, my lord," Gregg said, not sounding half as cocky as he had only a moment earlier.

Fast waited until the door closed and then crossed the room and took the woman's chin in his fingers, tilting her face toward his. "Well, Miss Fontenot, alone at last." He smirked as her green eyes widened at his cavalier treatment. He tipped her head to the side. "You've managed to hurt your pretty face. *Tsk, tsk,*" he murmured, shaking his head at the scrape and bruise on her lovely cheek. "We'll need to clean that up."

She jerked away from his touch and Fast let her go. He dropped into the chair closest to her, amused when her nervous gaze flickered over his shirtsleeves, worn buckskins, and bare calves and feet.

Something about his state of undress must have reminded her of what he'd been doing in this room before her rude interruption. Amusingly, her cheeks flushed a fiery pink as her striking eyes flickered around the room, darting from Fast to the closed door, back to Fast, and then to the bed, and finally back to Fast again.

"I do not like being alone with you, Lord Severn."

He laughed. "You should have thought about that before you decided to trespass and spy on me."

"Bringing me here to your lair of depravity is not proper," she persisted.

"No, darling, it most certainly isn't."

"Don't call me that," she snapped, bristling like an angry cat. "Since you agree with me, you should let me go."

"Should I? Because I don't see it that way. At all."

Her fetching little chin jutted aggressively. "What way do you see it?"

"You should have thought about the ramifications of your actions before you scaled the walls of my establishment and peered into my bedchamber." He gestured to the gaudy room around them. "You wanted to look in here so badly. Well, here it is." He cocked his head. "Tell me, did you see anything that interested you while you were peeping?"

Her skin flushed crimson one moment and then paled just as suddenly, her lush lips pinching into a prunish moue that communicated prim horror as effectively as if she wore a placard around her neck that said: *Disapproving Prude.*

"I saw enough to tell me that your sobriquet is well-deserved."

"Oh? And what *sobriquet* is that, pray? There are so many, you see."

"None so apt as *King of the Rakes.*"

Fast gave an appreciative chuckle. "Now *there* is an ancient cognomen. I've not heard it for at least sixteen years." Once, long ago, the moniker had possessed the power to annoy and even pain him. But now it amused him to hear the old nickname trip off Miss Fontenot's prim little tongue.

"I don't know why you look so proud, my lord."

"No? Do I?" he mocked.

"Although"—she broke off, scrutinizing him with an arch look.

"Although?" he urged.

"I don't think the name is exactly accurate."

"Really? And why is that?" he asked, genuinely curious.

"A *rake* is a philanderer, but the female I saw kneeling at your feet and—and *servicing* you is one of society's downtrodden wretches. A woman who has absolutely no choice in her depravity. That sort of behavior isn't rakish, Lord Severn, it is predatory."

It just so happened that Fast agreed with her assessment. He'd not fucked a whore since his very first time with a woman, when he'd been fourteen.

He could have admitted as much, but Miss Fontenot was a spying, prying, judgmental little scold who'd not earned the right to know his opinions about prostitutes or any other matter.

Besides, teasing her was fun. He couldn't recall the last time he'd met a person who lunged so enthusiastically for every baited hook he cast out.

"Predatory? Is that so?" he taunted.

Her look of scorn should have burnt the hair off his body. "How like a man to believe that a woman reduced to selling herself to keep body and soul together actually desires one of her abusers and takes pleasure in such debasement."

He laughed, thinking about the wealthy, sensual woman who'd just been kneeling for him.

Miss Fontenot gave him a look of pure loathing. "I'm so pleased that you find the thought amusing."

Yet again, he could have easily set her straight. Lady Mansfield was surely one of the wealthiest peeresses in England and was greatly enjoying her widowhood. She wasn't in any hurry to remarry after she had only just liberated herself from her husband a few years earlier. Fast wasn't her first or only lover and he knew he wouldn't be her last.

If either of them was exhibiting predatory behavior, it was Meg, who had no compunction about regaling all her friends with explicit tales of her amorous exploits with Fast.

Fast, on the other hand, was not the sort to kiss and tell.

Had he not respected the countess's privacy, he could have shared Meg's identity and wiped the sanctimonious scowl from Miss Fontenot's face.

But he didn't have the desire to set Miss Fontenot straight in her misapprehension; largely because it amused him to see the way her eyes spit fire.

"You seem to know a great deal about the subject of *servicing* men, Miss Fontenot."

Her lips thinned and her jaw muscles knotted with visible effort. For once, she remained quiet and did not snap for the bait.

Fast smiled at her in a way he knew to be maddening and said, "It seems only fair that since you interrupted my entertainment with my *tart*"—he'd have to remember to share that description with Meg the next time he saw her—"that you should make amends."

Her eyes widened with confusion. "Amends?"

Fast spread his thighs wide and pointed to the floor between his bare feet. "Yes—*amends*. Kneel for me, open that pretty mouth of yours, and suck—"

"Lord Severn!"

He ignored her gasp of mortification and gestured to the bed a few feet away—he'd seen the way she'd been sneaking nervous glances at it—which was well-mussed from his pleasurable labors with Meg earlier that night. "If you'd rather, we could retire to the bed. You could strip off what remains of that gown, get on your hands and knees, and let me have my rakish way with your delectable body."

Her eyeballs threatened to roll right out of her head as she gawked at the huge four-poster bed and the sensual red and gold velvet coverlet.

"You are—" her voice broke and she cleared her throat, her pulse fluttering wildly beneath the thin skin of her throat.

"Well?" he asked, cocking an eyebrow. "What am I, pray?"

Her emotions were as easy to read as a child's primer and Fast could see the exact moment when she recognized the seriousness of her predicament. She was half-naked, captive in a brothel, and utterly at the mercy of a man she believed to be completely depraved.

"Are you going to—" again she broke off, moistened her lower lip with the tip of her tongue, and opened her mouth.

"Am I going to fuck you?" he asked before she could speak, purposely employing vulgar phrasing.

Her jaw sagged even lower, and her horrified expression was so comical that it was almost painful not to laugh.

"You *wouldn't*!"

"Only if you beg me."

Fast had not believed it possible for her to look even more appalled.

"I—you—how—"

As amusing as her horror was, he decided to have mercy on her. "You needn't worry, Miss Fontenot: I do not, as a rule, fuck virgins, so you are quite safe here." When she merely gawked, Fast gave her a look of exaggerated surprise. "Why, Miss Fontenot! Is that disappointment I see on your face?"

The mocking words acted like the prod of a red-hot poker, and she jumped to her feet, forgetting the state of her gown in her outrage. "It most certainly is *not* disappointment—it is disgust!"

Fast stood and gazed down at her, allowing himself a nice long look at her lush bosom, which was quivering with each labored breath, her ripe breasts threatening to escape her plain white stays.

"Lord Severn!"

"Hmm?" He reluctantly pulled his gaze from her delicious tits and stared into her furious green eyes.

"You—you cannot do this to me!" she sputtered.

"I can't? Because it seems to me that I can do whatever I wish to you."

"I—I—"

"You are in this situation thanks to your own reckless behavior, Miss Fontenot. I didn't force you to sneak onto my property and spy in my window."

"I demand you release me, my lord. Immediately," she added, her voice high-pitched but admirably stern.

"No."

She made a half-yelping, half-snarling sound but appeared to be stricken speechless.

He gestured to the chaise longue. "Sit down, Miss Fontenot."

She held her ground for at least a minute before giving an irritated huff and dropping gracelessly onto the chaise.

Fast resumed his own seat. "What do you want, Miss Fontenot?"

"I want you to release me!"

"And I want you to tell me why you are following me. Watching me. *Bothering* me and interrupting my amorous entertainments."

"I am a newspaperwoman, my lord. I am only doing my *job*."

"And that means you are allowed to invade my privacy?"

"I did not—"

"Why were you spying on me tonight?"

She glared mulishly, her lips tightly compressed.

Fast leaned closer, resting his elbows on his thighs. "If you don't give me some answers, I will have you thrown in gaol, Miss Fontenot." He had no intention of doing any such thing, but her reaction to that news—fearful yet rebellious—told him that she believed he would.

And yet instead of capitulating, as he'd expected, she said, "I am not at liberty to say, my lord."

Fast snorted. "Let me hazard a guess, then. Parker is eager to get revenge after he was forced to print that humiliating retraction last year."

"Not so much the humiliation as the monetary punishment, which almost drove him out of business," she conceded, not looking terribly torn up over the matter if Fast was any judge.

"I am *delighted* to hear that," he said dryly. "Parker is bloody fortunate that he was not compelled to pay any more than he did."

She opened her mouth, closed it, and then opened it again to say, "As it happens, I agree with you."

As tempted as he was to ask why she was still working for the scoundrel if that was her opinion of him, he stifled the question and instead said, "And yet even though Parker has been publicly rebuked and financially chastised he is *still* selling sensationalized accounts of my life to the scandal mongers and generally making my existence a misery."

Once again her cheeks flushed scarlet—a humorous response from a so-called hardened journalist—and she blurted, "I didn't have anything to do with that story he published about you and the twin p-prostitutes from Paris."

"Didn't you?" he couldn't resist teasing, amused by her stammering.

"I swear I did not!" Her brow furrowed deeply, and she added, "I do not understand why you did not bring a defamation action against him for that, as well."

"Because the truth is always a defense to libel, sweetheart."

"You mean—"

"I mean that being a twin, myself, I've always had a fascination with other twins."

Her jaw sagged and she gaped wordlessly for a moment. "That—that's—you are revolting."

It was all Fast could do to keep a straight face. "As much as I'd like to sit here and discuss my sexual proclivities with you, I still am waiting for answers, Miss Fontenot. The fact that you are currently sitting in my boudoir—at my mercy—suggests that Parker is employing you to pry into my affairs."

"Er, affairs?" she repeated.

He couldn't help laughing. "If that was meant to sound innocent, you failed spectacularly."

Her lips quivered slightly at his accusation, but she quickly masked her amusement.

Fast sighed. "What do I have to do to stop your relentless snooping, Miss Fontenot?"

Her expressive eyes suddenly lowered to the V of bare chest that his shirt exposed. More blushing ensued and she seemed to have difficulty looking him in the face.

"Answer me, Miss Fontenot!"

The sharp command jolted her from her fugue, and her eyes lifted to meet his. Rather than look shy or ashamed, she raised her chin and demanded, "Why do you live in a brothel when your family has a perfectly respectable house on Berkeley Square?"

"Why the devil do you deserve to know—or indeed *care*—where I live?"

She winced at his angry tone but quickly rallied. "I care because it sells newspapers."

"Oh, is that what those rags are called?"

"Call them whatever you like; that is how I earn my living."

"I wouldn't be so proud to admit that if I were you."

"I don't care what you'd do if you were me," she shot back. "Trust me when I say that you do not have a clue as to how you'd go on in life if you were a woman." She gave the room around her a scathing glance. "Do you think that you would enjoy earning your crust on your back—or your knees—like the women you employ? Do you really believe they *like* servicing you and your associates?"

"I find it fascinating that you can't seem to stop talking about me and the women who *service* me, Miss Fontenot."

Again, her cheeks darkened, but she ignored his taunt. "Why are you staying so close to the waterfront? What sort of activities require a lord's presence at a brothel?"

"Why is Parker hounding me?" he countered. "I've been gone for more than a decade and a half. I am old, stale news. Is there nobody else in England on which he can focus his salacious imaginings?"

"I'm not at liberty to—"

"Bollocks!" he shouted, any amusement he'd been feeling vanishing. "What does he want from me, Miss Fontenot? Tell me now, or you will join Parker on my list of people who've sorely displeased me. That list is a short one, by the way, so I will have plenty of time to devote to making you very, very sorry you ever met me."

***

The room rang with Lord Severn's threat, making Lori accept that the man across from her had been prodded beyond endurance.

So much for his reputation as a cold, emotionless rake. Something told her that the rage he was now exhibiting so openly was not new, but something that always simmered just below the surface of his civilized façade.

Given his occupation these past sixteen years—that of privateer—Lord Severn should have brought to mind a pirate. Instead, Lori visualized him sheathed head to toe in metal and mounted on a giant black charger. A warrior knight from a bygone era: implacable, relentless, and unstoppable.

And—right now—furious. At her.

Lori moistened her dry lips as she contemplated what to say. What could it hurt to tell him the truth? At least some of it.

David would not agree!

That was true, but Lori wasn't sure she agreed with all David Parker's actions, either.

She cleared her throat and said, "Mr. Parker received an anonymous letter indicating that your brother didn't k-kill himself." The last words were scarcely a whisper as Lord Severn's huge hands fisted at his sides. If she'd thought him angry before she had been sorely mistaken. The very air around them crackled, like the atmosphere during an electrical storm, causing the small hairs on her arms and neck to stand on end.

He dropped his voice so low that she could barely hear it. "Are you actually admitting to poking your nose into my *dead* brother's suicide?"

Well, when he put it in those words, it did sound rather appalling.

And cruel.

All the moisture drained from her mouth at the danger glittering in his eyes, which seemed to have lost any hint of blue and were the steely gray of a winter sky.

"Peop—" her voice cracked and she cleared her throat. "People deserve to know the truth." Even to her own ears it was a pathetic excuse, so she wasn't surprised when he gave a disbelieving snort. "And you should want to know it too," she added desperately. "If somebody was responsible for his demise then they should be brought to justice."

"You are spying on me in a whorehouse because you want *justice*?"

Lori's face flamed at his derisive laughter—which she most certainly deserved—and she recoiled from his obvious abhorrence.

"You don't give a damn about justice. You just want to rake up the muck and see what shit floats to the surface. You just want to sell newspapers."

"No—that's not true," she said, almost as horrified by his vulgarity as she was by his accusation.

"It might not be true for you—although I have my doubts on that—but I *know* it's true for Parker. The bastard hated me before I slapped him with that defamation suit and he hates me even more after I won." He stood and closed the short distance between his chair and the chaise with one stride, towering over her.

Lori craned her neck and stared up at him. She wanted to stand but he'd not left enough room to ensure she could do so without their bodies touching.

He pointed a finger at her. "I told you at Avington's betrothal ball—when you had the temerity to accuse me of stealing and selling children into prostitution—that I would not tolerate any more of your prying." He cocked his head. "Or did I dream that conversation with you, Miss Fontenot?"

Lori scooted back on the chaise, away from him, or at least she tried to, but there was nowhere to go. "Um, no, we—"

"I understand you were once an English teacher?"

She blinked at the sudden change in subject. "Er, ye—"

"Did I use any words you didn't understand? Do you need me to define any of them for you?"

His condescending sneer ignited her anger and Lori pushed to her feet, not caring about their proximity.

At least she didn't care until her breasts pressed against his impossibly hard chest and she had to bend her neck to an even more uncomfortable angle to hold his gaze.

"I understood what you were saying perfectly well, my lord. Perhaps it is *you* who do not understand?"

He lifted an eyebrow. "Is that so? Why don't you explain matters to me."

"Just because you give an order does not mean everyone must obey it. Let me make my point clearer"—she poked him in the chest with her index finger, earning a disbelieving scowl and a sore finger for her effort. "I am not one of your dependents who is obliged to grovel and leap to do your bidding. And I am not a—a *whore* or a servant in one of your grand houses. I pay my own way in this world, and I do not answer to any man."

"Except Parker, it would seem."

Lori ground her teeth at the accusation, which was truer than she would like. "He is my *employer*, my lord. When a person works for their crust, they invariable must obey somebody. Of course you wouldn't know anything about that," she couldn't resist adding.

His lips twisted into a truly malevolent smile. "You should have considered what I said at Avington's ball more in the way of a warning, rather than an order, Miss Fontenot."

"Well, fine then. Consider me warned." She crossed her arms over her chest. She had hoped the gesture, which caused her elbows and forearms to shove against his hard-as-iron torso, would make him step back. But he didn't budge so much as a hair.

He nodded slowly, menacingly. "Fair enough, Miss Fontenot; I consider you warned. You share lodgings with Lady Winifred Sedgewick?"

She frowned. "Why? What has that to do with this?"

His smile widened, until he seemed to have twice as many teeth as other people, and then he turned and strode toward the bed.

"What are you doing?" she demanded shrilly.

And then felt like a fool when he merely pulled the velvet servant cord hanging beside the bed. His sardonic expression made her face scald. "More wishful thinking?" he taunted. Before she could answer, he said, "You will wait here, and Mr. Gregg will take you home."

"I don't need his escort. If you just—"

"Don't come back here, Miss Fontenot." He opened a door that had been made to look like part of the wall paneling and closed it soundlessly behind him.

Lori's ears buzzed in the sudden silence, her thoughts as torn and tattered as her gown.

What had just happened?

And exactly what did he mean by asking where she lived?

Chapter 5

"I could go to gaol, David!" Lori waved the now crumpled letter from the two Bow Street Runners in front of her employer's face.

David Parker was sprawled lazily in a big chair behind a desk that was so cluttered with papers there was no hint of wood. His handsome but rather debauched face wore the sort of indulgent, superior smile that made Lori want to slap him. It was the sort of smile that said a woman was—yet again—overreacting and being overly emotional.

"You are overreacting, Lori," he said, confirming her suspicions.

She briefly imagined hurling his inkwell at his head, enjoyed the mental image, and then carefully tucked it away and said, "That is all very well for you to say as it is not your name on this letter."

The letter in question was from Lord Severn's solicitor. Or battalion of solicitors, rather, because the man had an entire building full of them.

"It is just a scarifying tactic employed by the rich and powerful to suppress the truth and intimidate journalists," David said in an irritatingly soothing tone.

"Well, it is working," Lori snapped and the turned her back on him before she *really* overreacted and said something that would both get her sacked and lose any chance of getting her wretched book in front of a publisher.

She strode to the filthy window across from his desk and glared out at the hustle and bustle of Fleet Street, chewing her thumbnail as her gaze absently flickered over the drably dressed men—and even a few women—who scurried about their business in the light rain.

Every publisher of any note was located within a stone's throw of David Parker's office. The smell of ink and ambition seemed to pervade the stones in the buildings, scenting the air with desire, not just for money, but for the knowledge and fame and immortality that often accompanied the printed word.

Lori *loved* being part of the publishing world. Thus far, unfortunately, most of the stories she had managed to get published were what David called *puffery pieces*—vapid society articles describing gowns and jewelry, and detailing attendance at *ton* balls—published under the *Miss Emily* byline.

Oh, she had contributed to plenty of articles, but never had she received credit for any. And yet she continued to struggle and scramble and obey his unethical orders in the hope that he would one day find somebody who wanted to publish her book.

Lori was no fool—at least not entirely; she knew that her desire for publication had made her a hostage to David Parker. At times like this she prayed for the strength to break free from the hold he had over her.

And yet she could not make herself say the words….

Instead, she turned on her heel and strode back to David, who was idly flipping through some journal that was open on his desk. "Do you know how I received this letter?"

He shrugged, boredom flickering across his face. "I assumed in the usual way."

"Is the usual way for not one, but *two*, Bow Street Runners to hand deliver a letter?"

His eyes, which would have been a lovely whiskey brown had they not been so jaded and bloodshot, widened. "*Two Runners*? That seems a bit—"

"Excessive?"

"I was going to say *bullying*." He heaved an exasperated sigh when she did not instantly concur. "Is this your way of saying this investigation is beyond your abilities?"

"You know that is not what I am saying."

"I gave you this story because I thought you could get the answers we are seeking."

"Don't lie to me, David. You gave me this story because I have access not only to the London docks but also the *ton* functions where Severn has been—increasingly—showing his face."

He shrugged again, unperturbed by her hostility. "That is true. Unfortunately," he said, his gaze turning cold, "that doesn't seem to be much of an advantage. You've been digging around for two weeks and thus far you've given me nothing."

"Lord Severn's brother has been dead for almost seventeen years, David. A good many of the people I meet at *ton* functions were in leading strings when Lord Perseverance died."

"These all sound like excuses, Lori. Perhaps I should give the opportunity to somebody more seasoned if you feel you cannot manage it," he said in a silky voice.

"I did not say I couldn't manage it, David. I said it would take time. I have already spent a great deal of money and eleven of the past fourteen days packed into crowded, smelly stagecoaches haring across Britain." Lori held up a hand and ticked off one finger. "I have traveled to the Marquess of Grandon's county seat and spoken to old retainers, villagers, and anyone else who did not actively chase me away with a torch or pitchfork. When I found nothing at Grandon Castle to lend any credence to your theory, I traveled all the way up to the marquess's estate in Scotland. Once again, I found *nothing* to indicate that Lord Perseverance did not die by his own hand. Incidentally, I was bodily threatened *three* times by villagers and tenants for prying into Lord Percy's death."

David sat up straighter in his chair, interested. "Threatened? If that is not a sign that you are getting close to something, I don't know what is."

"Rather it is a sign that I am dredging up painful memories about a man who seems to have been universally adored."

He scoffed.

"I am serious, David. Whoever is sending you these letters claiming that Lord Perseverance was the victim of foul play is likely causing trouble for their own reasons."

He set his jaw and shook his head. "I have verified the source personally and I am convinced of the veracity of his accusations. I am *positive* that Lord Percy did not commit suicide as everyone was made to believe. His grandfather tried to pass it off as a hunting accident even though one of the men who discovered the body reported that Lord Perseverance was found holding one of his own dueling pistols and the other pistol was lying nearby. Tell me, what man takes a pistol to go hunting, not to mention *two* of them? No," he said before she could answer. "Something is rotten in the state of Denmark."

Lori was amused by his Shakespearean reference. But not for long. "Why is your *source* so coy about offering evidence—or testimony—if they know something? Surely, they can at least provide some proof of what they are claiming?"

David leaned across his desk, giving her his complete attention for the first time since she had stormed into his office twenty minutes earlier. "What my source has provided is a *lead*, Lori. A lead for a *journalist* to follow. That is why I'm paying *you*. But thus far you have brought me nothing, making me wonder if you really possess what is necessary to do this job." He paused and then added grimly, "I am beginning to suspect you do not truly want my help with your novel, either."

It took all the effort she could muster to swallow down the savage response that beat against her teeth like a battering ram against castle gates. David would allow arguments and disagreements with his newspapermen, but he had a limit and—based on the glare he currently bent upon her—Lori had reached it.

"I am determined on both counts," she forced herself to say, pleased by her cool tone.

He grunted at whatever he saw on her face and turned to his desk.

Lori heard the jingle of keys before David reached into one of the drawers and withdrew a familiar bundle wrapped in oil cloth and bound with twine.

He thumped it onto the surface of his desk. "I received this back from Merrow two days ago. They politely declined to print it."

Merrow was the editor of a well-respected publishing house and David's words were like a knife to her belly.

Lori swallowed. "Another rejection."

"Yes. But I was just getting around to giving it to Jessop first, and then Lackington if Jessop is not interested." He tapped his fingers on Lori's manuscript, the culmination of four years of work. "Should I bother? You could always take this along to either of them yourself—you haven't talked to them yet, have you?"

Lori gritted her jaws. David *knew* that she hadn't approached Alfred Jessop because the man was notorious in his dislike of female writers. As for Lackington, she needed somebody like David to submit her work as Lackington didn't accept manuscripts without a recommendation.

David pushed the manuscript towards her. "Or perhaps you would like to submit it to Newman? He accepts submissions from anyone." He smiled.

He was referring to the owner of the Minerva Press, which published sensational gothic novels.

"I could give you a letter of recommendation for Newman," he goaded when Lori merely glared.

She chewed the inside of her cheek bloody to keep from saying something that would end their association without even a letter to the owner of the bloody Minerva Press.

David again tapped the bundle. "Well?"

You are so often your own enemy, my dearest Lori. The next time you are tempted to behave hastily, take just a moment to consider the result of your actions.

Lori clamped her jaws tighter as her friend Freddie's voice echoed in her head.

One thousand and one.

One thousand and two.

David lifted his eyebrows, his expression one of mild amusement mixed with impatience. "I'm waiting for an answer, Lori."

"Don't give the assignment to anyone else. I have some other ideas about Severn that I shall pursue," she lied.

Fortunately, David didn't bother to inquire as to what those ideas were. "Good," he said, his smile insufferable. "While I cannot share my informant's identity, he has assured me that the killer was somebody Lord Perseverance knew."

Lori's jaw sagged. "Are you saying you know who the killer is?"

"No, I am most certainly not."

"But your informant does? If that is the case, then why—" she broke off when his expression began to turn ugly. "At least tell me this much: are you leaning toward Lord Severn as the guilty party?"

"You won't get me to utter those words aloud—not even in the privacy of my office, my dear."

So, *yes,* in other words. Lori felt sick to her stomach at the thought.

"I take it that you are aware both Lords Percy and Stand Fast were in love with the same woman—Lady Louise Sibley—so you should look into that."

"She is recently deceased, so I probably won't get much out of her."

David's eyes narrowed at her sarcastic comment. "I wasn't suggesting you talk to her. I was pointing out all the rumors that swirled around about the three of them. Chiefly, that Lady Louise would have married Percy if not for his untimely death."

"I know that," she said, unintentionally echoing his own words and drawing a frown from him. She hastened to add, "Her father was pressuring her to marry Lord Percy because he was the heir. As things turned out, she married the Earl of Moreland after Stand Fast left England."

"Have you gathered any information about why Stand Fast fled so hastily?"

She knew that David wanted her to say that Stand Fast had been driven from England either by his own guilt or by his grandfather's banishment—or both—but Lori refused to utter the words. And she refused to believe it, either.

"I will keep looking," she said instead.

His lips twisted into a bitter frown. "Are you sure you are up to this?"

"Yes," she lied again. "I have information that Lord Severn's grandfather is coming to London for the first time in years. He will bring his household with him and many of those servants have been with the family for decades. I hope one or more of them will be able to offer insights into the relationship between the twins, especially right before Lord Percy's death." Lori didn't really believe the Marquess of Grandon's servants—especially old retainers—would be so loose lipped, but what else could she say? She would simply have to come up with some other idea. Hopefully.

David nodded and pulled her manuscript back toward him. "Good. That's the sort of attitude a newspaperman, er, *woman* needs if she is to succeed."

Lori clamped her jaws shut.

He took one look at her face and sighed. "You will need to learn to hide your emotions better than that if you have any hope of competing in a man's world, my dear."

Lori bit her tongue until blood flooded her mouth and forced a bland expression onto her face.

"Better, but still less than convincing." David gave her a long, piercing look, and then—evidently satisfied that he had put her in her place—said, "I want you to investigate another matter at the same time you are looking into Lord Perseverance's death."

Dread rendered Lori immobile. *Oh God. What did he want her to investigate now? Lord Severn's long-dead grandmother's sexual escapades?*

"Oh?" was all she could manage to choke out.

"I have information that Severn wasn't just engaged in capturing French vessels for their prize money during the war, but that he was neck deep in smuggling—not just contraband, but slaves, as well."

Lori opened her mouth to point out the obvious, but David slammed his fist onto his desk, causing the inkwell and other debris to jump.

"Do *not* say it," he warned her.

She closed her mouth.

"I *know* he weaseled out of any responsibility for that bloody child slavery ring," he all but snarled, his face an ugly red mask of fury.

Lori enjoyed a brief fantasy of reminding him that Severn had not only *not* been responsible, but he'd been praised to the skies as one of the people who'd helped to catch the vile filth who were guilty.

Wisely, she kept her taunting to herself.

If David wanted to stick his nose into Lord Severn's business again, after almost having it bitten off the last time, who was she to say *no*.

"Who is the source on this matter?" she asked, taking the small note pad and pencil stub from the pocket of her cloak.

He pursed his lips.

Lori groaned. "Good Lord! The same person who sent the anonymous letter about Lord Percy?" She wanted to weep when he just stared. "Please, please, please give me something more, David."

"No, my source is most adamant on that matter, so stop your damned begging. But you can trust me when I say the man is imminently reliable. He claims that Severn doesn't just own a brothel so that he has constant access to free whores, he likes to stay close to the waterfront to keep a hand in his illegal trading."

"But he has retired from privateering—indeed, he has given up life at sea entirely. I believe it is his former first mate, er"—Lori flipped through her notebook—"James White who is now captaining the *Vixen* for him. As for smuggling, I already checked with customs and the last few runs the *Vixen* made have been filled with legitimate cargo according to His Majesty's officials."

"First off, White wasn't Severn's first mate but his second. Piers Amory Gregg—a man who is possessed of such a mysterious past that he must be concealing an unsavory character—was for years Severn's first mate but has joined the viscount in whatever chicanery he is up to at that whorehouse. Secondly, Severn is hardly bringing slaves to the London docks, but he *is* running his operation from his vile nest at The King's Purse. It is your job to determine the structure of his enterprise."

Yet another impossible assignment. Most likely because there was no truth to it.

"By the way," he added before she could speak, "if you can find anything out about Gregg that will mean a bonus for you. I have already set several of my better journalists on the man and they've come up blank. Gregg is a ghost—a shade with no connections or history for all that he is obviously English."

Lori wanted to ask how she was supposed to ferret out anything about Gregg if all David's *crack* newspapermen had failed. Instead, she said, "If the *Vixen* isn't smuggling anything directly into England, then is your source claiming Severn has been running slaves to America? Because his ship hasn't made that journey in almost four years."

"If I knew the answer then I wouldn't be asking you, would I?" he asked acidly.

Lori glared sightlessly down at her note pad, willing herself not to explode.

"One more thing."

Good. God. She bit the inside of her cheek to keep from screaming, lifted her eyes to David, and said, "Yes?"

"The last journey Severn was on—after he left England last summer—his ship was alleged to have rescued a number of mutineers from the *Sea Ranger*."

"*What?*" she all-but shrieked.

David nodded smugly. "I have a signed confession attesting to the fact that he picked up several mutineers after they ran the ship aground on some godforsaken rock off the coast of South America."

"I do not believe it! Severn operated under a letter of marque; he would be honor bound to bring any mutineers back home to stand trial."

"I know all that, Lori," David said, not bothering to hide his annoyance. "But he didn't bring any mutineers back, did he?"

"You said he *rescued* them. What do you mean by that? Rescued them from what or whom? And if he didn't bring them here, where did he take them? And why?"

"Those are all excellent questions, and I look forward to the answers you find."

"Accusing Severn of abetting mutineers is a deadly serious matter." A great deal more serious than the accusations David had made against Severn last year.

David's smile was snakelike and reminded her of why she didn't trust him any farther than she could throw him. "Oh, my dear Lori, I'm not making any accusations. I will wait and do that *after* you do your job and bring me the evidence I need."

What a novel concept for a journalist, she wanted to retort. Lori held his gaze for a long moment before nodding. "Very well. I will see what I can find."

"Good." He abruptly broke eye contact and began to shuffle the papers on his desk, her cue to leave. "Now. If there is nothing else, you are free to leave."

Lori glared at the top of his bowed head for a long moment, willing it to combust. When her fantasy failed to materialize, she turned on her heel and left without another word.

David Parker was an infuriating, odious toad. The only way she could be rid of him—and get her book before a reputable publisher—was to find the information he had so arrogantly demanded. To allow his obnoxious behavior to drive her to do something reckless would only confirm his belief that she was incapable of the job she had been given.

As Lori stormed past his startled clerk, she swore to herself then and there that she would do whatever it took to prove the insufferable rodent wrong.

Or die trying.

Chapter 6

"Miss Fontenot went to David Parker's office immediately after receiving your letter," Gregg said, examining his neatly trimmed fingernails as he sprawled in the oversized wingchair in front of Fast's desk.

Fast smirked at that news. "I hope she went there to give the bastard a proper raking."

Gregg laughed. "I would not be surprised; she looked as angry as a hornet." Mr. Pouncefoot-Jones leapt onto his lap, and he absently scratched the big black tomcat behind the ears, his gaze suddenly growing distant. "I don't think Lady Sedgewick was in the house when the Runners called."

Fast frowned. "What has that to do with anything?"

Gregg shrugged. "Just an observation."

"You're not…er, interested in her, are you?"

Gregg's eyes narrowed. "What if I were?"

"You needn't snap my nose off!" he said, amused by the other man's baleful glare. Rather than be repulsed by Gregg's obvious displeasure, Fast said, "You may fancy whomever you please—it's certainly makes no odds to me—but you should know the countess earns her crust by grinding the spontaneity out of young women and training them to be demure, obedient wives who would never embarrass their aristocrat husbands."

"I am perfectly aware of what she does to earn her crust," Gregg said, his eyes harder than granite. "What, pray, is your point, Severn?"

"What I am trying to say, very clumsily, is that Lady Sedgewick is a stickler for propriety and would never spare a glance for a former privateer. No matter how handsome or wealthy the man might be."

"I am exceedingly flattered by your concern for me, Severn," Gregg said acidly.

Fast barked a laugh. "That's me put in my place." He had not wanted to speak of such matters to begin with but felt that Piers Gregg—a man unaccustomed to the ways of the *haute ton*—deserved to know the lay of the land.

And now that Fast had discharged that duty he could dismiss it from his mind and return to a subject that truly interested him: Miss Fontenot.

"How long was she at Parker's office?" he asked.

"If you're asking whether she stayed long enough for a fuck and cuddle, the answer is *yes.*"

"That was not what I was asking," Fast snapped, unaccountably irritated by the other man's observation.

Rather than appear abashed, Gregg grinned, his icy anger of less than a minute before—when Fast had meddled in *his* business—nowhere to be seen. "To answer your question, Miss Fontenot was at Parker's office for perhaps a quarter of an hour. From there, she toddled down the street to *The Times.*"

Fast sat up straighter. "Did she, by God? Do you think Parker gave her the sack and she is looking for work elsewhere?"

His henchman laughed—either at the question or Fast's hopeful tone—and said, "No."

"How can you be so certain?"

"Because I waited for her—for over three bloody hours—and then ventured inside to find out what our little spy had been getting up to." Gregg clucked his tongue. "You are not going to like this Severn."

"What?"

"She visited the archives and asked the clerk for all the issues that contained stories relating in any way to the *Sea Ranger* mutiny. She was especially interested in the names of the mutineers who were still at liberty."

"Fuck! Bastard! Shit!" Fast grabbed the first thing to hand—an ugly bronze paperweight—and hurled it across the room. It struck a shelf of books and made a distinctly unsatisfying *thunk*ing sound before falling to the floor with a clatter. "That fucking Parker knows about Joe Jensen! How the devil did he find out, Gregg? *How*?"

"I wish I knew, my lord," Gregg said, looking as grim as Fast felt.

Fast slumped back in his chair, too stunned to speak.

For more than sixteen years Fast believed that *he* was the reason his brother Percy had committed suicide. But a year ago Fast had discovered, to his utter shock that he had been wrong all that time. Percy hadn't killed himself; he had been murdered.

The truth had come to Fast through a man named Joe Jensen.

Jensen had grown up on a tenant farm not far from Fast's grandfather's country estate. They'd been close in age and had knocked around a bit when they were young boys, before Fast and Percy had been shipped off to Eton.

It had been at least twenty years since Fast had seen Jensen and he would have forgotten all about the man if not for the fact that he'd seen Jensen's name on the navy's list of men involved in the *Sea Ranger* mutiny.

Jensen was one of the fifty or so crew members who had evaded capture. Fast encountered him in a small port town in Venezuela where Jensen was eking out an existence tending bar at a wharf side tavern. It was doubtful that Fast would have noticed Jensen if the man hadn't dropped two pints of ale and sprinted from the pub the moment he'd seen Fast's face.

Naturally, Fast had been too curious not to follow him.

When he had read about the mutiny in the newspapers he'd greatly sympathized with the crew. He had met the captain of the *Sea Ranger*, Hugh Pigot, on several occasions and there was no denying he'd been a savage, cruel man who'd abused his crew abominably.

However, mutiny was mutiny, so upon discovering Jensen's identity Fast had been determined to bring him back to England to face justice.

Just as he'd been about to hand Jensen over to a local smith to be fitted for leg irons for his journey home, the man had blurted out that Percy had not committed suicide.

Flabbergasted and infuriated, Fast had grabbed Jensen by the throat and demanded to know what the hell he was talking about. Jensen had proceeded to spill one startling detail after another. On their own, none of the things he'd shared about Percy's death would have convinced him. But then Joe had admitted that it had been his very own brother—Albert Jensen—who had been hired to fire the pistol that killed Percy.

No amount of threatening or beating had been enough to convince Joe to divulge the name of the person who'd paid Albert. Nor was it possible for Fast to track down Albert and get the truth out of him as the man had died years before.

Joe had said that if Fast brought him directly back for trial, he would never tell him the killer's name.

In the end, Joe had offered Fast a deal. He was an extremely sick man and dying of consumption—visibly ill at the time—and agreed to accompany Fast as far as Gran Canaria, which was the *Vixen's* last stop before home. He promised to wait there while Fast discovered the whereabouts of Joe's mother and two sisters. When he found the women, Fast would also help them with money and shelter if they needed it.

Once Fast had taken care of his part of the bargain, Joe would return to England, hand over Albert's signed deathbed confession, and give himself up to the authorities and testify to the veracity of the confession.

With no other alternative, Fast had accepted Joe's offer. They had agreed that Fast had six months to produce Joe's family after he'd returned to England. That had been five months ago, and time was quickly running out.

"My lord?"

Fast looked up at the sound of Gregg's hesitant voice.

"I'm over my snit," Fast said, not entirely telling the truth but ready to get on with matters. "Who is feeding Parker all this information?"

Gregg inhaled deeply and then exhaled after a long moment. "Well, only nine of us were in the room with Jensen when we discovered his identity. You, me, Barker, White, Shaver, Norris, Chenier, Keating, and Joe Jensen, himself." Gregg snorted. "I think we can strike you and me off the list of suspects."

"Surely Jensen would never tell anyone?"

"Maybe he is hoping to extort money from the man behind your brother's murder?"

After a long moment Fast grudgingly said, "That is an excellent point. However—and perhaps this makes me a fool—I believe Jensen's dealings with me have been both honest and honorable."

Gregg nodded. "My gut tells me the same."

"I am relieved we concur. As to the other names on your list; I don't believe any of them would have betrayed me. They have all of them have been with me since my first voyage on the *Vixen.* I cannot accept that I have been so wrong in judging their characters after all these years."

"I happen to agree."

"So that means somebody else on the ship overheard my conversation with Jensen." Fast scowled. "Lord knows it would have been easy enough for anyone to press an ear to the wall of the wardroom and eavesdrop. The crew of *The Vixen* is between sixty and seventy men at any given time."

"Of that number between forty and fifty have been with you for at least five years. I feel certain your traitor is not among their number. Not just because they are loyal, but because they'd need to have rats in their garrets to jeopardize their jobs. Those men are well aware that you butter their bread, my lord, and they are extremely fond of how thick the butter is."

Fast snorted at the other man's terminology, but Gregg was right: he *was* generous with the prize money the *Vixen* took in and gave bigger shares than any other captain he knew. His actions weren't entirely altruistic, he also paid well because it helped him retain his employees.

"Assuming your reasoning is sound, that still leaves at least fifteen or twenty men who—"

"Remember those men we hired in Gran Canaria?" Gregg interrupted, his gaze intense.

Fast squinted as he trolled his memory. "I vaguely remember. Three men, wasn't it? But they were only with us for that leg of the journey."

"*Two* of them returned home but one came back with us—Emilio Garcia."

"Your memory is terrifying," Fast said.

"It is," Gregg admitted with a faint smile. "But in Garcia's case it isn't so surprising as he rather stands out. He wears two earrings in his right ear, gold rings joined by a short chain. It's distinctive."

"I recall him, now," Fast said. "I don't suppose you know whether Garcia signed on with James and left with the *Vixen*?" James White was Fast's erstwhile second mate and the current captain of *The Vixen* now that Fast and Gregg had left the privateering life behind them.

"I don't know, but I'll make it my business to find out right away. I'll draw up a list of the others who might be probable suspects as well."

"Then I shall leave the matter in your hands."

Gregg opened his mouth, but then closed it and began to stand.

"What is it?" Fast demanded.

"It's just—well, I'm losing hope that we will ever find Ellie Jensen. I'm not sure we'll even learn what happened to her."

They had discovered early in their search that Jensen's mother and older sister had both perished in a workhouse more than a decade ago. But the youngest girl seemed to have disappeared into thin air.

"Keep looking," Fast said grimly.

"What are you going to do if Jensen refuses to keep his part of the bargain, my lord? Will you just let him go as you agreed to do?"

"I don't know how far I'm willing to go," Fast admitted. "That thought keeps me awake at night. I just hope that Jensen wants to see the killer punished badly enough that he'll tell me regardless."

"And if he doesn't?"

He smiled grimly. "Then I suppose I will discover to what lengths I'm prepared to go to find my brother's killer."

Chapter 7

Several Evenings Later...

Lori waited until Freddie had a spare moment—not easy when her friend had her hands full with the beautiful, mischievous Conroy twins she was launching—before sidling up to her and saying, "Thank you so much for getting me into this ball."

Freddie turned her unusual fawn-colored eyes on Lori, the expression in them as unreadable as ever. "You are welcome, Lori."

"I was wondering—"

"If you could sneak away and eavesdrop and gather information for your *Miss Emily* column? Or were you hoping to slip away from the ball entirely and gather information for one of Mr. Parker's other stories?"

Lori's face heated. "Er," was all she could manage.

"*Er*, indeed. Of course you may go, Lori. But before you leave, I have one question."

Lori hated to ask, but… "Yes?"

"When were you planning on telling me that two Bow Street Runners visited our house?"

Lori grimaced. "Ah. I was going to tell you, I just, er… Well, I was waiting for the right time."

"What would have happened if Runners had come to call when one of my clients was sitting in our drawing room?"

Lori briefly closed her eyes. "I am *so* sorry to bring such trouble to your very doorstep, Freddie. I will move out. I can go and—"

"I don't want you to leave. And I don't want you to stop what you are doing, either. I just want you to be honest with me." The pain beneath her words was worse than anger would have been.

"I will tell you everything from now on, Fred. I promise."

Freddie made a ladylike sound of disbelief. "I don't need to know *everything,* just anything important—like Bow Street Runners."

There was no point in confessing that the Runners had been as big a surprise to Lori as they had to Freddie. The truth was that Lori *should* have known that trespassing on Viscount Severn's property could have such ramifications.

"I swear that I'll not let that happen again," Lori said.

"There is one other thing," Freddie said.

Oh, God. What now?

"Anything," Lori said, hoping it wasn't too painful.

"You have worn the same two gowns for months and they are beginning to look… tired. People know you are my housemate and friend, Lori. Many are also aware that you aid me in my work from time-to-time. As such, your appearance—"

"Reflects poorly on you," Lori finished, not wanting to make her friend say the words. "I know, and I am so—"

"I don't tell you this to make you feel ashamed, or to make you apologize. I just want you to give me both gowns for refurbishment."

"Oh! Er, that's terribly kind of you, Freddie. But, you don't—"

Freddie set a hand over Lori's. "I enjoy doing such things, Lori. It will not be a burden, but a true pleasure."

She saw the truth in Freddie's warm gaze and said, "Then I accept. Thank you."

Freddie smiled and they both turned and watched the dancers, entertaining their own thoughts in silence.

Lori had just opened her mouth to take her leave when an angel glided into view. "Good Lord, who is that?" she asked, riveted by the vision of perfection dancing the quadrille with the recently out-of-mourning Earl of Moreland.

Freddie did not need to ask who she meant. "That is Miss Demelza Pascoe, the only daughter of Bryok Pascoe."

"So *that's* the girl all the sporting books call the *Dry Goods Princess*!"

"That is excessively vulgar, Lori."

"Sorry," Lori murmured, wiping the smirk from her face. "She is the most beautiful woman I've ever seen. And so young! I feel ancient just looking at her. How old is she?"

"She had her seventeenth birthday only a few weeks ago."

"Is that disapproval I hear in your voice?"

"Yes," Freddie said without hesitation.

"Seventeen isn't a terribly early age to have one's first Season."

"It is for her."

"What do you mean?"

"Miss Pascoe's mother died giving birth to her and her father did not want to be bothered with the raising of her, so she has spent most of her life in a convent. The girl is as innocent as a kitten."

Lori gestured to Freddie's current clients, who were dancing as well. "The Conroy twins just turned eighteen so they are scarcely a year older."

"That is true, but the twins have spent the last two years attending country assemblies and moving in society, even if it was rather rustic. They haven't been torn from a nunnery and pitchforked into the *ton* with all the subtlety of a veal calf being led to the auction block."

Lori blinked at her friend's uncharacteristic vehemence. "I'm surprised Mr. Pascoe didn't ask you to launch her," she said after a moment.

"He did. I told him I would sponsor her if he waited, but he refused."

"He wouldn't agree to wait another year?"

Freddie hesitated, a delicate pink color staining her exquisite cheekbones. "I could not promise him next Season as I had already accepted a client. In any case, I advised Mr. Pascoe that it would be better to wait two years. The girl is beautiful *and* an heiress. She doesn't need to fling herself into a marriage right away."

"I pity her," Lori said, her eyes once again drawn to the beauty and her partner. "Especially as she has already attracted Moreland's eye. He is a handsome man, but I cannot like him for some reason. I daresay he's in the market for a new wife now that his mourning period is over."

Freddie clucked her tongue. "I did not know his wife personally, but I *do* know the poor woman was with child almost constantly for the past sixteen years and gave Moreland only daughters."

Lori snorted. "*Only* daughters. Lord, Freddie, I never believed you to be so harsh on our sex."

"You misunderstand me, Lori. If there is no son, then everything will pass to some relative and those daughters will be left to fend for themselves." Again, she spoke with unaccustomed vehemence.

Lori desperately wanted to ask Freddie if that is what happened to her, but she bit her tongue. Her reserved friend had never spoken about her past in all the years Lori had known her. It was doubtful that she'd suddenly share the most intimate details of her life in the middle of a ballroom.

Instead, Lori changed the subject. "You said you have already accepted a client for next year—who is it?"

Freddie's lips tightened until they were almost white. "The Duke of Plimpton's daughter."

"But I thought you had told His Grace *no.*"

"I had."

"What made you change your mind?"

"Honey wrote and begged me to reconsider my decision."

All Lori could manage at this fascinating intelligence was, "Oh."

Honey—or Honoria Keyes as she was professionally known—had been a teacher with Lori, Freddie, and four other dear friends who had all met at the Stefani Academy for Young Ladies.

After the school closed, Honey had flourished as a portrait painter, which is how she'd met her husband, the Marquess of Fairchild, the Duke of Plimpton's brother and heir.

Honey's relationship with the duke should have guaranteed Freddie's sponsorship for his daughter, and yet Freddie had rejected Plimpton's first request. Lori was certain the duke must have done something to anger Freddie, although she had not been able to discern what.

It was interesting that Honey had needed to write and change Freddie's mind on the matter.

Honey had lived with Freddie before her marriage to Saybrook. In fact, the house Lori and Freddie lived in still belonged to Honey.

"Did you feel compelled to accept the duke as your client because we live in Honey's house?" Lori asked.

Freddie gave her a startled look. "No, of course not; Honey would never coerce me. Indeed, she persists in trying to *gift* me the house." Freddie sounded frustrated.

Personally, Lori thought Freddie should accept the gift. Saybrook was wealthy and Honey hardly needed a modest house in London whereas it would represent a lifetime of security for Freddie.

Knowing Freddie's thoughts on the matter she wisely kept her opinion to herself.

"I am glad you are going to sponsor Lady Rebecca," Lori said after a moment.

Freddie raised her eyebrows. "But you think launching young girls into society is barbaric."

"That is true," Lori conceded. She grinned and added, "But you are a woman grown and no schoolroom chit, Freddie and the delicious duke is quite obviously interested in you for more than launching his daughter."

Freddie's blush and stern frown told Lori that she was not mistaken in her guess. "I cannot imagine what gave you such an idea," she said icily.

"It was Honey who told me that the duke wishes to remarry," Lori said, unable to resist a little smirk.

"That may be so, but it does not follow that *I* am his intended."

"You would make a lovely duchess, Freddie."

Freddie's expression became even more quelling. "In the highly unlikely event that *any* man asked me to marry him, I would say *no*." She pursed her lips in disapproval and then added, "I must say your attitude is something of a surprise given your views on marriage in general."

"The married state is not right for me, but that does not mean it is not a good choice for others."

You mean for women who have not already made such a shameful mess of their lives that no decent man would ever want them?

Lori ignored the old taunt, which still caused her a sharp twist of pain even after seven long years.

Some of Freddie's icy reserve melted. "But you *adore* children, Lori. Out of all of us who taught at the Stefani Academy you were the only truly natural teacher. Indeed, I don't think I've ever met anyone who is so good with young people."

Lori forced herself to smile and give an insouciant shrug. "I do not need my own children. I have my brother's five daughters to love and lavish with affection."

If she kept telling herself that often enough, maybe she would one day believe it.

You've been saying the same thing for seven years and you don't believe it yet…

Lori gritted her teeth and firmly shoved the subject of the children she would never have out of her mind.

She smiled at her friend. "You have deliberately led me away from the point, Freddie. We weren't talking about *me;* we were talking about Plimpton and his intentions toward *you.*"

"Ah, you must excuse me, Lori," Freddie said, turning toward the dance floor. "This set is finishing. I must speak to both girls."

Lori snorted. "This discussion has only been tabled, not finished."

Freddie pretended not to hear.

***

Even though the ballroom was packed more tightly than a crate of salted cod, Fast immediately spotted Miss Fontenot.

She was, in his opinion, one of the loveliest women at the ball. However, it had not been her beauty which had attracted his gaze, but rather her spectacularly dowdy ballgown. He recognized the dress, of course. It was the same one she'd worn last year at Avington's betrothal ball and at every *ton* function since.

She must have chosen the most unattractive material in England—a brownish beige shade that put him in mind of burnt porridge—and yet she still looked stunning. He suspected Lorelei Fontenot would look appealing dipped in mud and rolled in gravel, but he could not help imagining what she would look like in a gown that truly fit and flattered her.

Fast scowled at that last thought.

"You're a fool," he accused under his breath. Why the hell was he picturing the pestilential shrew garbed in a ballgown? She was a plague upon his house, and he shouldn't spare so much as a thought for her, not to mention a *positive* one.

And yet he could not pull his eyes from her.

At the moment Miss Fontenot's gaze was focused, like so many others in the ballroom, on Miss Demelza Pascoe, a woman so beautiful that it fairly robbed a person of breath.

Almost as startling as the girl's beauty was the fact that she was dancing with Fast's erstwhile chum, Bevil Norman, who was now the Earl of Moreland.

How could Bevil possibly be courting so soon after Louisa's death? Was he really finished mourning her so soon?

But then Louisa hadn't given Bevil an heir, had she? And Fast knew that Bevil would set great store by such a thing.

Although he had not spoken to his old friend since returning to England, he suspected that Bevil—who'd been something of an impoverished social outcast when he, Fast, and Percy were at Eton together—was fiendishly proud of his unexpected elevation to an earldom. He would not be content to allow the title to pass out of his hands to some distant cousin just because he did not have a son. Bevil would marry again and it seemed that he was determined to choose a wife who had many fertile years ahead of her.

And then there was the fact that the Pascoe chit was an heiress. Fast had heard rumors that Bevil was in debt and desperately needed money. Like so many others, Bevil had wildly invested in the Exchange these past few years and had come out a loser.

Regardless of his need for an heir or money, it irked Fast that Bevil could even think of another wife when Louisa had been dead barely a year.

Louisa.

All three of them—Percy, Fast, and Bevil—had made fools of themselves chasing after Louisa. Louisa hadn't just been lovely—a diamond of the first water—she'd been kind, clever, and witty. She had been everything.

And Bevil Norman—Fast's impoverished friend—had been the lucky man who'd married her.

Fast knew that his twin had deeply loved Louisa. But had Bevil? Or had he only wanted her because of what she would bring to him: status and a sizeable dowry?

For years he had hated Moreland because the other man had married the woman Fast loved. By the time Fast returned to England last year—more than a decade and a half after he'd left—his hatred had burnt down to glowing embers.

It hadn't taken more than a few weeks back home for his banked hatred to flare back to life. He'd expected that Moreland would keep a house in London and that he and Louisa would be engaged in the social whirl of the Season. He had dreaded that first meeting with his old love.

But the day had never come.

Instead, he'd discovered that Louisa had not been seen in London since her marriage. Moreland had kept his wife isolated on his country estate, where she had given birth year in and year out, until she was bed-bound, a shell of her former self according to the few people who had seen her. She'd been gravely ill last year and Fast's two letters to her had gone unanswered.

And now Louisa was dead.

And Moreland was courting another wealthy beauty. Like Louisa, Miss Pascoe was a diamond of the first water. But Louisa had been the same age as the three of them while Miss Pascoe was a mere child. Even in a ballroom filled with very young women she was notable for the purity she seemed to radiate.

Bevil Norman's wooing of such a young girl was more than a little revolting.

Somebody should stop the man, but it wouldn't be Mr. Pasco. The industrialist had made no secret of the fact that he was willing to trade his daughter for the grandest title.

Fast smiled to himself; the heir to a marquessate bested a mere earl, didn't he?

Not pausing to examine his actions too closely, he strode to where the Pascoe chit held court under the watchful gaze of her chaperone, Lady Sarah Jowett.

He elbowed his way through the flock of cockerels posturing for Miss Pascoe and presented himself to her chaperone.

A delighted expression flickered over Sarah's handsome face. "What a lovely surprise to see you here tonight, Lord Severn. It has been a long, long time."

Fast cocked an eyebrow. "*Lord Severn*, Sarah? Is that how you greet your long-lost cousin?"

She laughed. "Are we cousins? I thought the relationship was a bit more tenuous than that."

He grinned and bowed over her hand, scandalously kissing the inside of her wrist and earning another throaty chuckle. "I'm delighted to see a friendly and familiar face." He gave her hand a gentle squeeze and lowered his voice. "I was terribly sorry to hear about Benedict. He was a good man."

"Thank you, Fast. That he was," she agreed quietly, quickly shaking away her grief and smiling. "I daresay I know why you are here." Her sharp blue eyes slid to her charge.

"You mean other than saying *hello* to you?"

"Yes. *Other* than that." She chuckled and said to the angel beside her, "Demi, this is Lord Severn, a dear, dear cousin of mine—several times removed. He was the first person I danced with in my debut Season."

"I didn't think you remembered," Fast said. He certainly hadn't, but he kept that to himself. He turned to Sarah's charge. "It's a pleasure to meet you, Miss Pascoe," Fast bowed over the younger woman's hand with considerably more formality than he'd done with Sarah.

The girl—for that is what she was—dropped a graceful curtsey and dimpled up at him. "It is an honor, Lord Severn."

She had a sweet, soft voice and eyes that were the same shade of blue as Caribbean waters. She was every bit as stunning up close as she'd been from across the room.

And she was far, far too young and innocent for Bevil.

"Is it too much to hope that you might have a dance free for me, Miss Pascoe?"

The angel glanced doubtfully at Sarah, who nodded.

"I have the supper dance, my lord."

"Fortune has indeed smiled on me tonight, Miss Pascoe." He bowed to the girl and exchanged a grateful look with Sarah, who would have advised her charge to always save a few dances for late arrivals, and took his leave.

Fast had barely gone three paces when Bevil's voice came from behind him. "One moment, Fast!"

Rather than feel pleasure at the prospect of talking to an old friend, his stomach tightened unpleasantly. Fast was a bit startled by how much animosity he felt toward his erstwhile bosom beau. Was it possible that he was still jealous that Bevil had married Louisa? Even after all this time?

Abashed at the thought, Fast forced himself to smile before turning.

"Fast, old man!"

"Moreland, how good to see you. You barely look a day older than the last time I saw you." The earl had indeed aged gracefully, the only signs that he was nine-and-thirty the few silver hairs at his temples and faint crow's feet at the corners of his hazel eyes. Otherwise, he was as trim and elegant as ever.

"I could say the same thing about you—but, I daresay, for entirely different reasons." Moreland's mocking gaze lingered on Fast's shoulder-length hair. "Did nobody tell you that queues went out of fashion along with brocade frock coats and buckles on one's shoes?"

Fast merely smiled at the unsubtle dig. "I wished to tell you that I am extremely sorry for your loss. Louisa was a wonderful woman."

The earl's expression instantly turned somber. "It is tragic that you missed seeing Louisa by only a few months." He blinked rapidly, as if his emotions were threatening to overcome him. "It was a difficult year, and I hope I'm forgiven for neglecting to call upon you while I licked my wounds and mourned my beloved wife."

Fast felt nauseated by the other man words. And then immediately guilty at his reaction. Why was he thinking such hateful thoughts about a man who'd once been his friend?

"I know you were close to Louisa at one time." Moreland's lips twitched so faintly it was almost imperceptible. "Very close. As was Percy, if I recall correctly."

Fast's gaze narrowed at the disingenuous comment. The other man knew damned well that Fast and his twin had both been in love with Louisa. Moreover, Bevil had to know that if not for Percy's death and Fast's banishment Louisa never would have consented to marry him. Fast and his twin had left poor Louisa in a poor position. *Ton* society would not have been kind to a woman caught in the middle of such a scandal—no matter that none of it was her fault.

It was Fast's belief that Louisa had married Moreland because she'd had no other choice. In short, he had won her hand by default. Had Moreland punished her for that?

Perhaps the marriage had been a happy one, but Fast somehow doubted it. Bevil had kept Louisa pregnant and sequestered on his Yorkshire estate while he'd enjoyed himself in London. While it wasn't unusual for a peer to breed his wife to death in pursuit of an heir, it *was* unusual to keep a woman in a secluded location when she had once been the toast of the *ton*. Fast hoped Louisa hadn't suffered as much as he feared she had.

"Do you know that woman?"

Fast followed Moreland's gaze and was unsurprised to find it aimed at Miss Fontenot, who was glaring not at the earl, but at Fast.

"Only slightly," Fast said, inexplicably hesitant to bring her to the other man's attention.

Moreland snickered. "She certainly seems to know *you,* Fast. Is she another of your conquests? I understand you're cutting a swathe through the widow population of the *ton*."

"You are very well-informed regarding my activities."

"You're an extremely popular topic of conversation, but I'm sure you must know that." He laughed and then added, in an exaggerated voice, "*The King of the Rakes returns to England after a decade and a half!* Who can resist such a juicy story. Isn't that why you've avoided popping into White's—because you don't want to see your name in the betting book?"

"Not really."

The other man scoffed. "Come now! No curiosity at all to see what is being recorded?"

"None."

"There are bets on when you'll marry. *Who* you'll marry. Whether your grandfather will be making the choice for you. And many more besides."

"Thank you for making me aware."

"So, will he?" Moreland persisted, undaunted by Fast lack of interest.

"Will who what?"

Moreland gave him an exasperated look. "Will your grandfather choose your bride for you?"

"Alas, the Marquess is the one who controls the purse strings, so I daresay I'll do as my grandfather wishes if I want to go on in any sort of style." Fast felt no shame about lying so blatantly.

"Good Lord, Fast! All those years at sea on a privateer vessel and you are not a wealthy man? I was given to believe the prize money was like low-hanging fruit."

"Are you asking me how much money I made, Bev? How vulgar."

The other man flushed. "Just seems odd that you would have stayed away so long if you weren't successful."

"I couldn't come back until I was summoned, could I?"

Moreland opened his mouth to say something, but then froze, his gaze flickering over Fast's shoulder. "Don't look now, but the fierce female you hardly know is headed your way."

Bloody hell.

Fast sighed and turned to his tormentrix. "Miss Fontenot, fancy seeing you here." He bowed. "What a pleasure."

"Lord Severn." She dropped a curtsey so brief it didn't even merit the name. Her striking green eyes slid to Moreland. Again, he felt reluctant to introduce the two, but it would insult her not to do so.

"Bevil, this is Miss Lorelei Fontenot."

She dropped a far deeper curtsey. "It is a pleasure, my lord."

"The pleasure is all mine," Moreland said, his tone so pompous and condescending it set Fast's teeth on edge. The earl bowed over Miss Fontenot's hand in a way that would probably cause most virginal young misses to flutter and blush.

Miss Fontenot, who was made of firmer stuff, looked faintly amused.

But when Bevil didn't immediately release her hand, she gave it an unsubtle tug and then turned away from the handsome lord.

The earl frowned at the rude dismissal, but Miss Fontenot's attention was already fixed on Fast, so she did not notice.

"I was surprised when your two *friends* called on me the other day, Lord Severn."

He returned her smirk, amused by her fire; most people wouldn't be so sanguine to be visited by not one, but two, Bow Street Runners. "I'm so pleased to hear you enjoyed meeting them. I do hope their visit served its purpose."

"Oh, I think you might be surprised at the interesting repercussions that brief visit will yield." A taunting smile lurked in her eyes.

Fast raised an eyebrow at her barely veiled threat. "How intriguing that sounds."

"You two seem very well-acquainted," Moreland said. "How did you meet?"

Fast had forgotten they weren't alone and turned to find the earl eyeing Miss Fontenot in a way that made his hands curl into fists.

"Lord Severn came to my rescue in a time of need," Miss Fontenot said.

Could the woman have said anything that was more likely to pique a person's interest?

Moreland opened his mouth, no doubt to ask for details, but Fast didn't give him a chance to speak. "Miss Fontenot broke a strap on her sandal at Lady Marten's picnic and I repaired it for her," Fast lied. Where he'd met the woman—and why—was none of Moreland's damned business.

Miss Fontenot gave Fast a querying look—obviously curious as to why he had lied—but she did not contradict him.

Moreland, however, looked disappointed by his mundane answer and changed tack. "Fontenot is an unusual name."

"It's not so unusual if one is French," Miss Fontenot countered with the same casual incivility she'd always employed with Fast. Moreland's frown said he didn't find her dismissive treatment as amusing as Fast did.

Miss Fontenot either didn't notice or didn't care. Indeed, instead of soothing the earl's ruffled feathers, she heightened his displeasure by turning her shoulder to him and saying to Fast, "I need to talk to you privately."

"I'm not sure a ballroom is the best place to—"

"This next dance is a waltz. Do you have it free?"

Fast felt rather than saw Bevil's jolt of surprise at her bold words.

"Are you asking me to dance, Miss Fontenot? I don't recall that ever happening before."

Rather than slink away in shame as a *ton* miss would do, she boldly met his gaze. "I daresay manners have changed a great deal since you were a young man."

Fast laughed. "Well *done*, Miss Fontenot."

She grinned. "So? Will you waltz with me, my lord? Or is your dance card full up?"

Chapter 8

"I am sorry if I shocked your friend Moreland," Lori said as she and Lord Severn glided around the ballroom as gracefully as a pair of swans. For all his great size, the viscount was a remarkably elegant dancer.

"Don't lie, Miss Fontenot; you are not in the least sorry."

Lori laughed. "No, you are right: I'm not. He's rather full of himself, isn't he?"

Severn's striking eyes glinted with surprise—and something else… Interest?

"You have the loveliest eyes," she blurted. What in the world was wrong with her? Those weren't the words she'd been planning to say.

He raised his eyebrows. "Miss Fontenot, are you trying to put me to the blush?"

"I doubt that could be done." But she was doing an excellent job making *herself* blush.

"If there is a woman alive who could do it, I'm guessing you are she."

"I will take that as a compliment."

"Unfortunately, I suspect it wasn't my *lovely* eyes that you wanted to talk about," he said, thankfully moving the subject onto something less mortifying.

"No, you are right. I'd like to talk about the *Sea Ranger* mutiny." If Lori had not been staring fixedly into his magnificent eyes at that precise moment, she never would have seen them shutter. Otherwise, his expression didn't so much as flicker. He was very, very good at concealing his thoughts.

"I wasn't in the country at the time so I daresay you know a great deal more than I do."

"Oh, I doubt that."

"Your doubt does not make it any less true." He smoothly spun her into turn, startling a laugh of delight out of her. Yet again she blurted words she'd had no intention of speaking. "You are very good, my lord!"

He smiled faintly but made no response.

They danced in silence for a few moments, his steps as smooth as silk, his massive body throwing off heat like a forge. Lori hastily pushed aside thoughts of his body, or at least made the attempt, but he was far too close and real at that moment.

Nothing could have been more unfortunate than Lori's reaction—both her body and her mind—to Lord Severn whenever she was near him. In theory, he represented everything she despised about wealthy men. In reality, the odd sense of recognition—she had no other word for it—from the moment she'd first set eyes on him he had unnerved her and continued to do so. She told herself, over and over, that was why rakes were rakes: they cast an irresistible lure over women without even trying to do so. That was their evil genius. That meant Severn, the King of the Rakes, broadcast an almost crippling appeal. The thing of it was, Lori honestly doubted that he ever considered his effect on the female race. Like storms, droughts, and plagues, he just was.

Regardless of knowing all this about him, she could not help wanting to be near him.

"Ninnyhammer," she muttered.

"I beg your pardon?"

Lori's eyes leapt up to meet his. "Er, nothing." She was scrambling for some topic of conversation when her gaze was caught by the Earl of Moreland. He was standing with some other men who were chattering, but his eyes were fixed on them. Or, more specifically, Lord Severn.

"You've known Moreland a long time?" she asked.

His coal black eyebrows lifted enquiringly. "What makes you say that?"

"There is just something about people who've had a long acquaintance that shows in the way their bodies move. A sort of silent language."

"You are a student of human nature, Miss Fontenot?"

"I find people interesting—more interesting than anything else, in fact."

"*Hmmph.*"

"Don't you?"

"Some people are interesting but the vast majority of them are either annoying or boring."

She laughed. "Which category does Lord Moreland fall into?"

***

Miss Fontenot was persistent, Fast would give her that.

She had not asked the question he'd expected, either. Which was which category *she* fell into. At least that was the sort of vapid flirtation he was used to at *ton* functions.

But once again Miss Fontenot did the unexpected.

"Moreland falls into a category all his own," he said, and then knew the moment he'd said the words it was a mistake. If the woman had possessed antennae, his statement would have sent them twitching.

"What category is that?"

"He is my oldest friend."

"Oh." Her obvious disappointment at his prosaic answer was almost comical. But she rallied quickly. "I noticed you didn't say *closest* or *best* friend."

"Didn't I? Perhaps that's because I've been away so long that I can no longer claim that status with him, or anyone else in England."

Again, she looked thwarted.

And again, she rapidly came about. "Lord Moreland does not look at you that way."

"No? How is he looking at me?"

She took her time before answering. "He looks like a man who has opened a door to a room he believed was empty, only to find it occupied. Whether he's happy or vexed by the contents of the room, I cannot say."

Fast thought she'd hit the nail precisely on the head.

Miss Fontenot sighed. "Or perhaps I'm just being fanciful." She lowered her gaze until it was somewhere in the neighborhood of the top button on his coat, making him realize that her neck must have been craned at an uncomfortable angle. He'd not thought her especially short until that moment. But from this angle he could see the pins that had been shoved into her thick blue-black hair pell-mell.

Why did he find that so…*endearing*?

"—upon the mutineers?"

The word *mutineers* was like being doused with cold water.

"What?" he asked rudely.

"I asked how you'd come upon the mutineers? After all, the place they'd run aground is said to be exceedingly remote."

Fast stared down at her, darkly amused when her cheeks flushed under his gaze. "Am I dreaming? Did I somehow mention mutineers and don't remember it?"

"Are you denying that you rescued at least one survivor from the *Sea Ranger*?"

"Where did you hear such a thing? Parker?"

"I cannot reveal my sources." Her prim, smug tone made him want to turn her over his knee and spank the truth out of her.

The image was an enticing one and Fast visualized a big red handprint—*his* handprint, in point of fact—on what would surely be a soft, generous, pale buttock. His cock immediately began to harden. He added a few more handprints to the pleasing mental picture and next imagined her eyes no longer sharp and inquisitorial, but sensual and submissive.

"Why are you looking at me that way, my lord?"

The pleasing image wavered at the edges and then dissipated entirely. "What way?"

She squinted at him, taking a long moment before saying, "I can't describe it."

"I thought you could read the language of people's bodies. Can't you read mine right now?"

"I think you would hurt me if we weren't in this crowded room."

"I don't hurt women." He toyed with adding *not unless they like it* to his statement but recalled her virginal responses to his teasing when she'd crashed into the brothel and decided to spare her blushes.

For the moment.

"Who would have spread the rumor that you rescued men from the *Sea Ranger,* my lord? It seems like an exceedingly specific accusation to be entirely false."

"You are tenacious."

She smiled. "Thank you."

"That wasn't a compliment. You put me in mind of a badger, Miss Fontenot—a badger with Parker holding the leash. Tell me, is he your lover?"

Her smile turned brittle. "I thought you'd concluded that I was a virgin the last time we discussed the subject of"—she broke off and glanced around before hissing, "*fucking.*"

Fast hated the relief he felt at her words. But he loved the fiery pink blush that stained her cheeks.

"*Tsk, tsk,* that is no word for a little girl, Miss Fontenot. Somebody ought to wash your mouth out with soap."

Her eyes bulged and a vein pulsed in her forehead. For a moment, Fast really thought she would forget she was in the middle of a ballroom and slap him. Or punch him, rather, as Miss Fontenot seemed far too feisty for a mere slap.

But she collected herself with admirable speed, regarded him with the icy indifference of a duchess, and said, "I should like to see you try it, my lord."

Fast laughed. But his amusement rapidly dissipated when he recalled the subject of their current argument. "Parker is unethical. By following his direction, you are too. You need to stop this line of inquiry immediately, Miss Fontenot, before somebody gets hurt."

"Are you threatening me with more Runners, my lord?"

Thankfully the music drew to a close because their heated exchange had already begun to attract interested glances. "Let me escort you back to your—"

"I don't need your assistance to walk across a ballroom," she retorted, pulling away from him before he realized what she was doing.

Fast stood on the dance floor, trying not to look like a fool who'd just been arguing heatedly with his dance partner.

He failed miserably.

Chapter 9

"This is good," David said, looking up from Lori's article. "But it's also a serious assertion. If we're going to accuse Sir Vincent of illegally profiting from his seat on a parliamentary committee, then we must have proof that he is the silent partner in the syndicate that bought the property."

His lofty words were especially ironic given how little he cared about such proof when it came to any story about Stand Fast Severn.

Wordlessly, Lori handed him the pages of an agreement demonstrating clearly that Sir Vincent was a primary shareholder in the company in question.

David looked at the crinkled, stained parchment and then back at Lori, his eyes widening. "This is a contract for the sale of the property in question. How in the name of God did you get this, Lori?"

The expression of terror on his face was amusing and she was tempted to tease him, but men like David never seemed to have a sense of humor unless they were the ones making the jest.

"Did you break into Lord Vincent's house?" he demanded when she didn't answer quickly enough.

She laughed. "Of course not! I found it—and several more copies of the same—in his clerk's rubbish."

David's jaw sagged. "You—you went through Lord Vincent's rubbish?"

"Yes. Every day for weeks."

"That's—" he broke off, blinking rapidly. "That's excellent work, my dear. Most ingenious, in fact. Bloody brilliant," he muttered under his breath, adding in a much louder voice as he turned back to the story in his hands, "We can run this on the first page."

Lori perked up. "That pays better, does it not?"

"Indeed, it does; twice your usual rate." He unlocked the drawer holding his strong box and she heard the clink of coins.

Her *usual* rate was what David paid her for the *Miss Emily* columns. Although the tidbits of gossip did not pay a great deal, it was at least a constant source of income. Freddie charged her so little rent that she was able to put aside more than half of her earnings. Of course, the ballgown she was buying would cut into that, but—

"By the way," David said, glancing up and pausing his counting, "how is your story on Severn coming? Or should I say *stories*?"

"I have nothing new on either investigation." Indeed, she'd been hoping he'd forget the foolish *story* about Severn's brother's suicide completely. Evidently, she was not to be so lucky.

He glowered. "Because you haven't been working on either of them?"

Lori decided to address the mutineer issue, first. "I'm sorry, David, but I fail to see where I'm supposed to find information for an alleged incident that took place halfway around the globe, and which the individual in question denies ever happened."

"Did you talk to anyone down at the docks where his ship is berthed?"

"The *Vixen* isn't due back for several weeks, so there isn't anyone to talk to." An image of Mr. Gregg, Mr. Barker, and the other men she'd met at the brothel flitted through her mind. "Not that I think any of his crew will be eager to gossip about the man who controls their livelihood. I believe they are quite loyal to him."

"There is always somebody who will have an axe to grind and want to complain."

"But is that sort of person really a reliable source?"

"A ship's crew is in constant flux, Lori. There will be somebody willing to talk about Severn," David went on, ignoring her question, or perhaps not hearing it at all. Sometimes she wondered if he simply closed his ears to her. "Sailors like to drink and when they do, their tongues loosen." He gave her a hard look. "Or perhaps that is something you do not feel capable of doing?"

"What? Going to sailor's haunts? It is nothing I haven't done before," she said, not entirely truthfully. She'd gone into two pubs in her life, one in the small village where her brother lived. The second one had been not far from Viscount Severn's country home, Grandon Castle. That was the pub where three of the local men had—not very subtly—warned her against prying into the Marquess of Grandon's family.

"There are dozens of such establishments, David. Surely it is more prudent to pursue this line of questioning once the *Vixen* is—"

"I'm tired of your constant excuses!" David snapped. "You need to start asking questions *now*. You need to get out there and prod and poke *now*. This"—he held up the contract she'd found in the rubbish—"is excellent work. I want you to show the same initiative when it comes to Severn."

"I hardly think I'll find a murder confession in Lord Severn's rubbish—or a document admitting that he ferried mutineers around on his ship."

"Sarcasm does not become you, my dear," he said in a dangerously silky voice. "More to the point, I don't care to hear that tone from one of my subordinates."

"I apologize," she muttered.

He grunted and resumed his counting.

Lori went to stare out the window. What was taking him so long? You'd think the man was parting with his personal fortune rather than few quid.

"You mentioned the last time you were here that Lord Severn's grandfather was coming to London?"

She turned around at the sound of his voice. "I did."

"Find out why the old man is coming to town. Is he angry at his grandson? Perhaps he is coming to banish him again." He gave an abrupt laugh. "See, that's the sort of information that you're uniquely positioned to find at all these balls you attend. You must have more invitations than you accept?"

"Sometimes," she said, unhappy with where his question might be leading.

"You should accept everything that comes your way. That is the way to gather more information." He grinned insincerely. "That is how one pleases one's employer, Lori."

"I'm hardly equipped to accept every invitation," she said, unable to keep a hint of irritation from her tone.

"Not equipped? Do you mean mentally?"

Lori snorted. "Very droll."

David grinned. "Sorry, I couldn't resist. I assume you mean clothing?"

The question surprised her. Was he considering defraying her expenses? "That is exactly what I mean."

He waved one hand. "*Pffi!* You're so lovely you could wear sack cloth and ashes and be admitted anywhere you wished."

Lori's face heated; she was a fool for believing he might cover some of her expenses. "Clothing matters to these people, David. And my gowns set me apart. They are hardly likely to confide in me when they view me as an interloper."

As usual, David ignored anything he didn't want to hear. He closed the cashbox and held out her money. When Lori reached for it, he pulled his hand back. "One more thing."

"Yes?" she said, forcing the word through gritted teeth.

"I want proof of progress on both the Severn stories, Lori and I'm tired of waiting."

"The *Vixen* is supposed to return to London in a few weeks and—"

"Two weeks, then."

"David! That is hardly—"

"Three weeks, and that's final. No more excuses. In three weeks you will have answers for me or you can find somebody else to work for. Understood?" His unblinking stare required an answer.

"Understood," she repeated through clenched teeth.

"Good." He tossed the coins at her, catching her by surprise. Lori scrambled to catch them, but one fell to the floor. "Oh dear," he said, cutting her a smarmy, challenging look. "How clumsy of me."

Lori considered strangling him. It would *almost* be worth transportation. Only the fear of being hanged stopped her.

Don't let him taunt you into rash behavior.

The thought served to stiffen her resolve and she dropped to her haunches, picked up the coin, and stood before dropping it into her reticule.

David did not look at her. Instead, he pretended to be engrossed by one of the many documents that cluttered his desk.

Lori collected her cloak, satchel, and umbrella and said, "Goodbye, David."

He gave a dismissive wave and did not look up.

Just like she knew he would, he waited until her hand was on the door handle before saying, "One more thing, Lori."

"Yes, David?" she asked, not bothering to turn around.

"I've given your manuscript to Gordon Wright at G.B. Wright and Sons."

Joy exploded inside her like the pyrotechnic displays so popular at Vauxhall Gardens.

Lori bit her lip and hastily shoved her excitement aside, and said in an admirably cool tone, "I look forward to his assessment."

He grunted. "Yes, yes. Run along now."

Lori left before she could say something that would jeopardize his goodwill.

Once on the street, she hailed a hackney and gave the driver the address to a modiste's shop where she would immediately hand over her hard-earned wages and collect the ball gown she had purchased. It was an unwanted expense, but she hoped it would please Freddie to see her in something new for a change.

Her thoughts quickly slid back to David's last words as she stared unseeingly out the hackney window. As thrilling as it was to hear her manuscript was in the hands of one of the finest publishing houses in Britain, she couldn't help thinking about what she had to do to pay for that privilege.

If Lord Severn had indeed abetted any mutineers, then that was a subject the public deserved to hear about and she did not feel guilty about exposing his behavior. After all, he would one day have a seat in Lords and his actions should be subject to scrutiny.

The issue of his twin brother's death was not nearly so clear cut. Why did she feel so guilty investigating that?

Because who benefited more from Lord Perseverance's death than his younger brother and heir?

Lori flinched away from that thought.

You don't want to believe that because you fancy the man.

She closed her eyes and let her head fall back against the tattered squabs. She despised herself for falling prey to a libertine like Stand Fast Severn. He'd been a shocking womanizer in his younger days and showed no sign of having changed.

Even if a person discredited the gossip about how many lovers he kept on a string, there were enough of his illegitimate offspring scattered around the countryside to give evidence to his unprincipled raking. Indeed, Lori had discovered at least five different women who'd claimed the King of the Rakes had fathered their child.

Although none of the mothers would speak to Lori directly, she had confirmed that all five of them received money from Lord Severn—even during his years at sea.

Severn's assistance wasn't only limited to money. The oldest children—now between eighteen and twenty—had married respectably, which would not have happened without Severn's influence. The two boys had attended well-respected schools and he'd purchased a commission for one.

Severn might be a philandering, gambling, reckless rake, but he had never shirked his responsibilities when it came to looking after his by-blows.

Lori had seen the far-too-attractive viscount often in the two weeks since they'd danced that waltz. She had not asked him to dance again—or even spoken to him—and he had avoided her.

Indeed, he had not so much as glanced her way. Instead, he had joined the men who were baying after Miss Pascoe and her fortune like a pack of slavering hounds.

Lori scowled at the unpleasant pang in her belly. Why was she so disappointed that Severn wanted to marry the lovely young heiress? There was hardly an unmarried man—and a great many married ones—who *didn't* lust after either Miss Pascoe's person or money or both.

Honestly, Lori couldn't even blame the men. Demelza Pascoe had become fast friends with Freddie's twins, so Lori had spent quite a bit of time around the girl in recent weeks. Demelza wasn't just beautiful, she was also sweet tempered and intelligent.

Unfortunately, she was also shockingly innocent.

It disgusted her that Severn—a man who lived in a brothel—would go after such a child. The thought of him slaking his lust on Miss Pascoe's nubile body made her positively ill.

Liar. You're not positively ill. *You're positively green with envy that he's not running after you.*

"That's bosh," Lori muttered, glaring out the window.

Your feelings for the man are the same reason you don't want to look into his brother's death. Because you are afraid of what you might find.

She *did* like Severn—despite his deplorably rakish behavior—but just as a person, not as a potential lover.

Liar, the voice accused yet again. *You desire him.*

It was true she felt a certain attraction for him, but not desire!

You are infatuated with the man.

"That's hardly unusual given that he is a rake with twenty years of experience under his belt, is it? Indeed, it would have been unusual if I *didn't* find him attractive," Lori retorted, uncaring that she was arguing with herself aloud in a hackney.

He will likely marry Miss Pascoe before the Season is even over.

That was entirely possible. All of London knew that all Mr. Bryok Pascoe cared about was getting the most prestigious title for his daughter.

It was easy to understand Pascoe's motives—he wanted to buy into the aristocracy at the highest level possible—but Severn's were less clear. His grandfather was one of the wealthiest peers in Britain, so why was Severn chasing after an heiress with a vulgar father and less than illustrious pedigree? The current marquess was an infamous snob. Lori couldn't imagine that he would agree with his grandson's choice of wife.

The woman is female perfection; what other reason does a man need?

Yet another undeniable truth. Demelza Pascoe was gorgeous, sweet, and obscenely wealthy. Why would Lord Severn want any other woman?

You mean why would he ever want you?

Lori ignored the pang she felt at the taunting thought and stared out the window, the rain on the glass blurring her vision.

Chapter 10

Fast obeyed the voice of wisdom for almost two weeks before he threw common sense to the wind and asked Miss Fontenot for a dance.

"Is that a new gown, Miss Fontenot?" he asked as they took their positions for a waltz.

She looked amused. "I suppose it is a bad sign when even a man who sets Runners on me notices when I get a new dress."

"Will you never forgive me for that?"

"No."

He laughed.

"I can't believe you noticed my new gown, my lord."

"Oh? Why is that?"

"You are more a Corinthian than a tulip of fashion. I cannot believe you waste a moment's thought about what most people wear."

"In the main I don't pay much attention to other people's clothing, but I make the occasional exception."

She fluttered her eyelashes with mock coquettishness. "Why, Lord Severn, are you flirting with me?"

"I would never presume."

She snorted. "I was surprised when you asked me to dance after ignoring me these past weeks."

Fast was flabbergasted when he felt heat creep up his neck. Why the cheeky little minx had embarrassed him! Perhaps he'd be lucky and she'd not notice. After all, he was still darkly tanned and—

"Why, Lord Severn! I do believe you are blushing."

"Nonsense," he said gruffly.

She laughed, her eyes sparkling with delight. "Why did you suddenly decide to acknowledge me again? And don't tell me that my new gown is responsible for the gesture."

Fast could have told her that he'd asked her *despite* the frumpy new gown. But he suspected that even a woman with little regard for her appearance wouldn't care for that comment.

So instead, he said, "I got tired of waiting for you ask me again."

"Has it really been so long?"

"You are cruel woman, Miss Fontenot. Here I've been counting the minutes, and you didn't even notice."

She laughed again. "I can understand it now."

"Understand what?"

"Your reputation as King of the Rakes. You are dangerously charming when you're not threatening a woman with Runners."

He heaved an exaggerated sigh. "I'm disappointed that you've managed to bring that up twice in less than as many minutes."

"Not nearly as disappointed as I was the day those two hulking men showed up on my doorstep."

"You do hold a grudge, don't you Miss Fontenot?"

"I'm dancing with you, aren't I?"

"So you are," he said, dropping the subject. "Tell me, why have you been ignoring *me* these past few weeks? I've not seen you peering in my bedroom window, and the servants at Grandon House and those at The King's Purse have not spotted you rooting through the rubbish bins."

She pulled a face but did not look especially guilty. "I suppose Mr. Gregg told you about that."

Fast didn't tell her that he, too, had watched her climbing around in the big wooden dustbin behind Grandon House on one memorable occasion.

"It's making me nervous that you've become so scarce of late."

"Have you considered that I've not been scarce at all? That I've merely honed my skills and you haven't noticed that I've been lurking outside your window?"

"I can't imagine ever not noticing you, Miss Fontenot."

She gave another of her disbelieving snorts. "Oh, *do* leave off, my lord. Save your pretty words for somebody who might be taken in by them."

He grinned. "Tell me about yourself, Miss Fontenot."

"Why should I?"

"You know so much about me." He cocked his head. "Please don't make me come dig through *your* rubbish bin."

She laughed. "No, I wouldn't want that. Our housekeeper would chase you off with a broom and a few choice words. What do you want to know about me?"

"Where are you from? Do you have family? How is it that you came to be living with Lady Sedgewick? There, that should be enough to get started.

"I'm from a small village outside Liskeard. My parents died when I was very young, and my older brother raised me. He is a vicar and is married to a lovely woman and they have five daughters."

"Tell me about your brother."

"What about him?" she asked, narrowing her eyes.

"So suspicious! I am just making pleasant conversation, Miss Fontenot. That is what people do when they dance."

She didn't look entirely convinced, but said, "His name is Jeremy and he is older by more than ten years. I was an afterthought to my parents."

"But one I'm sure they were very grateful for."

"How gallant you are, my lord."

"You make that easy, Miss Fontenot." He lifted an eyebrow and gave her a hard look. "Did you just roll your eyes at me?"

"You earned it. Tell me about *your* family, my lord."

"I would have thought you ferreted out all my details in your visits to my grandfather's estates. Yes," he said at her startled look, "I know you visited both our family seat and the property in Scotland. Tell me, did you find what you were looking for?"

"If you know of my visits then I daresay you know the answer to that question, too. Your people are very loyal to you."

"They are my grandfather's people."

"The loyalty I encountered was directed toward you, not your grandfather."

"Do I detect a note of surprise that I might engender loyalty?"

"You're so *suspicious*, my lord. We are just conversing. It is what normal people do when they dance," she said, mimicking him so accurately it made him smile.

"Fair enough. To answer your question, only Percy and I survived. My mother had numerous miscarriages before we were born, but there were no attempts afterward as my father had done his duty and produced his heir and spare in one go."

"*His* duty? How arduous a man's part is in childbirth! What about *her* duty?"

He barked a laugh, the noise loud enough to be heard over the music. Several other couples glanced their way. One of them was Moreland, who was dancing with the lovely young Miss Pascoe.

Bevil gave Miss Fontenot a significant once over and then smirked, evidently unimpressed.

Good. The last thing Fast wanted was for Bevil to guess just how much he liked Miss Fontenot. The other man was not above adding something new to the betting book at White's.

By dismissing Miss Fontenot so summarily Bevil had, yet again, proven what a shallow, unobservant man he was. While her gown was an unattractive shade of blue and fit her like a shapeless sack with long sleeves—something Fast had never seen on a ballgown—her vibrant beauty still shone through.

The woman didn't need pretty clothing to be stunning, but Moreland was too much of a snob to look past an unflattering garment.

"I've heard you are in the lead in that particular race," Miss Fontenot said, interrupting his thoughts.

"I beg your pardon?"

"You know what race I'm talking about—the one for Miss Pascoe's hand, as well as the rest of her, including her money."

Fast laughed. "Do you just say *whatever* comes to mind, Miss Fontenot?"

"Do you always evade direct questions?"

"Oh, was that a question? Because it sounded like an observation. Or an accusation. What makes you think I'm even in the running for Miss Pascoe's delectable person and heaps of money?"

"It is well-known you came back to marry."

"Strange that I didn't know it."

"Are you denying it? I know your grandfather is soon coming to London for the first time in over a decade. What else could bring him to the city but to arrange the betrothal of his heir?"

She was right about that—or at least partly right. His grandfather *was* trying to use guilt to force Fast into *doing his duty*. But the last person in London he would confide any information in—not to mention *personal* information—was the woman across from him.

"What a fertile imagination you have, ma'am. You should be writing fiction rather than slaving away a David Parker's dreadful rag."

"Miss Pascoe will make a lovely bride." she retorted smoothly, ignoring his dig.

Fast chuckled. "You are a treasure, Miss Fontenot. Indeed, I can't recall when I've been so diverted. Or enjoyed a dance more than this one."

For a moment she looked flustered, and her lovely cheeks misted with pink.

Interesting. The little gossip monger could be disarmed by a compliment, whereas threats and Runners failed to disturb her cool, calm façade.

But the moment of shyness passed in the flicker of an eyelid and the hard-nosed newspaperwoman returned with a vengeance. "Why do you think somebody would accuse you of giving aid to mutineers, my lord?"

Again, he laughed. "You are *relentless*."

***

Even though Lord Severn had laughed, Lori thought it sounded a bit forced.

He shook his head. "Astounding."

"What is astounding?"

"You are always the newspaperwoman, even on the dance floor."

"Those of us who work for a living must spin hay into gold while they may."

"Ah, work. Something I wouldn't know anything about?"

"Are you saying you were forced to earn a living as a privateer, my lord?" she asked, not bothering to keep disbelief from her tone. "That's not really the same, is it? After all, you could always come home to grandpapa if you tired of playing at hard labor."

His eyes, which had become wary at her mutiny question, now glittered with genuine amusement. It appeared the man enjoyed being baited and insulted. How…odd.

"I should dearly love to set you straight on the matter, my dear." His lips flexed into a faint smile. "Alas, I am going to strenuously resist the urge to do so."

Lori cocked her head and stared up at him, desperately wishing she could see beyond Severn's mask to the man who lived behind it. "Why are you so resistant when it comes to talking about your past?"

"Why do I feel like anything I say to you will end up on the front page of *The Mercury* earning money for David Parker?" he countered.

She ignored his question. "Your ship operated under a letter of marque, so you are well-known to the government and the *Vixen* has been mentioned in newspapers—even respectable *rags* such as *The Times*—on more than one occasion, so what you've done is hardly a secret."

"The *Vixen* was never my ship; I merely captained her for the true owner. It is he you should interrogate."

She laughed. "Come now, I think we can drop that pretense. Everyone knows that the so-called owner of record is just the figurehead, that you are the real power behind the *Vixen*."

"What a shame we cannot continue this conversation, Miss Fontenot."

"Why can't we?"

He gave her an oddly gentle smile. "Because, my dear girl, the dance is over."

Chapter 11

"This just came for you, Lori. *Lori? Lori.*"

Lori's head whipped up. "More Runners?" she asked, jumping to her feet.

Freddie smiled. "No, my dear.

"Thank heavens."

"I regret having to raise my voice, but it seemed you were very far away from here."

Lori yawned and dropped back into her chair. "I'm sorry. I didn't mean to ignore you. I am just… struggling." She gestured to the pages covered with messy handwriting and rubbed her eyes, which felt like somebody had been sprinkling sand in them. When she looked up again, she realized that Freddie was holding a large pale pink box tied with a silver velvet ribbon. "What's that?"

"It just came by messenger and it's for you." Freddie set the box on the desk, which was covered with failed attempts at an article for David.

"Who is it from?"

"The delivery boy didn't know."

"There is no message with it?" Lori asked.

"Nothing but the box."

"That's strange."

"Open it."

Lori smiled at her friend's impatience and pulled off the ribbon, lifted the lid, and then peeled back the layers and layers of silvery-gray tissue paper.

"Oh, my goodness," Freddie murmured. She reached out and stroked the exquisite peacock blue-green gown with reverent fingers. "It's gorgeous."

Lori couldn't resist petting the material before snapping out of her worshipful fugue and glaring at her friend.

"What is the matter?" Freddie asked.

"You bought this, didn't you?"

Freddie laughed. "This is from Madam Thérèse's dress shop. I recognize her distinctive pink box and silver ribbon. Even if I were arrogant enough to purchase you clothing without consulting you, I am afraid Madam Thérèse's is a bit above my touch.

Lori lifted the gown from the box, her heart speeding as she took in the almost overwhelming beauty of the garment.

Freddie reached into the box. "Look Lori—there is a pair of opera gloves, as well."

Once again, she felt compelled to reach out and pet the garments. The leather was softer than butter and the rich teal color and multitude of tiny buttons on the inside of the wrist spoke of an expert glover's touch.

"*Gloves* does not seem like a grand enough word for them," Lori said, handing them to Fredie.

"They are exquisite," Freddie agreed. She draped the gloves over her lap and gestured to the gown Lori was holding. "Lift it up so I can see."

Feeling as if she were in a dream, Lori held the dress in front of herself, the whisper soft silk warm beneath her fingers.

"Oh, Lori," Freddie breathed, her eyes shining with admiration. "That color is absolutely *perfect* for you."

Lori turned until she could see herself in the mirror over the fireplace. Her lips parted in wonder; Freddie was right. It was the perfect color for her, the blue-green making her eyes look even greener, like sparkling emeralds.

"Who sent it?" Freddie asked.

"I have no earthly idea." Could David have bought it? After all, she'd mentioned not being *equipped* to attend so many *ton* functions.

Lori snorted at the thought.

"What is so amusing?" Freddie asked, coming up to stand behind her, their eyes meeting in the looking glass.

"I cannot believe that I entertained, even for a second, that David Parker might have purchased such a thing."

"You are certain that he did not?"

She gave a bitter laugh. "If David *had* bought me a gown—a possibility that truly defies credibility—it would be cheaply and poorly made."

Freddie did not look surprised. "You have no ideas at all as to the sender?"

"None. Unless…"

"Unless?" Freddie prodded.

"Do you think Honey or one of the others might have sent it? They all saw me last year at Miles's betrothal ball. Indeed, Honey tried to convince me to accept a new dress as a gift." Lori had been amused and touched by Honey's offer, but she had firmly refused the gift. The last thing she wanted to do was make a practice of accepting expensive gifts from her wealthy friends. She met Freddie's suddenly troubled gaze. "Has Honey said anything in her letters that might indicate it is from her?"

"I *did* mention in my letter to Honey that I was refurbishing your gowns—but only because she had asked me if I had time to do some needlework on a reticule she had made for her niece." A faint flush stained Freddie's cheeks. "I'm sorry, Lori—I did not mean to—"

"Hush, Fred! You needn't apologize for that. However, I *do* want you to write and ask her if she is responsible for this."

"Of course, I will ask her."

Lori turned back to reflection and sighed. "I hate to admit this, but I love this gown."

"Why do you hate to admit that?"

"Because I can hardly wear it if I don't know who sent it."

"You can't send it back if you don't know who purchased it," Freddie pointed out.

"I will go to this Madam Thérèse and see if I can get the information out of her." Lori sighed as she lowered the dress back into the box. "If she won't tell me, I will tell her that I will send the garment back. That is exactly what I'll do. It is what I *must* do."

"You sound as though you are trying to convince yourself."

Lori laughed. "That's because I am. My better angel is in ascendance right now, but my evil imp is poised to take control at the first sign of weakness."

Freddie took the gown from her and carefully draped it over her arm. "If you bunch it up like that it won't be fit to wear," she chided gently. "I'll have Mary lightly press it. Just in case you decide to keep it."

"But I was going to take it with me—to Madam Thérèse's."

"You can hardly drag this big box all over the city. Send it by messenger if she refuses to tell you."

Lori sighed. "Fine."

"It would be perfect for the Archer ball tonight," Freddie murmured, gazing almost lovingly at the beautiful gown.

"Are you saying that you like this gown better than the one I just purchased myself?" Lori asked with exaggerated surprise.

Freddie opened her mouth, but then closed it again, clearly not wishing to give offence.

Lori laughed. "I am teasing you, Freddie. I tell myself that it's not so much that I have horrid taste as that I'm a terrible nipcheese. I always go into a dressmaker's shop with the best of intentions, but I find myself quickly overset by the shocking cost of things. I chose that blue material because it cost a fraction of anything else."

"Yes, that is what I thought," Freddie said mildly, making Lori laugh again. She cast another admiring glance at the gown over her arm. "I truly hope you can't find out who gave this to you, Lori."

***

Two hours later—and after a heated discussion in French, with Madam Thérèse—Lori had failed to obtain the name of her anonymous benefactor.

She had also managed to delay writing her article for another day, a matter that weighed on her mind and wiped the mystery of the ball gown from her thoughts as she made her way back home.

Despite David's rather harsh directive to drum up an article about Lord Severn—either about the mutineers or his brother's suicide—she was instead working on a story about the Earl of Ashby and his disastrous curricle race to Brighton, which had resulted in the death of a thirteen-year-old boy who'd been walking beside the road when Ashby lost control of his horses.

None of the articles Lori had read mentioned that the peer had been intoxicated and whipping his pair into a bloody froth when he'd lost control of them. That was a piece of information Lori had discovered after talking with over twenty witnesses to the reckless event.

She hoped the story would take David's mind off his obsession with Severn and at least buy her a few weeks reprieve.

This was the sort of article she felt proud to write. Ashby deserved to be punished and if she were fortunate enough to get the truth published it would hopefully help build public sentiment against him.

Writing about the race without sensationalizing it had proven more difficult than she'd believed, but the boy deserved better than to have his death turned into nothing but a lurid piece of gossip.

But now the story would have to wait.

Lori sighed and glanced at the watch pinned to her bodice after she'd hung up her hat and cloak. She barely had half an hour and would have to hurry if she was to be dressed and ready for dinner on time.

She'd just finished a quick sponge bath when Freddie paid her a visit, holding the freshly pressed ball gown over her arm. "Well? What is the verdict, Lori? Do you get to wear it? Or will you break my heart and send it away?"

"That stubborn *Thérèse* woman wouldn't speak so much as a word, so it looks like I'll be keeping it." She narrowed her eyes. "Don't forget to ask Serena about it—and ask the others, as well—in your next letter."

"I won't." She hesitated and then said, "You could always write to our friends yourself, you know."

"I *do* write, just not every week," Lori protested. Or every month, truth be told. She knew it was more than a little ironic that the writer among their group was dreadful at correspondence.

Freddie laid the dress carefully across Lori's bed and then turned to her. "I'm going to arrange your hair for you."

"Oh, you don't have to do that, Freddie. I know you have the twins to—"

"The twins are having dinner with their grandmother, so they shall meet us at Lady Archer's."

"It will be just the two of us?"

"Yes."

"That's capital!"

"We will have to take a hackney rather than the Barton's fine coach," Freddie warned.

"It is worth a ride in a filthy hackney to get you to myself without the presence of your wittering charges."

Freddie ignored Lori's unkind comment and motioned toward the dressing table. "Take a seat and unplait your hair. I'll return with my beauty box."

Lori heaved an exaggerated sigh. "Very well, I will allow you to dress my hair. But absolutely *no* ringlets. Or curling tongs."

Freddie smiled. "No ringlets or curling tongs, I promise."

***

As usual, Fast ignored the cluster of young bucks who'd gathered around him the moment he'd entered the ballroom. Instead, he focused his attention on his erstwhile best friend, the Earl of Moreland, who was dancing with Miss Pascoe.

Just looking at his smug, handsome face set Fast's teeth on edge.

"Isn't that so, Severn?"

He jolted at the sound of his name. "What's that?" he asked, not bothering to hide his irritation from the Marquess of Dare—a tiresome youth who clung to him like shit on his shoe no matter how diligently Fast tried to scrape him off.

Dare smiled eagerly. "Er, I was just saying that the odds are currently in your favor when it comes to landing the Pascoe chit."

"Don't you know that wagering about ladies is bad form?" Fast barked.

The youngling's face puckered and for a moment Fast felt guilty, as if he'd just swatted a puppy on the nose with a newspaper. "Oh, er, yes. Just so."

"*I* haven't participated in any of that foolery," Viscount Melton said, cutting Dare a virtuous smirk.

"Being a kiss-arse is also bad form, Melton," Fast said.

All the other young men guffawed.

"Have any of you—" Baron Kearsley began, but Fast didn't catch the rest of what he said, the chatter around him falling away as the person he'd been waiting for all evening appeared across the crowded ballroom.

His mouth became as dry as the Sahara and yet he was suddenly perspiring like a bishop in a brothel. "Bloody hell," he muttered. He'd known Miss Fontenot would look good in that blue-green gown, but nothing had prepared him for just *how* good.

"I say," Dare squawked in his grating voice, "who the devil is *that*?"

Fast didn't need to ask who the young sprog meant. Before he gave into temptation and snarled at the young men to not so much as *look* at Miss Fontenot, Fast pushed off the wall and made his way toward where she was chatting with the Countess of Sedgewick and several matrons. He knew it wasn't possible, but the damned Fontenot woman seemed to draw all the light from hundreds of candles toward her.

As Fast had long suspected, the clinging silk of her gown displayed the sort of figure that men launched navies and declared wars over. The snug bodice was lower than she usually wore, but not so daring that it would offend even the most prudish sensibility.

Instead of the full-length sleeves she usually favored, Fast's creation featured short, delicate puffs of silk that left her pleasingly plump arms on display. Or at least *partly* on display.

His choice of opera gloves in a matching blue-green kid had truly been inspired. The supple leather hugged her pale, creamy flesh in a manner that was positively decadent and required him to pause and subtly adjust himself before resuming his journey across the ballroom.

Her glorious mass of blue-black hair was, for once, arranged in an attractive coiffure rather than brutally scraped back from her temples and pinned to within an inch of its life. Thankfully, she had not opted for either a cropped, teased fringe or the annoying sausage-like curls that so many young women preferred. Instead, her thick glossy locks were twisted into a simple but elegant chignon that managed to look smooth yet artfully disarranged, as if she'd just tumbled from a lover's bed.

Lady Sedgewick noticed Fast first and must have said something to Miss Fontenot because she turned to him, her eyelids lowering over her brilliant green eyes and her full lips curving into a mocking smile.

Christ she was lovely!

"Miss Fontenot, what a pleasure seeing you here tonight."

"What is the world coming to, Lord Severn?"

"I am almost afraid to ask what you mean?" he said.

"Who would have believed that *you* would have sought out *me*?"

Fast laughed. "I must be a glutton for punishment."

Her smile grew into a smirk, and she turned to her friend. "Freddie, this is Lord Severn. Lord Severn, the Countess of Sedgewick."

Fast was amused by her unconventional mode of introduction and suspected she did it on purpose.

Lady Sedgewick gave a curtsey of surpassing grace. "It is a pleasure to meet you, my lord."

Fast bowed over her hand. "The pleasure is all mine. I knew your husband about half a lifetime ago."

Her eyes, an unusual fawn color, shuttered, and the slight amount of warmth he'd seen in them turned to frost. "Indeed."

Fast couldn't say he was surprised by her reaction. He'd known Sedgewick well enough back in the day and the man had been a cad who'd had some rather unsavory perversions. He suspected his widow was all too aware of what her husband had been like. He would have thought Sedgewick's death was a happy release but clearly the countess had been left penniless if she was forced to launch Cit's daughters to earn her crust. She was a lovely woman but had all the warmth of an iceberg. Lord only knew what Gregg saw in her to fascinate him so.

He turned to Miss Fontenot. "You look lovely," he said, amused by the pink wave that suffused her from the swells of her delicious breasts right up her swanlike neck. A neck that only sported a rather sad-looking pearl necklace he suspected was paste. Damn! Fast knew he should have included some bauble that matched the gown.

"Thank you, my lord."

"Did you have any plans to ask me to dance?"

She laughed. "Odious man! You should not have mentioned my shocking behavior in front of Freddie. She will be horrified."

"But not surprised," Lady Sedgewick said dryly.

"I believe there is a waltz next," Fast said. "Will you honor me with a dance."

"Oh, but the honor would be all mine," she purred.

The small hairs on the back of his neck stood up. Bloody hell, what was she planning to grill him about this time?

Chapter 12

"I want the supper waltz, too," Fast said only seconds after they'd begun to dance.

Miss Fontenot laughed. "What makes you think I have it free?"

"If you promised it to somebody else, tell them you forgot that you'd already given the dance to me. But I don't think you have."

"For shame! Are you saying that I am not taking the *ton* by storm, my lord?"

"You're taking me by storm, and that is all that matters." Her lips parted and Fast smiled at the adorably flustered look. When she didn't speak, he added, "I have only ever seen you dance once before—and that was with Avington last year. As far as I've seen—and I have certainly been paying attention—you have not danced with anyone else except me this year. Although I suspect that is from choice rather than circumstance."

"You are flirting with me again."

"I can't help myself. You look downright edible tonight."

Twin streaks of red stained her cheeks so suddenly that she looked almost as if she'd been slapped, but her voice was even and calm when she said, "Is that all it takes to interest you in a woman, my lord? An expensive gown and a fancy coiffure?"

He lowered his caressing gaze to her upper arm. "Those gloves don't hurt, either." Before she could reply, he said, "To answer your question, what you wear doesn't make a damned bit of difference to me. I'd still be interested in you if you wore a burlap sack." He gave her an evil smile. "Or better yet: nothing at all."

"If you're trying to make me blush you have already succeeded and can stop."

Fast would have liked to tease her all night but decided to have mercy. "What is the occasion?"

"Occasion?"

"For the new gown."

"Perhaps I am on the catch for a wealthy husband."

Fast laughed.

"Why is that so amusing?"

"You strike me as a woman who has no use for a husband."

"What do you mean by that?"

"I mean I cannot see you promising before God to obey any man."

"And that is how you view marriage—as an opportunity to exert dominance over your wife?"

"If you were my wife, I'd enjoy establishing a bit of dominance over you."

She gave a startled, breathy laugh and looked away, for once disconcerted by his crude, suggestive comment.

Fast experienced a rare twinge of guilt for teasing her. She might be a sophisticated newspaperwoman, but she'd as much as admitted that she was still a maiden. "I apologize, I shouldn't be so vulgar."

Her head whipped around. "Why not? Because I'm a woman?"

"That, and also because you're young." *And likely a maiden.*

"I assure you, I am not a child."

He smiled. "No? How old are you?"

"It is rude to ask a lady's age."

Fast laughed at her quick retort.

"How old are *you*?" she asked.

"Given your investigative skills I suspect you already know the answer to that, Miss Fontenot."

She laughed, her intensity giving way to amusement. "I do indeed. And far more besides."

"I don't doubt it," Fast said dryly.

"So, you don't talk to other young ladies the way you talk to me?"

"No."

"Not even Miss Pascoe?"

"No."

"Why is that?"

"Because she's not the sort of woman who'd climb a mountain of packing crates to peer inside a brothel. Tell me," he said, changing the subject, "why haven't you been shadowing me lately?"

"Why? Do you miss me?"

"I'll admit that your attention adds a sort of zest to my days. And nights."

She snorted, clearly uninterested in flirtation, no matter how mild. "Why does Parker hate you so much?"

"What, you don't know the story?"

"Would I ask if I did?"

Fast sighed. "He wrote a story about my grandfather years ago—this is when I was still a lad—and, as usual, he got a great deal of it wrong. My grandfather sued Parker's employer and won. I dare say it was not pleasant for him, even though the money came out of somebody else's pocket. So, I suppose the answer to your question is *revenge*. Which makes me suspicious as to why he has suddenly stopped haunting my every move."

"You aren't the only source of news in the city, my lord."

"I'm glad to hear that he finally realized that."

"Oh, he still wants stories about you, but I have my own fish to fry."

"Indeed? What lucky fish they are to have your attention."

She tilted her head. "Is that the best the King of the Rakes can manage?"

"You want my best?"

"Of course."

"I save my best for the bedchamber, darling."

She rolled her eyes.

Fast laughed. "I deserve that."

"You do," she agreed. "Tell me, why aren't you asking Miss Pascoe for the supper dance?"

"What makes you think I haven't and she turned me down?"

"I suspect she has been sternly instructed to reserve that set for the heir to a marquessate."

He clucked his tongue. "That does not speak highly of my personal charm."

"It wouldn't matter if you had the charm of a chamber pot; Bryok Pascoe is determined to have you for a son-in-law."

Fast laughed. "Thank you, Miss Fontenot."

She shrugged. "It wasn't meant to be an insult; it is merely the truth."

"So young and yet so cynical."

"I prefer the word *pragmatic*."

"For your information, Miss Pragmatist, you are the first woman I have asked for the supper dance."

She stared at him appraisingly, and Fast could almost hear the gears churning away in that clever mind of hers. "May I ask you something, my lord?"

"I am shaking in my dancing slippers, Miss Fontenot. You have never asked permission before; it must be a truly offensive question."

"What if I promise not to include anything you say for the duration of this dance in any article? What if I promise you confidentiality? Will you answer my questions honestly?"

"Why, Miss Fontenot! Are you feeling ill?"

She gave him an exasperated huff. "Why don't we just talk? I've heard that normal people do that on occasion."

"Touché. Go ahead and ask and I'll decide if I want to answer."

"It's common knowledge that the *Vixen* belongs to you, and yet I've never seen your name mentioned anywhere when it comes to prize money."

Fast didn't reply.

"You don't want to answer that?"

"Oh, was that a question? Because it sounded like a statement."

"And *you* sound like a grammar teacher."

"I own the *Vixen* in conjunction with a partner, he has been content to accept all the fame and acclaim."

"Piers Amory Gregg? Notice the way my intonation went up on the word Gregg, indicating it's a question."

"Yes, Gregg is my partner."

"Interestingly enough, I've not been able to find a single piece of information about Mr. Gregg, for all that he claims to be English."

"That *is* interesting."

"Are you refusing to talk about him?"

"Questions about Mr. Gregg are his affair. I'm sure he'd be delighted to be the subject of one of your articles—why don't you ask him?"

"I think he's even more secretive than you are."

"*Secretive* has such negative connotations. I prefer the word *private,*" he said, his words an echo of her earlier statement. "Why are you so curious about prize money, anyhow? Are you trying to discover how wealthy I am, Miss Fontenot?"

"I wouldn't mind knowing."

"If you want to know for personal reasons, then I will be happy to tell you."

"Personal reasons? You mean am I hunting for a husband?"

"That is the second time you've mentioned yourself and husband hunting in the same sentence tonight. Dare I hope?"

She pursed her lips and shook her head, but a smile crept into her brilliant green eyes. "I may not be interested in matrimony, but I *do* hope some clever woman eventually hunts, traps, and takes your tail for a trophy."

Fast laughed.

***

"Are you committed for the next set?" Lord Severn asked Lori as he led her off the dance floor."

"That would be *three* dances you've asked me for in one evening. Even I know that is the *ton* equivalent of an instant betrothal."

"Have no fear, Miss Fontenot, I'm not trying to trick you into marriage. I thought we might have a walk in Lord Archer's garden rather than dance; it is one of the nicest in London."

Lori cut him a sideways look. "Why are you being so polite and attentive to me?"

"I should hope I am *always* polite. As for attentive? Well, for purely selfish reasons."

"Which are?"

He lowered his voice and leaned close enough that Lori felt his hot breath on her temple. "Because I enjoy your company."

Lori shivered.

"Are you cold?" he asked, his voice rich with humor.

The blasted man *knew* he was the reason she was shivering. Arrogant rake.

"I will go for a walk with you," she said. "My wrap is on my chair."

He led her back to where she'd been sitting with Freddie—who was nowhere in sight and must be off with her charges—and picked up the lovely scrap of silk and draped it over her shoulders.

"There," he said, offering her his arm.

Lori took it, feeling remarkably conspicuous as she walked beside him toward the French doors. No doubt that was just her nerves talking; after all, there were numerous other couples leaving the stultifying ballroom to take the air. But there was no denying that the viscount was a magnet for attention—especially the female kind—and they were attracting more than their fair share of speculative glances.

"Let us get away from the throng," Severn murmured once they'd reached the terrace.

"You've been here often?" she asked as he escorted her toward a path lighted by lanterns that had been placed at enough distance to offer some privacy.

"Severn House is at the opposite end of the square—which I'm sure you know. When Percy and I were young, Lord Archer's son was one of our playmates. We spent hours in this garden."

"It's beautiful out here," she said, the air pleasantly crisp and intoxicatingly floral.

He stopped beside a fountain and turned to her. "*You* are beautiful."

Lori wished her heart didn't behave so recklessly when he said things like that. She swallowed down the nervous flutters and looked up at him.

His hard mouth softened into a smile when she met his gaze. "Why do you write for Parker?"

"You've asked me that before. Why do you find it so astonishing that I work at a newspaper? Because I'm a woman?"

"No, because you seem far too clever to do such work."

She refused to feel flattered by his words. "I work for him because he pays me." Lori hesitated, and then added, "That money allows me to write the things I really like to write. Those things, unfortunately, don't pay."

"Oh? What do you like to write?"

She chewed the inside of her cheek, marveling at her own resistance to answering his question. Her aspiration to become a novelist was not a secret—not by any means—so why was she so reticent with this man?

"Novels," she said, before she could lose her courage.

"What sort of novels?"

"Why do you care?"

He gave an exasperated laugh. "So very prickly! Why on earth would I ask if I didn't care, Lorelei?"

"Who gave you permission to use my Christian name… Stand Fast?" she countered, pleased the quaver in her chest didn't make itself known in her voice.

"*Mmmm*," he rumbled, his pale eyes narrowing. "I like the sound of my name on your tongue."

For some reason the word *tongue* sounded very wicked when he said it. "Your name is unusual, my lord." It was a stupid observation, but all she appeared to be capable of at the moment.

He nodded slowly, his gaze suddenly dark and predatory.

Lori couldn't stop swallowing, her mouth flooding with moisture as his pupils swelled. "Is it a family name? Was somebody in—Oh!" she broke off with a yelp when he reached up and cupped her jaw, the tips of his warm fingers resting on the back of her neck.

She didn't move away. Indeed, it was a struggle not to take a step closer. "What are you doing?" she whispered.

"I want to kiss you," he said, lightly caressing her cheek with his thumb. "Do you want me to?"

God help her; she did. "Yes." Lori worried that she'd spoken so quietly that he might not have heard her.

But he must have, because his mouth lowered over hers.

Given his reputation, she had expected a forceful, aggressive claiming, but his lips were soft and gentle as they drifted over her mouth, learning the shape of her with a light tracery of kisses, teasing her until she pressed her lips against his.

He gave an approving murmur and angled his head so that she could reach him more easily.

So…this is what kissing was like.

"Lorelei," he murmured, the word a warm feather brushing over her cheek. "Are you a siren… luring me to my doom?"

If he expected an answer to that question—or any other—he was destined to be disappointed, because a wordless grunt was all she could manage.

He chuckled softly and then claimed her mouth again, harder this time, his tongue slicking along her lower lip, his teeth gently nipping. The second kiss quickly grew more intense, his touch commanding and demanding and she quickly found herself towed beyond her depth.

One of his hands slid to her waist, pulling her closer while he cupped her head with his other hand, angling her for his pleasure. His body was enticingly hot and hard, and her hands behaved with a will of their own, stroking the fine wool of his coat, her fingers closing over his lapels so she could tug him lower and closer.

Lori gave a whimper of surprise when his tongue probed her slightly parted lips.

"Let me in, Lorelei," he murmured.

How…shocking.

She opened to him and his hands molded her body to his, his tongue slick and hot. The myriad sensations that flooded her were as enticing as they were confusing and at first Lori felt overwhelmed, as if she'd been caught up in a sensory cyclone. But then…gradually, without even realizing it, she began to not only respond, but explore, caressing his tongue with her own and nipping his firm lower lip.

Lori's mind was rarely still; even when she slept a non-stop parade of dreams consumed her. But right then, for the first time in her life, she was entirely in the moment, the masculine scent of his cologne mingling with the faint taste of port and the warmth of his hands until every single part of her felt *alive.*

And then he pulled away.

He chuckled when she tried to follow him, his big hand firm on her waist as he steadied her, the slight clench of his fingers commanding in a way that aroused, rather than annoyed, her.

Lori wrenched her gaze from his reddened, slightly parted lips to eyes. The startling blue of his iris was a mere sliver, swallowed by twin black pools of desire.

Desire for her.

The pulse at the base of her neck fluttered hard enough that she felt it. His gaze dropped to it briefly before lifting back up to her eyes.

"Come home with me, Lorelei."

Chapter 13

Fast regretted the words the moment they left his mouth. Bloody hell! It had been years—decades—since he'd bungled so badly.

Lorelei, rightfully, looked as if somebody had just tipped a bucket of cold water over her head. She took an unsteady step backward, the sleepily aroused expression of only a second earlier already gone.

"Ah," Fast said.

She bristled. "What do you mean *ah*?"

"You've come back to yourself. For a moment I thought—" He broke off and shrugged. "Just *ah*."

"What did you think? That I would go to your house"—her eyes widened— "or perhaps you thought to bring me back to the brothel?"

Fast couldn't help smiling at her anger. "There, that is more like it." Strangely enough, he hadn't liked seeing her flustered and uncertain—especially not when he'd been the one to wrong-foot her.

"Why are you looking at me that way?" she demanded.

"What way?"

"Pityingly."

He gave an exasperated huff. "Has it ever occurred to you that you might be misreading me?"

"No. I recognize that superior, pitying look. Is that because I won't leave this ball with you? You think because I'm a woman who works that I'm also a—a—"

"Yes?" he asked, curious to see what she thought he thought she was.

"A female with loose morals. A—a Jezabel."

He laughed, amused by the antiquated word.

She lifted her hand, as if she might slap him, but then clenched it into a fist and dropped it to her side. "Are you courting Miss Pascoe?"

Yet again, Lorelei had surprised him with a question he wasn't expecting.

"You are, aren't you?" she demanded, mistaking the reason for his pause. "You are in pursuit of one woman but believe you have the right to bed another."

"I am not betrothed to Miss Pascoe."

She gave him a scornful look. "You think women are put on earth to amuse you—that we are nothing but your playthings. And when the result of your—your *raking* arrives nine months after you have taken your pleasure you are already long gone, leaving some poor woman to live with the consequences."

The irony of her accusation was enough to make him laugh. Wisely, he didn't.

"Why are you smiling, my lord? Do I amuse you?"

"It is not so much *you* I find amusing as this conversation, Miss Fontenot."

"I'm so pleased to be a source of mirth. But I am finished entertaining you." She spun on her heel.

Or at least she would have done if he'd not caught her upper arm, the feel of warm silky skin and cool soft leather teasing the pads of his fingers.

"You should not go—not like this, Lorelei."

She jerked her elbow away and Fast immediately released her. "Why not?" she demanded, crossing her arms and rubbing the spot where his fingers had just been.

"Because your eyes are throwing sparks, and your lips look freshly kissed, and your cheeks are delightfully flushed. If you enter the ballroom in such a condition everyone will know you've just been soundly kissed in the garden." He smiled. "By me."

"And that would reflect poorly on you because you are supposed to be pursuing Miss Pascoe, aren't you?"

"It wouldn't look good for either of us," he said, not bothering to deny her accusation. It was better for her if she was suspicious of him. Especially since Fast couldn't seem to control his thoughts or hands or mouth around her. No, she shouldn't trust him.

Her jaw flexed and he suspected she was rapidly trying out responses and just as rapidly discarding them, her rattled behavior once again telling him that she was scarcely more than an innocent when it came to sexual dalliance—or even mere flirtation. He felt a sharp pang of regret that there could never be more between them.

She was a stunning woman and not just her looks. Standing near her was like standing beside a lightning bolt; never before had he been so completely aware of another person.

But she was not of his world; she was a newspaperwoman, not a member of his class. No, she was not meant for him. He'd forgotten that fact briefly when he'd held her in her arms. He'd been a bloody fool to ask her to go home with him. He was relieved—if also disappointed—that she'd come to her senses.

This needed to be the last time he allowed himself to linger in her company.

The last.

After tonight, he would avoid the woman like the plague. For her good, as well as his own.

***

"My goodness," Freddie murmured as she gazed down at the contents of the now familiar pale pink box. "It is—"

"Magnificent," Lori finished for her.

Freddie looked up from the gown at Lori's brittle tone and she frowned. "You look angry."

"I *am* angry."

"Because Honey said it wasn't her and you still have no idea who sent this?"

"Yes."

"And you went back to Madam Thérèse again?"

"Yes." Lori flung up her hands. "The woman refused to budge an inch. Being in the dark one time was amusing, but this is…"

"Is what?" Freddie asked, her eyes turning back to the gown as if they were on leading-strings.

"It's annoying. And frustrating. And embarrassing."

"Embarrassing?"

"I am a newspaperwoman, Freddie. I ferret out the truth for a living and yet I can't even find out who is sending me gowns. I look like a fool."

Freddie gave Lori one of her rare smiles. "I can see how that might be awkward for you. But, at the same time, you can hardly expect Madam Thérèse to betray the confidence of one of her clients. Especially one who spends so much money." She cocked her head. "Weren't you the one who told me that the people who contribute information to your stories deserve to have their identities protected, if that is what they want?"

"Please stop being so logical!"

Freddie laughed.

"But I haven't shown you the worst of it yet." Lori lifted the gown from the box, exposing a beautiful marquetry box.

Freddie reached for the box but then stopped, her eyes darting to Lori.

"Go head and open it," Lori said.

Freddie flipped up the lid and caught her lower lip with her teeth.

She had already stared at the necklace, bracelet, and earrings for a full half hour before her friend had come home and discovered Lori standing in her room like a slack-jawed yokel.

"Are those what I think they are?" Lori asked.

"Emeralds?" Freddie said, and then picked up an earring and held it to the light. "I'm no expert on gemstones, but they are lovely, whatever they are."

Lori tossed the gown over the jewels and pressed the heels of her hands against her pounding temples. "Good Lord, Fred! What in the world am I going to do?"

"Wear it. All of it—the dress and the jewels," Freddie said, without so much as a second's hesitation.

"But—"

"You don't know who sent it and that person has obviously gone to a great deal of effort to make sure of that. You can hardly be accused of accepting gifts from someone when you don't know who that someone *is*. You have three options: give it away, sell it, or keep it. That necklace alone must cost hundreds of pounds, Lori. You cannot *give* it away. You could sell it, but you would still be profiting from an anonymous gift, so why not wear it? At least wear it once before selling it," she amended. "And just *think*, Lori: selling it all would give you enough of a nest egg to live on for a long, long time. Having pride is all well and good, but we are women of uncertain means, Lori. And right there"—she jabbed a finger at the box— "is one way to remove that uncertainty. You would be a fool to throw away such a windfall. And I know you are not a fool."

Lori watched in open-mouthed wonder as her friend—often referred to as the *Ice Countess* behind her back— paced back and forth, her cheeks flushed and her breathing rapid. "I beg your pardon for becoming overly emotional, Lori, but I am angry," she said, startling Lori with her raised voice. "These gifts are probably from a man but we, as women, are told all our lives that we cannot accept gifts from men who are not our husbands or fathers. And why is that? Because it offends our honor. But does it not offend our honor to need a man's protection and money to live respectably?" She made a very rude, un-Freddie noise and shook her head. "Why should *men* be the only ones to make all the rules? Or break them," she added under her breath.

Lori had never seen such fire in the other woman's fawn-gray eyes. For years Lori and the other teachers who'd worked at the Stefani Academy had believed Freddie was too calm and controlled. It couldn't be good for a person to suppress every emotion. And here Freddie was letting her emotions bubble over for the first time that Lori had seen and on the subject of anonymous gifts.

Interesting.

Something told her that if she tried to pry—however gently—Freddie would close up as tightly as a clam.

Instead, she considered her friend's argument.

If Freddie, who was considered an arbiter of taste, fashion, and manners, not only by Lori and the rest of their friends, but also most of the *ton*, believed that she should keep and wear the gifts then she would.

"Very well. I shall wear the gown *and* the jewels."

"Excellent. It is most propitious the gown arrived today. you can wear it and the jewels tonight."

"Tonight?" Lori repeated. "I did not think we had any engagements?"

"I accepted two invitations for this evening. On both our behalf."

"Two? But I hadn't—" she broke off at Freddie's narrow look. "Er, what are we attending tonight?"

"Lady Russell's ball first, and then we shall stop in at the Countess of Rutland's."

"I can come to the first one, Freddie, but there really is something I need to do later."

"There is something you need to do at midnight?" Freddie repeated.

"Er, yes."

"Something dangerous?"

"Of course not," she lied.

"Am I going to read about whatever you are doing in tomorrow's newspaper, Lori?"

"It's nothing like that, Freddie." At least she certainly hoped not, although Lori knew that David would, without compunction—indeed, quite eagerly—publish a story that reported the arrest of the Countess of Sedgewick's housemate at one of the most salacious and dangerous wharf front taverns in London.

"I will only be gone a few hours, Freddie. And it is completely harmless."

Freddie stared for a long moment before nodding. "I hope so."

So did Lori.

***

Miss Fontenot's green eyes sparkled up at Fast, the glitter in them putting the emeralds around her neck to shame. "You look perturbed, Lord Severn. Should I not have asked you to dance tonight?"

Fast *was* angry—and disgusted—but at himself rather than Miss Fontenot.

First, for buying her the damned gown and jewels that he was currently imagining tearing from her body.

Second, for coming to this ball in the hope that she would be here.

Third, for saying *yes* to her cheeky request for a waltz.

It was time to face the truth: where Miss Fontenot was concerned, Fast was weakness itself.

He'd lied to himself and said that he needed to come tonight if he was to continue irritating Moreland by courting Miss Pascoe.

He'd told himself that Miss Fontenot would still be so angry with him about the last time they'd spoken that he would get to watch her from afar without risking another exchange between them.

He was an idiot.

"My lord?"

"Hmm?" he murmured, deftly guiding her around a pair of dancers whose enthusiasm for the waltz was greater than their skill.

"Are you perturbed that I asked you to dance?"

When he looked down, he saw a glint of something that looked like concern in her eyes.

"I wanted to dance with you," he said.

"Then why do you look so grim?"

Because you should stay as far away from me as possible, and I should help you by avoiding you at all costs.

He immediately ignored that advice and said, "Tell me, what do you do when you are not working, Lorelei?"

"I don't recall giving you permission to use my Christian name."

"You didn't."

She snorted softly and then said, "Nobody calls me that."

"Oh? What do they call you?"

"Miss Fontenot."

"I meant what do your friends call you?"

"But we are not friends, my lord."

"Are you still angry about the last time?"

Her eyes flickered and she glanced away, but then quickly dragged her gaze back to him. "Oh that. I'd already forgotten."

They both heard the lie in her voice.

Fast left that dangerous subject behind and said, "You look lovely tonight. Another new frock?"

"Yes," she said shortly.

"You look annoyed."

She pursed her lips.

"What is amiss?" he persisted. "Why do you look like such a squeeze crab?"

"*Squeeze crab*?"

Fast smirked at her amused outrage. "If the shoe fits."

"Don't worry, my lord. For once, it's not you."

"What a relief. Then what is it?"

She paused for so long that he thought she'd ignore his prodding. "It is this dress," she eventually admitted.

"What is wrong with it?" he asked with altogether too much heat.

Fortunately, she did not notice his strange reaction. "Nothing is wrong with it."

She was right about that; she looked bloody gorgeous.

"Somebody gave it to me."

"Oh? Is that bad?" he asked carefully.

She shook her head, her cheeks turning that dark rose shade he'd grown to love. "Never mind."

"You can't just dangle an interesting tidbit like that in front of me and then say *never mind.*"

"Says who?"

"Says me."

She stared at his chin for a moment before lifting her eyes to his. "Somebody has been sending me gifts."

"Like the gown?"

"Yes. This gown, the one I wore last time, and other… things."

Fast inwardly smiled at her dismissive use of *other things* for the fortune in emeralds currently festooning her delicious person. "A secret admirer, then?"

"I don't know that the person admires me."

"What other reason could he have for sending you gifts?"

"Why would you say *he*?"

"It was just a figure of speech."

She grunted.

"Don't you like the gifts?"

"Of course I like them. They are beautiful—and perfect! That isn't the issue."

Perfect.

Fast allowed himself a tiny, smug smile at her admission. He liked seeing his gifts on her body very well indeed, but it was nice to hear that she liked them, too.

"So, what is the issue then?" he asked.

"I don't know," she admitted.

She looked so disgruntled that Fast wanted to laugh. But he suspected that he would gain more information with silence than mockery.

And his patience was rewarded when she said, "I'm supposed to be a newspaperwoman adept at digging up information and I haven't been able to discover a thing about the gift giver's identity."

Fast made a mental note to give Thérèse a bit extra when he settled the next bill.

"Surely you must suspect somebody?"

"I"—she bit her lip and then vigorously shook her head. "No."

"You were going to say somebody—whom?"

She gave him the irritable scowl he treasured almost as much as her blushing. "I've already said too much."

It irked Fast almost beyond bearing that there was somebody else in her life she suspected of giving her such gifts. And the fact that he was irked was even more… irksome. Naturally, she must be combing through her acquaintances and looking for a probable suspect. And just as naturally Fast would not be among that number. She'd said it herself: they weren't even friends. Indeed, she viewed him as nothing more than source material for a newspaper story.

It was Fast who'd given in to a flight of fancy and developed not just lustful imaginings, but *romantic* ones.

Bloody. Damn. Hell.

He needed to do something to keep the shocking state of his thoughts in check because Gregg was already beginning to suspect there was something amiss. He hated to think what his long-time business partner and friend would say if he ever guessed that Fast had been brought to his knees by a woman whose only interest in him was exposing his family's darkest secrets in his enemy's newspaper.

And he *never* wanted Gregg or anyone else to guess how arousing he was finding it to clothe this woman. Even Fast thought himself more than a bit unhinged to be deriving such pleasure in choosing garments for her—or even just thinking about her wearing garments next to her skin that he'd selected for—

"At first I thought it might be Mr. Parker—*ow*!" Miss Fontenot glared up at Fast when his fingers tightened around her waist.

"I beg your pardon," he muttered. "It's just difficult to believe you'd think that tasteless money-grubbing cad would select such a lovely garment.

She cut him an irritable look. "You're the one who asked me who I thought it was. Don't ask me questions if you're going to become so huffy about my answers."

"Huffy?"

"Yes, huffy. Besides, you hardly know anything about the man, so you're not in the best position to judge."

He was too angry to trust himself to speak, so he resorted to his characteristic grunt. She suspected Parker? Unbelievable!

"And don't think that you can force me to talk more by making those bestial grunts or maintaining a mysterious silence."

Fast grinned. "You've got me all sorted out, haven't you?"

An expression flickered across her face, but he'd be damned if he knew what it meant.

Before he could tease an answer out of her, what must have been the shortest waltz in history drew to a close.

"Do you have the supper dance available?" Fast asked, inwardly cursing his mouth.

"Lady Sedgewick wishes to leave before supper."

"Ah, the life of a social butterfly."

She smiled but didn't disabuse him.

Fast was disappointed but told himself it was for the best. He would have stayed for supper if she'd been free, but the truth was that he needed to get down to the wharf and help Gregg interrogate Garcia—their main suspect for whoever was selling information to Parker. The man had evidently been spotted by one of Gregg's many informants and Gregg was to set a trap for him later tonight.

While he regretted that he'd not get to spend more time with Miss Fontenot, he could not deny that he was very interested to question Mr. Garcia and discover if he was the man they'd been searching for. If Garcia was the one who'd blown the gaff about Jensen, then Fast would make excellent use of him before dishing up his just deserts.

Fast grinned at the prospect of feeding Parker some misinformation of his own devising. Christ but he'd like to get a few steps in front of despicable newspaperman for a change!

Chapter 14

Lori had never known just how acute her sense of smell was until that moment.

Nor had she known how cloying the scent of roses could be.

"'Ere ya go, luv," Ella said, draping something over Lori's shoulders that might once have been velvet but was now so threadbare and discolored it resembled a mangy, piebald cat.

"Er, thank you." Lori adjusted the shawl around her shoulders and stared in fascinated horror at her reflection in the mirror.

Behind her, the prostitute—Ella Clent—smiled and nodded. "A sight for sore eyes, ye are."

A sight to *make* eyes sore would be more like it, but Lori forced a smile. "Thank you."

"Moy pleasure," Ella said, adjusting one of Lori's curls.

Ella had teased Lori's hair and then formed it into sausage-like ringlets that had been gathered into two clusters, one on either side of her head. She'd then rouged her cheeks and lips and heavily kohled her eyes. As a crowning gesture, she'd put a patch at the corner of Lori's mouth.

Lori pointed to the large black dot. "Are you sure about this?"

"It's true that it's been years since they was in style, but the gents like 'em," Ella assured her.

And Lori's gown…

Well, it was also something that hadn't been in style for years. The bodice was boned and tight with exposed lacing, shoving her breasts up in the neighborhood of her chin, until they resembled a very fat baby's.

The skirt and petticoats were composed of acres of fabric and rustled whenever she moved, scenting the air with a musty rose smell, as if somebody had stored flowers in a trunk and then buried the trunk under six feet of dirt for half a century.

Lori would never be able to stomach the scent of a rose again.

"Ye look a treat," Ella assured her.

"*A treat.*" Lori repeated, laughing. "Well, that's good. Now, let me see if I can walk in these shoes." Lori stalked back and forth in Ella's small room, her feet making a clomping sound in velvet shoes with scuffed carmine heels and flaking gold buckles.

Already her ankles hurt just from a few jaunts across the room.

She shook her head. "I will just wear my own ankle boots. Nobody will notice them beneath the gown."

And it would also allow her to run, if need be. But Lori kept that thought to herself. Indeed, it felt cowardly to entertain such a notion. After all, Ella walked the same streets and entered the same drinking establishments every night of the week while Lori would only be visiting once and for a short time and a different business entirely. Poor Ella would be forced to sell her body until the day she died.

"We needs to 'ave a plan if a gent wants some trade," Ella said as Lori sat and changed her footwear.

"Trade? You mean if some man wishes to engage my, er, services?"

Ella laughed. "Aye, that's wot oi mean, ducks."

It was difficult to imagine any man wanting a woman who was wearing so much face paint, but then Ella herself wore a great deal—with *two* patches—and she claimed to make a decent, if not luxurious, living.

"I could tell anyone who approaches me that I'm on my courses," she said as she buttoned up her boots.

Ella gave another of her cackles. "Men don't care about that, luv."

"Really?" She sat up straighter and grimaced when the boning dug into the side of her breast.

"Nah. Most men would fuck a knot'ole in a fence."

Lori winced. "That is very vivid imagery." She stood and took the money she'd pre-counted before arriving at Ella's cramped little hovel. "Here is half of what we agreed upon. I'll give you the rest once we've visited the last of the taverns."

Ella nodded, took the small purse of money, and tucked it into her bodice.

"There is also a piece of paper in with the money that has an address written on it. If anything should happen to me, I'd be obliged if you'd let the lady who lives there know where you last saw me."

Ella frowned. "Anyfing? Like what?" she asked, visibly perplexed as to what could possibly befall two unattended women wandering around down at the docks after midnight.

"I don't know, Ella. But if I can't get back home at the end of the evening, that is the address where I live. My housemate should be made aware if I have any problems." Lord. She hated the thought of somebody bothering Freddie, but who else did she have? Not David, that was certain.

Ella shrugged. "Awright. You ready?"

"As ready as I'll ever be."

***

Fast checked his watch and then lifted a hand for the serving wench, who sauntered over to his table with a come-hither smirk on her face.

"Aye, milord? Wot can I get ye?"

He smiled up at her rather haggard face, not surprised that she knew who he was. "Can you keep a secret?" he asked her, sliding a shiny gold coin across the table.

A spark of interest entered her deadened eyes as she stared at the sovereign, a coin that had barely rolled out of the Mint. "These're new, aye? I ain't seen one yet."

"Well, you have now. And it is yours."

Her eyes narrowed. "Wot do I got to do fer it?"

"What is your name?"

"Cora, milord." She dropped a curtsey, her eyes flickering back to the coin.

Cora had been pretty not too long ago but life on the water's edge was not kind to women. Fast suspected the men she normally had commerce with hadn't been too kind either, based on the hardened crew drinking at tables all around him.

"I need an extra set of eyes and ears, Cora."

"Er, who is it you're lookin' for, milord?"

"He might have changed his name, but he was called Garcia. He crewed his way here from Gran Canaria and will speak with a heavy accent." He smiled at her look of disbelief. "I know, I know—there are a great many foreigners milling about down here with heavy accents, but not so many are Spaniards. Do you know the accent?"

"Aye, milord."

"If you come across him—even if you are not certain—send a message to The King's Purse immediately. Ask for me or Mr. Gregg. You know him?"

"Aye, everyone knows Mr. Gregg, sir."

Fast gestured to the sovereign and then stood as she tucked the coin away. "And Cora?"

"Yes, my lord?"

"This is just between us. If this man learns I'm looking for him he'll go to ground."

"I understand, sir."

Fast made his way out of the bar, aware that dozens of eyes followed him out the door. That wasn't unusual. He was an oddity on the docks—a peer who owned a whorehouse and had for years captained a ship. People knew who he was, which made it difficult to do anything without drawing attention. But they were running out of time, and he could no longer afford to be subtle.

The Virgin Queen—the bar he'd just left—had been his fourth tavern that night, and he'd handed out four sovereigns. But there were dozens of shady bars all along the waterfront.

Unfortunately, Gregg's carefully devised trap for Mr. Garcia had fallen through earlier that evening. While it was true that Garcia had been snared, it had been the *wrong* Garcia. Even so, the meeting hadn't been utterly useless as Mr. Garcia was, in fact, acquainted with the man they were seeking. Indeed, he claimed to have seen their quarry a scant hour before at the Jolly Taxpayer, a truly desperate tavern.

Gregg and Fast had hastened to the disreputable watering hole only to discover that Garcia had gone. They had decided to continue their canvassing, but to split up. Fast was working the establishments by Bell Wharf while Gregg was—

"Take your hands *off* me!"

Fast's head whipped around at the sound of the familiar voice, which came from the alley he was just passing. Disbelief momentarily froze him in place before a feminine cry rang out and he sprang into action, bolting down the alley toward the source of the distress.

"You are hurting me!"

"Now, now, hen. Just come along wiff me nice an' easy-like. All my guv wants is to 'ave a word wiff you," a male voice soothed. "If ye'll juss—*aaargh,* you bitch! You *bit* me!"

"If you lay so much as a finger on her, it will be the last thing you do," Fast said as the hulking brute raised his ham-sized fist, which was indeed bleeding.

The man went rigid, his forehead furrowed. "Oo the devil are you?"

He ignored the question and strode toward the giant, who was taller even than Fast and had another two stone on him. "Let her go. *Now.*"

The huge brute lifted his bloody fist, but in a placating gesture, keeping a grip on Lorelei's upper arm with his other hand. "Ere, then. No need to come the ugly, guv. I'll pay the dibs if she belongs to you."

Miss Fontenot gasped. "I do not belong to any—"

"Release her and step away," Fast barked.

The other man's small eyes suddenly widened in comprehension. "Yer Lor' Severn, ain't ye?"

Fast lunged for him and the man stumbled back, shoving Miss Fontenot toward him. "'Ere! Take 'er!"

"Get behind me," Fast snapped, relieved when she obeyed without any argument. He glared across the filthy alley at the giant, who'd raised both his hands, his posture defensive rather than aggressive. "You said your employer wants to talk to her. Who do you work for?"

"I wasn't gonna 'urt 'er."

"What did you want from her?"

"I jest…" The man's jaws snapped shut.

"You just what?"

"Er, nuffink. I jes reconnoitered that she's the wrong bird."

Fast narrowed his gaze at the other man, who'd begun to back away. "Where do you think you're going?"

Rather than answer, the man spun and ran full out.

"Damnation!" Fast gritted out, furious that he could not follow—not without leaving Miss Fontenot alone—and staring in seething frustration as the giant disappeared into the night before turning and getting his first good look at the woman who had been occupying far too many of his thoughts recently.

Fast stared down at her, rendered speechless. If he'd not heard her voice, he never in a hundred years would have recognized her.

"What the devil have you done to yourself?" he finally managed.

She pursed her lips and set about straightening her hideous clothing. "I am incognita." She sounded normal enough, but he could see her hands were trembling, so she wasn't as sanguine as she wished to appear.

"Why are you wearing those clothes? And why, in the name of all that is unholy, are you down here on the docks?"

"Why, pray, are either of those matters any business of yours, Lord Severn?"

He gave an unamused bark of laughter. "There is gratitude for me."

"I'm sorry," she said, not sounding it. "I ought to thank you."

"I shan't hold my breath." Fast pointed to her hand. "You are bleeding."

She examined the back of her hand. The scratches—likely from the rough brick—went up her forearm.

"Come with me," he said. "Those need seeing to or you will have an infection."

She opened her mouth.

"I am offering you help. You would be wise to take it."

Her mouth snapped shut and she nodded.

Fast took her arm and led her out of the alley.

"Where are we going?" she asked when they began to walk in the opposite direction from The King's Purse.

"A hackney driver waits for me behind *The Virgin Queen*."

"Is that where you were coming from when you heard me?"

He ignored her question, instead gesturing to her lewd garments. "*This* is why you couldn't dance the supper dance with me tonight? Because you were planning to wander the docks alone? What the devel are you looking for now, Lorelei? What could be so damned important that you would risk not only your virtue, but your life?"

She gave an exasperated sigh—the sound of a woman pushed beyond reason. "I cannot tell you that, my lord. I am investigating a matter for a story I'm writing. Until it is published, I won't chatter about it as if it was the newest fashion for hats."

"Does it have to do with me?"

She laughed, but Fast thought it sounded forced. "Not everything is about you, Lord Severn."

"I dearly hope that is the case."

"But it just so happens I *was* looking into something that involves you," she added after a moment.

"You are nothing if not predictable."

She glared at him. "If you spoke to me, I might be able to ensure the story fairly represents your point of view, my lord."

Fast ignored the comment.

They rounded a corner and discovered the hackney driver leaning against a post chatting with a pair of whores. Or perhaps they could have been two more newspaperwomen in disguise for all Fast knew.

The thought amused him.

"Why are you smirking in that odious way?" she demanded as he handed her into the hackney.

"Oh, am I smiling? Back to The King's Purse," he told the driver, and then climbed inside and took the seat across from her.

"I demand to know what is so amusing, my lord."

"I do not think you would be similarly amused."

Her lips compressed and she shook her head. "You are the most provoking man it has ever been my misfortune to encounter."

Fast laughed. "Coming from you, that is quite rich. Tell me, where did that big brute back there want to take you, Lorelei? Just who wants to talk to you badly enough they would send a ruffian to abduct you?"

The thick maquillage on her forehead creased as the skin beneath it puckered. She lifted both hands in an oddly distressing gesture and then let them drop limply back into her lap. "I don't know," she admitted, looking and sounding so forlorn that Fast actually believed her.

Fast reached out and took both her small hands in his before he could consider what he was doing. It was a sign of her abstraction that she did not pull away. Fast lightly squeezed her slender fingers. "You are angering people, Lorelei—and not just me."

Something very much like fear flickered across her face.

Fast suffered an unpleasant twisting sensation in his gut at the sight and he softened his tone. "Tell me about this story you are investigating, Lorelei. If I am so inclined, I might give you the information you seek."

Her eyes snapped to his, wonder rather than fear in her eyes. "You would?"

"I might." His lips twitched into a smile. "Perhaps then you won't feel the need to come poking around the docks at midnight dressed like a prostitute from the reign of George the First."

Chapter 15

Lori bit her lip and glared across at Lord Severn, unable to tell whether or not he was jesting. Not about Lori looking like a whore of yore—that was indisputable—but about telling her the truth regarding the mutineers. Would he really talk to her openly and honestly about such a matter?

Don't be a ninny! His only object is to get you away from the docks with as little fuss as possible. The last thing the man wants is for any of tonight to end up as food for some newspaper article.

Lori could accept that Severn did not want to be embroiled in scandal, but she did not believe that was all that motivated him. She'd seen in his eyes that he was also genuinely concerned for her safety.

She would never admit it aloud, but Severn was justified in excoriating her behavior tonight as dangerous and foolhardy.

The worst part about being trapped in that alley with her monstrous assailant hadn't been the groping Lori had endured. It had been the knowledge that *she* was responsible for her situation.

She should have known the man was trouble when he approached *her* claiming to have information about Lord Severn and his dealings with a mutineer from the *Sea Ranger.*

Rather than ask how he knew that she wasn't the whore she was pretending to be, Lori had gone along with him as trustingly as a lamb to slaughter. Instead of waiting for Ella—who'd stepped out a short time before to *do a bit-o-business*—she had followed the huge brute out to a dimly lighted alley, desperate to learn what he knew.

Nothing. That was what he'd known. At least nothing about Severn. But he had known plenty about Lori, including the story she was working on. During their terrifying, but brief, scuffle she had wondered if Lord Severn had been the brute's employer.

Lori had been ashamed by the thought when the man himself had come along and rescued her. Rather than thank him, she had immediately commenced brangling once he'd driven off her captor.

She frowned, suddenly conscious of the astounding coincidence of his arrival.

What in the world had brought Severn to the exact spot at the exact time that she'd been there?

"Come, come, Lorelei." His voice jolted her from her unpleasant thoughts. "If you don't tell me what you are doing here, then I'll send my men out. They will quickly discover what you were asking about." He lightly squeezed her hands, reminding her that he still held them.

Lori jerked her fingers from his grasp, strangely hurt when he allowed her to do so. "What are *you* doing here?"

"I live down here."

Lori blinked. Well, that was true.

"I've answered your question; now it is your turn, Lorelei."

She decided to ignore his use of her name. "I am still curious about the mutineer or mutineers you picked up."

"And I'm still curious about who told you such a thing?"

Lori considered reminding him that she couldn't expose her sources but decided—with his offer of a few moments before still on the table—that maybe sharing a bit of information might show good faith on her part. "I honestly do not know who it was, my lord. All I do know is that Mr. Parker received a letter on the subject. And—and I believe the sender was anonymous, although I would not swear as to that last part."

"Is that all it takes to make something newsworthy? A letter—and an anonymous one, at that? Perhaps *I* should send a letter claiming that I saw Parker abetting mutineers?"

Lori didn't blame him for his bitterness. She, too, thought David was chasing his tail with this story. But she also needed this job, so…

"I agree that some of the information my employer chooses to act upon is… vague. But you must admit that this accusation is rather specific. And it seems bizarre that it has arisen from nothing. It brings to mind that old adage about smoke and fire."

Instead of the hot denial that she had anticipated, he turned and stared out the widow, his profile carved from stone.

Lori felt a flutter of excitement. "There *is* something to it, isn't there?"

"I think all this prying you're doing on Parker's behalf is putting you in danger."

She'd begun to suspect the very same thing back in that alleyway. "How funny you should say so. I was thinking the same thing."

He turned and fixed her with a look of disgust. "You think I am the one who sent that brute to—"

"I don't think that," she hastily assured him, realizing as she said it that it was true. When he merely stared moodily, she smiled and added, "If you wanted to abduct somebody, you would do it yourself, not send a minion."

There was a slight thawing in his eyes at her words, but he did not speak.

"You must understand that I can't stop investigating this story? Especially not now that I know I must be close to something." Even though it scared her. "Until tonight, I'd not believed that Parker's source could possibly be correct. That man back in the alley makes me believe I must be on to something. You mentioned talking to me earlier—was that all a jest?"

Lord Severn heaved a sigh. "No, it was not. I'll talk to you, but I want you to give me your word that Parker doesn't know I'm the one who gave you the information."

Lori's pulse sped. "I promise."

His eyebrows rose. "You didn't give that much thought. Are you sure?"

Could she write a story and withhold the name of her source from her employer?

Before she could answer, the carriage rolled to a stop.

"We're here," Lord Severn said, opening the door, hopping out, and flipping down the steps before offering her his hand. When she hesitated, he said, "I thought you wanted to talk to me?"

Lori eyed the brothel and recalled her last humiliating visit. "I do. It's just that I thought we might have this discussion… elsewhere."

"Like where? Back at the *Virgin Queen*?"

"No, of course not. Just—"

"Do you want your story or not?"

Her gaze slid to the building looming behind him.

He laughed at her hesitation. "Has the intrepid Miss Fontenot suddenly turned craven?"

"Quit trying to manipulate me," she snapped. "Do you give me your word that you will tell me the truth?"

"I promise that everything I tell you will be the truth."

Something about his careful wording made her pause.

"I will make it worth your time," he added.

"Fine. I'll come inside. You'd better not be toying with me," she added and hopped out, ignoring his hand.

***

Lori glanced around the room, surprised by the quiet elegance of the décor. The walls were covered in crème silk and the furniture upholstered in a coffee brown leather that looked both supple and well-worn. It was the sort of room one would expect to find in an aristocrat's house, not in a brothel beside the Thames.

And it was nothing like the room she'd visited last time, that erotic bower where she'd briefly witnessed his lordship in the midst of pleasure.

Lori experienced the annoying clenching between her thighs that always assaulted her whenever she thought about that night.

"What is wrong?" Severn asked, as if he possessed a sixth sense that alerted him when a woman was entertaining thoughts of him. "You look like you just sucked on a lemon."

"Nothing is wrong," she snapped.

He lifted his eyebrows at her hostile reply.

Lori forced a civil tone into her voice. "It is just that this room is very… different from the last one."

"Do you want to go to the last one?"

"Absolutely not!" she retorted, and then noticed the smile lurking in his pale eyes. "Very droll, my lord."

He merely pulled the servant cord, and then gestured to a table with several decanters and asked, "Would you like something to drink?"

"I'll have whatever you're having."

He poured two glasses without comment.

"So…what is this room?"

"Part of my living quarters—a study of sorts." His eyelids lowered slightly. "You've already visited my bedchamber."

"I like this décor a great deal more," she said, refusing to be drawn.

He hesitated, and then said, "I have had this room made over to suit my taste."

"Hmmm."

"You think the red, black, and gold bedchamber more suitable for a man of my sort?"

Lori didn't, but she needed to get her jabs in where she could, so she said, "You looked very much at home in that other room."

He chuckled and held out her glass. "Here. Sip it slowly as you are unaccustomed to it."

"How do you know what I'm accustomed to?"

"Do you drink whiskey often?"

She met his amused gaze, and an answering smile formed on her own lips before she could stop it. "No. This is the first time." As tempted as she was to be a contrarian and toss the contents back in one gulp, she wisely took a small sip.

"Well?" he asked.

"It is surprisingly pleasant and invigorating, but not something one should quaff."

He laughed. "Quite true."

"Tell me about the mutineers, my lord."

Just then there was a knock on the door.

"Saved by the bell," he said lightly. "Come in."

The door opened and a maid hovered on the threshold. "You rang, my lord?"

"My guest has a rather nasty scratch. Please bring some hot water and something to clean and bind the wound."

"Yes, my lord."

The instant the door closed Lori said, "You were talking about the mutiny, my lord."

He grinned, took a drink, and then absently turned the cut crystal around and around with surprisingly elegant fingers for such a large man. "What do you know about the mutiny itself?"

"The ship was a frigate—one of the fifth class, so a smaller ship. She had a crew of approximately one hundred and seventy. There were fewer than a dozen marines and none of them took action against the mutineers when the violence began. The core leadership of the mutiny was thought to number about twenty-five or thirty men. They comprised the group that killed the captain and all but three of his officers. They then sailed the ship to Spanish controlled waters and turned the vessel over to the authorities. They claimed to have put the captain and his officers on a lifeboat which they set adrift. That lie didn't hold up for long as there were so many survivors. The Spanish re-christened the ship and twenty-five of the original crew stayed on. Since then, a system of rewards has led to the capture of thirty-five of the crew. Of those, twenty-four were hanged. Obviously, there is still a large number of the conspirators at large."

His eyebrows had crept higher as she'd spoken. "You have an astoundingly detailed memory."

She shrugged off the compliment. "The subject is fresh in my mind as I recently read all the newspaper accounts at the *Times*."

"What do you know about Captain Pigot?"

"He was considered a harsh captain by—"

Severn gave a bitter laugh. "Harsh. That's one way to describe him."

"If you know more, please tell me. I am only sharing what I've read."

"Did you know he had ordered eighty-five floggings on that one journey alone."

"*Eighty-five*? Surely that must be… excessive."

"It is *extremely* excessive," he agreed grimly. "Of those eighty-five men, two died of their punishment."

"That is truly barbaric—and surely criminal," Lori said, feeling vaguely ill. She met his brooding gaze, her eyes widening when she deciphered his expression. "Good Lord. You believe the mutiny was justified!"

"I met the man once in Baltimore," he said, ignoring her question. "He was holding a court of sorts on the deck of his ship. He had a midshipman named Davis before him on his knees—as if it were some sort of biblical tribunal—and was trying to force the man to publicly beg forgiveness for some infraction or other. When Davis refused, Pigot had him bound to the whipping post and personally administered twelve lashes. As if that wasn't enough, he also disrated the man. Do you know what *disrating* means?"

"It means his career in the navy would essentially be over. But I ask you again: is that a reason to mutiny?"

"That is not what I'm saying."

"What *are* you saying?"

"Pigot demonstrated a cruel capriciousness that made life for the men serving beneath him a daily terror. Do you know what Davis—an experienced junior officer by all accounts—had done to incur Pigot's wrath?"

"No."

"Pigot noticed that a sail had not been secured properly by one of the sailors under Davis's supervision. He confronted Davis with the infraction and Davis apologized and took responsibility for his subordinate's actions himself. And for that, his life was ruined."

"Pigot was undeniably a horror, my lord, but I'm not sure that justifies the crime of treason, not to mention several murders."

"As far as the law is concerned it certainly doesn't." He shrugged and drank deeply from his glass before saying, "But I have my own code."

"And what does your code dictate?"

He fixed her with a piercing look. "I collected some of the mutineers—I refuse to disclose the number to you, Miss Fontenot, so do not ask—and transported them to a neutral location."

Lori's jaw sagged. "So Parker's informant wasn't lying at all."

"It is true that your anonymous correspondent might know a thing or two," he conceded, and then set down his glass with an audible *thump* and leaned toward her. "So, I have answered some of your questions. Now I have one for *you*: what is the name of the person feeding all this information to Parker?"

The hairs on the back of her neck lifted at the quiet menace in his voice. It was the same voice he'd used in the alleyway earlier that night, but now it was directed at *her*. Lori suddenly understood why that hulking brute had capitulated so quickly. "I told you already: I do not know," she said in an admirably level voice.

"But you could find—"

A brief knock interrupted him, and an expression of vexation settled onto his stern features before he barked out, "Come!"

Lori met his gaze as a maid entered the room and forced an arch smile before echoing his earlier words, "Saved by the bell, my lord."

Chapter 16

Put the tray on my desk, please," Lord Severn instructed the servant before nodding his dismissal at her and turning back to Lori. "Come and sit here and I will clean your wounds."

"I can do it. I don't need—"

"Lorelei."

He didn't raise his voice, but something in his tone made her pulse quicken and her body began to rise from the chair with no instruction from her brain.

Lori mentally chided her traitorous flesh, crossed her arms, and pressed her bottom firmly back down on the chair. "You like to order people around, don't you?"

He rolled his eyes. "*Please* let me help you with this. In addition to your arm there are scratches on your face. It will be easier for somebody else to care for both. If you like, I can ring for the maid, and she can assist you."

His patient tone was more annoying than his commanding one.

"Fine." She thrust to her feet, stomped over to the chair, and dropped into it gracelessly.

"Good girl."

Lori bared her teeth.

Predictably, he chuckled at her glower and then proceeded to carefully bathe the side of her face and neck. "I beg your pardon," he said when she flinched. "Is it very painful?"

"No, only a little sore. Does it look bad?"

"The scratches will probably heal quickly but I think you will have some bruising." His jaw flexed and his pale gaze slid from the grazed flesh to her eyes. "I wish I had apprehended the brute earlier and spared you this."

Lori swallowed at the intensity in his eyes. "I am just grateful that you were there at all."

He gave her a long, brooding look and then turned back to the wound and applied a medicinal smelling salve. His touch—as businesslike as it was—sent sparks of heat skirling through her veins. He was such a large man, and yet so very gentle. Tender, almost. Soothing…

"You seem adept at treating wounds," she said, choosing to speak—even if it was something stupid—before she began to moan. Or purr.

"I must have a natural aptitude as this is my first foray into the world of nursing," he said, a small smile tugging at his lips. Once he replaced the lid on the tin of salve, his eyes flickered over her, and he frowned.

"What is wrong?"

"I have made a clean spot on your face. I am going to wash off the rest of this muck."

Lori had forgotten all about the horrific cosmetics. "You don't have to do that. I can—"

"Lorelei."

Again, the word was soft yet too compelling to ignore.

"What?" she asked in a stupidly breathy voice, unable to look away from his eyes.

"Let me do this for you. Please."

After a moment, she nodded, unwilling to trust her voice.

He added more hot water to the basin and proceeded to wash her with the same care he'd used to tend to her injury. He snorted softly when he peeled off the black beauty spot. "I haven't seen one of these since I was a boy. I had a great-aunt who wore them."

"I had only seen them in stage plays until this evening," she admitted.

When he'd cleansed her to his satisfaction, the water in the basin was cloudy.

"That is revolting," Lori said, eying the flannel cloth he'd used, which had been white and was now a sickly gray. "Why on earth would people tolerate wearing cosmetics all day, every day?"

"Probably because they did not possess skin as lovely as yours."

Heat immediately crept up her neck at his compliment—which seemed all the more flattering for the matter-of-fact way in which he delivered it—and Severn smiled.

She gave an exasperated laugh. "You said that on purpose! Just to make me blush."

"Yes, I did. But that does not make it any less true. Hold still, there is just one last thing."

Before she could ask what, he began plucking pins out of her hair, his large hands quick and deft.

There was such a feeling of unreality to it—Lord Stand Fast Severn, the King of the Rakes, serving as her lady's maid—that Lori couldn't think of anything to say or do except sit there and watch, rapt, as he carefully deconstructed the horrendous coiffure.

Dorian, her only lover, had never tended to her with such tender care—or any care at all, really. And Dorian had never—not even when he'd been rutting in her—caused a fraction of the bewildering and pleasurable sensations currently rampaging through her body like a fever.

She was sweating and her lungs felt the way they had when she'd fallen off those piled up packing crates and knocked the air from her chest. Thinking—at least thinking any rational thoughts—was impossible. All she wanted to do was feel more of his big hard body against hers. She desperately wanted him to touch her the way he had done that night at the ball, when his hands and mouth had roamed her person with a possessive intent that made Lori regret refusing his shocking invitation to go to his house every night since.

"If you keep looking at me like that, I'm not going to stop at just removing your face paint and hair pins." He punctuated his words by tossing aside the last pin with a soft *ping*.

"Loo—" Lori's voice cracked like an adolescent boy's. She cleared her throat. "Looking at you how, pray?" Her attempt to sound chilly was dismal.

"You know how."

"What—what might you do if I don't stop?"

His lips tightened and he slowly slid his fingers into the sausage-like curls, capturing her gaze as he gently raked his hands through her heavy tresses. "You have beautiful hair," he said, his disconcerting eyes finally releasing her and moving over her face until he was regarding his fistful of curls which he then lifted higher, until he could bury his nose in the tangled locks. His eyes drifted shut as his chest expanded and he murmured, "Even that hideous rose perfume can't entirely hide your scent."

Lori gawked. "You—you know my scent?"

He opened his eyes. "Why do you smell so damned good?"

"I, er, wasn't aware that I did. My sister-in-law makes soap with calendula and—"

"You smell like summer." He inhaled another lungful. "And fresh bedsheets."

Lori laughed. "Bedsheets? That doesn't sound very—"

"You drive me mad." He growled, releasing her hair and moving his hands to her waist.

The room rocked around her.

Except it wasn't the room, but Lori who was moving as Severn lifted her onto his lap as easily as if she were a toddler.

"What are you—"

His lips crashed down over hers and she opened her mouth to let him in, not waiting to be asked.

His chest rumbled with approval, and he stroked into her with suggestive thrusts.

Lori did something she wanted to do since the very first time she'd seen Severn and carded her fingers into his jet-black over-long hair. Although their hair was alike in color, the texture of his was far silkier and finer than her own coarse strands.

He purred when she grazed his scalp with her fingernails. "Yes, please," he muttered against her parted lips before resuming his kissing.

She lost herself in a blizzard of sensations, reveling in the erotic caresses of his hands on her waist, hips, and back, drowning in the heat and hardness of his chest and luxuriating in the way his big body completely surrounded hers, dominating her with his size and strength.

And then—just as suddenly as he'd fallen on her—he put her at arm's length, his expression raw and aroused. "*Damnation!*"

"What?" she asked, the word sounding as woozy as she felt.

"Regardless of what you've heard about me, I don't deflower virgins."

Lori frowned and yanked her hands from his hair, not caring when she snagged some strands and made him wince. "I never claimed to be a virgin."

One of his eyebrows shot up.

She couldn't help laughing at his skeptical expression, although it was a laugh borne of annoyance rather than humor. "Do you really think I would lie about something like that just so you would keep touching me?"

He opened his mouth, but Lori scowled both at him and her stupidly heating face, and said, "Let me go!" But when she tried to push off his lap, his hands encircled her waist easily holding her in place. Not that she struggled terribly hard.

"You didn't even know how to kiss properly that first time," he said.

"Just because I'd never *properly*"—she sneered as she spat the word—"k-kissed a man before doesn't mean I am an innocent," she retorted, stung and mortified at the thought that he'd noticed her lack of skill.

"Of course not. I beg your pardon for saying such a stupid thing." His pitying look was almost worse than his disbelief. "I know not all men care for such intimacies." And then he hesitated, opened his mouth, but then closed it.

Again, Lori tried to back away, and again he held her in place. She settled for crossing her arms and jabbing her elbows into his chest. Lovely. Now she would have sore elbows to go along with her bruised feelings. "What?" she demanded, annoyed when he continued to stare at her. "Just say whatever it is you want to say, my lord."

"Were you forced?"

"No, I was not. So you can take that careful, pitying look off your face—as if you are anxious that I might shatter like glass if you do or say something wrong. I've had a lover, my lord—only one, unlike some people"—he snorted, but she ignored him. "But it wasn't"—Lori broke off and chewed the inside of her cheek, just what words was she looking for? How could she explain the paltriness of her sexual experience without sounding even more pathetic than she already did?

After a moment, Lori gave up looking for careful words and simply said, "The man I—I *fucked*"—she gave him a mulish look, daring him to comment on her vulgar language— "was a selfish clod and kissing wasn't the only thing that did not hold any interest for him." Her face flamed, but she plunged onward. "Let me just say that my experience didn't make me want to rush out and repeat it."

"Did he not give you an orgasm?"

Yet again, Lori was rendered speechless by the raw, direct words he used.

Severn mistook her startled silence for a lack of comprehension and said, "Women can experience sexual climaxes just the same as—"

Lori shoved at his massive chest, but he didn't budge so much as an inch. "I know that you dolt!"

His lips quivered slightly, making her want to hit him again. "I beg your pardon. I had no inten—"

"What he did or did not do is none of your concern. Perhaps I should interrogate you about *your* sexual history."

"I will answer anything you like."

"I thought gentlemen did not kiss and tell?"

He smiled. "I never said I'd give you a list of names."

Jealousy at the thought of him having a *list*—and how long it likely was—stabbed at her, twisting a knife in her chest. "What a lovely offer. But I believe I will decline your generous offer. Any discussion of your *amours* would be a long one—surely lasting well into the New Year—and I have more important matters in my life."

Rather than be offended, he grinned. "Maybe not that long." His smile slid away. "But I don't want to talk about past lovers right now. I don't want to talk about anything." His hands closed on her hips, and he brought her closer, the action spreading her legs wider, until her sex was pressed against something impossible to mistake. "I've been hard for you since the first moment I laid eyes on you."

"My lord exaggerates."

"Not by much." He lifted his hips slightly and her eyelids fluttered when he grazed her in exactly the right place. Or the wrong place—unless she wanted to lose her few remaining wits.

"Stop trying to pull away, Lorelei."

Her body became pliant at his command, an involuntary physical response that was infuriating and one she should immediately take steps to root out. Lori squared her shoulders, scowled, and said, "Stop barking orders. You already said that you did not—"

"Shut up, Lorelei," he murmured, and then claimed her mouth with a kiss so enticing and commanding there was no possible way Lori could have resisted, even if she'd wanted to.

He released her an indeterminate time later, and she was foolishly pleased to see he was breathing every bit as hard as she was. "There is one more thing that needs—"

"Shut up, Fast." Lori indulged in a brief, smug smirk as she used his own words against him. "You needn't say it. I already know what *thing* you mean." After all, she'd heard it before from Dorian, hadn't she? True, Dorian had waited to share the brutal truth with her until *after* he had taken her maidenhead.

Lori supposed she should look on the bright side. Lord Severn, for all his rakish ways, was at least not promising to love her forever as a way to lure her into bed.

"What *thing* do you think I mean?" he asked, his brow creased.

Lori no longer recalled the exact phrases Dorian had used to shatter her innocence and transform her from an openhearted, trusting girl into a scarred, cynical woman, but she would never forget the gist of his cruel words. And she never *ever* wanted to hear the same sentiment—either unexpurgated or dressed up in pretty language—from another man's lips as long as she lived.

She met Severn's questioning gaze with a blasé smile she was far from feeling. "I know that you want the same thing I do."

"And what is that?"

"A few hours of mutual pleasure and nothing else."

He blinked. "Er, that's all I want?"

Lori gave a derisive snort. "That is all *any* man wants from a woman like me." He opened his mouth, but she went on before he could offer up some weak demurral and irritate her. "Don't worry, my lord. You needn't fear that I am on the catch for a husband. I don't believe in marriage."

"I think you might have mentioned that once before." He stared at her, his expression…odd and unreadable.

"Why are you looking at me like that?"

"What am I looking like?"

"Like a stunned carp."

He laughed. "No! Was I?"

Lori shrugged away both his strange expression and playful banter and said, "I understand what we are about here, my lord. We are from two distinct social classes and this"—she gestured from his body to hers— "is the only sort of association there can ever be between us. I may be inexperienced, but I am not a fool. Nor am I such a ninny that I need you to look out for my *honor.* I am the only one who gets to determine when and with whom I share my body. I give you my word that I have no expectations of you beyond tonight." She paused for emphasis, and then said, "Understood?"

He hesitated, and said, "I understand you."

Lori ignored the pang of disappointment she felt at his quick, easy acceptance—as if she had wanted him to argue and insist that he wanted something more…meaningful from her.

She was such a romantic fool.

Lori thrust aside her disappointment and said, "And there is one other thing."

"Yes?"

"I do not want to fall pregnant." Lori hadn't considered that possibility when she'd been with Dorian seven years ago and it had just been sheer dumb luck that she had not conceived.

His mouth pulled up on one side and he lifted a hand and cupped her jaw on the unscraped side of her face, his warm palm oddly reassuring. "I promise I won't make you pregnant," he said, lightly caressing her cheek with his thumb.

She scowled. "How can you promise something like that?"

"Because I don't have to put my cock inside you to give us both a great deal of pleasure," he said, the heat in his eyes palpable.

Lori's heart skipped at his confident, vulgar, and enticing claim and she opened her mouth so she could draw in more air.

His thumb slid across her cheek to her mouth, and he lightly traced the shape of her lips. "I'm going to make you feel so good, Lorelei." He pressed his thumb against her lower lip and when she opened for him, he slid inside. "Suck."

Her breathing hitched as she closed her lips around him, the skin salty and slightly rough.

A low growl issued from his chest and a muscle ticced in his temple. For a moment he looked like a man who was wrestling with some incomprehensible mental puzzle.

As quickly as the expression had appeared it vanished and was replaced by a slack, almost lazy smile. "You saw me that night when you peeked inside." It wasn't a question, which was just as well because Lori was in no position—either mentally or physically—to answer just then. "You saw the woman kneeling at my feet." He paused and then added, "*Servicing* me."

Lori *had* seen, and it was a mental image that had intruded on her—both during her waking and sleeping hours—with worrying frequency in the weeks since.

He began to slide his thumb in and out of her mouth. "Suck me harder—use your tongue."

Lori's sex clenched, the action setting off a distracting cascade of pleasure. Why in the world was sucking his thumb so very arousing?

"Yes, just like that," he praised, making her realize that she wasn't just sucking him, but tonguing and nibbling him as well. "You have beautiful lips, Lorelei. As arousing as they look and feel on my thumb, I would love to see them wrapped around my cock."

There was that word again: *cock*. Her eyelids fluttered and her heart pounded so hard it felt as if a horse was galloping over her ribs.

"Shhh, don't look so worried. I am not going to ask you for that," he said, misreading the reason for the shudder that ran through her body. His lips curled up at the corners. "At least not tonight." He withdrew his thumb, rubbing the moist pad on her lower lip with an almost yearning look before lowering his hand. "I want to use my mouth on you."

Lori had a vague idea of what he meant, of course—she had read about cunnilingus—but was, yet again, shocked that he would put such a thing into words. Not that she didn't like his naughty suggestion—or want what he was offering. Indeed, at that moment, she could not think of anything she wanted more. But when she tried to force out the word *yes,* she discovered her throat had closed up. So she nodded.

He smiled. "Use your words, darling. I want to hear you say you want it."

Lori's face burned, but she refused to let him have the last word. "I want it."

Once again, he moved with impressive speed and strength, lifting her with him as he stood, turned, and then set her gently on the chair he'd just been occupying. Heat kindled in his eyes as he sank gracefully to his knees in front of her. "Spread your thighs for me."

Lori glanced around the room. While it wasn't brightly lit, it certainly wasn't dim. "You mean to do it…*here*?"

"Yes, here. Open for me."

She unclenched the muscles in her legs but couldn't seem to make them move.

"There is no shame in changing your mind, sweetheart."

"I haven't changed my mind," she retorted, and then saw by his faint smile that he'd known exactly what to say to goad her into doing his bidding. She snorted and shook her head at him, amused despite herself. And then she did as he bade her, feeling exposed even though layers of petticoat and skirt covered her sex.

"Very good," he praised in a quiet voice as he eased between her knees, nudging them wider. "Tell me, Lorelei—are you wet for me?"

In keeping with her inarticulate behavior this evening, she gawked at him in open-mouthed stupefaction.

He chuckled. "Sorry, love. Did that shock you?"

"You know it did," she shot back, far angrier at her incessantly blushing skin than at Severn and his naughty taunting.

"But in a good way, hmm?"

"I refuse to feed your already oversized self-esteem."

He grinned, the expression so boyishly wicked that he looked like some other man for a moment—some younger, more carefree version of himself. "I know you would never lie to me, but I think I should check and see for myself." He slipped his hands beneath the layers of fabric. But rather than reach immediately for her sex, his fingers closed around one of her ankle boots first, and then the other.

"Shouldn't I remove my boots?" she asked.

"Absolutely not."

Lori couldn't help thinking that his big hands felt like hot manacles as he gently but inexorably spread her wider.

Chapter 17

Fast felt as though Christmas had come early this year as he caressed from Lorelei's trim ankles up her shapely calves to the soft, yielding flesh of her thighs.

"Bloody hell you have beautiful legs! They should be on display in a museum." He stroked up and down slowly, reveling in their curvaceous magnificence.

She laughed. "I have already agreed to tonight, my lord. You needn't shower me with compliments to persuade me."

Fast frowned and his hands froze just above her knees, their ultimate destination forgotten for the moment. "Who was it who taught you to believe that compliments were nothing but tools to pry a woman's thighs apart, Lorelei?"

She colored slightly but collected her wits with the celerity to which he had become accustomed. "I just meant—"

"I know what you meant," he said, resuming his stroking. "As it happens, I enjoy telling you what I like about you—probably more than you like hearing it."

She pulled her lips between her teeth for a moment, as if struggling to stifle a smile, and then said, "I like hearing it."

Fast nodded his approval and allowed his hands to continue their journey. This time he did not stop at the border where cotton met flesh but explored higher and higher. He felt the heat of her cunny even before his fingers reached the damp, springy curls that guarded her sex. "My God, Lorelei." Blood roared in his ears as he slid a finger between her slick folds. "You aren't wet—you're drenched." He lightly flicked her engorged nub before she had a chance to respond to his crude words and was rewarded for his audacity when a muffled cry tore from her slack lips, her full, shapely hips lifting in silent appeal as Fast teased the source of her arousal. Her thighs, which she'd clenched so tightly only moments before, strained as she opened herself to him.

"Look at me, darling," he ordered when her eyelids began to drift shut, amused and aroused by the quick way she responded—even though it was clear that her inclination to rebel against authority warred with the sensual pleasure she took in submitting.

Fast was truly looking forward to taking her apart.

But first, he needed to get her out of her horrid clothing.

Although it pained him, he withdrew his hand, needing both to shove the voluminous petticoat and stiff panels of her gown up to her waist. "Christ," he muttered. "These damned skirts." He fumbled with the fastenings before finally just tearing the faded, worn material.

Rather than chide him for his roughness, she helped him and together they ripped and tugged on the garments until all she had on were her chemise, short stays, stockings, and ankle boots.

Fast shoved aside the mountains of petticoats and skirts and then looked up at her.

He'd worried that the brief foray into practicalities would bring her back to her senses, but she merely watched him from beneath lowered lids, her lips parted with what looked to be anticipation.

Ah, here was his intrepid newspaperwoman.

He caressed up her stocking sheathed calves until his hands rested beneath each knee. "Over the armrests."

Her eyes widened as she realized the view that would afford him.

Fast watched with interest as she struggled, modesty fighting with curiosity and desire.

Primitive hunger roared through him when she complied, jerkily lifting one knee and resting it over the armrest, and the other.

He didn't allow himself to look down yet, keeping his gaze fixed on her face. "Now slide your bottom to the edge of the chair. More."

She caught her lower lip with her teeth and complied.

Fast stroked her thighs, the strained and stretched muscles twitching beneath his palms. "Are you uncomfortable?"

She shook her head, her breasts straining above the plain corset as she angled herself in a way that she could see what he was about.

Only when she was settled did he allow himself to look down. He released an explosive breath at the sight that met his hungry gaze. Although the chemise covered her, a dark triangle was visible beneath the thin muslin, which was almost transparent from many washings.

Rather than lift the shift and expose her, he pulled the fabric taut, until her mound was imprisoned beneath the muslin, the erotic details of her wide-spread sex limned in a way that both exposed and teased.

Fast lightly caressed her over the damp muslin, glancing up and pausing his gentle petting when a needy sound tore from her throat.

Her jaws had clenched until the muscles and sinews stood out beneath the flushed skin of her throat. Her hips lifted until she nudged his hand.

Fast gave her what she wanted, circling the rapidly swelling bundle of nerves until the muslin was soaked and small, animal grunts slipped from her mouth with each flex of her hips. He waited until she was maddened by lust—until she'd forgotten about her wanton sprawl or the man fingering her or anything but the need to climax.

That's when he lowered his mouth and sucked her stiff little nub between his lips.

The result of his action was both immediate and explosive. Her hands fisted his hair and held him in place—as if he had any intention of ever leaving—and her hips bucked as she ground her cunt against his eager lips and tongue.

Fast could not recall a more beautiful sight than prickly, combative Lorelei Fontenot losing control after barely a touch from his tongue. He gently massaged the straining muscles of her thighs as her contractions became less and less violent, until finally her hips stilled.

She opened her eyes, blinked blearily, and then tensed. "Oh," she muttered, and then tried to pull her legs closed.

Fast easily held her open. "Do your thighs hurt?"

"No, but—"

"Then hush and stay as you are. I am not finished."

Her brow furrowed. "I don't unders—"

"Lift your chemise. I want to see you."

Only the hitch in her breathing told him that his words affected her. "You are so… bossy."

"I am," he agreed without hesitation. "And that excites you, doesn't it? And you cannot fathom why that is." He could tell by the scowl on her face that he was right on both counts. "Raise your chemise," he commanded in a low voice before she could argue.

With clenched jaws and shaking hands, she lifted the slip of muslin higher, exposing herself inch by delicious inch.

It was Fast's turn to breathe harshly. "Good God, Lorelei." He caressed the taut cords of her thighs and used his thumbs to spread her lips and expose that most sensitive part of her to his hungry gaze.

"Look at you," he murmured, leaning low and flicking her bud with the tip of his tongue.

When she gasped, he looked up at her. Her eyes were wide, her lips parted as she breathed raggedly. He extended his tongue slowly, holding her gaze as he curled the tip around her tiny organ.

His balls, already aching and hard, clenched at the low, animal keening noise she made as she yet again raised her hips, offering herself to him.

Fast tongued her too lightly to give her what she needed, teasing and taunting and tormenting her until she shook as though a fever were raging through her body.

"Please," she whispered. "I need—" she broke off with a guttural moan.

"I know what you need," Fast said.

And then he lowered his mouth and gave it to her.

***

For the second time that night Lori lost control. The tension that had been coiling inside her suddenly released like a spring. The pleasure was truly excruciating. One second, she wanted to run from it, the next she was grinding herself against Lord Severn's mouth.

She told herself that *this* time would be the last. But then just when she began to regain control, to remember where she was—who she was—he once again drove her toward the cliff and ruthlessly shoved her off the edge.

Time blurred and she lost track of everything except sensation, extreme bliss rippling through her body again and again and again.

Lori was languidly lazing on yet another cloud of ecstasy when the soft, wet heat of Severn's mouth disappeared.

No. It didn't disappear, it moved lower.

And lower.

Lori opened her eyes and looked directly into Lord Severn's heavy-lidded black gaze.

The corners of his mouth curled up at whatever he saw on her face—likely witless befuddlement—and then he brazenly breeched her entrance and slid his tongue inside her.

The unspeakably carnal sight caused her greedy body to ready itself for yet another climax. Severn did not disappoint, his rhythmic, suggestive thrusting propelling her once more toward rapture.

Watching him was even more arousing than the feeling of his skilled lips and tongue. Lord Severn, the Rake of Rakes, was kneeling between her thighs, giving her pleasure she'd never dreamed was possible.

But then just when she teetered on the edge of another orgasm Severn sat back and smiled, his lips and chin slick with… *her.*

She lifted her hips and bumped his hand before she could think what she was doing.

He laughed and lightly flicked her clitoris with the tip of his finger. "Stop begging."

Lori hissed in a harsh breath, aroused rather than chastened by the careless gesture. She had to savage the inside of her cheek to keep from pleading—no, *demanding*—that he finish what he'd started.

"Such a greedy girl," he murmured, resuming his stroking, but missing the one place she wanted him far too consistently for it to be accidental. "Be patient and I will give you more of what you want."

She gritted her teeth to keep from snarling *get on with it.*

Judging by his knowing smirk, she was less than successful at hiding her frustration. "I want to feel inside you." He lightly probed the place where his tongue had just been and lifted a querying eyebrow.

Lori nodded.

His gaze lowered to his finger as he breeched her. "God you look beautiful." His eyes flickered between her face and her sex as he worked her. "You're so tight and wet," he said, his voice harsh with need, his eyes black pools of lust as he pumped her deeply again and again and again.

She groaned when he slid a second finger alongside the first, the ache of being stretched both pleasurable and mildly uncomfortable.

"Look how good you take me," he said in a hushed, almost reverential tone.

And then he lowered his mouth and worked her with fingers, lips, and tongue.

This time—with part of him inside her—the contractions felt twice as intense as any that that had gone before, and the climax went on and on and on.

Lori had no idea how much time had passed when she finally opened her eyes to find that Severn had lowered her legs from the armrests and now sat between them lightly massaging her thighs.

Lori blinked at him. "Did I fall asleep?"

"For a little while." He smiled. "Now that you've rested, perhaps you are ready for—"

She set a limp hand on his shoulder when he began to lower his head again. "Please. I just… can't—"

He chuckled. "As you wish." He got to his feet and then slid his arms beneath her.

"I can walk," she protested feebly.

"I know." He carried her across the room, pausing long enough to open and then shut the door behind him.

Wake up! the voice of reason shouted. *You came here to question him, not to… well, not to do whatever it was that he just did to you.*

Lori knew the voice was right, but she was so *bone weary* that she didn't protest when she felt the unspeakable softness of velvet bedding beneath her bare bottom.

"Rest for a bit," Severn said, his deft fingers once again moving over her person, this time unbuttoning her boots, which she'd forgotten she was still wearing.

"I need to go," she said, but made no effort to move.

He untied her garters and rolled down each stocking.

"I can't stay," she said, a yawn distorting her words. Cool, butter-soft sheets that smelled faintly of Lord Severn's elusive cologne were tucked in around her naked torso. She'd never slept nude before. It felt exquisite.

"Just rest, Lorelei."

"I have to be…somewhere," she murmured.

"Sleep," a low voice said.

And that was the last thing Lori heard.

Chapter 18

Lori yawned and stretched, turning over in bed. It felt too good to get up. The sheets had never felt so soft. Almost like silk against her bare breasts and belly.

Her bare breasts and belly.

She was naked.

Her eyes popped open, and she stared around at the dimly lit room. It took a few seconds before she recalled where she was.

And how she'd gotten there.

Images of Lord Severn between her thighs, face slick, lips wet and swollen—

Lori groaned, squeezed her eyes shut and slammed her palms over them, as if that could erase her behavior from the night before. But the images were ten times more vivid behind her eyelids, so she immediately opened them.

Before the shame could snowball and grow into something crushing, she firmed her jaw and said in a low voice, "You have nothing to be ashamed about. You haven't done anything worse than thousands of men do every single day. Sensual desire is as normal as anything else the body craves."

She repeated that same mantra—but in her head—until the tension leaked out of her. And then she tugged the sheet off the bed and wrapped it around her like an ancient Roman toga. Once she was properly shrouded, she tried to open the door. It was locked. She was about to start pounding on it when she saw the other door.

Ah.

She twisted the handle, fully expecting it to be locked also, but it turned easily, and she opened it to the study from the night before.

Her eyes immediately went to the chair where she'd sat sprawled and—

"Oh, God," she mumbled, assaulted by images of her naked body wantonly spread before Lord Severn. His lips slick and passion-bruised, his eyes dark and brooding as he—

Lori yelped when the door suddenly opened and a maid with a full tray hovered on the threshold.

"Oh! You're awake. His lordship said not to disturb you if you were sleeping."

Lori waited until the maid nudged the door shut with her foot to ask, "Where is my clothing? And Lord Severn? And what time is it?"

The maid blinked at the rapid fire questions and carefully set down the tray before saying, "There are clothes in the armoire in the bedchamber. Lord Severn has gone out, but he wanted you to know he'd return shortly. It is just after seven o'clock."

"*Seven o'clock!*"

The woman winced. "Yes, Miss Fontenot."

Oh, God! Whatever would Freddie be thinking? She would be worried sick.

"I need to leave." She brushed past the maid and yanked open the door to the bedchamber.

The maid's footsteps sounded behind her. "Er, Lord Severn wanted you to wait until—"

"I need to leave! I should have done so hours ago," Lori shot back. She flung open the armoire and riffled through the hanging garments before turning. "My gown isn't in here."

"No, Miss."

"May I have it back?"

"I'm afraid not."

"Why?"

"Because—"

"Because I had it tossed into the rubbish bin," Lord Severn's voice came from the doorway.

"You had no right to do that!"

He ignored her and said, "You can leave, Dolly."

The maid scurried out of the room without a backward glance.

"Breakfast is in the other room. Why don't you come and—"

"I want my clothing," she demanded, fear mingling with anger at his high-handed behavior.

He gave her a cool look. "I told you: it is gone."

"Well go and get it!"

"That's not going to happen. Besides," he said with humor lurking in his eyes, "we rather destroyed that gown last night. Or don't you remember?"

The memory of that destruction came back in a flash, and with mortifying clarity. But Lori refused to acknowledge it. "Then find me some other clothing."

He gestured to the wardrobe. "There are—"

"You expect me to wear your whore's clothing?"

He shrugged, unperturbed by her rudeness. "There are a number of dressing gowns in there." His pale eyes flickered over her body, making her remember that she was dressed in a sheet. "Although I must say you look fetching as you are."

"Very droll, my lord. I want—" she broke off when he strode toward her, not stopping until he was close enough to lay a finger across her lips.

"Shh."

Her jaw dropped, but no sound came out.

"That's better." His large hand spread across her lower back, and he gently propelled her toward the doorway.

Lori took a few steps before her wits returned and she whirled on him. "Don't you *shush* me! This is not amusing. I want my clothing and I—"

"And I want you to sit down and have a civil conversation with me."

Her mouth snapped shut as she was, yet again, silenced by a voice that was scarcely above a whisper. His eyes were even paler today. Or perhaps they only seemed that way because his pupils had shrunk to pinpricks. Although his expression was mild, there was no doubt in her mind that he was displeased that she had the gall to disagree with him.

Lori wanted to tell him to go to the devil, but it struck her rather sharply that she was without clothing, money, or any means of getting out of a building that belonged to him, filled with servants loyal to him.

She clamped her jaws shut.

He nodded, his harsh expression softening slightly. "Good girl. Now, have a seat."

Lori bristled at his patronizing *good girl* and it took every drop of self-control she possessed not to hit him.

Instead, she sat in the chair he indicated.

He gestured to the tray on the table. In addition to tea, coffee, and numerous covered dishes there were several newspapers. "Will you make the tea? I like mine black and strong," he said once he'd taken the seat across from her.

She wanted to argue, but she also desperately wanted tea.

And so she commenced with the familiar ritual. By the time she'd poured out her tea—she liked it weak and milky—her pulse had slowed to a normal rate.

Once the tea had steeped until it was an almost oily black, she poured a cup for Severn and met his penetrating gaze.

"Thank you," he said, all the coldness from a few minutes earlier gone, his features now those of a pleasant, gentlemanly host.

But Lori wasn't fooled. A cauldron simmered inside him and the lid had temporarily been dislodged—*she'd* been the one to dislodge it. It shamed her to admit it, but she wasn't in a hurry to see that same cold expression on his face again.

He took a sip and gave a contented sigh. "This is good."

"When can I leave?"

"I am worried about that man in the alley last night," he countered with hardly a pause.

Lori opened her mouth to stubbornly repeat her question, but the glitter in his eyes stopped her. Instead, she said, "It won't happen again as I won't be going down there again." It was a lie, but she didn't owe him the truth.

"Did he give any indication who his employer was? What he wanted to talk to you about? Anything?"

"I've already told you *no*. You heard what he said."

"*Hmm.*" He took another sip of tea.

Lori set down her untouched cup and saucer. "When can I leave… Fast?"

He looked amused by her use of his pet name and Lori cursed her clumsy effort at manipulation.

"Who do you think is feeding Parker all his information about me?" he asked.

"I don't know—as I've said at least five times already. Even if I did, I wouldn't tell you. What are you hiding, my lord? How about you answer that?"

"I'm sorry." He gave her a look that was tinged with regret.

Lori blinked. "Sorry? What are you sorry about?" Dread slithered down her spine.

He ignored her question. "You had better make yourself comfortable."

"What? Why?"

"Because you will be staying here as my guest until I decide otherwise."

***

Fast knew it was childish, but he couldn't help enjoying the way Lorelei's mouth opened and closed just like that of a landed fish.

"What do you mean?" she managed after a moment.

"Just what I said. I'll be keeping you here so I can make sure you don't get into any trouble."

"But"—she made a flustered huffing sound, like a broody hen, and shook her head, and then spluttered, "You can't do that!"

"Yes, I can."

"People know I am here. They will come looking for me if I don't return."

"People like Ella?"

She gaped. "How do you know about her?"

"You needn't worry, my dear. I have already compensated Ella for her silence. She will not be going to Lady Sedgewick's house."

Her eyes threatened to start from their sockets. "There are others! She wasn't the only one. I told—"

"You are a dreadful liar."

Her already red face darkened even more at the accusation and her mouth worked, but no words came out. That was fine; Fast had plenty to say. "You are staying here until it is safe to let you out again."

"Safe? What in the world do you mean?"

"Just what I said."

"You can't do that! I'll—I'll—"

"You'll *what*?"

She jumped to her feet, forgetting about the sheet she was wearing.

He watched with interest as she trod on the bottom of the fabric and dislodged the makeshift toga. She had lovely, lovely breasts and he regretted not exploring them more fully the night before. Judging by the way she was scowling at him, Fast would not be getting a second chance to enjoy her body.

He got to his feet, and she hastily stepped back, bumping into the chair behind her, and then edging around it, until she was clutching the chairback with both her hands. "You can't just keep me here."

Before Fast could answer there was a knock on the door. "Who is it?" he called out staring at Lorelei.

"Gregg."

Fast's gaze slid over Lorelei's barely clad body—a body he didn't want anyone but himself to see.

"One moment" he called, striding toward the door.

"Where are you going?" she demanded shrilly.

He ignored her and opened the door. Fast knew by Gregg's expression that something was amiss, so he stepped outside and shut the door behind him.

Lorelei's voice, raised in anger, came through the thick wood. "Severn! Where are you going?"

Gregg looked amused as Fast lightly held the handle while she yanked on it and continued shouting.

"I want any room she's in to be locked at all times and station a man outside it," he said, needing to raise his voice to be heard over the racket.

"Very good, my lord."

"You'd better have one posted outside the window, too."

Gregg smirked as he fished a key from his pocket and stuck it into the lock.

The door handle rattled. "You let me out this instant!" Fast winced when the door shook. She would hurt herself if she kept flinging herself against it like that.

"If you have something to tell me, tell me quickly."

Gregg glanced at the vibrating door. "I think it would be better not to speak of it right here."

Fast sighed and jerked out a nod.

"Will she be staying in your quarters?" Gregg asked as they strode down the corridor.

"Only until the Queen's Chambers have been secured. Then I will move her in there."

Gregg laughed. "Oh, she'll like that."

"I don't care what she likes. It will be far easier to keep her contained in that suite. There are too many goddamned doors in and out of my rooms."

The Queen's Chambers, as the rooms were laughingly called, had been equipped for every perversion known to mankind. The room also had bars on the window and only one door. For all that it was locked up tighter than a Newgate cell it was luxurious. Lorelei would be comfortable, if scandalized.

"Oh, and from now on," Fast said, "I don't want any of the maids to go into her room alone. She had poor Dolly terrified."

Gregg looked amused. "Of course, my lord."

"I want you to be the one to accompany the servants."

"You don't trust the lads?" Gregg asked, his eyebrows arched.

"Oh, I trust the lads. It's her I don't trust."

Gregg laughed and then opened the door to his own suite of rooms.

Fast disposed of himself in one of the chairs. "So, then. What is the need for such secrecy?"

"It was Moreland."

Fast frowned. "What about Moreland?"

Gregg opened his mouth, hesitated, and then said with a grim look, "It was Moreland who had your brother killed, my lord."

Fast stared. And when Gregg merely stared back, Fast gave a sharp bark of laughter. "The devil you say! Somebody is having you on, Gregg."

But Gregg didn't laugh with him. "I'm afraid not, my lord. Barker tracked Garcia down and found his lodgings. Unfortunately, he also found Garcia. Dead. Somebody slit his throat for him and then tossed his place. Not that there was much to toss. But it was obvious that whoever did it was looking for something."

Fast shook his head. "But… but this makes no sense. How could Garcia tell Barker it was Moreland if he was already dead?"

"Because there was a witness to Garcia's murder, my lord."

Fast laughed again. "Now I *know* somebody is lying if they said they saw Moreland slit somebody's throat. Bevil Norman faints at the sight of blood—he always has. He might kill a man, but not with a knife."

Gregg rubbed his temple. "I'm making a mess of this."

"You bloody well are," Fast agreed. "Tell me straight what happened."

"It wasn't Moreland the witness saw, but a huge bloke who is one of the earl's servants. A man named Edward Carey, who is as big as you."

"What did he look like?" Fast asked, a sick feeling already blooming in his belly.

"A scar through his eyebrow with salt-and-pepper—"

"Damnation! That was the man who had Lorelei cornered in that alley last night."

"A neighbor saw Carey enter Garcia's flat, heard sounds of a scuffle, and saw Carey leave covered in blood."

Fast shook his head in perplexity. "But…why?"

Gregg pressed his lips together and shrugged. "That, I don't know. Barker and two other men are holding Carey captive in a corder's shack on Bell Pier. It took a lot to soften him up, but he finally broke and confessed it was Moreland who sent him to kill Garcia." Gregg snorted. "Not that there was much chance of him getting out of it. In any event, he swears that he knows nothing about why Moreland wanted Garcia dead. It seems the earl hasn't taken him into his confidence to that extent."

Fast shook his head, unable to credit what he was hearing. "And you really believe that Carey is working for Moreland?"

"Barker will be able to tell you the whole of the man's confession, but there is no doubt of it, my lord. Carey has lived in a cottage on the Earl of Moreland's estate for years and is well-known about the place. Moreland obviously placed a great deal of trust in him." His jaw flexed. "Moreland is the man who paid Albert Jensen to kill your brother. And it makes sense to assume that he had Garcia killed—and his rooms searched—hoping to find the confession. I daresay Garcia has been bleeding him."

The words echoed strangely. Fast could hear them, but it was simply too difficult for his brain to grasp. It was too…fantastical to accept that a man who had once been his best friend—and Percy's too—was responsible for killing his brother and all but destroying Fast's life.

He stilled his rampaging thoughts and took deep, controlled breaths. After a moment, he unclenched his fingers as his shock began to evaporate like fog under a hot sun.

"There's something else." Gregg's voice seemed to come from a far way off.

"What?" he demanded irritably, grappling with rage now that shock had passed.

"Carey said that he found the girl."

"Girl?"

"Jensen's younger sister."

Fast's head whipped up. "Good God! Ellie Jensen is alive?"

"She *was* alive when Carey brought her to Moreland. But he hasn't seen her since delivering her several weeks ago."

"Did he say where Moreland was holding her?"

"He doesn't know."

Fast shifted his jaw from side to side, his mind racing. "You think he's keeping her to get Jensen to hand over the confession?"

"I don't know, but Carey claims he didn't find anything in Garcia's rooms. And *yes,* before you ask, I do believe him. So that confession is still out there." Gregg shoved a hand through his thick ash blond hair. "Damnation but I wish we'd been able to talk to Garcia. I wonder…" he trailed off and shook his head. "No. It is too farfetched."

"What?"

"What if Garcia took that letter from Jensen before we even left Majorca? What if he didn't just tell Moreland about it, but *showed* him and that is why Moreland is willing to kill to get his hands on it?"

Fast pondered the notion for only a few seconds and then shook his head. "Jensen would have sent a letter if he'd been robbed. If not because the bargain he made with me, then because he would be worried that the killer might seek out his mother and sisters." He scowled. "Which is exactly what Moreland did."

"But Jensen couldn't have sent word if Garcia killed him when he stole the confession."

Fast blinked, stunned that he'd not considered that possibility. "Good God!" he said, lifting his eyes to Gregg. "If Joe Jensen is dead and his brother's confession is missing, then…"

"Then you don't have a signed confession or a witness to attest to it," Gregg finished for him.

Fast felt as though somebody had punched that air from his lungs. This simply could not be happening! Moreland could *not* evade justice.

If you can't bring him before a jury of his peers, then you will simply have to seek justice yourself.

"It doesn't matter if I don't have evidence," Fast said. "Because I'm going to kill Moreland." He would use his own two hands, and he would enjoy it. He would do it slowly. He would—

"What about the girl?"

"Girl?" he repeated, his chest aching with the effort of containing the anger that was roiling and swelling and pulsing inside him.

"Ellie."

Fast forced himself to concentrate on something else besides squeezing Bevil's neck until it snapped. "Do you think she is still alive?"

"I don't know. There is far too much we don't know."

"You're saying I shouldn't kill him.

"Er, maybe not yet, my lord."

Fast flexed his hands. "No, you're right. I can get some answers out of him first."

Gregg leaned toward him and opened his mouth.

Fast raised a hand. "Let me guess. I can't kill him *or* beat answers out of him."

"Not yet, sir. We might still find the evidence you need to see him face justice. Isn't that what you want for your brother? Justice?"

"Killing Moreland *will* be justice."

"It will also make you a murderer."

"That doesn't bother me one iota."

"And what about your grandfather? Will it bother him?"

Fast ground his teeth. "That is a low blow, Gregg."

"Perhaps, but it doesn't make it less true." Something like pain flickered in the other man's dark brown eyes. "You don't want to live out your life on the run, my lord."

"Of course I don't. But I am smart; I'll leave no trace."

"Let's say you do kill him and don't get caught. If word of this scandal were to gets out—and we don't know how many people are in on this secret now—you will be in the same position as Moreland; which is to say ripe for extortion."

"So what the hell do you propose, then? That I do *nothing*?"

Gregg opened his mouth, but then closed it.

"Oh, for Christ's sake! Speak, man."

"Death is quick, my lord. Some would say it is the easy way out for what Moreland did."

"But torture before death can be long and drawn out," Fast retorted. And it would be. He would take days—maybe weeks—to kill Bevil Norman.

"Yes, but it seems to me that would be letting his sort of man off too easily. It seems to me—based on what you've said about him—that he would suffer more by losing all his money and status first."

Fast's jaw twitched. "So you're saying I should make my information public? With what evidence?" He snorted. "And even if I do find that confession, now that I know Percy's killer is a bloody *peer*—ha!" he laughed bitterly. "The word of a dead man, a killer's brother—a known mutineer—would never bring down an earl, Gregg."

"I'm not talking about making what you know public."

"Then what the hell are you talking about?"

"Moreland is hurting for money, my lord."

"I know that. So what?"

"Why not destroy him before you kill him?" Gregg hurried to explain. "You've got the upper hand when it comes to the Pascoe chit. If he marries her, his money troubles are over."

"That's just one heiress. There are dozens of them dangling for a peer. It might frustrate Bevil to lose a woman like Demelza Pascoe, but he wouldn't suffer for long."

"Surely there are ways to discredit Moreland so badly that no wealthy Cit would allow his daughter to marry him. Even if he *is* an earl?"

Fast fought against the unfettered, rampant hatred churning inside him. He knew Gregg had a good point—several of them. He didn't want to spend his life running from a murder charge. Moreland's situation was a case in point in how bloody difficult it was to keep such a thing a secret. And then there was the fact that such an accusation would kill his grandfather.

Killing Moreland won't get Percy back.

No, nothing would.

How would Percy want you to deal with this? Shouldn't that weigh in your decision?

Fast gritted his teeth against the deviously clever voice. His brother wouldn't have wanted Fast to destroy what remained of their family. And that is exactly what he'd be doing if he turned himself into a murderer. For all that Percy could be selfish and thoughtless, he had *always* taken the responsibilities of being the heir seriously. That is what had made it so hard to believe that he had killed himself.

We belong to the family first and then ourselves, Fast, Percy had said on more than one occasion. *Even our father knew that. I could hardly be worse than him, could I?*

Percy had been right. Their father had done his best to drain the marquessate of its money and bring shame to the name, but he had married an acceptable woman and provided the obligatory heir and spare.

"My lord?"

He looked up. "What?"

"You mentioned the Countess of Mansfield was having a house party."

"Yes. What of it?"

"Her country estate isn't far from Moreland's, is it?"

"An hour or two away." He frowned. "Why? What are you driving at?"

"If you were to accept the countess's invitation—"

"I rejected it already."

Gregg grinned. "You know she would be delighted if you were to change your mind."

"Probably," Fast accepted. "But why would I?"

"How many properties does Moreland own?"

Fast shrugged. "Lord, I don't know. He still has a bit of acreage near my grandfather's estate. And his wife, Louisa, brought at least one property to the marriage. I'm guessing there are several minor estates that came with the earldom. Why?"

"Because if he is holding Ellie, certainly it would be at one of those places."

Fast nodded slowly.

"And if you went to Lady Mansfield's party you could sneak over one or two nights and look around his estate, couldn't you? Perhaps drop some blunt to see if anyone who lives around there knows anything."

"I could."

"You could also tell Moreland that you had some investment opportunity for a dear old friend—bait a trap for him, as it were. I can throw something together before you go, just enough to whet his appetite."

"That is all assuming I can look at him and talk to him without killing him, which I'm not entirely sure I could do. And keep in mind that he won't be at Meg's party—not when he lives so close."

"But aren't the Pascoes going to be there?"

"Yes, that is true," Fast admitted, suddenly recalling a conversation he'd had with Meg about her inviting the industrialist and his daughter to her party. "I have lowered my standards and invited an obnoxious Cit because it is the only way I'll be able to lure you to attend," she had retorted. "Everyone knows you have your sights set on Miss Pascoe for the position of Viscountess Severn. If you don't come, Moreland might very well steal a march on you."

Fast looked up at Gregg and nodded. "Yes, Bevil will make sure to join in the festivities if the Pascoes are there."

"Well, there you have it. A perfect opportunity to take care of several problems at once."

Fast heaved a sigh. "Christ. Am I really considering going to a party to be near my brother's murderer?"

"Think of the goal, my lord. And also think of Ellie."

"Damn you, Gregg; you are right. I shall need to get going today as that bloody party starts the day after tomorrow." He snorted and then met his friend's curious gaze. "If I leave then you will be in charge of Miss Fontenot in my absence." Fast felt a pang at the thought of leaving her, which was only more proof that the less time he spent with *that* far-too-appealing young lady, the better.

Gregg gave Fast a pained look. "Why, thank you, sir."

"I suppose there is nothing in London that cannot wait until my return."

"I can hold down the fort here until the *Blue Devil* returns in ten days—two weeks at the most."

"I'll bloody well be back by then," Fast assured him.

The *Blue Devil* was the ship Jensen was supposed to take to England. If the man was still alive, of course. Fast would have felt guilty asking the *Blue Devil*'s captain to transport a mutineer if the man hadn't already been delivering a hold full of contraband.

He would have brought Jensen over on the *Vixen* if the ship wasn't under so much scrutiny thanks to David Parker.

And Lorelei Fontenot.

He snorted softly. Yes, and her.

Fast turned to Gregg, who'd paused and was staring at him strangely. "Out with it," he ordered.

Gregg smiled wryly and said, "Even if spending time with Moreland this coming week makes you decide that destroying him piece-by-piece is too difficult, you've waited nine months to avenge your brother. Perhaps you might remind yourself—when your temper begins to fray—that it would be advisable to wait until after the *Blue Devil* arrives to kill him."

Fast gave an unamused bark of laughter. "Damn you and your cool, calculating mind, Gregg. But you are right. I will wait for the *Blue Devil* before I do any killing. Satisfied?"

A slow, evil grin spread over Gregg's face, and he rubbed his hands together. "Indeed, I am, sir. You leave it to me to come up with a nasty little financial snare for Moreland. I anticipate having a great deal of entertainment at his lordship's expense."

Chapter 19

Lori paused her frantic pacing and glanced down at the scrapes and bruises on her knuckles, frowning at her own stupidity.

She should have stopped abusing the door far sooner than she had—especially as she suspected that Lord Severn wasn't even out there to hear her pounding and shouting—but it had been the principle of the thing. Now she had swollen knuckles for her stubbornness.

The sound of a key turning in the door lock made her turn.

"Hello, Miss Fontenot," Gregg said, grinning from the doorway.

"Where is Severn?"

"He's not here. I'm to take care of you until his return."

"And when is that, pray?"

Gregg shrugged. "He doesn't answer to me." His smile broadened. "Or to you." He stepped back and gestured to the doorway. "Come with me."

Lori frowned. "Where are we going?"

"To your new quarters."

She considered arguing, just for the sake of it, but then decided she'd rather be anywhere else than in his lordship's private chambers.

Gregg walked slightly behind her and directed her through a series of turns and through several doors before they stopped in front of a black door strapped with wide iron bands and studded with big nail heads, like something you've find in a medieval prison.

Gregg inserted a large skeleton key into the lock. "This suite is called the Queen's Chambers." He turned the handle, flung open the door, and gestured for her to enter.

"Why is it called—" Lori broke off when she'd taken five steps into the room. "My God!" She stared in fascinated horror at the walls, which were festooned with manacles, whips, crops, and other less immediately identifiable paraphernalia. In the center of the room stood the most massive four poster bed she'd ever seen. It was black wood with black leather bedding, and there were chains and iron rings set into the frame.

Lori spun toward Gregg. "You can't mean to leave me in *here*!"

"Aye, this is your new home until his lordship says otherwise."

Lori wrenched her gaze off one especially wicked looking whip and opened her mouth.

"I'll answer no questions about Lord Severn, so don't even ask." His normally amused expression had fled, replaced by a stare that was as cold and hard as a gaol cell.

She swallowed down her flood of questions, instead saying, "Somebody needs to send word to my housemate, Lady—"

"Sedgewick," he interrupted, an odd light glinting in his dark brown eyes. "And don't you worry your head about that, Miss Fontenot. It has already been taken care of."

"What do you mean?"

"Never you mind." He turned and went to the door.

"Where are you going?"

"Somewhere else."

"When will his lordship return?"

"When he gets here."

"Wait!"

He turned. "Yes?"

Lori discarded the brave front that had become harder and harder to maintain. She also discarded her pride and begged, "Please, Mr. Gregg. You don't have to do this. Let me go. Don't leave me here. This is—"

He opened the door and then shut it in her face.

"Mr. Gregg!" she shouted.

The only answer was the sound of the key turning in the lock.

The fear she'd been feeling exploded into anger. He thought she'd sit here and behave? She glanced wildly around the room. The window was barred and there was only the one door. The suite was composed of two rooms: a small sitting room—if you could call a room that had whips and weapons and lord-knows-what hanging on the walls a sitting room—and the bedchamber.

Staring at all the implements only served to make her woozy, so she turned away and stared at the bed, instead.

That wasn't much better, except… "Aha!" she muttered. Smiling, Lori marched across the room and yanked on the thick black velvet servant cord beside the big four poster. Then yanked again. And Again.

It took ten minutes before key turned in the lock and Gregg entered. He gave her the same smirky look. "You have been a bad girl, Miss Fontenot."

She crossed her arms and seethed. "I am not a girl."

He snorted, opened the door wider, and gestured a man with a ladder into the room.

Before she could ask what was going on, the man set the ladder beside the velvet rope she'd just been yanking non-stop, scaled up the rungs, and quickly disconnected the servant pull.

"Isn't that a bit excessive?" she demanded as the man carried the ladder and bell pull from the room. "What if there is an emergency? A fire? How am I supposed to summon anyone now?"

"You can yell through the door. There will be somebody stationed outside your room at all times."

"Please," she pleaded softly. "Do not do this."

He lifted one eyebrow at her but didn't say a word before closing and locking the door.

"*I will see you thrown in gaol for this!*" she shouted.

Silence was her only answer.

***

Mr. Gregg returned at midday, accompanied by a maid bearing a tray, and again at dinner. Both times he behaved as if Lori didn't exist when she pelted him with questions and demands.

Lori hadn't had the heart to abuse the poor maid, who'd looked as terrified as a mouse, and ate both meals more for something to do—there was nothing to read and nothing to write with—than because of any real hunger.

The implements on the wall had held her attention for no more than an hour and soon she was pacing the room like a caged animal—quickly having passed through the stages of fear and worry and rage and now deeply mired in boredom—when the door opened and the maid entered to exchange a tea tray for Lori's dinner tray.

Gregg followed behind the girl and was holding two books and what looked to be a cloak—*her* cloak, in fact—over his arm. "This, I believe, is yours. And these are for you."

Lori took the cloak, trying not to smile at the thought of what she'd left in the inside pocket. "Thank you."

"I've taken the liberty of removing your pen knife and coin purse from the cloak pocket. You will get it back when his lordship releases you," Gregg said, smiling in a way that made her want to hit him. He held out the books, and Lori gave them a suspicious look. "I just thought you might be bored." He shrugged and began to retract his offer. "But if you aren't—"

"No! I want them." She reached out with both hands and took them from his unresisting fingers. A quick glance at the spines showed one to be a traveler's account of Italy and the other a history of Massachusetts.

When she looked up, Gregg was already closing the door.

"Wait!" she called out.

He paused.

"Thank you."

"You are welcome."

"Might I also have a newspaper if there is one?"

Gregg hesitated and then nodded. "I'll have one sent up with your breakfast."

"Does that mean Lord Severn won't be returning tonight?"

Again, he hesitated, and then said, "I don't believe so." The hard, almost satyrish, angles of his face softened slightly. "Try to get some sleep, Miss Fontenot."

Lori stared at the door long after it closed and then set down the books. She was simply too agitated to read. Instead, she resumed pacing, her mind racing from subject to subject, always returning to the two worries that consumed her the most: how was she to get her story to David, and what would happen to her novel if she did not deliver.

When the clock on the mantle chimed two in the morning, she sighed and climbed onto the gothic black leather bed. She had expected to toss and turn, but she must have fallen asleep immediately because the next thing she knew a pale gray light was filtering between the heavy black velvet drapes that covered the room's only window.

Lori stared up at the canopy, her thoughts no longer in the same turmoil as the day before.

It was impossible to deny the truth of her situation: she was being held hostage in a brothel by a man who had been her lover.

Lori bit her lip as a memory of her abandoned behavior flickered through her mind's eye.

"Oh, God," she murmured, closing her eyes and squeezing them so hard that she saw stars instead of the erotic images that had burned themselves into her brain.

Did she really possess such antiquated notions of morality that she regretted taking a lover? Hadn't it been Lori who'd said to Freddie and Serena—the two women she'd always been closest to in her small group of friends—that there was no shame in enjoying sensual pleasure. Just like any man.

Well, it was time for her to take her own advice.

Lori forced her eyes open. "I refuse to be ashamed for what I did." The words were loud in the quiet room and Lori wasn't sure exactly who they were for.

Besides, engaging in carnal acts with Lord Severn was hardly her most pressing concern at this point. There was also the not insignificant matter of how she was going to escape.

She absently chewed on a broken fingernail, considering her options as she glanced around the gaudily appointed room, her gaze lingering on an especially medieval looking whip and manacles that appeared to be lined with thick black fur.

Who would have guessed there was a room even more vulgar than the bedchamber Severn used for his *amours*. Did he use this room, too? Did he use the implements that covered the walls? What did he do in this massive black bed?

The possibility that he used this room to have sex with other women caused a confusing and twisted ripple of desire and jealousy to assault her body.

Lori scowled at her reaction to his prurient behavior, and then was immediately irritated by her knee-jerk shame. Hadn't she just finished convincing herself that there was no shame in sensuality? Wasn't it natural that she would respond in such a way? It didn't mean there was anything wrong with her.

She shoved back the bedding, swung her feet to the floor, and shrugged into the gaudy dressing gown she had worn yesterday.

The room's only portal to the outside world wasn't just barred, it also faced the river. The pier, which had been empty the night before, was today crawling with dock workers. Lori squinted at one man who wasn't working, but just leaning against one of the pier posts. And staring right up at her.

Lord Severn had posted a guard *outside* her room!

There truly was no escape. She was his prisoner. His to do with as he pleased.

Yet again she experienced a pleasurable tingling between her thighs.

Wonderful. She was Severn's prisoner and secretly lusting for him.

Not so secretly.

She caught a glimpse of her scowling face in the mirror on the opposite wall and her expression turned to horror.

"Good Lord!" Lord Severn had removed much of the face paint two nights earlier, but not the kohl around her eyes. She'd gone to bed last night without even looking at herself or washing her face. The black had smudged and her hair—which his lordship had loosed—sprang out from her head like so many black snakes.

And then there was the emerald and gold dressing gown.

It clung to her body like oily green water. She might have been nude, her nipples hard and puckered against the fine silk.

Lori groaned.

No wonder that cad Gregg had been staring at her.

She wanted to yell and scream at somebody, but the person responsible for her current situation was none other than the fool in the mirror.

She had strolled right into Lord Severn's clutches as easily as a child who'd been offered a sweetie.

Fool! Fool! Fool!

Lori wanted to deny the accusation, but she couldn't. This was all her fault. She was such an idiot.

The jingle of a key in a lock was like the lighting of a fuse and she rushed the door, the sudden, desperate need to escape overriding any rational thought.

Rather than a maid with a tray, she slammed right into a rock-hard chest.

"My, my, my," a deep voice rumbled beneath her cheek as arms like steel bands tightened around her waist. "Look who is excited to see me."

Lori glowered up at Lord Severn. "You—you *swine!* Unhand me!"

He released her so suddenly that she staggered back and would have fallen if he'd not reached out and steadied her.

She slapped his hand away. "I thought you'd left."

"Not yet, love, but soon. I'm sorry I couldn't be with you last night, but—

"I didn't want you with me! You odious, arrogant, bas—"

"*Shhh.* Gently bred ladies don't call their lovers such names."

"*Lover!*" she shrieked.

He winced. "Darling, if you don't moderate your voice then I'll be forced to—"

"To what?" she yelled even louder. "Just what will you do? Tell me, my lord!"

"—put you over my knee and spank you."

Lori backed away from him, until she was stopped by one of the posts on the massive bed. "You wouldn't!"

"Would, too."

"I *dare* you to even *try* to come near me. I will scratch out—"

"Ooh, I just adore a dare." He closed the distance between them with breathtaking speed, not stopping until his body pinned hers against the post. "And I'll tell you another thing I would adore, Lorelei. And that is spanking that lush bottom of yours." His thin lips curved into a hungry, taunting smile. "And so would you."

Her jaw sagged. "I would nev—"

"Hush. Now, listen to me. The sooner you accept your position here, the better it will be for you. Because I am not letting you go until your life is no longer in danger."

"In danger from who?"

He frowned. "Shouldn't that be *whom*?"

"Lord Severn. If you believe I find this amusing then, you are—"

"You don't need to know the name of the person who sent the ruffian after you. All you need to know is that you are in danger."

Lori wanted to scream and stomp her feet, but she knew that would only amuse him more. "I will stop investigating the story if you let me go," she said in an admirably calm voice.

"That is a lie."

She opened her mouth to deny it.

"And even if it is not a lie, it does not matter. This is no game you are involved in, Lorelei." He lowered his hands on to the thick wooden post behind her, until his body was caging hers, their torsos pressed tightly from hips to chest.

Lori made a sound like a startled hen. "I can't believe you would use your superior physical strength to intimidate me, my lord."

"Believe it." He bent his head, until his face was barely an inch from hers. "Or do you need further convincing? I could overpower you in other ways if you need further—"

"No—no, I believe you."

He pouted. "That is too bad. I was looking forward to showing you how cruel, unfair, and inventive I can be."

"You are despicable."

"Yes, I am. But not for the reasons you think."

She blinked. "What do you mean?"

His eyes, which had begun to darken, roamed her face. "I mean that I want to stretch your naked body out across this big bed and finish what I started the other night."

"You didn't f-finish?" she gasped, thinking she would not have survived much more.

"No, I did not. My goal is to kiss, lick, and/or suck every inch of you."

Lori squeaked.

The hunger blazing from his eyes caused an explosion of flutters in her chest. "I want to see just how wet I can make you. And I want to give you so many orgasms that you beg me for mercy."

"You—you wouldn't dare." She'd meant to sound outraged, but she could tell by the amused glint in his eyes that she'd failed miserably.

"No, I wouldn't. At least not today." His smile slid away. "Not because I lack the desire, but I don't have the time. I'm afraid I must go." He stepped away and it was all she could do not to reach out and grab him and pull him back.

She tucked her willful hands behind her to keep them from disobeying and said, "Where are you going?"

"To a house party."

"A *house party*?"

He winced at her shriek. "Yes. Will you miss me?"

"You *cannot* be serious! You are keeping me here while you go to a *house party*?"

"I am very serious. But it will be Mr. Gregg who will do the keeping until I return."

Lori was so angry that silver sparks filled her vision. Never had she wanted to hit anyone so badly. She clenched her fists, forced down her fury, and prepared to demand—or even beg—that he let her go. Instead, what came out of her mouth was, "Whose house party?"

She briefly squeezed her eyes shut as she bit back a howl of fury. What on earth was *wrong* with her? Now she wanted to hit *herself*.

He chuckled at her question. And then proceeded to ignore it entirely and say, "Try to behave yourself. Mr. Gregg doesn't have my sense of humor and won't be amused if you—"

"Somebody will come for me, my lord."

"I doubt that. But if they do, Mr. Gregg will convince them you are not here."

Lori ground her teeth. "How long do you plan to keep me prisoner?"

"I am not sure."

"Meanwhile, you'll be galivanting all over the country attending house parties."

His grin spread slowly across his face. "You are jealous."

"And you are an arrogant arse," she shot back, outraged that the odious man was right.

He laughed. "If it is any consolation, I wish I could take you along with me, sweetheart."

"You are a loathsome, conceited, odious—a *poltroon*!" she finished lamely.

"A poltroon?" His eyes shone with amusement. "There is one I've not been called before." He strode toward the door, pausing and turning after he had opened it. "Be a good girl while I'm gone, Lorelei."

"Go to hell!"

He laughed again. And then shut and locked the door behind him.

Chapter 20

Two hours later Lori was using the butterknife from her breakfast tray to pry the bolt off one corner of the bars on the window when she heard the telltale sound of the key in the lock.

She sprinted to the bed and tucked the knife behind a pillow, hurriedly dropped into a nearby chair, and picked up the book on Massachusetts.

When the door opened, Mr. Gregg entered. "Hello, ducks."

She scowled up at him. "Go away."

"Are you sure?" He lifted a very familiar looking valise. "Shall I take this with me?"

Lori stared at the battered leather bag. "Wait! Is… is that *mine*?"

"I don't know. Why don't we have a look and see?" He shoved his hand inside the bag and pulled out something white. "*Hmm*, pretty. Is this yours?" He waved Lori's nicest chemise in the air.

She charged across the room and snatched the garment out of his hands. "Where did you get this?" she demanded, grabbing the valise, and taking a few steps back, even though Gregg showed no signs of trying to take the bag back.

"Your housemate packed it for you." He grinned. "Indeed, Lady Sedgewick handed it to me herself." He gave a low whistle, his eyelids lowering. "Now *that* is a lovely lady."

"Why in the world would she give my things to you?"

"Because you wrote to her and asked for them."

Lori narrowed his eyes at him. "I most certainly did no—"

"Oh, yes you did." He reached into his exquisitely tailored clawhammer coat and pulled out a few folded pieces of parchment. Lori came close enough to snatch them from his hand.

She gave an outraged squawk when she saw the three messages—all the same, with varying degrees of success when it came to copying her handwriting. "You forged a letter from me!"

"Guilty as charged."

She pulled her gaze from his smirking face and read the brief message.

Dearest Freddie,

I'm afraid I need to be away from home for a few days. Would you mind terribly packing a bag for me? You can give it to the man who delivered this message—Mr. Gregg—and he'll bring it to me. Don't worry, Freddie, I'm not in any trouble. I'll send you a message by Mr. Gregg every day to let you know things are well. You may trust him implicitly with any messages for me.

Thank you, my dear.

Lori

She looked up, shaking her head. "You *swine*! I may trust you *implicitly*? You are without shame."

Gregg looked delighted by the accusation. "Utterly and completely."

Lori rooted through the bag, relieved when she saw not only fresh undergarments but her two favorite day dresses. Wearing nothing but a fancy dressing gown did not do anything for her morale.

Nor your morals, either.

She scowled at the taunt and looked up to find Gregg leaning against the doorframe, his expression strangely pensive as he stared at the scattered newspapers and half-eaten meal on her breakfast tray.

"What do you want now?" she demanded rudely, hoping her angry tone hid the nervous quaver in her voice.

"Where is the butterknife?"

"What butterknife?"

He strode directly to the window, lifted the corner of the heavy velvet drape, and made a *tsking* sound as he turned to face her. "You'll never get those bolts out of the wall. The knife, Miss Fontenot."

She gave an exasperated growl. "On the bed, under the cushion."

He found the knife, tossed it onto the tray, and then strode to the door and opened it, handing the tray to whomever was waiting outside before turning back to her. "I want you to stop trying to escape."

"No."

He laughed. "Would you really have tried to climb out the window if you'd managed to get the bars off?"

"Yes."

"Even if the man I put on guard had fallen sound asleep and didn't see you—which wouldn't happen, by the by—you might have broken your neck in the fall. Or been scooped up by some shifty character."

"You're one to talk of shifty characters."

"Stop trying to escape."

"All right. I'll stop."

He blinked and his lips parted, the expression of startlement making his almost sinister features look boyish.

Lori smirked and added, "If you let me walk out the door."

"No. Tell me about Lady Sedgewick."

"*What?*"

"You heard me; I want to know about her."

"Why?"

"It's nothing nefarious."

Lori snorted. "Why don't I believe you?"

He lifted a hand and laid it over his heart. "You have my word."

"Why should I tell you anything?"

"Because I'm asking nicely" He gave her a smile that wasn't entirely pleasant. "And because you could use a friend right now, and it seems I'm the likeliest candidate."

"A friend who keeps me prisoner? I don't think I need that kind of friend."

"A person can always use more friends." He leaned against the doorframe and crossed his arms.

There was movement at his feet and the black cat who'd knocked her off the stack of crates rubbed against his calf.

"You!" she accused, pointing a finger and glaring at the offending creature.

The cat paused and gave her a smirk that was a great deal like Mr. Gregg's.

"You should be honored Mr. Pouncefoot-Jones has deigned to pay you a visit."

Lori ignored his taunting. "Will you help me escape if I tell you about Lady Sedgewick?" She had no intention of telling him anything, but it would be interesting to see how far he would go to get information about Freddie.

"No."

"So, then what will you do for me?"

"I could tell you some interesting things."

"Such as what Lord Severn did with the mutineers he picked up?"

He chuckled and shook his head. "I won't say anything about Severn."

"Then what? Give me a sample of the *interesting things* you could share."

"Did you know the Earl of Barrington is pockets to let?"

"*Pffft!* Everyone knows he is broke thanks to ill-advised investments."

"Did you know Barrington is dabbling in illegal slave trading to refill his family's coffers?"

Lori's eyebrows shot up. Barrington was an extremely powerful, well-connected man. Parker would love to print such a story, but even he would want more than innuendo to go after such well-regarded peer. "I would need proof," she said. "And lots of it."

He nodded slowly. "I have proof."

"And you'll give it to me if I tell you about Freddie?"

He nodded again.

"I'm not going to tell you anything she has confided in me."

"I don't want to pry into any confidences," he said. "Was her marriage happy?"

Lori frowned.

"Well?" he prodded.

"I don't know," she finally said, more than a little ashamed that it was the truth. "She was widowed years before I met her."

"Does she have a lover?"

She opened her mouth to tell him he was an impudent scoundrel for asking such questions, but then realized she could give him a truthful answer without betraying her friend. "I don't know anything about that." She paused and added, "And I wouldn't tell you even if I did."

Humor glinted in his dark eyes at her answer. "What about the Duke of Plimpton?"

Lori was startled by the question. "What about him?"

Gregg sighed and gave her a pained look.

"Are you asking me if Plimpton is Freddie's lover?"

"Is he?"

"I already told you that I don't know anything about Freddie's *lovers*."

"And you wouldn't tell me if you did," he said, a wry smirk curving his lips.

"Yes, that is correct."

"So then who is Plimpton to her?"

"Why do you think he is anything to her?"

"I saw his carriage leaving her house when I called to get your valise."

"Oh." Lori studied him for a moment. What could it hurt to tell him that Plimpton was Freddie's client? It wasn't a secret. "Freddie will be launching Plimpton's daughter next Season."

He nodded slowly, but didn't look especially surprised.

"You already knew that, didn't you?" she accused.

He kept nodding.

Lori flung up her hands. "Why are you wasting my time and asking me things if you already know the answer?"

"Do you have something better to do?"

She snorted. "Excellent point. What else do you want to know?"

"What about her marriage to Sedgewick?"

"I already told you I don't know if it was happy or not."

"You must know *something*."

Lori wracked her brains for some bit of information that would not be a betrayal of her friend.

"Do you want to exchange information, or not?" he asked coolly.

"Would you rather I make something up?" she demanded, goaded less by his picking at her than the realization that her friend's past was such a mystery to her after so many years.

"How is it that she doesn't live in the dower house on her dead husband's estate?"

"*Is* there a dower house?" Lori retorted, intrigued.

Gregg frowned.

"I don't know why that is," she admitted. "I—I just know she is not on easy terms with the man who inherited the earldom. Evidently his is some distant cousin."

"I find it had to believe this is all you know about your own housemate."

"She is an exceedingly private person. I doubt she's told anyone about her marriage," Lori snapped. "But if she has, it would be Miles Ingram."

"That's the Earl of Avington—the bloke who taught dancing at that girl's school?"

"How do you know all this?" she asked, more than a little worried about how much this man seemed to know about Lori's friends.

"Why would Avington know? Were they lovers?" he persisted.

"You seem to have *lovers* on the brain," she shot back.

"Answer my question or I'm leaving."

Lori gave an exasperated growl. "I *told* you already that I don't know if she has had any lovers. Do you work for the Spanish Inquisition by any chance?"

His lips twitched slightly at that. "What about the rest of her family?"

"She never mentions them," Lori said rather lamely. Did she really know so little about a woman who was probably her best friend?

"Nothing?"

Lori didn't blame him for sounding skeptical. "She has never mentioned any siblings or her parents. I assume there is nobody left, or she would not have been forced to fend for herself."

Gregg stared for a long moment and then turned to leave.

"Wait! When will you give me the information about Lord Barrington's smuggling?"

"Before you leave here."

"And when will that be, pray?"

"When Lord Severn says you may leave."

"When will he return?"

"That is a matter for him to decide."

Lori looked for something to throw at Gregg's head, but he opened the door and stepped into the corridor too quickly.

The cat strutted across the room and hopped up onto the bed.

"You're forgetting your cat," she called to Gregg.

He was in the act of closing the door but glanced at the sinuous black beast, which was sprawled across the supple leather bedspread as if he belonged there.

"Mr. Pouncefoot-Jones doesn't belong to me. He's his own cat." Gregg shut the door with a firm *click* before she could come up with a response.

Lori stared at the cat, who stared back at her from beneath lowered lids and then yawned.

"Fine, you can stay," she said after a moment. "But I get the right side of the bed."

***

Two mornings later the maid entered Lori's room without Gregg in attendance. She shut the door behind her and deposited the tray on the usual table.

For the first time, there was no sound of a key turning in the lock.

Lori perked up; what was going on? Where was Gregg? Was the woman alone?

She swallowed down her excitement and smiled in what she hoped was a winning, rather than scheming, way. "Hello," she said to the young woman who eyed her nervously. "I see you every day and yet I don't know your name."

"Er, it's Lucy, ma'am." She fiddled with the tray a little and slid an anxious glance toward the closed door. Was Gregg waiting on the other side of it to lock up after Lucy left? Or was he elsewhere this morning, hence the girl's nervousness?

"You don't have to call me *ma'am,*" Lori said, pushing off the bed and moving slowly toward the maid, approaching her as she would a skittish animal. "Just *Lori* is fine."

"Aye." Lucy gave a hesitant nod and began to back away.

"Wait! Don't leave just yet."

But the girl darted toward the door.

Lori hurried after her and was right on her heels when Lucy flung open the door. She made it no more than two steps into the corridor before she slammed into a hard, broad chest.

"Now, now, Miss Fonty-Not, none of that," Mr. Barker chided, one of his massive paws gently but inexorably closing around her upper arm.

Lori watched helplessly as Lucy scurried off down the hall before glaring up at Barker. "You can release me now."

"Not until yer back inside. Go on, now," he said, nudging her backwards into the room.

She growled at him but shuffled back two steps. "Where is Mr. Gregg this morning?"

"Somewhere else." He jerked his chin at her tray. "Go'won and eat yer food afore it's cold."

"Care to join me?"

He chuckled. "I awready ate, Miss Fonty-Not."

"It's pronounced *fon-te-no*," she corrected. "No *t* sound at the end."

"Ain't that wot I just said?"

She couldn't help smiling. "It was close."

He began to shut the door.

"Wait!"

He paused and lifted an eyebrow. "Aye?"

Did every man in the whorehouse know how to raise one eyebrow? Was it a prerequisite for being a privateer?

"I'm bored," she said.

His brow furrowed. "Er—"

"Why don't you come inside and keep me company?"

He gave her a startled look before comprehension dawned. And then he laughed. "Oh, no, miss. 'is loreship would 'ave me guts for garters, 'e would."

Lori smiled slyly. "He can't get angry at what he doesn't know, can he?"

Barker laughed, his easy dismissal of her offer reminding Lori that she was employing her very elementary seduction technique on a man who was living in a brothel, surrounded by prostitutes.

She tried a different tack. "Surely he wouldn't get angry at you just for talking?"

"You ain't wantin' to talk, are ye?"

He looked so amused that she couldn't lie.

"No. I was hoping I might somehow trick my way out of this room."

He chuckled. "Aye. And get me sacked in the bargain."

"Oh, very well," she said, making a point to look chastened and defeated. She gestured at her head. "My hair is a disaster. I need somebody to help me wash and dress it properly," she lied. "Couldn't you send one of the maids up? Perhaps Lucy?"

"I'll ask Mr. Gregg."

Lori feigned a look of surprise. "Does Mr. Gregg count ladies hairdressing among his many skills?"

Barker gave a full belly laugh and waved a huge forefinger at her. "Yer a caution, you are! I'll fetch a lass fer ye."

"Could I also have some paper? Ink? A desk?"

He looked perplexed, his mind obviously sifting through her request and trying to figure out how she could use any of those items to escape. After a moment he said, "Er, I don't see why not, but I'll need to ask Mr. Gregg."

"I'd like to take a walk—get some exercise," she added desperately as he moved to shut the door.

"I'll—"

"Ask Mr. Gregg," Lori finished for him.

Barker gave her a crooked, oddly charming smile. "Aye, miss. Now eat yer food." And then he shut the door.

Lori heaved a sigh and turned to her meal. Not even the sight of three fresh newspapers lying on her tray could cheer her.

She could dress her own hair—she'd never had a maid in her life—but she desperately wanted to talk to somebody who lived at the brothel. Even if she couldn't convince anyone to help her escape, at least she could learn a little about the place. She hadn't lied about being bored. The last few days had been the first in years when she'd not had to work. Reading and lounging were lovely pastimes, but she needed something to occupy her mind—especially when all she had to think about at the moment was how she was probably out of a job and had lost any chance of ever getting her book published.

Sighing heavily, she sat down and ate her meal before it went cold.

She had just poured a second cup of coffee when there was the sound of the key turning in the lock.

When the door opened, a woman a few years older than Lori entered, Barker standing in the open doorway behind her holding a large cannister of steaming water. "This be Dinah and she'll 'elp ye." He jerked a nod at the woman, who was holding a slim lap desk. "There's yer writin' things." He set down the water and then closed and locked the door before she could thank him.

"Hello," Lori said, taking stock of the woman who was certainly taking stock of her. "I didn't really need help dressing my hair, I'm just bored and lonely."

Dinah gave a startled laugh. "Mr. Barker said as much, miss. That's just as well, as I'm not really a maid. I was just one of the few people awake at this hour."

"Call me Lori." She gestured to the other chair at the table. "I'm sorry, but I only have one cup, or I'd offer you some coffee."

Dinah set the writing desk down but didn't sit. "I've already had plenty of coffee," she said, regarding Lori with open curiosity. "The lads say you're a newspaper lady?"

"I am. But I'm afraid being prisoner here is cutting into my job. What lads do you mean?"

Dinah got a wary look. "The ones who came with his lordship."

"So…you, er, work here?" Lori asked, when it was clear the other woman wasn't keen to disclose more information about Severn's men.

"I'm a whore, if that's what you're askin'," Dinah said, her expression mulish.

"I'm very curious about what it is like to work here," she admitted. *Have you ever lain with Lord Severn?*

Dinah snorted. "You a maiden, then?"

Lori was momentarily taken aback by the direct question, but it only seemed fair that she needed to share something about herself if she expected the other woman to confide in her. "No."

Dinah's eyes widened in surprise, but she looked less evasive. "What part about workin' here did you want to know about?"

"I guess… all of it. Would you mind answering a few questions?"

"What sort o' questions?"

"You don't have to answer anything you don't feel comfortable with."

"And this will be in a newspaper?"

"If I chose to write a story about it, your answers might be mentioned."

Dinah's eyes shuttered and she firmly shook her head. "No. I could never 'ave my name in the newspaper. Mrs. Marlowe would be most displeased."

"Mrs. Marlowe? Who is she?"

Dinah opened her mouth and then closed it. "Er, I shouldn't say."

"I could write a story and change your name."

The other woman frowned, mulling over Lori's offer. Suddenly she looked much younger than she'd seemed at first.

"How old are you, Dinah?"

"Nineteen."

Lori scrambled to hide her shock. Dinah didn't look four years younger than her. In fact, she would have guessed the other woman as at least five years *older*.

"How long have you worked here?"

"I'd have to ask Mrs. Marlowe before I say anything more," she repeated.

"I understand. Er, when do you think—"

Dinah stood. "I can ask her right now."

"I thought you said everyone was still asleep."

"Oh no, she's always up early. And up late." Dinah pulled a face. "To own the truth, I don't know when she sleeps. If you don't mind waiting, then—"

"Not at all." What else did she have to do?

"I'm not sure when I'll return."

Lori smiled. "Don't worry, I'm not going anywhere."

Dinah's eyes bulged and then she gave a surprised sounding laugh. "No, I s'pose not." She knocked on the door.

It opened immediately and Dinah murmured something—to Barker, Lori supposed—and the door shut. Once again Lori heard the sound of the key in the lock.

Lori sighed and glanced at the water Barker had left. She might as well use it while it was still hot.

An hour or so later, after washing her hair and tidying her room, she was just sitting down to examine the contents of the lap desk when she heard the jingling of keys at the door.

When it opened, it wasn't Dinah, as she'd expected, but an older woman—perhaps in her mid-thirties—who was breathtakingly lovely.

"I am Mrs. Marlowe and I'm in charge of this establishment."

Lori stood and held out her hand. "My name is—"

"Lord Severn told me who you are," Mrs. Marlowe said, lightly clasping Lori's hand before releasing it.

"Did he also mention that I'm an unwilling captive?"

The older woman smiled faintly. "He told me you were to be treated as an honored guest."

Lori laughed. "You know that holding a person hostage is illegal?"

"Yes, I know that. But Lord Severn owns this building and employs everyone in it. If we were to allow you to leave, he would be extremely displeased. The truth is that he has asked very little of me or anyone else here so I am inclined to do as he asks so long as he doesn't abuse his power."

"And depriving me of my liberty is not an abuse?"

"Miss Fontenot, you are in a whorehouse. The women who live here have an entirely different, and more realistic, definition of what constitutes abuse."

Lori's face heated and she shut her mouth.

"Now, Dinah said you wanted to ask her some questions?"

"Yes."

"About what?"

"About what it is like to work here—what her life is like."

"I see. And I assume you would publish the results of your, er, interview?"

"I might."

"I cannot encourage any of the employees to cooperate with you if you are going to mention the name of the establishment." Her full lips turned down at the corners and her dark blue eyes narrowed. "Drawing attention to ourselves in the newspaper would lead to unwanted attention—perhaps we would even be shut down."

Lori didn't point out that that is what *should* happen. "Provided his lordship doesn't kill me and eventually releases me, then there's nothing to stop me from writing a story, whether you agree to help me, or not."

The other woman's lovely face hardened. "No, of course you may do whatever you wish." She turned to leave.

"Mrs. Marlowe—please wait a moment."

"Yes?" the madam asked coolly.

"I—I don't want to make your life difficult."

Mrs. Marlowe didn't look convinced.

"What if I agreed not to mention the brothel by name?"

"I have a better idea."

Lori perked up. "Yes?"

"You can ask all the questions you like, but you must allow Lord Severn to read your story and agree to its contents before publication."

"*What?* No! That's—"

Again Mrs. Marlowe began to turn. "I can see that you don't care for that idea, so—"

Lori felt any chance of a story slipping away and blurted, "Fine. I will agree to your terms."

Mrs. Marlowe paused. "That is easy to say, but how do I—"

"I give you my word of honor. I know that is not something we women are taught to offer each other—as if we possess no honor, or it has no value—but why shouldn't our word count every bit as much as any man's?"

The madam hesitated, and then nodded slowly. "Very well, I accept your word. You will not publish anything that doesn't have the viscount's approval?"

"Yes."

"Good. Then I shall tell Dinah—"

"Wait—could I ask you a few questions first?"

Mrs. Marlow's golden-brown eyebrows lowered. "About what?"

"Just general questions about the brothel."

Rather than prod her, Lori waited.

A moment later, her patience paid off. "I'll answer questions as long as you promise me one thing."

"You mean one *more* thing other than allowing Severn to have veto power over my article?"

The other woman gave her a small, but genuine, smile. "Yes, in addition to that. I want you to promise me you will tell the truth without sensationalizing it—making it… titillating."

"That is one thing I can guarantee you, Mrs. Marlow. Please, have a seat." She gestured to the same chair she'd just offered Dinah. "I will take some notes if you don't mind?"

"No, I don't mind."

Lori set out the bottle of ink and inspected the quill nib while she talked. "You run this business?"

"I manage the day-to-day matters, but I am an employee, like everyone else."

"You mean—"

"I mean the business belongs to his lordship and I work for him."

"Could you tell me how long you've, er—"

"Been a whore?" Mrs. Marlowe asked wryly.

"It might help me if I knew the preferred nomenclature."

"I prefer the term *whore*. It's jarring, but more honest than *courtesan* or *demimondaine* or any other pretty words."

Lori nodded, although she wasn't sure *whore* was a word she could use.

"Like many of the others here I came to this line of work as a last resort. It is the same tired old story," she went on, before Lori had to ask. "My father is a gentleman farmer, but he was blessed with too many daughters—there are seven of us—so several of us had to find work. I've never been especially good with children, so I chose to hire myself out as a lady's companion. I worked for a woman who was young, bedridden, and dying. I had an affair with her husband." She glanced toward the window, her eyes vague. "He said he loved me and would marry me… after his wife died and a proper mourning period." She shrugged. "Before that could happen, I fell pregnant and had to leave." Her voice was toneless, as if she were reciting a grocery list. "He gave me some money to live for a while, but then no more came. I lost the baby and when I tried to see him, his servants turned me away. His wife had died, and he married another woman before even a month had passed. I needed to find work, but nobody would hire me without a recommendation. I could not tell my family." Again she shrugged. "It was an unpleasant period of my life. I'd just been evicted from the boarding house where I'd been living when I encountered the midwife who'd delivered my stillborn child." She paused, her jaw tightening. "She told me about an establishment that took on gently bred women such as myself. The place looked like any banker or solicitor's house. The woman who operated it was fair and vetted the clients to make sure they weren't violent or visibly diseased. I worked there for three years, until the owner died and her son took over." Her lips tightened. "He was not like his mother. Instead of adult women, he was interested in the money to be made from the far more lucrative virgin trade. And so I looked elsewhere and ended up at The King's Purse." She looked up from her thoughts and seemed almost surprised to find Lori in the room. "That was four years ago."

"I know you don't wish me to list the names of anyone to do with The King's Purse, but if you told me the identity of the virgin exploiter, then I might be able to do something about him."

Mrs. Marlowe's lips curved into a small, cold smile. "That business has been closed down." Her gaze sharpened as she stared at Lori. "Thanks to Lord Severn and the Earl of Grandison."

Lori frowned. "You mean it was one of the brothels written about in the papers last year?"

"Yes."

"Severn had only been back a little over a month when all those arrests were made. How did he manage to get involved with Grandison on such a matter? I know Lord Grandison has made the eradication of the virgin trade a goal of his for years. Why would he join up with the owner of a brothel?"

"You'll need to ask his lordship about that."

Lori wasn't surprised by her answer. All Severn's employees seemed loyal to the core. "So…what can you tell me about?" Lori decided to ask after a moment's consideration.

"Let me give you a little background about this establishment."

Lori nodded.

"The man who used to own The King's Purse had once been relatively decent. But that changed as his addiction to the gambling tables grew worse. When I first started working here, the house was clean and well maintained. By the time Lord Severn won the business in a card game it was—" she broke off and made a sour face. "Let's just say it was grim. All that began to turn around after Lord Severn took control. The changes have been nothing short of miraculous."

"Women are still forced to sell themselves, aren't they?"

"Nobody who works here now is *forced*. Every woman now keeps the majority of her fee and also decides *who* she services. Back when the last owner was in charge, a woman had no choice. He and his cronies used all of us—often without paying—as if we belonged to him, body and soul."

"And that doesn't happen with Severn?" Lori asked, not sure she really wanted the answer.

"His Lordship doesn't use any of the women's services—even though there are a goodly number who would be delighted. And his men always pay their way."

Lori's eyes narrowed. "You're saying that Lord Severn *never* uses any of the—the whores who work here?"

Mrs. Marlowe gave her a wryly amused look. "You have grown so heated, Miss Fontenot. I didn't think that newspaper journalists were supposed to become so emotional about the subjects they write about. I thought they were supposed to maintain a certain degree of neutrality."

Lori gave a forced-sounding chuckle. "You are correct. I should not let my own opinions color my investigation. It's just that—well, I saw Severn with one of your employees the last time I was here. I'm sure you've heard about that?"

"You mean when you were peeping in Lord Severn's window?"

Lori hadn't thought her face could get any hotter. "Yes, that time. In any case, what I saw in the window was proof that his lordship is hardly an angel of mercy. To me he looked more than willing to exploit his own employees for his pleasure."

Mrs. Marlowe's smile grew.

"What? Why are you smiling like that?"

"Because I would like to tell you something. But it must go no further than the two of us—not into your article or anywhere else. Is that possible?"

If she agreed to what this woman was asking, then she would have to abide by it, regardless of how useful the information might be. She stared hard at Mrs. Marlowe, who merely waited, expressionless.

"Fine. I give you my word that I won't tell anyone else what you are about to tell me."

Mrs. Marlowe looked pointedly at the quill in Lori's hand.

She laid it down.

"The woman you saw him with was not an employee. She was a lover from his own class. And he didn't bring her here, she followed him and all but forced her way into The King's Purse."

"From his own class?" Lori couldn't keep the disbelief from her voice.

"Yes."

"Are you saying that was a *peeress* I saw kneeling and—er, well, are you sure?"

"Yes. I even know *which* peeress, but that is something I will *not* tell you."

Lori had to bite her tongue to keep from begging. Just who would be brave enough—or careless enough with their reputation—to come down here? Other than Lori—of course—but then she wasn't a peeress, was she?

She opened her mouth.

"I will not tell you the woman's name."

"I wasn't going to ask," she said, only lying a little bit. "So, you're telling me that he's never had sexual relations with one of the women here?"

"Not to my knowledge. And not very much happens in this building that I don't know about, Miss Fontenot."

Lori could believe that. "So… then why does his keep this place?"

"I don't know. He doesn't take any profits and allows me to operate it the way I wish."

"He doesn't take any money at all?"

"None. And yet he put a great deal of money into the enterprise."

"That is… Well, I can't believe it."

"You have my word of honor that I'm telling the truth." She lifted her eyebrows. "Or doesn't a woman's word carry any weight with you?"

Lori laughed. "Touché, Mrs. Marlowe. You said he lets you operate the business your way?"

The other woman nodded.

"And what way is that?"

"I have final approval over our clients, which means there are no violent or openly diseased men. I don't sell children or virgins or anyone who is unwilling. If somebody comes here out of desperation, I offer them other choices instead of exploiting their need."

"What sort of choices?"

"Lord Severn lends his name to letters of reference for anyone who wants to go into service or work in one of the manufactories he invests in. All they must do is show willing to work hard and learn whatever trade they wish to pursue. Most of the time that's not difficult as so many girls were already in service when their master—or their master's offspring—took advantage of them and destroyed their lives."

Lori was rendered speechless. Lord Severn didn't exploit the women at The King's Purse? He found respectable jobs for the ones who wanted to get away?

It sounded like a fairy tale. Could Mrs. Marlowe be lying?

"You can talk to any of the other women here if you don't believe what I'm saying."

Lori jumped at the offer. "I would like to talk to anyone who is willing."

"Under the same terms you already agreed to."

Lori nodded. "Yes."

"I will agree to that. In exchange for one thing."

Lori laughed. "You really are quite a haggler. What do I need to concede now?"

"Mr. Gregg mentioned you'd used a butter knife to pry off the bars. Don't try to escape. It will make my life a great deal easier."

"Why? Because you fear Lord Severn's wrath?"

Mrs. Marlowe gave an exasperated sigh. "No, Miss Fontenot, not because I fear him. He's been good to us, and I'd like to do something for him in return." Her eyes narrowed. "And another thing. If he is keeping you here, I daresay he has a good reason."

Again, Lori felt heat creeping up her neck, but she held her tongue.

They held each other's gazes. Lori didn't know why she didn't just agree to the other woman's terms. Especially since she'd already decided to wait around for Severn's return. Even if she managed to escape—which was doubtful—she'd still have no money and be stranded in a part of town that wasn't kind to women.

Besides, after languishing at The King's Purse for the better part of four days she had no hope that she still had employment with David. He would be furious that she'd not checked in when the deadline for her story arrived and went.

While she felt a sharp, painful regret about the future of her manuscript—although *future* was an inaccurate word at this point—she couldn't help feeling relief that she no longer had to torment her principles by working for the man.

All she had to look forward to upon leaving the brothel was the agonizing process of finding a position with another newspaper. And *that*, she was in no hurry to face.

Besides, she was curious about Severn and what he was up to. And now, after learning of his strangely humanitarian bent when it came to the brothel, she was doubly curious to grill him when he returned.

Lori met the other woman's patient gaze and nodded. "Very well. I give you my word that I won't try to escape."

***

Lori's promise to Mrs. Marlow turned out to be far easier to keep than she ever would have guessed.

The madam didn't just answer questions, she also allowed all of her employees ample time to talk to Lori if they were so inclined.

To Lori's astonishment, every woman in the place—and even the few men who worked there—spent several hours talking about their lives and what had led them down this particular path.

At first, she had thought only to write an exposé on the subject of prostitution—something she could sell to one of the more reputable newspapers like *The Times*—but the more time she spent taking notes and learning peoples' stories the more she envisioned something that was both larger in scope while at the same time less…limiting.

Because there was no denying that if she wanted to sell something to a newspaper, she would need to heavily censor many details. Even if she did so, the subject was one that could too easily be made into something that titillated rather than informed.

A novel, on the other hand…

It did not take long for that idea to take hold.

She continued to interview during the days—when most of the workers were at leisure—but at night, when the huge house around her came to life and everyone went to work, Lori wrote.

Indeed, she didn't just write, she scribbled more furiously than she'd ever done in her life, the words pouring from her quill as if they could not wait to make their way onto a piece of parchment.

Day after day, night after night, passed this way—time flowing in a blur as she composed something so compelling that she was almost afraid to look at it for fear it might only be a product of her fevered imagination.

It was on the seventh night after she'd first spoken to Mrs. Marlowe—late, perhaps four o'clock in the morning—that she reached the end of an extremely rough draft of her story.

A novel in scarcely a week! How was that even possible?

But her aching hand—fingers swollen and sluggish—was a mute testament to her labor.

She tossed aside her quill and stared at the not insubstantial stack of parchment on the desk in front of her. The story was rough, but it was all there—all laid out and ready to be polished. It was, without a doubt an excellent start.

And you owe it all to Lord Severn.

Lori pulled a face at the thought, but knew it was true enough. Not that Severn had locked her in this horrific room so that she could write a book. She looked around at the walls, laden with sexual implements, and shivered slightly, unnerved by the sight of them even after all these days. No, he had left her in the Queen's Chambers hoping to offend every sensibility she possessed.

Instead, he has managed to stimulate more than just your interest…

"Oh, *do* shut up," she muttered.

But it was true. Looking at whips and leather straps and—and things she could not identify—had fed her desire to understand what she was missing.

Lord Severn will doubtless be willing to educate you in such matters.

"Ha! If he ever returns."

He'd been gone a week. What was he doing at the wretched house party? Was he paying midnight visits to eager lovers—as hedonistic aristocrats were said to do at such gatherings, which were no better than orgies?

Lori hated to think about it.

When was the man coming back?

It suddenly occurred to her that she'd scarcely spared a thought for the fact that she had probably been sacked from her job at *The Mercury*. Honestly, that was a relief, even though it meant she would need to find some other way to earn her crust. She was beginning to think she should seek out another teaching position, not that they were thick on the ground in London, which would mean moving somewhere else.

She would hate to leave the City, which she found vibrant and inspirational, and she would truly dislike moving out of the house she shared with Freddie.

Not to mention moving away from Lord Severn…

Lori sighed, genuinely dispirited at that last thought. Yes, she would hate to leave Lord Severn. Although what she expected could ever come of their association, she did not know.

Oh yes you do! You know.

She caught herself up sharply, refusing to allow her thoughts to travel down that path—a path that ended with Lord Severn in her life for the long term.

Instead, she turned back to her manuscript and carefully straightened the stack of pages, wishing for a moment that she could straighten her emotions as easily.

***

The following day...

Fast stared out the post chaise window, not really seeing the scenery that sped past, but instead imagining the same beautiful, willful, green-eyed face that had haunted him almost hourly since he'd left Lorelei Fontenot at The King's Purse a week ago.

It was Lorelei's face he'd seen whenever Meg had tried to lure him to her boudoir.

It was Lorelei's face that had materialized in his mind's eye whenever Bryok Pascoe had—with a complete absence of finesse—repeatedly thrown Fast together with Demelza.

And, most surprisingly, it had been Lorelei's face that had given him strength to resist strangling Bevil Norman at the blasted house party from hell.

While Fast had agreed in theory with Gregg's proposition that he take his time and destroy Bevil piece-by-piece, a week in proximity with the man had severely eroded his commitment to that plan. In truth, if he could have gotten away with killing Bevil in a house crawling with amorous, room-hopping peers and peeresses, he would have done so.

When he returned to London, he would need to revisit his plan with Gregg.

But that was for later. For now, he was free. Free to go back to The King's Purse and make an even bigger fool of himself over Lorelei Fontenot.

But first he had to make a brief stop at Grandon Castle and retrieve something from the family vault.

And then you will truly *be prepared to make a complete and utter besotted jackass of yourself.*

That was the truth, but Fast did not care. He was going to Grandon to fetch jewels his mother had left him. It was an extremely valuable set that he was then going to hand over to a woman who was likely even now drafting a newspaper story about Fast which she would joyously sell to David Parker in the flicker of an eye.

"Bloody hell," he muttered. "I *am* an idiot."

While Fast had returned to England this year determined to marry—not only to please his grandfather, but because he also desired a family—he had never believed he would fall in love again. The sort of marriage he had envisioned was a cordial but bloodless union between two people of the same class. Oh, he'd hoped that he would marry a woman he would learn to love over time, but he'd had no thoughts of passion or being *in* love. He would not have married any woman based on her birth or position alone, but those two factors would have influenced his decision.

Instead, he'd been struck by lightning, or by a green-eyed vixen, rather, who had captivated him with her sharp tongue, lively mind, and irrepressible spirit from almost the first moment he'd met her. True, his initial reaction to her had been mostly defined by fury over her relentless stalking and the story she'd threatened to publish, but even when he had wanted to strangle her, she had occupied far too much space in his head.

He had hoped that almost a year away from England—and *her*—would have erased the woman utterly from his thoughts. But he had been secretly pleased when, as soon as he'd returned, he'd discovered her rooting in his rubbish and spying in his bedroom, both actions that had given him good reason to pursue their acquaintance. Who would have believed that setting Bow Street Runners on a woman would have proved more effective than traditional flirtation methods?

Fast couldn't help a wry chuckle at the thought.

Was Lorelei beautiful? Undeniably. But the appeal of her exquisite physical appearance was easily rivaled by her sheer liveliness and her—and her—

"Damnation!" Fast couldn't seem to find the right word for exactly what it was about her that had grabbed him by the scruff and showed no sign of turning him loose.

"What difference does it make if you can't find the word? You're still suffering from the affliction."

Affliction? *Addiction* might be a better word for how she had ensorcelled him. Matching wits with her in boring *ton* ballrooms and imagining what she looked like under those ugly gowns she wore had been stimulating enough. But then he had made it all the worse by spending a night with her!

"Lord save me," he said, sounding so pathetic that his face heated in mortification even though there was nobody to hear his pitiful whinging.

A week away from her—spent at the house of his erstwhile lover—should have driven the fever called *Lorelei Fontenot* from his body.

But it had *not* worked. In fact, the distance had only seemed to magnify his symptoms.

He closed his eyes and allowed his head to fall back against the soft leather squabs, exhausted by his relentless thoughts.

All this fretting was pointless. Fast would soon be reunited with the fascinating, maddening, unsuitable object of his obsession. If he was fortunate, he would discover that he had grossly exaggerated both her myriad charms and his attraction to her. If that was the case, then they could engage in a bit of mutually enjoyable bed sport and then go their separate ways once it was safe for her to leave the brothel.

But somehow, Fast did not believe it would be that easy.

Chapter 21

Did Miss Fontenot behave while I was gone?" Fast asked Gregg. The two of them were in Fast's dressing room while he was finishing dressing for dinner.

Gregg's eyes glinted with amusement. "Absolutely not."

Fast chuckled and held out his left hand to Bixby, his valet, who carefully pared and buffed his fingernails. "Oh dear. What mischief did she get up to?"

"She tried to organize a worker uprising among your employees."

Fast laughed. "Indeed?"

"She told them to agitate for higher pay like those mill workers did last year."

"Am I about to get hit with a strike, Mr. Gregg?"

"Thankfully Mrs. Marlowe reminded the girls that they made more than twice what they did before you took over. You wouldn't think they'd need it pointed out that you allow the damned place to operate like a bloody charity," he muttered under his breath.

"I didn't hear that last part," Fast lied.

"Er, nothing, my lord."

"How many times did she try to escape?" he asked when Bixby released his hand and disappeared into Fast's dressing room to fetch his coat.

"Actually, she hasn't tried anything since the first few days."

"Really?"

"She's a fearless little thing but she knows when not to throw effort at something that's impossible."

"*Hmm.*" Fast wasn't so sure of that. Part of him believed that Lorelei was enjoying her little adventure and not in any hurry to end it too quickly. Not to mention that she was probably always on the lookout for opportunities to snoop about and find more information about his private activities while she was his *guest.* At any other time, it would have been amusing to allow her to sniff about. But given the sensitive matter that was currently underway… Well, he'd need to be careful not to give her anything she could massage into a newspaper story.

Not that David Parker was in any condition to print anything she wrote, even if she *did* go back to work for the worm.

His mouth flexed into a cruel smile at the thought of the man who'd put Lorelei's life at risk. Fast glanced at his knuckles. They were still a bit swollen, but the cuts that had opened when he'd beaten Parker to a pulp had mostly healed over the past week.

As Bixby helped Fast into his coat he wondered if he should tell Lorelei just how crooked Parker was—especially where she was concerned.

But no, now wasn't the time. She'd find out soon enough and he knew she'd feel betrayed by what the man had done to her. Besides, he couldn't tell her yet. Not until he was sure that his interference had yielded the results he hoped.

"—if that is agreeable to you, my lord?"

Fast realized that he'd missed the first part of what Gregg had just said. "I beg your pardon?"

The other man smirked. "It seems like you are distracted this evening, my lord?'

Fast snorted at Gregg's sly look and turned to the mirror. "What were you saying?"

"I was asking if I might use your invitation to the Duchess of Chorley's ball tomorrow night."

Fast's fingers froze on his neckcloth, which had become slightly askew when he'd put on his coat, and he turned away from the looking glass and met Gregg's gaze directly. "You want to attend a *ton* ball?" Fast narrowed his eyes at the other man.

He was about to ask why on earth he wanted such a thing, when Gregg's sharp features hardened and he said, "Aye, that's right. You owe me," he added in a voice edged with hostility.

"Are you serious, Gregg? *This* is the first of your favors?"

Gregg's jaw tightened. "You're getting off cheaply, my lord."

"Yes—I'd say I am," Fast said, laughing to hide his surprise more than from any humor he felt at the situation.

Piers Amory Gregg—although Fast doubted that was even his real name—had saved Fast's life many, many years ago. In return, Fast had promised the man three favors—anything Gregg wanted, whenever he wanted. And this was the first favor: an invitation to a ball?

Although he and Gregg had traveled the world together for over a decade and a half, he sometimes felt that he scarcely knew more about him now than he'd done all those years ago. Gregg had never offered to tell him the truth about his past and Fast—who'd had plenty of secrets of his own to protect—had never pried.

"An invitation to a ball that I have no plan to attend is of no importance to me, Gregg. You may have it without calling on a favor. Although you may have some difficulty using it as my name is on it." He shrugged. "But the invitation is in my study on the desk."

"Actually, it's right here." Gregg patted the front of his coat.

Fast snorted. "Pretty damned sure of yourself, eh?"

"I was pretty damned sure about how little you care for attending *ton* balls."

Fast could have told him that he had even less interest than usual given that the only woman he wanted to see was currently in the same building as him.

A woman who has been stewing for more than a week…

Fast snorted at the thought and turned back to the mirror, giving his cuffs a tweak. He heaved a sigh and said, "Well, I suppose I can put off the grilling no longer."

He was startled by the excitement that built in his chest as he strode toward the Queen's Chambers.

He paused and jerked a nod at Rufus, who was standing guard beside the door. "If you hear me screaming for mercy, you'd better intervene. Otherwise, see that the door stays locked, and nobody enters."

Rufus grinned. "Aye, my lord."

Fast steeled himself, entered the room, and then frowned when the woman was nowhere to be seen. "Lorelei?"

Her head popped up on the far side of the bed. Before he could ask her what she was doing, her arm moved in a blur and she snarled, "You!"

Fast ducked, narrowly avoiding being struck in the head by the ankle boot that came hurtling through the air.

"Did you miss me?" he asked, barely sidestepping the second boot which followed with impressive speed and accuracy.

She gave him a look of pure venom.

Fast crossed the room toward her once he was sure that she had no more projectiles.

He gestured to her. "Although it is gratifying to see you on your knees and showing the proper respect when you greet me, you don't need to remain kneeling for the duration of the evening." He grinned as her expression grew even more thunderous. "I never expected you to prostrate yourself before me, but I could certainly grow to like it, darling."

***

Lori sneered up at her captor. "I wouldn't get used to it if I were you. And don't call me *darling,*" she retorted, despising the way her belly tightened at the mere sight of him. And then he grinned—which exposed his prominent canine teeth and made him look every inch the wolfish rake he was alleged to be—and the tightness in her stomach sank a bit lower.

She didn't wait for a response from him before ducking back under the bed and squinting into the gloom. "*Aha*!" she muttered when a pair of glowing eyes blinked near the wall, positioned in such a way that she'd have to climb all the way under the bed to reach them.

Fast's voice came from above. "Whatever are you doing down there?"

Lori ignored him and called in a pleasant, but forced, tone, "Here kitty, kitty." She made kissing noises and crooned, "Good kitty."

The vile beast just stared at her, slowly blinking its huge eyes.

She cursed under her breath, pulled her head from beneath the bed, and sat back on her heels, glaring up at Severn. "Your fiendish cat is toying with my garter beneath the bed."

The man had the nerve to chuckle. "Ah, you've attracted Mr. Pouncefoot-Jones' attention, never a good idea. Or at least not a comfortable one."

"I've been around cats all my life, but I have *never* seen one as—"

"Mischievous?" Severn suggested.

"That is too benign a word. I was going to say evil, or malevolent."

When she began to get to her feet, he offered her his hand. "Allow me."

Rather than flail about clumsily, Lori accepted his help and allowed him to help her stand. But she immediately yanked her hand away once she was on her feet.

"You're welcome," he said, smiling politely.

Lori ignored his sarcasm and pointed to her right foot. Already her stocking was bagging around her ankle. "I am in need of a garter." She hated how her face heated at speaking the word *garter,* as if she were some schoolroom ninny and not a seasoned newspaper woman currently living in a brothel.

"Don't you have another pair?"

"I had *two* pairs, but your beast took the others, as well."

He laughed. "You need to stop leaving such things lying about." He strode to the door, rapped on it, and said something in a low voice to Rufus, her guard of the day.

Lori collected her ankle boots from where she'd thrown them and dropped into a chair to put them on.

"I sent Rufus to borrow a garter from one of the ladies."

"Why don't you be a gentleman and reach under the bed and retrieve mine?" she asked with false sweetness.

He laughed and held up his hands. "Oh, no. What Mr. Pouncefoot-Jones takes; he keeps. I'm not sticking my hand under there."

"Coward."

"Yes, and not ashamed to admit it, either." He showed her the back of his hand, which had four faint white scars. "See these?"

Lori smiled at the claw marks.

"Find that amusing, do you?"

"I do. How did those happen?"

"I tried to take back one of my stockings."

"*You need to stop leaving such things lying about, hmm?*" she mimicked.

"If that was an attempt to sound like me, you failed spectacularly."

He was about to withdraw his hand when Lori noticed something and grabbed it. She ignored the fluttering in her belly that even the slightest touch of his appeared to ignite and studied his knuckles. "I know Mr. Pouncefoot-Jones is vicious, but your knuckles are swollen. What happened?"

"Nothing."

"It doesn't look like *nothing,*" she said, releasing his hand.

There was a brief rap on the door before it opened, and Rufus entered and dropped something into Severn's outstretched palm. "Here's a pair from Dinah, my lord."

"Thank you, Rufus. That will be all." Once the door had shut, Lord Severn held up intricately embroidered garters, one between each forefinger and thumb. He wore a mocking smirk that reminded her of a little boy taunting a little girl. "*Hmm*, what is it that has been embroidered on here?" He squinted exaggeratedly at the garter in his right hand. "It looks like people. What on earth could they be doing?"

Even from a foot away Lori could see that a needlework virtuosa had embroidered nude men and women engaged in coitus.

She snorted. "I thought you were forty, not fourteen."

He scowled. "Nine-and-thirty, Miss Fontenot—nine-and-thirty."

Lori laughed outright this time. "Oh, I beg your pardon. Did I lacerate your delicate self-esteem?" She grabbed at the garters, thinking to catch him unaware.

"*Uh-uh-uh*," he chided, not releasing the garters as a decent man would do. Instead, he tugged hard enough to pull her forward, requiring her to brace a hand against his chest to avoid a full body collision.

Lori couldn't resist flexing her fingers a little, shivers running through her at how little give there was.

"Feel anything you like?"

She jerked her hands away and stepped back.

"Here." He grinned down at her and held out the garters, but then jerked them back again when she reached for them. "Unless you would like help putti—"

"Give. Them. To. Me," she said through clenched teeth.

He laughed and handed them over. "I'll turn my back so you can tie them on."

Lori stared suspiciously at his broad back for a few seconds. When it appeared he wasn't lying, she lifted her foot to the chair, hiked her skirt, tugged up her stocking, and tied on the garter, pausing to examine the erotic scenes depicted. They really were quite stunning—not to mention scandalous.

Once she'd secured the stocking, she thought about her other garter and sighed. No point in having unmatching ones, although who would ever know?

You're worried that his lordship might find out later on. Or hoping, rather…

She gave an exasperated sigh at her own idiocy, switched legs, and changed out garters, tucking her own boring singleton into the hidden pocket in her petticoat.

"You may turn around now."

He turned and eyed her up and down, a slight pucker on his forehead.

"What?" she demanded.

"It has just struck me that you are not dressed for dinner."

She crossed her arms and fixed him with a scathing look. "I am a prisoner here, my lord, so I'm afraid I didn't come prepared for formal entertainments. It scarcely matters what I wear as I've been a prisoner in my room for the entire time."

Lori thought she saw something that looked very much like sheepishness on his face before he smothered it and held out his forearm.

She stared at the proffered limb. "What am I supposed to do with that?"

"I thought you might want to get out of this room." He began to lower his arm. "But if you don't—"

She grabbed him. "Yes, I very much want to get out of this room."

He led her toward the door and rapped on it.

Rufus unlocked it and nodded to them as they passed down the corridor, through a set of double doors into a much shorter hallway with only two doors. Severn opened one and gestured her inside. Lori recognized the room as the one she'd been in right before the viscount had gone off to his house party.

She glanced around, confused.

"What is it?" he asked, motioning her toward a table set with crisp linen, sparkling crystal, glittering silver candlesticks, and a bottle of wine.

"I feel like I came from this room a different way the last time."

"You did. This suite has several different entrances, a few of them concealed."

"Why?"

He pulled out her chair. "I would guess they were used when a lot of smuggling went on here. And no," he quickly added, giving her a dryly amused look, "none of that goes on now."

"I wasn't going to ask," she protested. But only because Mrs. Marlowe had emphatically denied there was smuggling of any kind at the brothel.

Lori waited until he'd poured them both a glass of wine before asking, "So, did you enjoy your house party?"

He grinned, appearing, for once, delighted by one of her questions. "You sound put out, Lorelei. Did you miss me?"

"If I sound *put out* it's because I've been imprisoned in this house for days. When do I get to leave?"

"I'm not sure."

"You can't just keep me here forever."

"Actually, I could."

Before she could contrive an answer to his shocking statement the door opened and Lucy and Dolly entered bearing trays loaded with covered serving dishes.

Severn politely thanked the two women once they'd set out all the dishes, turning back to Lori after the door had closed behind them, the key turning audibly in the lock.

"You have somebody else lock and guard the door even when you're in here with me?" she scoffed. "Are you afraid of me, my lord?"

"Let's just say that I respect your ingenuity, Lorelei. I wouldn't put it past you to brain me with a candlestick, steal the key from my pocket if I were so foolish as to carry it on my person, and then stab poor Rufus with a butter knife once you'd escaped the room."

"Ha! I would have more luck trying to brain a rock."

He laughed. "My grandfather would agree with that assessment. Now, let's pretend this is a pleasurable meal between two people who want to get to know each other. And once the meal is over, we can talk about other—less pleasant—matters."

"Such as my liberty?"

"Yes. Such as your liberty."

Not far behind his genial expression was a wall of granite that said she would neither charm nor badger him into changing his mind.

"Fine. I'll eat and act pleasant, and you can tell me about this house party."

He uncovered a large oval platter that held two bowls of still steaming soup. "Let me serve you."

"Do you always avoid questions like that?"

In answer, he slid a bowl in front of her. "Try some, before it is cold."

She ate a mouthful and set her spoon down with a clatter.

He ignored her pettish behavior and commenced eating his own soup, giving a hum of approval. After a few mouthfuls he set down his spoon with far more grace, smiled at her, and said, "The house party was at the Countess of Mansfield's country estate."

Lori paused, the spoon halfway to her mouth. She'd heard stories about the lovely, wealthy countess, whose name had been linked with Lord Severn's in the gossip columns. Indeed, *Miss Emily* had been among the first to note the connection.

She deliberately raised the spoon the rest of the way, swallowed the contents, and then lowered it before savagely shoving down the jealousy threatening to choke her and saying, "That must have been interesting. Who else was there?" She smiled sourly. "Or was that it? Just a special party for two?"

Lord Severn smiled. "No, it was a regular house party. Let's see, there was Miss Pascoe and her father," he paused at her snort, and then continued, "Lord Moreland—"

This time Lori laughed outright. "A house party at the estate of a woman rumored to be your lover—or at least one of them—with a woman you and Moreland are both openly vying for? Goodness! It has all the makings of a French farce."

He smiled again and ate a mouthful of soup.

"You must have had a lovely time choosing which bedroom to visit. That *is* what happens at house parties, isn't it? Bedroom hopping? I would not know, you see, as I have never attended one. But I've heard plenty of stories." It was as if her mouth had developed a will of its own and Lori couldn't stop the petty, jealous words from spilling out of her. Severn's expression—blandly smiling—just heaped more fuel on the fire. "Did you have an enjoyable time?" she asked in a waspish, peevish tone that made her cringe.

"Not really."

"Oh dear! And why is that? Because Moreland was in ascendance with Miss Pascoe?"

"No. Because the only woman I could think about was you."

Her jaw sagged. "I—I beg your pardon?"

"I *said* you are the only woman I could think about. Why do you look so surprised?"

Lori could only stare. He'd thought about her? *Only* her?

"Even at the best of times I'm not the house party type," he said, when she didn't speak, calmly spooning up the last of his soup and then gesturing to her half-eaten bowl.

"I'm finished," she said through strangely numb lips, watching him with bemusement as he cleared away their bowls and placed two covered dishes before each of them, removing the silver lids with a flourish.

Lori couldn't pull her gaze away from his face long enough to look at the food. Besides, she could eat tree bark at this point and not taste it. His words from a moment earlier—*The only woman I could think about was you*—kept echoing in her head.

"If you don't like them, then why did you go?" she finally managed to ask.

And why did you leave me here while you spent days and days with a beautiful heiress and lovely, wealthy widow?

He gave her a gently teasing smile. "Well, you see, Lorelei, adults often need to do things they don't like."

His words surprised a laugh out of her. "Very droll."

"That is better," he said.

"What is better?"

"You had your stern newspaperwoman face on. Now you look like a delightful young lady."

"And the two are mutually exclusive in your opinion?"

"As to that, I don't know. But I do know that I would much rather have a conversation than be interrogated."

"I don't interrogate!"

He cocked his head and raised an eyebrow.

"Fine, maybe I interrogate sometimes. But that is only because men refuse to take a woman seriously otherwise."

"I take you very seriously." The humorous glint from only seconds earlier had vanished.

Lori swallowed self-consciously at the unmistakable heat in his gaze. "If you take me so seriously then stop fobbing me off with excuses and tell me why you left me a prisoner in a brothel while you went off to cavort at a party?"

"I told you: it's because I take you seriously."

She shoved away the plate in front of her. "Quit feeding me these vague answers. I want the truth, or you can take me back to my room."

"But you haven't even touched your pheasant, Lorelei."

"I am in earnest… *Fast.* What is going on? I've waited patiently. You owe me the respect of an answer."

Something flickered in his eyes at her use of his name. He sat back and lifted his wine and took a sip before saying, "You're right. I *do* owe you some answers." He set down his glass. "In addition to your safety—which really *is* a concern—I'm keeping you here because I have something very important that needs to happen and I can't have you muddling about and destroying months' worth of work and planning."

"Putting aside for a moment how draconian and illegal your behavior is, just how long do you estimate this *something* will take?"

"I'm hoping it won't be much longer. In fact, it should be over within the next few days." He smiled grimly. "One way, or another."

"Would you let me go today if I promised not to pry into your affairs for the next few weeks—a month, even?"

He smiled and she suddenly noticed the fine spray of lines around his striking eyes was more pronounced, the furrows beside his prominent nose deeply graven in his lean cheeks. He looked… exhausted and yet strangely alert, as if he were on edge and waiting for something to happen.

"I can't protect you if I let you go," he said. "You've already meddled in something you don't understand—no, I *can't* tell you about it. Not yet," he spoke over her when she tried to interrupt. "I will make you a bargain, Lorelei. If you will—"

"*Another* bargain? All I seem to do is give in to the people here."

Rather than look angry at her rude interruption, his mouth pulled up on one side. "You mean like the bargain you made with Mrs. Marlowe to interview all the employees while I was away?" He chuckled. "She tells me that you have been scribbling like mad—filling enough pages of parchment to make a book. It sounds as if you should be grateful that your captivity has provided you with such inspiration."

Lori was indeed grateful for the last few days, which had been some of the most inspiring and productive of her life. But she was hardly going to tell *him* that. "I'm delighted my sudden spate of productivity amuses you." He didn't bother to deny it. "However, I have to point out that any stories I want to write are subject to your approval—another *bargain* I made."

"I need to protect the people who work here, you must understand that?"

"I do understand. And I want to protect them, too. It would be nice if you believed me. If you didn't think I'd just destroy innocent women's lives to get my story in a newspaper." She raised a hand when he opened his mouth. "And if you are going to mention last year, then—"

"I wasn't going to mention that business with the child slavery article," he said, no longer amused. "I knew full well what Parker believed, and I did nothing to deny his accusations. I *did,* however, try to warn you not to get involved."

Lori scoffed. "Oh, and I was just supposed to take your word—the word of a stranger at the time—that you were telling the truth? Don't you think everyone facing exposure tries to threaten their way out of it?"

"I *do* trust you," he said, ignoring her question. "As for the story you are writing, if the people who spoke to you give their approval of how you've depicted them then I won't interfere. Is that fair?"

It was more than fair, but Lori wanted more. She wanted what she'd foolishly come up to his room expecting all those nights ago. "I want you to tell me what is going on. Why you came back to England—the real reason."

"So you can publish it in the newspaper?"

"If it's newsworthy."

"No."

"That's not fair!"

"Life isn't fair, I'm sure you've heard that before."

"You've kept me here against my will. How am I supposed to support myself while I'm imprisoned?"

He laughed. "Come, come. If you've not drafted an entire literary work during your stay, then you must be close. I suspect there is nothing quite like a story about a brothel to sell books, Lorelei."

It annoyed her that he was right. She was so excited about her new book that she had decided days ago to tell Parker that he could go to the devil. She also planned to demand that he give her back her manuscript. She would publish the damned thing with a vanity press if she had to. Indeed, she would do anything before whoring herself for Parker, which is what she had been doing.

But none of that was Fast's business.

Truth be told, she had questions that had nothing to do with newspaper articles.

"I have a question—this is just for me, not for publication."

A look of caution flickered across his face. "Very well."

"Are all the illegitimate children you've claimed to sire really your own?"

He turned from wary to furious in a heartbeat. "That is an intensely private matter and not a subject for a newspaper story."

"I just said I wasn't—"

"It wouldn't just be my reputation that would suffer if you wrote about such a thing; it would also damage the lives of several innocent people."

She lifted her hands in a placating gesture. "I am not writing a story about it, Fast."

"Then why the devil would you investigate such a matter, Lorelei?" There was not only anger in his voice, but betrayal.

Lori could not confess her real motivation—that she hated to think of him as the sort of man to leave a trail of illegitimate children in his wake—because then he would want to know why she cared so much. And *that* was something she didn't even like to admit in the privacy of her own mind.

Instead, she said, "I have spent so much time investigating your brother and your family that I just want to know the truth. For myself, not for Parker."

"I will answer your question, but this is *just* between us. If you *ever* tell anyone else and my grandfather learns of it, it will kill him."

"I already gave my word."

"Fine. Then here is your answer: None of those children are mine."

Lori nodded, unsurprised. "You believe they are your brother's, don't you?"

He blinked, his eyes narrowing. "I don't just believe it; I know they are Percy's. Isn't that what Parker told you?"

"I—" she bit her tongue.

"You what?" he prodded when she stopped.

Lori would need to tell him the truth eventually, but not until she had confronted the children's real father.

"Lorelei? What is it?"

"Why would you take the blame for children your brother sired?" she asked, ignoring his question. "Please. I just want to understand. For me—not for anyone else."

He gave her an angry, exasperated look and pushed to his feet. "I need something stronger than wine if I'm to talk about this."

Chapter 22

Fast rang for a servant and once the food had been cleared away, he gestured to the decanters. "Would you care for something to drink? I'm sorry; I should have asked the maid to bring the tea tray. I will ring for one if you—"

"I would have some of that whiskey you gave me before," Lorelei said, primly smoothing the skirts of her plain gray gown.

Fast wrenched his gaze from her—something that was hard to do even for the few seconds it took to pour the drinks. Christ but he had missed her! It had been torture to stay away.

Even so, you should *have stayed away. Instead of returning to The King's Purse—and the temptation of her—you should have gone to stay at Severn House.*

Probably. Already his mind was too curious about those naughty garters he knew held up her prim white stockings.

It isn't too late…you can still do the decent thing.

He could. And he *would.*

Liar. You have no intention of going anywhere other than to bed with the woman who has been dominating your thoughts for days. You are going to draw her deeper into your web even knowing that you very well might kill a man next week and have to run for the rest of your life…

Fast scowled at the unwanted voice and shoved the stopper into the decanter with unnecessary before turning around.

"Thank you," she said when he gave her the whiskey.

Once this conversation was over, he *would* bid her a firm *goodnight* and go to Berkeley Square.

He would just have this one drink and then leave.

He lowered himself into the chair opposite her and lifted his glass. "Here is to both of us getting what we want, Lorelei."

"I can drink to that."

Fast found the way she pursed her lips after taking a tiny sip enchanting.

That was another thought he quickly thrust away.

He sighed and shoved a hand through his hair; the strain of spending the last week in close proximity with Bevil Norman and not killing him had worn him to a nub.

"You look tired, my lord."

"My lord? Are we back to that again? Say my name if you want my story."

Her pale cheeks tinged a delicate pink. "You look tired, *Stand Fast*."

It tickled him to hear his full, ridiculous name on her prim lips. "I am fine," he assured her.

She cleared her throat. "So, you were saying…"

"Who told you the children were Percy's and not mine—and I don't mean Parker's anonymous source, I mean who confirmed it for you?"

She took a sip of whiskey, her gaze evasive. "I don't want to get my source in trouble. She only told me because I gave her my word that I wouldn't write about it."

"You seem to have done a great deal of that recently."

She gave a brief, wry laugh. "Yes, I have. I'm not much of a journalist." Before Fast could argue with her on that subject, she said, "Tell me why you have claimed them as yours."

Fast stretched out his legs and absently examined the tips of his Hessians, forcing his thoughts back more than two decades to the first time his brother put a child in one of his lovers, when Percy had been only seventeen.

"You have to know what growing up in our family was like to understand why I did what I did. The demands that were piled on Percy from the moment of his birth were crushing. My grandfather—and my mother to a certain degree—expected Percy to make up for my father's dissipated, wastrel ways. It was to be my brother's job to not only rescue the family name from the trampling it had endured beneath my father's boots, but Percy was also supposed to sacrifice himself—his *life*—on the altar of matrimony to revive the family coffers." He gave a bitter laugh. "Hell, even my father thought it was Percy's duty to clean up the mess he'd made."

"I understand your father had several illegitimate children of his own."

"Several?" He snorted. "More like a dozen. My father was the very definition of a charming rake. And he *was* charming—as long as you didn't have to rely on him for anything. He was a reckless gambler, an inveterate womanizer, a careless steward of the family fortune and reputation, and on and on. To be frank, it is fortunate that my grandfather survived him because the marquessate would not have survived too much more of my father."

Fast stared at the whiskey in his glass and considered his next words. When he looked up, he saw she was not only patiently waiting, but the expression on her face was one of compassion. She was listening to him not as a journalist, but as a human being. That kindness decided him. "Tell me, do you know how my mother died?"

"I don't know much about either of your parents."

"It was the pox."

She swallowed. "Oh."

"My father—happy-go-lucky-philanderer that he was—managed to pass the disease along to her but never suffered any ill effects from it himself." He threw back the rest of his drink, set down the glass with a *thump*, and said, "You're probably wondering what any of this has to do with my brother's by-blows?"

"I'm in no hurry, Fast."

He sighed and resumed his story, "From a young age Percy was always a bit fragile. If there was an influenza in the neighborhood, he would catch it. And his afflictions were always more severe. When he was seventeen, he developed scarlatina and we thought he was going to die." Fast still felt an anxious clenching in his belly at the memory—even though it was more than twenty years ago, and his twin was long dead.

"He recovered but he was bedridden for months. He was never robust afterward and the doctors said his heart had been damaged by the long illness. They said he would have a longer life if he lived more carefully." He snorted. "I'm sure you can imagine how that advice was received by a seventeen-year-old man who carried the expectations of his entire family on his shoulders. Rather than comply with the advice, he rebelled. He was determined to live life to the fullest. I know it's no excuse for his behavior, but—to be fair to Percy—he never wanted me to assume any of the responsibility for his offspring; I was the one who insisted. By the time the first child was born I had already been thrown out of Eton and refused to go to university. Instead, I was embracing a life of reckless hedonism and getting up to far more trouble than Percy ever would. I was running headlong into disaster as my father had done before me. I refused to listen to anyone and had a head like a brick"—

he smiled when she laughed— "that's not an exaggeration. I was like a wild animal, out of control and heedless of any attempts to rein in my behavior."

He raised his empty glass. "Would you like another?"

She shook her head.

Once he'd refilled his drink he dropped into his chair with a sigh. "Unlike me, Percy rarely gambled, never outspent his allowance, didn't engage in public—and scandalous—wagers, and obeyed our grandfather like a good grandson should. The only arena in which he could not seem to exercise any restraint was when it came to women."

Fast sipped his whiskey, allowing thoughts of his twin to take possession of his mind, not something he permitted very often as it always left him feeling gutted and dispirited.

"My brother loved women, and they loved him right back." He smiled wryly. "He was the handsome one."

"Oh," she said, clearly nonplussed. "I thought you were identical."

He chuckled. "I was jesting; we were identical, although after he was ill it was easy to tell us apart. When I say he was the handsome one, I mean that he had a sweetness—a gentleness—about him that attracted people."

He swirled the amber liquid in the glass, his eyes on the past. "Women were mad for him, and because my grandfather kept him close—denying him a university education to keep him swaddled in cotton wool at home—the women he met were those who lived on the family estates." Fast looked up and met her gaze. "I can see the disapproval in your eyes."

"It's not for me to approve or disapprove," she said, but didn't deny his accusation. "But I still don't see why you thought you should take the blame?"

"At first, I did it for our mother. She'd had such a horrid time with my father and her greatest fear was that we'd both turn out to be just like him. Percy was her favorite—and my grandfather's as well—and it would have killed her to know he'd followed in our father's footsteps. She was very ill for most of our childhood and died when we were barely sixteen. By that time my reputation as a hell-born babe was fixed and it was just easier to go on as I'd begun."

"You mean with you taking all the blame because you were the King of the Rakes," she said, the irony in her voice telling Fast that she had gone from thinking him a complete villain to shifting a large part of the blame to his dead brother.

"Believe me, Lorelei, while I did not father any children, I committed plenty of other sins to justify my reputation."

She pursed her lips, as if she were holding something in.

"What is it?"

"I'm starting to question your *King of the Rakes* façade entirely. For days I've spoken to the women who work here. I've heard horrific things—stories of degradation, exploitation, and tragedy. But not once have you figured into any of those stories as anything other than a port in a storm. In fact, you most often feature as a savior."

"Keep in mind they are my employees, so they have to say that, or I might decide to sack them."

"That's a lie, too. It took me a good deal of time and effort, but I finally got the truth out of Catherine Marlowe. She started off insisting you were the owner here. Only when the holes in her story began to grow did she finally confess that you signed this business over to her, with an agreement that she share any profits with the other employees, regardless of how humble a position they occupy. All you have ever asked for is that this set of rooms be at your disposal while you do whatever it is that you are doing down here at the docks. Which is *not* smuggling or anything else illegal as far as I can tell. Just what *are* you doing?"

"I'm disappointed in Catherine," he said, ignoring her question. "I asked her to keep our business arrangement confidential. And yet you managed to weasel it out of her."

"Why do you want people to believe the worst about you?"

"I never said I did."

"You certainly don't try to set anyone straight."

"No, that is true." Fast knew he shouldn't encourage that admiring glitter in her gaze, but he had to admit that it was far better than the way she'd looked at him before she knew the truth. "I might not be the villain others believed me to be, but my thoughts about you—and the things I'd like to do to you—are less than sterling."

The ivory column of her throat flexed as she swallowed hard. And then swallowed again. "You mean things like the night before you left?" she asked, her voice amusingly squeaky.

"That was only the beginning of what I want to do to you."

Her lips parted and Fast could hear the hitch in her breathing even from where he sat.

"Is Lady Mansfield your lover?"

"If you're asking me whether I engaged in sexual relations with her while I was at her house party, the answer is *no.* Nor did I visit anyone else's room. The only woman I want is you, Lorelei."

***

Lori knew it was only in her mind, but it suddenly felt as though the temperature in the room had soared.

Fast sighed and set down his unfinished glass of whiskey. "I probably should have kept that to myself, but it's time I share a few truths. I am a hypocrite, Lorelei. I say I'm keeping you here for your safety—which is true—but I'm also doing it to satisfy my own pleasure. I'm falling in love with you, darling." He smiled at the startled noise she made. "It surprised the hell out of me, too—not because you aren't exceedingly loveable, but because I wasn't sure I had it in me to feel this way. The last time I felt anything even remotely similar for a woman was more than sixteen years ago."

"Do you mean the Earl of Moreland's wife?" she asked, feeling a twinge of jealousy for at least the third time that night, this time for a dead woman.

He shook his head, an expression of amused exasperation on his face. "You've found out everything about me, haven't you?" Before she could deny it, he asked, "Have you ever been in love, Lorelei?"

"No."

He laughed. "At least you gave the question some thought before answering."

"I can answer quickly *because* I've given it thought." A great deal too much thought, she might have told him. What she'd felt for Dorian had been a desire to belong—and giving her body to him had been the key to belonging. Of course she had believed it was love at the time. It was easy to sneer at her behavior in hindsight, but she'd been seventeen and lonely.

"It's selfish of me, but I'm glad to hear there had been nobody else," Fast said, pulling her thoughts from the past.

Lori was glad she'd never felt genuine love for Dorian. It would have made what he did to her even more heinous.

As for what she felt for Fast? Well, that was far more complex. Part of her wanted to embrace the emotions roiling inside her—to revel in the sensuality and excitement of being wanted by such a man.

But a larger part of her couldn't forget the gulf between them. Especially since he'd been the one to mention the nature of their relationship the last time they'd been together. He might love her, but Lorelei was not the sort of woman an heir to a marquessate would marry.

Not that she *wanted* to marry, of course.

Yes, keep telling yourself that. Maybe one day, you will actually believe it.

Well, regardless of what she wanted, Fast would not marry her. Even if he could overlook her lack of breeding and connections, he would change his mind quickly enough when he learned the truth about Dorain.

"I've been having a lot of selfish thoughts when it comes to you," he said, once again pulling her from her uncomfortable musing.

"Selfish how?"

Fast's pale eyes flickered over Lori's body in a way that only added to the heat in the room, her skin prickling and the bodice of her favorite day dress suddenly tight and uncomfortable.

He held out a hand. "Come here, Lorelei."

Lori wrenched her gaze from his icy blue eyes and looked at his hand. If she took it, she suspected there would be no turning back. Not because he would force anything on her, but because she wouldn't want to let go of him.

Until he moves on to some other woman, one who is suitable to be his wife, the relentless voice in her head reminded her.

Yes, until then. I can be his lover until he marries…

She pushed away the painful thought even as she reached out and his warm fingers engulfed her much smaller hand.

"Your hand is shaking," he said, rubbing his thumb lightly over the thin skin on the back of her hand. "Are you nervous?"

"I'm not shaking," she lied.

Thankfully, he did not laugh or scoff.

"Come and sit." His booted feet slid apart, and he patted his thigh with his free hand.

Lori's emotions warred with each other, the desire to crawl into his lap and take what he was offering vying with the urge to protect her heart and run as far and as fast as she could go. He'd just told her that he loved her; either he was manipulating her for some reason—and she didn't believe that was the case—or he genuinely cared for her. Was wanting him so very bad? He was an intoxicating blending of danger and mystery and allure, like those places on ancient maps that depicted the frightening unknown: *here be monsters.*

How could a woman possibly say *no*?

She stood and went to him, lowering herself on shaking legs. His thigh was hard and warm beneath the thin muslin of her gown.

His arm slid around her, and he pulled her close. Her leg rubbed against his groin, and she jolted when she realized what she had inadvertently grazed. He was aroused. *Very* aroused.

"*Shh,* it's all right." He stroked her lightly, the same way one might gentle a nervous horse.

What are you doing? He might care for you, but he will leave you. You will be crushed far worse than you were with Dorian because this time you—

"Would you like to go back to your room, sweetheart?" he murmured, his breath hot on her shoulder.

It would certainly be safer there.

He cupped her jaw, turning her face until she was forced to look down at him. Viewing him from the slightly raised angle threw shadows across the chiseled planes of his face, making him look like a stranger for a moment. But then he *was* a stranger, wasn't he? They hardly knew anything about each other—at least nothing that wasn't common knowledge.

And yet…for some reason he didn't seem like a stranger. How odd; when had that happened? When had Fast turned from a notorious rake into somebody Lori didn't just respect, but also liked a great deal?

"Such serious thoughts," he murmured, smiling. His thick black lashes were a striking contrast to the pale crystalline blue of his eyes, and she could see the beginning of his night beard prickling his tanned skin.

"I want to make love to you, Lorelei."

Her lips parted and he gently guided her face to his and lightly kissed her, his lips and breath warm and soft. "Will you come to bed with me?"

Chapter 23

Wasn't it you who just—not even an hour ago—promised that you were going to leave The King's Purse and go home to Berkeley Square after your drink?

Yes, it had been him. And that had been Fast's intention, too. Yet here he was, breaking his word to himself yet again.

Fast had known Lorelei Fontenot was trouble from the first time he'd seen her. He'd felt the spark of desire for her even last year at Avington's betrothal ball, when she'd been covered from toes to chin in a hideous gown that looked like it belonged to somebody's spinster aunt. Even when she'd had the audacity to accuse him—in the middle of a *ton* ball, for pity's sake!—of engaging in child prostitution.

True, the spark he'd felt for her had quickly been overwhelmed by fury, but it had been there all the same.

He should have gone back to Berkeley Square tonight rather than come here. He should have danced attendance on his grandfather, who was already seething that Fast wasn't living in the family house.

He should have kept her prisoner somewhere else. Perhaps at his family's estate in Scotland. Somewhere far, far away from him.

He should have done just about anything other than come back to The King's Purse and immediately—*immediately*—arrange to have dinner with her.

Quite frankly, the list of things he should have done was almost as long as the list of things he was about to do to her.

Fast shrugged off what he *should* have done and gave himself up to the pure sensual pleasure of having her in his arms, reveling in the feel of her full sweet lips pressed against his and her soft, curvaceous bottom balanced on his thigh.

How in the hell could a man resist such temptation?

He groaned when she suddenly pulled away. "What is it now?" he asked with a distinctly sulky tone in his voice.

"Yes," she said, her pupils all but swallowing the magnificent green of her irises.

"Yes, what?"

She laughed softly. "Yes, Fast. I will go to bed with you." She paused and then added, "Yes, I will m-make love to you."

Fast stroked the sweet curve of her jaw. "You know if we have intercourse there is always the chance you might conceive, even if I am careful?"

She nodded.

"You needn't do this just to please me, darling. There are other ways we can amuse ourselves. We don't have to—"

"I want to."

Fast shot to his feet, lifting her along with him and making her laugh. "I want to see all of you this time," he said, carefully lowering her to her feet.

"I want to see all of *you*," she shot back, reaching for his coat, her fingers fumbling slightly with the buttons.

"I suspect that could be arranged," he said as he began to pull the pins from the elegant coronet of hair. "I like this style a great deal more than the one you wore the last time," he murmured, unraveling the thick plait and running his fingers through the strands until they fell in a wavy black curtain to her hips. He buried his nose in a fistful of it. "It smells better, too."

She laughed. "It took two washes to rid it completely of that horrid rose scent. Now, step back," she ordered, shrugging out of his grasp so she could push his coat and waistcoat from his shoulders.

"So impatient," he chided, amused by her intent stare and urgent hands.

When he reached for the buttons on her gown—the practical sort that fastened up the front—she pushed his hands aside. "No. I want to undress you, first."

"As you wish."

She cut a quick glance up at him and snorted.

"What is so amusing?" he asked, turning his wrists up so she could remove his cufflinks.

"You don't look at all shy at the prospect of being nude."

"Should I be?"

She ignored his question. "How many women have undressed you?"

Fast took her hands in both of his and stilled them. "Look at me," he said when she stared down at her feet, her jaw clenched. "Lorelei."

Her head whipped up. "You enjoy using that bossy tone with me, but I'm not one of your sailors."

"Believe me, sweetheart, I have never mistaken you for one of my men. As to the other matter, I have been with a great many women. But right now"—he transferred her wrist to his other hand, easily holding both her arms with one hand so that he could cup her face. "Right now, I'm only thinking of one woman—and that is you."

She glared for a moment, but then jerked a nod.

***

Lori couldn't believe that she was stripping Lord Stand Fast Severn naked.

And he was letting her.

You should put a stop to this now. *You will be devastated when this is over…*

The joy she'd been feeling began to shrivel.

"What is it?" a deep voice rumbled beneath her fingers. "You look as if you swallowed a fly, Lorelei." He stilled her hands. "Look at me," he ordered yet again.

"What?" she retorted, not caring how rude and petulant the word was.

"We don't have to do this. You can change your—"

"I don't want to change my mind."

"Then what made you look so dejected?"

"I wasn't dejected," she lied. "I was just thinking."

"About?"

"It's a bit embarrassing to engage in *love making* when a person knows so little about the matter. I'm *bound* to be a disappointment after all your experience." It wasn't what she'd been thinking about, but it wasn't a lie, either. She might have lain with Dorian a half-dozen times, but she'd taken nothing away from the rushed, furtive encounters.

"Hush," he murmured, pulling her closer. "You couldn't disappoint me if you tried." He claimed her mouth with one of his wits obliterating kisses, his strong hands stroking her back in a soothing way while his lips and teeth and tongue slowly broke her into a thousand little pieces.

When he began to withdraw, she chased his retreating tongue, first sucking him into her mouth and then exploring him the way he always did her.

He rewarded her boldness with a low growl that sounded so much like the purr of a huge cat that she laughed and pulled away.

He grinned down at her. "See what you do to me? You turn me into an animal." He purred again.

"A larger version of Mr. Pouncefoot-Jones?"

He nuzzled her neck. "But I won't steal your garters."

She laughed.

"You don't need to worry about a lack of skill. Trust me. My cock is hard for you all the time, even when you're pestering me with questions I'm suffering for the want of you."

"What a martyr you are," she accused, a reluctant smile twisting her lips.

He laughed, released her, and pointed to his cravat. "Get back to work."

Still smiling, she pulled off his neckcloth. For some reason, the action made her think of something else entirely. "I believe Mr. Gregg has designs on my friend Freddie."

His eyebrows shot up, but something about his surprise didn't seem real. "You wish to talk about this *now*?"

"You already knew about his interest in her, didn't you?"

He shrugged.

"He's not the right sort for her—not even as a lover."

"They are both adults, Lorelei. I'm sure Lady Sedgewick can put him in his place if Gregg steps out of it."

Lori grunted and then reached up and unbuttoned the single button that held his collar closed, an action which caused his shirt to fall open, exposing a delicious expanse of golden-brown skin.

"What is it?" he asked when she stared.

"You've got hair on your chest."

He smirked. "Guilty as charged. Why do you look so startled?"

"The drawings I saw didn't have hair."

"What drawings were those?"

"Never you mind."

"Didn't your lover have any hair on his chest?"

"That's none of your concern," she said, not wanting him to know that Dorian had never bothered to do more than unbutton his fall, as if Lori was a whore he'd encountered in a Covent Garden alley. What had seemed like passion when she'd been seventeen now looked like what it was: selfish haste. Lord, but she had been foolish!

"Lorelei? Is aught—"

"Lift your arms," she ordered.

When he complied, she tried to tug his shirt over his head.

"Oye! Not so violently or you'll tear off an ear," he complained, his voice muffled by the cloth over his face.

"Bend lower so I can reach."

He obeyed and she pulled off the garment.

Lori did not bother to hide her interest in his torso, which was indeed glorious—hair and all. His body was not as dark as his face and neck, but it was clear he'd spent time in the sun. "Did you go about on your ship without a shirt?"

He blinked at the question. "On occasion. Er, you're wrinkling that. Bixby will be most displeased and scold me."

She tore her gaze from his nipples, which were a darker pinky-brown than her own and absurdly tiny. "What?"

He gestured to the shirt that she'd not realized she was clutching in a death grip. "My valet gets personally affronted if any of my clothing comes to harm."

Lori couldn't have cared less about his valet. She was fascinated by the way the hair grew on his chest, swirling around his nipples and then thinning to a fine line that led between the fascinating musculature of his abdomen down to his navel.

But it didn't stop there.

It continued in a much finer line that disappeared beneath his low-slung breeches.

A big warm finger slid beneath her chin and tilted her face up and up until she met his warm, amused gaze. "You appear to be fascinated by my body hair. Does it revolt you?"

"No." Her face heated but she forced herself to say, "No, it doesn't revolt me. I like it."

He nodded slowly. "Good."

Lori gave his chest a shove. "Sit," she ordered. "Boots next."

***

"Give me your foot," Lorelei ordered.

Fast complied and she turned and straddled his calf, the sight of her bottom pressed against the thin fabric of her gown making him wish like hell that he'd stripped her naked first.

He gripped the armrests as she yanked on the boot hard enough to pull him half-way out of the chair.

Once she'd repeated the process a second time, she sank to her knees in front of him and reached for his placket.

Fast gritted his teeth to keep from groaning when the heel of her hand bumped his erection. He had to grit even harder while she methodically worked the five buttons that held his breeches closed.

Once the last button had been opened, he lifted his hips and she pulled down his breeches slowly, her eyes licking over him like fire as she stripped him, until only his monstrously tented drawers remained.

And then she spent an inordinate amount of time carefully folding his breeches—as if she'd suddenly been stricken with shyness—before turning back to him, her gaze snagged by his cock.

Amused by her rapt stare, Fast reached down, curled his fingers around his shaft, and stroked himself from root-to-tip.

Her eyes instantly leapt to his. "Does that feel good?" she asked in a raspy voice.

"Not as good as if you were doing it."

She caught her lower lip with her teeth, her eyes riveted to him, but her body motionless.

"Touch me, Lorelei."

She hesitated only a few seconds before reaching for him, her long, elegant fingers twitching slightly before they closed around him.

Fast's eyelids fluttered. "Yessss," he hissed when she commenced petting him, her awkward touches by far the most erotic he'd ever felt.

"I want this off," she said a moment later, not taking her eyes from his muslin sheathed shaft.

Fast pulled the tape on his drawers and pushed the material lower. Her eyes widened as she stared down at his exposed cock. When she did not move to touch him, Fast stroked himself until the foreskin slid back to expose the sensitive, bulbous crown. And then he squeezed.

Lorelei sucked in a breath when a bead of liquid formed on the tiny slit.

Fast aimed the swollen head toward her and said, "Will you take me in your mouth, Lorelei?"

Chapter 24

Lorelei's gaze jumped to Fast's face at his shocking request. His lips were slack, and his pale eyes glittered beneath lowered lids while his hand languidly stroked, the erotic gesture causing muscles from his forearms to his chest to ripple and flex.

"Have you done it before, Lorelei? Sucked a man's cock?"

Her sex—already throbbing with arousal—tightened at his crude question, and the erotic contraction sent ripples of pleasure through her body.

"Yes, I've done it." Her eyes lowered to his *cock*, an oddly appropriate name for the organ thrusting almost proudly into Lord Severn's fist. "I—I wasn't any good." That was an understatement. She could still hear Dorian's rough curses when she'd accidently grazed him with her teeth.

He stilled his erotic stroking and cupped her face with his other hand, his thumb lightly rubbing her lower lip, his nostrils flaring. "I find that difficult to believe. Do you want me to teach you how to pleasure me?" His lips pulled up slightly on one side. "How to make me beg?"

Her mouth, which had been watering from the moment she'd begun to undress him, experienced a flood of almost Biblical proportions. "Yes," she murmured, recalling all too clearly the way *he* had made her beg the last time they had been together.

"Taste me, Lorelei," he murmured, resuming his stroking, the action causing more moisture to bead at the tip.

Lori leaned forward lightly touched her tongue to the tip.

His big body tensed, and he groaned in a way that shot straight to her womb. He was salty, slick, and musky, but it was not unpleasant.

And the reaction from him was enough to mask her uncertainty. Looking up at him, she found his eyes riveted to her.

Emboldened by the naked hunger in his gaze, she leaned forward and ran the flat of her tongue up the thick shaft to the fat mushroom shaped head.

His nostrils flared and his breathing suddenly became ragged.

"Tell me what to do," she said.

"You're doing just fine on your own," he assured her tightly.

"But I want to make you climax."

He smiled and she couldn't help noticing how strained the expression was. "You will." When she hesitated, he asked, "Did anything I do to you feel bad?"

"No," she quickly said.

"It will be the same for me. Trust me, darling—I wouldn't lie."

Lori felt as if a world of expectations slid away as she turned her attention back to his fascinating appendage.

Which is when she noticed what was beneath them.

Testicles. She knew the word, but had no idea they would look so… fragile. The tight pouch was lightly furred, like his chest. His free hand rested beneath them, and his thumb lightly stroked, the gesture so natural she suspected he didn't even realize he was doing it.

Testicles were too much for her brain to sort out just then, so she shifted her attention back to the slick head.

He shivered as she licked and kissed and explored. Emboldened by her success, she stretched her jaws to see how much she could take inside her mouth. When her teeth grazed him, his body stiffened.

"I'm sorry!" she gasped.

"It didn't hurt," he assured her. "I was just startled. Don't stop. Please.""

Using more care, she tried again but was still unable to take any more than the fat crown inside. But it appeared to be enough based on the almost agonized groan that tore out of him.

"Yes, Lorelei, that's so good." His hand came to rest on the back of her head and he carded his fingers through her hair. He smiled down at her, his eyes heavy and his expression one of sheer masculine pleasure. "Use your upper lip on top and your tongue to shield me from your bottom teeth," he urged, lifting his hips slightly and sliding deeper and deeper, until she felt like she would choke. Just as she began to gag, he pulled out and she could breathe. "Yes, just like that," he murmured, his fingers lightly caressing her scalp, his eyes fixed on her mouth. "You should see how beautiful you look with those plush lips wrapped around me."

She blushed at his words and preened at the hunger in his voice.

"Wrap your hand around me to control how much you take, Lorelei." He nodded approvingly when she gripped the base of his root.

"Stroke a little. *Ungh*. Christ! Perfect." One of his hands drifted to his belly and then up to his chest.

Lori thought her eyes would roll right out of her head when he pinched one of his tiny nipples and groaned, his hips lifting and pushing his shaft deeper. "You're making me feel so good." His hips rolled, resuming their subtle thrusting. "Show me you can take a little more."

His praise sent a warm wave flowing through her body and she opened wider, suddenly wanting to demonstrate just how much pleasure she could give.

Rather than be disgusted by her own compliance, there was something about responding to his commands that was causing the sensual tightening in her sex that she knew led to a climax. How was that possible? Why should she take pleasure in performing such a debasing task?

And then it struck her: because it *wasn't* debasing when she could see how much pleasure it brought her lover. If anything, it made her feel powerful to cause this big, strong man to shiver and groan.

"God, Lorelei! I'm so close to exploding, but I don't want to end this yet." His fingers tightened in her hair, until he held her immobile. "That's enough for now, sweetheart."

For a moment, Lori resisted.

He smiled, controlling her body with an ease that should have frustrated her, but only made her more aroused. "We'll do more of this later. Trust me," he said, gently withdrawing all the way. He stood, lifting her to her feet as if she were a feather.

"Let's get this off you," he said, his deft fingers reminding her of how many hundreds of times he'd probably removed a woman's clothing. Just how many lovers he'd had and the ones he'd likely have after she was gone and—

"Don't," he ordered, forcing her to meet his gaze.

"Don't what?"

"Start thinking about things that don't matter right now."

"How do you know what I'm thinking?"

He raised his eyebrows. "Was I wrong?" he asked, returning to the buttons and then sliding the gown off her shoulders.

"Smugness is not an attractive attribute," she said, stepping out of the circle of her gown.

He laughed and reached behind her to loosen the laces of her half-stays. "Lift your arms."

When she did, he raised not just her corset, but her chemise along with it, leaving her naked one step sooner than she'd expected.

He stepped back and studied her. Not covering her breasts with her hands was one of the most difficult things she'd done.

"So beautiful," he murmured, and then dropped to his haunches and speedily removed her boots. But when she reached for the garters, he stayed her hand. "No. Those you leave on." His gaze darkened even more. "Those wicked garters are lovely on you." Before she could think of a retort, he stood and held out his hand. "Come, let's go to bed."

***

"Up you go," Fast said, lifting her by the waist and smiling at her startled gasp. "On your back, darling," he said, amused when she was too surprised to argue and immediately complied.

"You're staring," she said, a hand across her breast and another resting over her mound.

"Yes." Fast allowed her to cover herself—for the moment—and reveled in the sight of her.

No matter what happened between him and Lorelei in the future, he would never, as long as he lived, forget the sight of his innocent lover sprawled over the decadent red velvet that covered the bed, garbed only in white stockings and those naughty garters.

"Bloody hell," he muttered.

"What is it?" she asked, her eyebrows drawn down.

"You're just so damned desirable."

She blushed and this time he could enjoy the way it spread all over her body.

"You like to embarrass me, don't you?"

"Yes," he said. "Legs apart," he ordered, even more smug when she obeyed without hesitation.

"I can't believe I just did that," she muttered.

Before she could snap them shut, Fast dropped to his elbows, braced his forearms against her thighs, and dragged his tongue up her slit, probing the seam of her lips just enough to taste her. An animalistic growl tore from his chest. "God, I love seeing you squirm and blush."

"Yes, we have already established—oh!" she gasped when he parted her pouty lips and sucked her engorged pearl into his mouth.

All her modesty flew out the window and she sank both hands in his hair as she had done the time before, her eyes riveted to his. She was already so close to her climax that he'd scarcely begun to enjoy himself when she bucked like an unbroken horse beneath him, her back arching off the bed, breasts thrust high and legs shaking as she came.

Fast could feel the relaxation in her body as she slowly drifted in the aftershocks of her orgasm. She was so deep in her bliss that she didn't even notice when he made his way up her body, his arms caging her as his knees pushed her thighs wider.

He stroked his nose alongside hers. "Are you sure you want this?" Fast lightly pulsed against her tight opening, gritting his teeth against the pleasure that shot up his cock at the slick friction. And then he stilled his gentle thrusting and tried to be a better man. "We can wait for another—"

"I want you." Her legs spread wider, as if to bolster her claim.

He shallowly probed her and hissed. "You're very tight."

"Is—am I too tight to do it?" she asked, her brow furrowed with concern.

He chuckled softly. "It's not possible to be too tight, love. At least not for a man." Fast breached her and made them both gasp. "How does it feel?" he asked, remaining still inside her and allowing her to accustom herself to the invasion. He was in no hurry. Indeed, he would have liked to make this night last all week, but his self-control was already stretched to its limits.

"It feels like you can't possibly fit."

He laughed. "Trust me, darling, I'll fit."

Lorelei's breathing quickening as he slowly filled her. "There," he murmured once he was hilted. "That is all."

"It don't recall it being so, er, snug before," she said in a strained voice.

He couldn't help chuckling. "Thank you."

"I wasn't trying to flatter you."

"I know," he said, leaning low to nuzzle her jaw. "That makes it even better. Relax," he urged. "Your body is so tense." He showered her with light, gentle kisses. After a moment, he felt her body relax.

"Lorelei?" he asked, when she just stared blankly over his shoulder. "Is something wrong?"

"No. I was just thinking."

"That sounds dangerous," he teased. "About what?"

"I was just thinking about the first time."

Fast struggled for something to say and came up with, "Oh?"

"Sexual intercourse—especially the first time—is something that defines a woman's life, and yet it is over so quickly." Her brilliant green eyes came back into focus. "I'm sorry. You probably don't usually talk this much during, er, coitus."

"No," he agreed, "but it does not matter what I *usually* do." He leaned down and kissed her soundly. When he came up for air, he withdrew from her slowly, his body shaking with the effort of behaving like a gentleman rather than a dog in rut.

"You are shaking. Is something wrong?" she asked.

"Nothing is wrong. In fact, everything is right. The reason I'm trembling like a leaf is because I'm having to exert more effort than I've done in years—two decades, as a matter of fact."

"What do you mean?" she asked as he sank back in, hissing his pleasure and briefly closing his eyes.

He worked her deeply with each slow thrust. "I mean that I've not been with a woman this way since I was nineteen years old."

Her eyes bulged. "What do you mean?"

"Just what I said," he said, his hips refusing to obey his brain, his cock developing a mind of its own. A mind that ordered his body to plunge and take and dominate.

"I—I don't understand."

Fast gave a strained chuckle. "Might we wait until *after* to talk about this, darling?"

"After," she agreed, her body rising to meet his on the next thrust.

He slid his hands around her thighs, lifted her legs until her feet were flat on the mattress, and bottomed out in her tight heat.

"Too much?" he asked when she groaned.

She shook her head. "S'good," she muttered, wrapping her legs around him right before he drove her into the mattress, her body taking him even deeper.

Fast's thin control snapped. He was vaguely aware the woman beneath him had only made love a few times, years before, and deserved more finesse, but after two decades, he could not restrain himself.

The voice of reason intervened at the very last moment, shrilly shrieking: *No baby*! Fast withdrew just as he came apart, pumping ribbon after ribbon onto her soft belly.

His arms, so sturdy only seconds earlier, could no longer bear his weight and the room seemed to rock from side to side. "Just going to close my eyes a moment," he muttered as he lowered onto her, using the last of his strength not to drop down like a lead weight.

***

"Just going to close my eyes a mome…" The last word was swallowed by a soft snore, the weight of his big body pressing Lorelei into the mattress.

He'd pulled out so abruptly that Lori had been startled. It was a good thing that at least one of them had remembered that she didn't wish to get pregnant. Dorian had certainly never let that concern him. Of course, neither had Lori. She'd been so desperate for acceptance and affection that she'd given no thought at all to the repercussions of her actions.

She scowled at the canopy over her head. Why on earth was she thinking about Dorian now?

Lori firmly pushed thoughts of her first lover from her mind and turned her attention to the man currently crushing her in the most pleasurable of ways.

She frowned; what had he meant about two decades of abstinence? Or perhaps she had misunderstood?

Lori knew that he'd had lovers since returning to England. Why would he lie about such a thing?

Yet again, she shoved away the unpleasant thought. She'd have plenty of time to mull over the matter obsessively when she was alone.

Fast's weight should have been uncomfortable, but there was something oddly comforting about it. His breathing was heavy and deep, that of a man who'd had far too little sleep of late.

Emboldened by his near-comatose condition, Lori laid her hands on his back and lightly caressed him. He fidgeted a little at her touch but didn't wake, so Lori massaged the muscles of his back more firmly, marveling at the sheer size and bulk of him.

Her hands moved down and down until they reached a part of him that she'd not yet seen: his bottom.

She cupped a tight round globe of flesh in each palm and lightly squeezed.

Her hands froze when he gave a low murmur and shifted. When he didn't wake, she resumed her exploration, entranced that such a large man would possess such narrow hips and small buttocks. Her own bottom was fleshy and broad, and her hips seemed to spread alarmingly with each year that passed.

There was a delicate fuzz—like a peach—on the otherwise smooth skin and it tickled her palms as she caressed him.

He grunted when one of her fingers skimmed the crease that divided the two cheeks and Lori dropped her hands to her sides.

"*Hmm*, what's that?" he asked, pushing up onto his elbows.

"I didn't say anything."

He blinked blearily down at her. "Lord! I must be crushing you," he mumbled, and then rolled off her before she could say anything.

He had been crushing her, but the experience had been exceedingly pleasurable.

"Was I too rough, sweetheart?" he asked, pushing up onto his elbow and staring down at her.

Before she could answer, he slid a hand over her hip bone and dipped a finger between her lower lips.

"Lord Severn!" Lori grabbed his arm and tried to tug it away. It was like trying to move a boulder.

"What?" he asked, trying to look innocent and failing spectacularly. His lips curved wickedly, and he made no effort to remove his hand. He also showed no trace of the sleepiness of only a few seconds before. "Let me," he said, his voice a low purr.

"Let you what?"

"Let me make you come. I know that you did not achieve release when I selfishly rutted you for my own pleasure."

"I'll l-let you do that if you tell me what you meant."

He lifted an eyebrow, the erstwhile irksome gesture squeezing at her heart for some reason. "You mean about not having had another woman for twenty years?"

She nodded.

He glanced significantly down to where her hand still gripped his arm.

When she released him, he said, "I meant exactly that." He slid a thick finger between her netherlips and circled the sensitive bundle of nerves with a skill and ease that said *that* hadn't been something he'd given up for the past twenty years.

Frankly, it felt so good that she shamelessly didn't care.

"Spread your legs a little for me, love."

She narrowed her gaze at him.

"I promise I'll keep talking. Just let me play."

Lori spread her thighs wider. "Tell me why you'd do such a thing?" she asked in a voice that did not sound strained. No, not at all.

His lips flexed into a frown and his gaze went vague, but his finger never faltered in its mesmerizing rhythm. "I wasn't any better behaved than Percy—I was just more fortunate." He gave her a wry smile. "I made the vow after Percy got the first girl pregnant that I would not add another bastard to the family line."

"And that means—"

"That means I have not had sexual intercourse for more than twenty years."

Lori stared.

"Why do you look so flabbergasted?" His finger lightly nudged her in such a way that she tensed and pushed her hips at his hand.

"It seems not to fit with your rake status," she admitted in a not entirely steady voice.

"Is this not rakish enough for you?" he asked, caressing a part of her so sensitive that she gasped and threw back her head.

He chuckled, his finger moving away from the too-sensitive spot and drifting lower, toward her opening.

Lori bit her lip when he lightly probed her.

"You are sore," he said.

She nodded.

His finger continued its journey down. And down.

Lori tried to snap her thighs shut, but he rolled over, moving with startling speed, until he was once again between her legs. This time he pushed his knees wider, to keep her thigh spread.

"What are you doing?" she demanded as he resumed his stroking. "Fast!" she yelped as he prodded a part of her that she'd most certainly never seen and had only ever touched by accident.

He ignored her question and slowly, deliberately, lowered himself onto the bed until his elbows kept her legs apart. And then he lowered his mouth to her clitoris, although his finger still practiced its startling caresses.

Lori soon stopped caring about his distracting digit, her body racing toward bliss almost before she knew what was happening.

After she had climaxed not once, but twice, he rolled back to the side, his big hand lightly cupping her sex, the possessive gesture so arousing that she didn't want to contemplate what that meant.

He wiped his mouth with the back of one hand and smiled. "I'm sorry, you were asking—or trying to ask—something when I distracted you."

For some reason, Lori was suddenly too mortified to put her question into words. Some newspaperwoman she was turning out to be!

He lightly stroked her sensitive folds before sliding toward that taboo place. "You want to know if I ever put myself in *here*." He pressed the damp pad of his finger against the sensitive pucker.

"You haven't," Lori said. And then, "Have you?"

"Oh yes."

"But… *why*?"

"Because it feels wonderful. For both parties."

A shocked, scoffing snort slipped from her mouth. "I find that hard to believe."

"I look forward to convincing you."

Her jaw dropped. "I would never let you do that!"

He released her sex and slid an arm around her, pulling her close and planting a firm kiss on her mouth. "I think you will change your mind about that, love. But for now, it is time to sleep." Fast stretched to snuff the candle on the nightstand, throwing the bed into a comfortable half-darkness. "We'll leave the others burning because I'm too lazy to get up," he said, and then fitted her back to his front, pulled the covers up over them, and kissed her ear. "Go to sleep, my enchanting lover."

"I'm not tired," Lori protested, her eyelids suddenly so, so heavy.

"I know. But I am."

"Because you're old and need more rest."

He gave a startled huff of laughter. "Vixen," he muttered, his chest a hard wall of heat against her back. "Sleep tight, Lorelei."

Chapter 25

"Wake up, my lord. *My lord!*"

Fast pulled Lorelei closer. "It's not time yet, love," he mumbled.

"Lord Severn!" a distinctly masculine voice hissed in his ear.

Fast's eyes flew open. "What the dev—"

Gregg leaned over him and laid a finger over his lips. "Miss Fontenot," he whispered.

Fast blinked and then nodded, suddenly wide awake. And wondering what the fuck Gregg thought he was doing barging into his bedchamber.

The other man must have seen the anger in his eyes. "I didn't see anything," he promised quietly, backing away from the bed.

Fast scowled, checked to see if Lorelei was fully covered—she was, the sheets pulled up to her chin—and carefully extricated himself.

He quickly pulled on his breeches and followed Gregg from the room, shutting the door behind him with a quiet *snick* before saying. "What could be so important that you couldn't wait until morning?"

Gregg took a deep breath and said in a rush, "The *Blue Devil* is here. Jensen is dead, my lord."

Fast sagged against the door. "Good God! When? How?"

"Evidently somebody murdered him not long after we dropped him off in Majorca."

"Christ! The letter?"

Gregg shook his head. "The woman who operated the boarding house where Jensen lived packed up his possessions and gave them to Captain Evans when he came to collect Jensen for the journey home. I've already gone through everything, sir, there is nothing."

Fast shook his head. "So…Garcia didn't have it, and it wasn't in Jensen's belongings. And—if Moreland's brute Carey is to be believed—Moreland doesn't have it, either."

"Maybe there was no confession?" Gregg suggested.

Fast had considered that, too. "Well, that doesn't much matter any longer. Without Jensen, the confession would lack conviction. "I wonder if Moreland knows that Jensen is dead," he mused, his mind speedily waking up.

"I can't imagine how," Gregg said. "If Garcia—or somebody he was working with—killed him then the last thing he would have wanted to do was tell Moreland about it."

"I agree. Let's send him a letter. If he knows Jensen is dead, then it can't make matters worse. But if he doesn't know, we might be able to lure him out."

Gregg nodded. "What do you want me to write?"

"Say that Jensen just arrived in London and has the confession in his possession. And that he was supposed to sell it to me, but that he has changed his mind because Moreland has his sister."

"I'll do it right away," Gregg said. "Anything else?"

Fast shook his head. "No. If we are fortunate, Moreland will take the bait and produce the girl."

"And if he doesn't?" Gregg asked.

Fast met his friend's concerned gaze and smiled grimly. "Don't borrow trouble, Gregg. We've got plenty of that already."

***

Lori drifted in the shallows between sleep and wakefulness, her body humming in a way that was becoming pleasurably familiar to her.

If she opened her eyes, it would stop—she just knew it would.

But when she reached down to rub herself harder and encourage more of those feelings her knuckles encountered something hard.

"Ow!" a muffled voice muttered, yanking her from her dozy state.

Broad shoulders pressed against her inner thighs, warm, strong finger stroked the intimate folds between her legs, and a hot, insistent mouth sucked and licked.

Her lips curled into a smile when she realized she'd not been dreaming at all. She carded her fingers through his messy hair and ground herself against his mouth, focusing his tongue exactly where she needed it.

Rather than be annoyed at her rough, demanding usage, he chuckled and slid a finger inside her, pumping her with hard, deep strokes as his wicked mouth worked its magic.

Lori's hips began to jerk and then buck as the most powerful orgasm she'd yet experienced gripped her in its punishing fist.

She was lost for a time, only vaguely aware of his tender kisses and gentle stroking. As she came down from the ecstatic heights he crawled up her body, until his messy head emerged from beneath the covers.

"Good morning, my delicious lover," he murmured, kissing her with lips that were swollen and slick and tasted salty and musky. Of *her*.

He chuckled, once again reading her mind with an ease that was disconcerting. "You taste good, don't you?"

"Not as good as you," she retorted, and then bit her lip, shocked at her own words.

"Mmmm," he rumbled. "I'm so glad you feel that way." His hips thrust lazily against her thigh, the hard length of him making her shiver.

Lori opened her legs in silent invitation.

He paused his sensuous frottage and arched an eyebrow. "Are you sure you're not too sore?"

"I wasn't a maiden, you know."

"I know." He smirked, easily moving up her body. "But then you've never encountered a… specimen as huge and impressive as mine before, have you?"

Lori laughed. "Oh dear. I can see it was a mistake to say such a thing aloud. You're going to get a big head, aren't you?"

"I've already got one," he murmured, pressing the blunt head of his erection against her opening.

They both laughed.

"That was terrible. I'm sorry," he said, "I just couldn't resist." He kissed her jaw and then lightly bit the spot and kissed it again. "I can't resist you, either," he growled.

She did feel an unpleasant stretch when he breached her, but it was superseded by the bliss of having him inside her again. Once more, she couldn't help comparing her experience with Dorian with the way she felt with Fast.

"Such a wet, tight pussy," he murmured, and then chuckled when his wicked words made her clench her inner muscles. "Touch me, lover," he said, his thrusts easy and slow.

Lori eagerly complied, massaging the compact muscles that she'd surreptitiously stroked last night.

"Ah, God," he groaned, his tight bottom bunching and flexing. "That feels so good. Harder—you can't hurt me."

Lori dug her fingers into the taut flesh.

"Yessss," he hissed. "So good—so perfect." His strokes became rougher, less controlled, and the massive bed jolted with the power of his thrusts. "I don't want to come, but you're going to make me—*Lorelei*!" His body went rigid just before he withdrew from her.

This time Lori was paying attention and watched as he spent. He gave himself only a few brutal jerks and then his head dropped back as ribbon after ribbon jetted from the tiny slit, the muscles of his chest and abdomen so defined that she could see the individual striations with every spasm and thrust.

Once there was nothing left, he did as he'd done the night before and collapsed with an exhausted groan. This time, her arms slid around him without hesitation, and she held him tight to her body.

Lori must have fallen asleep because the next time she opened her eyes she was alone in the bed and the light coming through the window was bright yellow rather than the weak gray light of dawn.

She yawned and stretched, a smile stretching her mouth as she remembered last night and the words he'd spoken.

He loves me.

No. He's falling *in love with you*, the pedantic voice in her head corrected.

For once, Lori could laugh at the chiding voice. So what if he'd said *falling*? It was enough that he'd given voice to the feelings that had been swirling around inside her for weeks.

Lori sat up and swung her feet off the bed before noticing her uncharacteristic nudity. And then she recalled why she was without a stitch of clothing that morning and smiled.

Still smiling, she glanced to the end of the bed, where she usually kept her dressing gown. Only then did she recall that she was not in her gaudy black bedchamber, but Fast's gaudy red one.

Instead of a robe on the footboard bench there were two familiar pale pink boxes tied with silver ribbon. She stared uncomprehendingly for a long moment.

And then the truth came to her in a rush: It had been Fast who'd bought her gowns and jewels. Lori had never once considered him. But then why would she have suspected him?

His words from last night came back to her: *I think I'm falling in love with you*. Just how long had that been going on?

And why had he purchased dresses for her? Because her clothing was so dismal?

She felt a stab of disappointment but quashed it; why should that upset her? It was certainly true. Her dreadful taste when it came to sartorial matters had always been a source of amusement among her friends. There was no denying that the gowns Fast had chosen suited her perfectly. How could such gifts be insulting?

Lori pushed aside her unease as well as the bedclothes. She found her garments in a neatly folded pile on one of the chairs and slipped her chemise over her head before slowly going toward the boxes, as if she were approaching a dangerous animal rather than luxurious gifts.

But then wasn't what was in the box dangerous—the expensive gowns and valuable jewels, both items a wealthy man gave a mistress—and her hand hesitated on the lid of the top box.

So, that is what you are, isn't it?

Lori yanked her hand back from the boxes when she heard the door open. She turned, expecting to find one of the maids with her breakfast.

But it was Fast. "Ah! You're awake," he said, hitching the door shut with his foot as his hands were occupied carrying a tray that was twice as big as usual. "I was hoping to catch you still abed," he added, setting down the tray. His smile grew bigger when he saw what she'd been looking at. "Oh, good. I wanted to watch you open them."

"You gave me those other gifts."

His smile faltered at her accusatory tone. "Yes."

"Why?"

His brow furrowed. "What do you mean?"

"I mean why did you think I needed new gowns and expensive jewels?"

His lips parted and, for the first time since she'd met him, he looked uncertain. "I gave them to you because I wanted to. And because I thought you'd look lovely in them."

"Because I didn't look *lovely* enough in my usual clothing?" she asked, wishing that her tone had not turned quite so shrewish.

"I believe I said before that you would look beautiful in sackcloth, Lorelei." The furrows in his brow deepened. "Are you angry with me for giving you gifts?"

Was she?

"Or are you angry that you didn't discover who'd given them to you?"

She opened her mouth to deny that, but then paused, her eyes on his face. He'd looked so happy—joyous, even—when he'd come into the room. And now he looked shuttered, wary, and—yes—hurt.

And all because he made the mistake of being generous to you.

Lori drew in a deep breath and then exhaled slowly, bewildered and annoyed by the emotional whirl in her head. "I am not angry."

"But you're not happy, either."

"I'm… concerned."

"Concerned that I gave you some gifts?

She nodded.

"Why?"

"I'm…not sure," she admitted. "It is only that giving gifts—especially items like clothing and jewelry—is something a man does with his mistress."

He folded his massive arms over his chest and his frown turned into a scowl. "I thought I made my feelings for you clear last night, Lorelei."

I think I'm beginning to fall in love with you.

Lori bit her lip, suddenly seeing her behavior from his point of view. She had assured him on their first night together that she understood what *this*—their affair—meant: that it was nothing more than temporary physical gratification.

She had also assured him—repeatedly and emphatically—that she had no other expectations of him, certainly not marriage!

He had not lied to her, not like Dorian had done at first, when he had sought to seduce her. All along Fast had been open and honest. And now she was accusing him of treating her like a mistress when that was exactly what she was.

You are furious at him because you want more.

She was. And her behavior—her desire for something more permanent—mortified her.

Lori forced herself to meet his gaze, hating the reserve that had entered his icy eyes. Eyes that had been warm only moments earlier.

And it was her fault for treating him as if he were Dorian.

He deserved better.

Lori took a step toward him. And then another, until she was standing close enough to touch him. That short walk was one of the hardest things she'd ever done.

"I'm sorry, Fast."

Chapter 26

Fast told himself not to feel like she'd just slapped his face. He'd known all along that she had a proud, prickly side. Evidently the gift giving had brought that out in her.

She came toward him slowly, and with an entirely un-Lorelei-like hesitancy in her step. "I'm sorry, Fast."

The sense of ill-use he'd been feeling disappeared at her abashed expression. "Come here, you darling hedgehog." He slid a hand around her waist and pulled her to him. She came willingly, all but flinging herself at him, her soft body as taut as a bow. Fast stroked her back and held her close. "You are trembling! What is wrong, my love?"

"I have to tell you something embarrassing." Her words were muffled as she spoke them into his coat. When Fast tried to move back so he could look at her, she shook her head. "No, I don't want you to see me when I say this."

"Very well. I'm listening," he said, resuming his stroking.

"I was a tomboy when I was a girl. In fact, until I was thirteen, I refused to accept that I wasn't just another boy.

Fast smiled, easily imagining a younger, more coltish, version of Lorelei. "What happened at thirteen."

"I grew breasts."

She sounded so woeful that he was glad he hadn't laughed.

Her arms, which had been tight around him like bands of wire, loosened and she set her hands on his hips and moved back enough that she could tilt her face and see his. "You probably think that is amusing."

"I think I'm glad you grew them, but I can certainly understand how it made it difficult for you to be just another lad."

"I still tried, but it became more and more difficult to fit in with the group of boys who'd been my playmates. When I turned sixteen my sister-in-law, who'd all but raised me, convinced me to go to a dance—ball is too grand a word—at the local squire's house." She chewed on her plump lower lip, her expression pensive as her gaze slid again to his. "The boys who'd been ignoring me suddenly noticed me."

Fast's hands tightened on her slender waist; he would just bet they did.

"To make a not very interesting but intensely mortifying story shorter, the local lord's son—I don't want to use his real name, so I'll call him *William*—singled me out for attention. William was the leader of the group I'd always tagged after, so it was something of an honor to gain his notice. At first it was just small things he did to distinguish me. He brought me some boiled sweets, or a book I wanted but couldn't afford, things of that nature."

Again, she chewed her lip, this time so viciously that he wanted to stop her before she hurt herself, but he didn't want to interrupt whatever was so difficult for her to say.

"My brother kept only one old horse—a relic of his youth—in his small stables and allowed me to ride the poor beast. When poor Dancer came up lame on one of my rambles, William said that it would be no bother to mount me from his father's stables. His lordship breeds horses and had more than his family could use at any given time.

Not convinced by William's offer, my brother approached his father. His lordship very kindly said I would be doing him a favor by riding one of his horses as he'd otherwise need to have one of his grooms exercise the animal. Yet still my brother wasn't comfortable accepting such an offer." Her lips twisted into a bitter smile. "I now know exactly why that was, but at the time I begged and pleaded and badgered poor Jeremy." She cut Fast a guilty look. "I was a little toad and essentially shamed him into granting his permission by not so subtly hinting that I should not suffer for his inability to buy me a proper horse."

She inhaled deeply, and then went on, "William and I were childhood friends who'd always ridden together, usually in a group with other neighborhood children. The only difference was that I now rode a horse from his father's stables."

Fast's stomach tightened when she paused. He slid a hand around her jaw and tilted her face to his. "You don't need to tell me this if you don't wish to, Lorelei."

"I don't want to talk about it, but…I want you to know why I am so wary of men."

He nodded, but the unease in his belly grew even worse at her words.

"More and more when we rode out William managed to separate me from the others. I felt some unease about what we did—a bit of touching—but…he told me that he loved me—that he wanted us to be together and was only waiting until his last term at Eton was over to divulge the truth about us to his father."

Her hands idly caressed Fast's hips in a way that he would have enjoyed if he'd not dreaded where this story was headed.

"You became lovers," he said, hoping to save her some pain.

She snorted. "I don't think the clumsy, hurried, and ultimately humiliating fumblings we engaged in made us *lovers*."

His hands tightened on her shoulders. "Lorelei, did he—"

"He didn't force me. Everything I did with him, I did willingly. If I sound bitter, it's only because I regret being so foolish and believing that he ever loved me."

I am falling in love with you…

Fast's words from the night before came back to him, and he suddenly understood why she was telling him this story.

"It's not foolishness to seek love and affection, Lorelei. It just means you are human. For anyone—a man or a woman—to use the promise of love to get what they want is…well, it's reprehensible."

But Lorelei did not seem to hear him, her eyes vague as she stared into her past. "I engaged in sex with him not just once, but several times. The worst part of it was that I never even enjoyed it, but I kept doing it to please him." She frowned and gulped, blinking rapidly. "Actually, that wasn't the worst part. The worst was that I continued meeting him, even when it was clear that he'd lost interest in me. I only did so because I knew that when I stopped, that would be the end of all my so-called *friendship* with not only him, but the rest of the group." She gave a slightly hysterical laugh. "As if any of them were worth it."

Fast grimaced. "Good God. Please tell me he did not—"

"He did—he told them what we had been doing." Her voice broke on the last word and two fat tears slid down her cheeks.

"Oh, Lorelei," he murmured, stroking her back.

Lori angrily brushed her tears away with the back of her hand. "I have no idea why I'm crying now."

Fast pulled her close, holding her so tightly it had to be painful. But Lorelei just burrowed closer.

"It was *so* humiliating, Fast."

"You were an innocent trusting girl, and he took advantage of your generous heart, Lorelei. He behaved like a selfish arsehole."

She gave a watery gurgle of laughter. "You are the first person I've ever told—I never even confessed it to Freddie. I wanted to tell my brother because I hated seeing how William smirked and simpered and behaved as if he were an angel in Jeremy's presence. But I couldn't say anything," she said, the words hot puffs of air against his throat. "My brother owes his living to William's father, and I was afraid of what Jeremy might do if he found out," she said, her voice choked. "And the worst part of all was that he became betrothed a scant two weeks after he finished with me. He had never cared for me—he'd known all along he would marry somebody else. I hated him so much, Fast, but I was far angrier at myself for being so stupid. My brother knew something had happened when I stopped riding his lordship's horses and stopped seeing William or any of the others, all of whom had been sniggering behind my back for weeks, laughing about the vicar's whore of a sister who'd been spreading her legs for a man who'd tossed her aside like a piece of rubbish to marry somebody better."

Her shoulders shook with silent sobs and Fast held her while she wept.

***

Lori sniffed tiredly and turned her head to look up at the man who'd held her quietly and patiently throughout her emotional outburst.

"I'm sorry for that," she said, her voice nasally and eyes watery and no doubt shot with red.

"*Shh*," he murmured, not pausing his soothing stroking. "You have nothing to apologize for."

At some point during her emotional storm, he had carried her over to the settee and she'd sobbed out her heart while resting her head in his lap.

"I never cry. It's been years—not since my mother died," she said. "I don't know what came over me."

"There's no shame in it. Everyone needs a good cry once in a while."

She chuckled. "Oh really? And when was your last cry, pray?"

"When my brother died."

Lori gasped. "Oh, Fast! I'm so sorry. I didn't—"

"Hush. I know you didn't mean anything." He stared down at her, but his magnificent eyes had a blank look in them and she knew he was seeing something else.

"For almost sixteen years I thought I had killed my brother."

"*What?*"

"Oh, I didn't hold the gun to his head, but I felt as though I might as well have." His gaze flickered and then gradually sharpened. "We had a falling out over a woman. It hadn't been the first time we'd both fancied the same girl, but it was the first time we allowed our emotions to come between us."

Lori sat up and faced him, taking his hand in hers and waiting patiently.

"Regardless of the fact that Percy was far kinder and had a much sweeter disposition—not to mention that he would inherit the title and everything that went with it—Louisa fell in love with me. Percy was furious when I told him that I'd asked her to marry me, and she'd accepted." His lips turned down at the corners. "It turned out he had every right to be angry as Louisa had—weeks before and unbeknownst to me—promised to marry him." He snorted. "Not only that, but while I had been saving myself for our marriage, Louisa and Percy had been lovers for months. I'm not proud to admit that I struck him at that point, hitting him hard enough to knock him unconscious. I was terrified that I'd killed him. I hadn't, but I *had* fractured two of his ribs and he had a concussion from the fall.

"My grandfather was furious at me, but nowhere as furious as I was at myself. I confronted Louisa and discovered that Percy had not lied. She claimed that her parents had exerted pressure on her to accept Percy even though it was me she loved. The betrothal was to be kept a secret until her eighteenth birthday. Louisa swore that she was working up to telling them all the truth. And she also admitted that she'd been Percy's lover the entire time."

"Oh, Fast," Lorelei murmured, squeezing his hand.

"Don't feel too sorry for me, darling. I'm not proud of what I did next; I told her that our betrothal—which wasn't even a day old—was over. I said that if I had to choose between her or Percy, the decision was easy. I was cruel and I wanted to hurt her. I hope that I would have eventually forgiven her—and apologized for my unkind words—but I never had the chance. Three days later—when Percy was able to leave his bed—he went into the woods and shot himself. Immediately afterward I argued with my grandfather who essentially told me he never wanted to see my face again."

"And that is why you stayed away all these years?"

"Yes. Until my grandfather wrote asking me to return." He stared at their joined hands, an unreadable expression on his face.

Just when he looked on the verge of speaking, he seemed to shake himself and look up, his eyes blank as if he'd just woken from a trance.

Lori opened her mouth to ask what had changed—why his grandfather wanted him to return, but all of a sudden Fast released her hands and got to his feet.

"Where are you going?" she asked.

"To bring your gifts to you, so I can watch you open them." He carried the boxes back to her and set one on the table and the other in her lap. "Open it," he ordered, taking the chair across from her.

She gave him a pained look.

"What is it, Lorelei?"

"It's just that I've never given you anything."

"Oh yes you have. Open your gifts, please."

***

Fast was bloody grateful that he had snapped out of the powerfully confiding spell that had wrapped around him before he'd blurted out the truth about Bevil Norman and his part in Percy's death.

It wasn't that he didn't trust her, but rather because he was so uncertain of what his future held. If he could not bring Moreland to justice in the accepted way, he would kill the man. Something told him that Lorelei would be less than eager to ally herself with a murderer.

Not only was the situation with Moreland a problem, but Fast believed Lorelei when she said she did not wish to marry. If he were given enough time, he knew that he could convince her that spending the rest of their lives together would be worth sacrificing some of her Wollstonecraftian ideals.

And then there was the issue of his grandfather, who would also need a great deal of careful handling. Although the old man was a stickler in many ways, Fast felt sure he could talk him around to his position in the end.

But he could hardly engage in either conversation when he might be a fugitive from the law, wanted for the murder of a peer, before the bloody week was out.

What he needed was some time to sort out one problem before turning to another. Not that being married to Lorelei was a problem. Indeed, he was fairly certain they would deal very well together once they'd got past a few minor hurdles—such as her hatred of the institution of marriage and his grandfather's near-obsession with a lineage that could be traced back to the Conqueror.

Fast put the matter out of his head for the moment and enjoyed watching his lover open her gifts.

Her cheeks were flushed as she pulled the ribbon and lifted the lid off the box, rustling through the tissue paper before giving a small gasp and lifting a hand to her mouth.

He sat forward in his chair, his eyes fastened to her face. "Do you like it?"

She stroked the gauzy silk fabric, which was the same rich shade of red as the fruit of a pomegranate.

"It is magnificent," she said, cutting him a quick, shy look. "I've never worn this color before."

"Hold it up in front of yourself so I can see if I chose well. I argued quite fiercely for this color as Madam Thérèse said you couldn't wear this shade."

"How did she know what color I—" she broke off. "Ah, she saw me."

He laughed. "Indeed, she saw far more of you than she liked. I think she was on the verge of capitulating the last time you interrogated her."

She stood and lifted the silk which flowed like a scarlet waterfall from her hands.

When she held it up, Fast nodded, smugly pleased. "Just as I thought. Go look at yourself in the cheval glass. It is just inside my dressing room."

"Well?" he called out, when he heard no sound from inside the adjacent room.

She came out slowly, her eyes downcast, her cheeks almost the same red as the gown.

"You don't like it," he said flatly.

"I love it. You were right; the color is perfect."

"Then why won't you look at me?"

Her eyes, when they finally lifted to his, held an expression of shyness that was foreign on her beautiful face.

He stood and went toward her, cupping her face in both hands. "*You* are perfect." He claimed her mouth, delighted when she returned his kiss with as much passion as he felt. What a dolt this *William* was that he'd never bothered to kiss this magnificent woman. He felt a flare of rage at the thought of a man abusing her trust so. He would need to find out the identity of the unprincipled cad and—

"Is something wrong, Fast?"

He glanced down at her and smiled. "Nothing except it is past time for you to open the other box."

She caught her lower lip with her teeth. "It is too much, I can't—"

"I thought we'd finished with that tedious subject, Lorelei."

She pursed her lips and inhaled until her lovely breasts pressed enticingly against the thin material of her chemise. "I shall let it rest for now." She wagged her finger at him. "But don't buy me anything else."

"I'll damned well buy you whatever I please," he retorted. "I've done nothing for the last decade but pile up money like a dragon in his lair. You are the first person I have wanted to spend any of it on. Don't be selfish. Let me spoil you. Now, open my gift."

She heaved an exaggerated sigh and carefully laid the gown over the back of the settee before picking up the smaller box.

When she pulled off the ribbon and lifted the lid, she gave him a wry smile at the lacquer box nestled within the box and lightly stroked the lid. "This looks very old—and beautiful. And it has peacocks on it, which seems to be a theme with you."

"Open it," he ordered again.

"So impatient," she muttered, but lifted the lid. Her head immediately whipped up and yet again she opened her mouth.

Fast knew it wasn't to say *thank you*. "Remember. You can argue later."

She snapped her mouth shut and snorted, shaking her head as she turned her gaze back to the ruby necklace, earrings, and two bracelets in the box. "This is… well, I don't have words."

"Who could have envisioned such a day?" he mocked, sotto voce.

She cut him a scowl. "I suspect you paid a fortune for it."

"It's rude to speculate on the cost of a gift," he chided. Fast suspected that she would be astounded if he told her that he had not paid anything at all for the set, which was, indeed, worth a fortune. It had been his mother's. Not part of the Grandon jewels, but a set that she'd brought to her marriage. She had given it to Fast a few weeks before her death, telling him to give it to a woman he loved, no matter whether he married her, or not. The look on her face as she lay dying had told Fast plenty. He'd always known his parents' marriage was arranged, but he'd never guessed that his mother had been forced to give up a man she loved to marry Fast's father.

The jewels had been locked away in the family vault at Grandon Castle since his mother's death and Fast had fetched them on his way back from Meg's wretched house party, already imagining how the glittering stones would look with the gown he'd ordered from Madam Thérèse.

"Thank you," she said quietly. "Your generosity humbles me. I don't know what to say."

Fast took the box from her hands and tossed it aside. He sat down beside on the settee and then lifted her onto his lap. "I don't want words." He smiled slyly. "I want you to give me a proper *thank you*."

"And what would that be?"

"A kiss."

She lifted her eyebrows. "That's all?"

"And also let me put my hand beneath your chemise."

She laughed and the sound was so warm and uninhibited that it squeezed his heart.

He kissed her hard, as if he could somehow imprint his stamp on her. Bloody hell but he loved this prickly, difficult, never predictable woman.

She broke the kiss and began to stand.

"Where do you think you are going?"

"I'm not going anywhere." To his utter delight she swung one knee over his thighs, until she was straddling his lap.

"*Mmm*, I like this a great deal, Lorelei."

She swooped down on him, her mouth hot and demanding as she took control of the kiss. At the same time, she guided his hand under her chemise, which had ridden up her hips. Fast moaned when she placed his palm over her mound and then raised up high on her knees, making herself more accessible.

He didn't hesitate to accept her invitation and slid a finger between her lower lips. "My God, Lorelei, you're so wet! Is that for me?"

She nodded primly and then kissed him again. Their tongues jousted lazily, and she nipped and nibbled, teasing him into a frenzy while he stroked the source of her pleasure, until his hand was drenched with her desire.

"Take me out of my breeches, Lorelei," he murmured against the damp skin of her neck once they'd broken their kiss to draw breath. "I want to be inside you."

She freed him in seconds, yanking his breeches and drawers down to mid-thigh before closing her hand around him and pumping him with clumsy but firm strokes.

Fast groaned and stared into her darkening eyes while they stimulated each other with hands and fingers.

"Tell me what feels best," she ordered in a voice that was rough with passion.

"The crown is the most sensitive, and right below it. Wet your palm with my slick and stroke me hard."

She immediately followed his directions, and he gasped, his hips jerking so hard that his buttocks lifted off the settee. "God, yes! Just like that, darling."

"I like it when you call me that."

"I like calling you that."

She laughed.

"And I really like it when you laugh."

She bit her lip, as if embarrassed. Why she was embarrassed of laughter and yet fearlessly straddling his lap and fisting his cock was beyond him.

His Lorelei was a puzzle, and it would take years to put all the pieces together. But that was for later, right now he needed her.

"Ride me, Lorelei." His lips curved into a wicked grin. "Imagine that I am an especially willful horse that needs breaking."

She choked on a laugh, positioned him at her entrance, and slowly lowered her body.

"Oh God, *yes*." He took her hips and lifted his own body off the settee, thrusting hard enough to lift them both off the cushion. "You feel so damnably delicious that you are destroying my resolve."

"What resolve?" she teased in a breathy voice, and then gasped and grabbed his shoulders to hold on as he began to buck beneath her.

"My resolve to make this last," he hissed through gritted teeth.

"It is not as if we cannot do it again, is it?"

Her expression was so adorably serious that Fast threw back his head and laughed with pure joy.

***

"Wake up, my sleeping beauty…"

The low, soothing voice caressed Lori like a warm hand.

No…wait, that *was* a warm hand, caressing up her thigh.

Her eyes sprang open and met a brilliant blue pair mere inches from her own.

"Hello darling," Fast murmured, kissing her temple and lightly cupping her mound, which reminded her that she was naked.

"Is it morning?" she asked, pulling the bedsheet up to her chin.

He looked amused by the gesture and, after giving her sex a light squeeze, released her. "It is very early and I should not have woken you, but I have a surprise for you."

"A surprise?" she repeated stupidly.

He pointed across the room.

Lori pushed up onto her elbows and squinted. "Oooh! Where did that come from?" she demanded, looking from the huge steaming copper tub to the man beside her. "I have been dying for a bath!"

"Well, what are you waiting for?" He made a sweeping gesture with one hand toward the bath.

Lori shoved back the sheet and quickly, before she could lose her nerve, scrambled out of the bed and quickly strode naked across the room, telling herself to ignore the view she must be giving him. Why should she care if he saw her bountiful bottom? He had seen it before, after all.

Lori paused just long enough to dip a toe in the water and then groaned. "It's perfect," she said, and then eased first one leg and then the other, into the water before lowering slowly. Only then did she look up at him.

"Why didn't I know you had this tub?" Lori demanded, greedily surveying his body as he stripped off his shirt and breeches and eased himself in on the opposite end.

"I don't want to give away all my secrets," Fast said.

The tub had clearly been built for two people, but probably not with a man of Fast's dimensions in mind. That meant only Lori could completely stretch, her feet resting on his chest while his knees poked above the water.

It was heaven.

Lori had a sudden sense of unreality. Here she was, lying in a bathtub in a brothel with a man who'd taken her prisoner. She *should* be angry—she'd certainly raged against her situation enough at the beginning of her captivity—but she couldn't honestly say she regretted this experience. How could she? Not only had the last twelve hours been among the most enjoyable of her life, but the week before had been one of the most productive seven days of her career.

While the novel that had all but flowed out of her fingers onto the page was not yet fit for print, it was as solid a first draft as any she had ever made. And in only a fraction of the time! Lori did not think she flattered herself that it was better than anything else she had written. The first thing she was going to do when she left The King's Purse was march into David Parker's office and demand her manuscript back.

The second thing she was going to do was polish up the book and then submit it herself rather than—

"What are you grinning about over there?" he asked, gently rubbing a soapy cloth between her smallest and second smallest toe.

"You never told me how you got your name?" she said, not wanting to talk about her book.

He cocked his head. "Why do I think that is not what you were thinking about?"

"It wasn't, but…I don't want to say what I was thinking about. Don't worry, it didn't have to do with you."

He clutched his heart. "I am crushed."

She snorted. "You were going to tell me about your name."

"We were named after a set of twins on my mother's side." He smiled. "Puritans, as I'm sure you've surmised."

"So, your mother's family are Puritans? They must have fought with the Roundheads?"

"I'm sure the first Stand Fast and his brother would have fought with Cromwell had they remained in England, but they'd fled England several years before the war started. My mother was always fascinated by her radical nonconformist ancestors, hence the names." He moved to the next toe and glanced up at her. "I visited them when I was in Massachusetts, you know."

Lori frowned. "Them?"

"The descendants of the original Stand Fast and Perseverance. They thrived in America and Makepeace furniture is highly sought after."

"You are related to *those* Makepeaces?"

He nodded. "Indeed, I am."

"Even I—ignoramus though I am in all matters of fashion, sartorial or décor, have heard of them."

"I am proud to say their goods fill the cargo holds of several of my ships.

"Wait a moment—several? You have *several* ships?"

He gave her an exaggerated wide-eyed look. "Are you telling me there is something about me that you don't know?"

"I suspect there is a great deal I don't know about you," she said dryly.

He merely smiled and occupied himself with washing her arch and heel.

Lori closed her eyes and let her head rest against the sloped tub. She was so relaxed that she could have fallen asleep if not for the ugly secret still weighing down on her like a pallet of bricks.

Perhaps you don't need to tell him the truth? He has taken care of those children knowing they aren't his. Can this information really make any difference?

But it *would* make a difference, that's why she feared telling him so badly. Aristocratic men were prickly about matters of pride—insanely, murderously so—and it was entirely within the realm of possibility that Fast would demand some sort of satisfaction on his brother's behalf.

Lori chewed her lower lip, torn.

"What is bothering you, Lorelei?"

She opened her eyes. "How do you know something is bothering me?"

He gave her an exasperated look. "You should never, ever try your luck at a card table. Your every thought flits across your face."

She sighed.

"Out with it."

"It is about your brother's children—and it is not pleasant," she warned.

He paused his ablutions and fixed her with a suddenly frosty stare. "Have you already sold the story about Percy's illegitimate children?"

"Of course not!"

He grunted. "Then nothing else will bother me."

Lori seriously doubted that.

"Tell me," he barked.

"Do you always give orders?"

"Most of the time."

"And people just jump to obey them."

"You tell me." His lip pulled up on one side, his heavy-lidded look reminding her of the way Lori herself had instantly obeyed him on more than one occasion…when the command was an erotic one.

Lori tried to scowl at him but failed miserably. "You're incorrigible."

"And you blush more than any woman I've ever met."

"I know. And I hate it."

"I don't. Now, tell me what is bothering you."

She heaved a sigh. "I want you to promise me something before I tell you."

His eyebrows pulled down over his nose, making him look even fiercer than usual. "I don't like this game, Lorelei."

"It's not a game. And I'll only tell you if you promise me first."

"Promise you what?" he asked in that menacing tone that gave her shivers.

"Promise me that you won't sack any of the people who spoke to me—and gave me information."

The corner of his mouth ticced, but he jerked out a nod. "I give you my word."

"And also promise you won't fight in any duels over what I tell you."

His expression turned to one of comical confusion. "Why would you think I'd engage in a duel?"

"I've read about the things you used to do."

"That was almost twenty years ago!"

"Then it shouldn't be difficult to promise me *now*."

The muscles in his jaw knotted. "You know something so—so *heinous* that you think I might engage in a duel?"

Lori couldn't believe how hard it was to meet his gaze when he had that wall-of-ice expression on his face. "The subject is a…volatile one."

He pushed up from the tub so suddenly that he sent water flooding over the side.

"Fine! I give you my word that I shan't go out and get in a duel. Now *tell me*," he demanded, towering over her.

She took a deep breath before for saying. "You are frightening me."

The chagrin on his face was immediate. "I'm sorry," he said tightly, lowering back into the tub, his posture no longer relaxed. "You must know that I would not hurt you. I've never laid a finger on any woman in anger in my entire life."

"I know. But fear is not always rational. And…and I know this will be unpleasant."

His jaws flexed—as if he were biting down on something—but he merely squeezed the water from the washcloth and draped it over the tub before saying, "Go on."

"The woman who told me about your brother told me something else, too." She swallowed. "She said that she'd also had sexual relations with Lord Moreland. She said he wasn't an earl back then, just the son of an impoverished landowner."

Lori didn't think it was her imagination that he'd gone pale beneath his normally glowing tan. "Are you saying one of those children might be Moreland's."

Lori pulled her lips between her teeth, mentally girding herself for what she was about to say.

"Not just one of them. All five of them."

Chapter 27

The fury that had blazed up inside him at her words died away almost as fast as it had flared, replaced by an icy calm. He had experienced the same phenomenon in the past, but only when his ship had engaged in a skirmish with another vessel.

Fast refused to capitulate to the primitive response. He had already frightened Lorelei, if he gave in to his berserker rage, she would be terrified.

And so Fast inhaled deeply, held it a moment, and then exhaled and said, "Go on," his voice neither hot nor cold. Just… flat.

She regarded him through anxious eyes, like an animal preparing to flee.

"I'm not angry with you, Lorelei."

"I know."

"But I want to hear all you know about this. Including who told you."

She licked her lips nervously.

"Don't worry; I won't punish the messenger."

"The woman who told me is Martha Sheldon."

"When did you talk to her?"

"I met her weeks ago, when I went up to your family's estate."

Fast frowned. "And you've known the truth all this time?" Again, anger crept into his voice. This time it was almost overwhelmed by disbelief.

"No. She refused to talk to me. Then. She came here to see me five days ago."

He shook his head. "I don't understand. How would she have known to find you here, of all places?"

"She is, er, involved with one of your men—she met him when you went to your grandfather's estate."

"Who?" he demanded.

"You promised not to punish anyone."

"I didn't know my own damned crew was covered by that promise!"

She flinched, making him realize he was shouting again.

"Fine," he snapped. "Who is it?"

"Rufus."

Fast stared unseeingly, a series of images flickering through his head—Rufus laughing and chatting with Martha, who lived on his grandfather's estate. Bloody hell!"

"You look angry."

"I gave my word not to exact retribution, and I will keep it." He wouldn't sack or thrash the loose lipped idiot, but that didn't mean he wouldn't give him a proper bollocking. "Just tell me the rest of it."

"Martha said that the very day that she, er, laid with your brother, Lord Moreland—or Bevil Norman as he was evidently called back then before he inherited his title—cornered her." She swallowed, her face taut. "I know he is your friend—"

"Never mind about that. Just tell me." He forced the words through gritted teeth, struggling to remain calm.

"She said that Moreland…forced her."

"He raped her," he repeated flatly.

"Yes."

"And you believe her?"

"I do. She said that he threatened to destroy her family if she said a word to your brother. Evidently her father was a tenant farmer on Moreland's father's land back then. At least that is what it sounded like."

Fast nodded. "Yes. Moreland's father—John Norman—wasn't an earl. The current holder of the title, Bevil Norman, only inherited when the three men who stood between him and the earldom died." Three deaths that Fast was quickly beginning to suspect had not been accidents. "In any case," he went on, "John Norman had been the biggest landowner in the area, after my grandfather, but the feckless fool lost everything at a card table shortly before my brother's death." Fast seethed at the memory. "Percy was so sorry for Bevil—for losing everything—that he convinced our grandfather to use his influence to get him a position at the Home Office." And Moreland thanked Percy for his kindness by having him killed.

"Fast?"

He blinked and looked up through a haze of red.

"Is—are you all right?"

"I'm fine," he said roughly, unclenching his fists, and picking up the thread of her story. "And so Martha was only with Percy that one time?"

She swallowed. "Er, no. Moreland ordered her to continue seeing Lord Perseverance. He said that she should do nothing to make him suspicious. If she did, then Moreland, would make her family suffer."

Fast had no words.

Lorelei stared at him a moment, and then went on. "She continued to have sexual relations with both men and became pregnant. When she approached Moreland, he came the ugly with her and said he'd accuse her of lying if she tried to blame the child on him. He told her to go to your brother—that Lord Percy was a soft-hearted f-fool," she stopped and eyed him nervously before adding, "And that he would claim the child."

Fast bristled at Moreland's dismissive insult, but shoved down his rage and said, "Go on."

"She was scared of lying to your brother, but she didn't know what else to do. Evidently Lord Percy saw no reason to disbelieve her. But before he could make arrangements for the child you stepped in. Martha felt guilty about the lie, but she kept her mouth shut because Bevil Norman terrified her."

"So, why did she come to you? And why now?"

"Because she met Alice Knoll."

"Christ," Fast muttered, shaking his head. "The mother of my brother's second child. Let me guess, the two women compared stories and found some similarities?"

She nodded. "Once they'd discovered that he had done the same thing twice, it didn't take much imagination to think he'd done it to the other three women." She grimly met Fast's gaze. "All five women had the same story."

"Why did Martha tell you this?"

Her forehead creased and she shook her head, visibly perplexed. "I'm not really sure. I think part of it was that she'd read about how you helped to destroy the child slavery ring. And then of course Rufus told her about all the good you did at The King's Purse." She shrugged. "I suspect she simply felt guilty for taking your money for a child that might not even be related to you. I think she wanted to confess the truth to somebody. And of course, I encouraged them to confide in me by promising to keep all five women's names a secret."

Fast couldn't help raising his eyebrows at that.

"I know, I know—not much of a journalist, am I?"

Fast didn't know what to say to that, but he knew he had to say *something*. "You've said that before, Lorelei. I just don't think it is true. You are persistent and inventive and you've protected Parker's sources for him. I think sometimes, life is not just black or white, love. I'm sorry you gave your word and broke it, but I will never use the information you gave me against those women. Now *Moreland*, on the other hand…It was a bloody shame a person couldn't be killed more than once."

"Thank you," she said, her voice small and somber.

Fast nodded, his mind racing in at least three directions.

"Fast?"

"Hmm?"

"Why do you think Moreland would have done something like that?"

Fast had been wondering the same thing himself.

"Could it all have been envy?" she asked.

"I have no idea."

"Everyone I spoke to talked about what close friends the three of you were—all the way from boyhood."

A sick picture was slowly coalescing in his mind's eye, but he couldn't bring himself to believe it.

Even if he could get his hands on Albert Jensen's confession it wouldn't tell him *why* Bevil had done what he'd done. Nothing would tell him except the man, himself.

Gregg's notion of taking apart Moreland's life piece by piece—making him poor and shaming him—was all well and good when it came to making him suffer slowly. But Fast would never get the truth out of Moreland by wrecking him financially.

He wanted answers. And the only way to get those was with his bare hands.

Fast realized he was seething again and forced his emotions back into the boiling, bubbling pot of rage where he'd kept them ever since he'd learned that Bevil Norman was the man who'd murdered Percy. He slammed the lid on the cauldron nice and tight.

And then he exhaled slowly and looked up and smiled at Lorelei. "I'm sorry if I frightened you. That's the last thing I'd ever want to do."

"I understand. You have every right to be angry."

He reached out and took her hand and kissed the slightly wrinkled tips of her fingers. "The water's getting cool. Shall we get out and dress for dinner?"

"Isn't it a bit early?"

"I'm looking forward to seeing that dress on you."

She pursed her lips and flushed. Fast could see she was still uncomfortable with the idea of expensive gifts, but he could live with that. For now.

He stood and then took her hands and lifted her to her feet, until their wet bodies were pressed tightly together. "Besides," he murmured, kissing the top of her damp head, "the sooner we have dinner, the sooner I can strip the gown off you and carry you back to bed."

Chapter 28

Fast had not been jesting about carrying her back to bed immediately after dinner. In fact, he hadn't even waited until the dessert course was over to make good on his promise.

Not that Lori had complained.

It had been wise to have an early night as Mr. Gregg had knocked on the bedroom door at one-thirty—interrupting what had been a very pleasant cuddle—and Fast had left the room to talk to him.

Lori had immediately fallen back to sleep, only to be kissed back to wakefulness an indeterminate time later.

"What is it, Fast?"

"I'm sorry, sweetheart, but I have to nip out for a few hours."

"Now?" she'd woken fully at his odd declaration.

He'd kissed her so deeply and thoroughly that—for a moment—she had believed he was going to crawl back beneath the covers.

But he had eventually pulled away. "Go back to sleep, sweetheart. If all goes as planned I'll be back beside you by morning. If not then, then certainly by tomorrow night." He hesitated, kissed her, and then added, "We'll have a good dinner and a nice long talk, love."

"Mmm, talk?" she'd mumbled.

"Yes, darling. You've been patient, and it's time—well, we'll talk later." He'd kissed her again. "I have to go."

She had wanted to ask what they would talk about, but he'd gone before she could come up with the words.

That had been more than six hours ago. Lori glanced at the clock as she stretched and blinked the sleep from her eyes. It was almost eight-thirty and he'd not returned.

She heaved a sigh and pushed back the covers.

Fast had had all her clothing and her writing desk moved to his room the day before, so she slipped into the dressing gown that was laid at the foot of the bed and then pulled the servant cord.

Lucy arrived a few minutes later. "Oh, you're awake. The master told the kitchen not to send breakfast up at the usual time, but to wait until you rang. Shall I fetch your tray?"

It was just like Fast to think about her even after he'd had a long night. "Did his lordship just get back, then?"

"No, miss. He never came back. He told Mrs. Marlowe last night, before he left."

"Ah." The house was so well-insulated and quiet that Lori tended to forget that the real business of King's Purse didn't even get started until after midnight.

"I'll have hot water sent up when I fetch your tray," Lucy said.

"You needn't bother with that. There's plenty in the pitcher still."

"But it's cold!"

"It will wake me up. Thank you, Lucy."

Lucy bobbed a curtsey, murmured, "Of course, Miss Fontenot," and then scurried from the room.

No matter how many times Lori had told the girl to call her by her first name, Lucy insisted that his lordship and Mrs. Marlowe wouldn't like her taking such liberties.

The cool water did indeed wake her up and by the time Lucy arrived with a heaping tray of food a scant quarter of an hour later she was famished.

Lucy gestured to the stack of newspapers on the tray, which was twice as thick as usual. "Mrs. Marlowe thought you might want yesterday's papers as well as today's as you didn't have a chance to read them."

Lori's face heated when she remembered exactly *why* she'd skipped her morning ritual yesterday.

"Thank you, Lucy. And thank Mrs. Marlowe for me."

Lucy curtsied and then fled in her usual headlong way. Only when she was gone did Lori realize that she'd not heard the telltale sound of a key turning in the lock. Nor had she heard it earlier.

She caught her bottom lip with her teeth and went to the door, hesitating a moment before twisting the knob. She was so startled when it turned that she didn't pull it all the way open, instead peeking out the crack to where her gaoler usually stood. As if he wouldn't notice her opening the door if she were stealthy enough.

But there was no guard.

Lori paused, and then quietly shut the door, slumping against it, her mind in a whirl.

She was free, or near enough.

Her feet were already moving toward the armoire that held her valise when she stopped. Why was she running off? She had already decided not to sell any stories about Fast to Parker—or anyone else—which meant her employer would likely sack her on the spot.

Even if he didn't, Lori had already decided to leave his employ. She felt a rush of relief at the thought of never having to see the odious man again. And of never again needing to work on a story that shamed her.

She wouldn't look for a new job right away. It made excellent sense to stay at The King's Purse until she'd finished her first draft of the article. That way she could easily speak to any of the women if she needed to verify any information.

And then there is the fact that Fast lives here…

Yes, there was no denying that was a greater lure than any other. As much as it scared her, it was time that she faced her feelings for the man: she loved him and had for some time. She'd been a coward not to admit as much when he'd declared his love for her.

She'd had another opportunity last night, when he'd again told her he loved her before falling asleep with his arms around her, and yet again she'd taken the coward's way out and not answered.

Lori dropped down into a chair and closed her eyes. What a relief to finally admit it, if only to herself. She loved him. And he loved her back. The thought was both thrilling and a little frightening.

After her terrible experience with Dorian, Lori had not believed that she was even capable of falling in love. It wasn't that she did not trust men—although she was far less trusting than she'd been before—but more that she had discovered her own judgement was suspect where love was concerned. Even after all these years she still felt ill when she recalled how she'd foolishly believed that Dorian had cared for her.

Lori hadn't been able to make herself confide to Fast the crowning humiliation in her tawdry little affair: How Dorian had laughed in her face when she had confronted him after learning that he was betrothed to another woman.

"How long have you been committed to this marriage, Dorian?"

"Almost a year," he'd answered without hesitation. "We didn't want to make an announcement until Lady Lenora was seventeen."

"You knew all this time and yet you led me to believe there was the possibility of some future between us?"

The glance he'd given her had been a blend of annoyance and amusement. "*Me* marry a vicar's sister? And an immoral bluestocking willing to spread her legs, to boot?" He'd laughed. "I knew you had some barmy ideas, Lori, but I didn't think you were stupid."

She had slapped him then, only surprised by her own violence for a second before his retaliatory slap—more of a punch—had driven her to ground.

"Be grateful I did not hit you harder," he'd snapped as he'd glared down at her. "If you know what is good for you, you'll scurry home with your tail between your legs and keep that clever mouth of yours shut. I'd hate to be the one to convince my father that his vicar is harboring the village tart under his roof. It would be unfortunate if your brother were forced to seek a position elsewhere."

The threat had chilled all the rage in her belly. Her brother had a wife and four children, soon to be five. He would never be able to find a new position if Lori's behavior became known.

Dorian had left her there, sprawled on the ground. Lori *had* scurried back to the vicarage with her tail between her legs, hoping that she'd be able to lick her wounds in private. After all, Dorian was an earl's son, and they hadn't moved in the same social circles. Indeed, the only time she'd seen him had been when *she* had made an effort to seek him out.

Unfortunately, Lori had been forced to look at him every Sunday in church, but at least he had been in no more of a hurry to talk to her than she was to him.

As it turned out, it wasn't Dorian she had needed to worry about avoiding.

Scarcely a week after they had exchanged blows, the squire's son, Daniel Fenton, had accosted her on the way home from delivering a care basket to one of her brother's homebound parishioners.

Lory had never especially liked Daniel—although he'd grudgingly accepted her, he had always treated her with marked disdain—but she'd been so grateful to be included in the group that she'd failed to notice the cruel gleam in his eyes whenever they rested on her.

Well, Lori certainly noticed it that day.

She had stopped when he'd called out to her, pathetically pleased that not all her former *friends* had given her the cut direct. Lori had smiled and greeted him in a friendly manner. He'd responded by shoving her against a tree and thrusting a hand down her bodice.

Only by clawing his face and stomping hard on his foot had she got away. As she'd fled, her eyes blurring with tears, he'd yelled obscenities after her—threating her and her family with dire repercussions.

Lori had known then that she couldn't continue to live in her brother's house. Although Jeremy and his wife Sarah hadn't heard what Lori had done yet, they soon would. Dorian's friends—like Daniel—would make sure of that. Jeremy might never hear anything directly, but there would always be rumors if she stayed there.

There was a slight chance that people might forget if she went away. That was all she could do to spare her family.

Lori's mother and father had left her a small annuity; it would not have been enough to live off, but it was enough to afford a few years of schooling. She'd begged Jeremy to let her use that money on school, arguing that she would eventually need to find employment, likely as a governess, and that more tuition would help her in that endeavor when the time came.

She spent two happy years at Miss Lincombe's School. During her final semester, she was fortunate to secure a position teaching literature at Ivo Stephani's Academy for Young Ladies.

Although Lori had always loved teaching young children—she had for years volunteered at the village school in her brother's parish—she had been delighted to discover that she had a true aptitude for teaching older students, as well.

Her few years at the Stefani Academy had been the best in her life and Lori had made a new home with the tightly knit group of teachers. A home that had been shattered when Ivo Stephani had absconded with the school's money, leaving his wife, Portia Stefani, to pick up the pieces. Portia had eventually closed the school, and Lori had been faced with the prospect of going back to live with her brother if she couldn't find a job.

Right as she was preparing to swallow her pride and move back to Jeremy's house in Moorcross, she'd received an offer for a companion job. The woman, a widow named Mrs. Holmes, lived less than an hour from her brother and his family. That meant she would be close enough to visit, but far enough not to worry about encountering anyone from the village. At least she'd believed that for almost a year, until her employer's nephew had visited with a friend of his—none other than Daniel Fenton.

Lori had packed her bags the very same evening that Daniel had arrived, telling her employer that she needed to see to a family emergency. The way Mrs. Holmes had sneered made it clear that Daniel had already filled her ears with lies. Indeed, the old woman had told Lori not to return and had paid her for the days she'd worked and not a penny more.

Lori had known then that she could never return to Moorcross to live. That had left her with only one real choice, which was to accept Freddie's offer to share her London house. She'd encountered Parker one day when she'd been wandering the stacks at The Temple of the Muses—the magnificent bookstore that served as a sort of meeting place for authors and publishers. David had seemed so kind—so interested to hear about her book.

And so eager to hire her when he had learned that she lived with Lady Winifred Sedgewick, the well-known companion and matchmaker to the *ton.*

The *Miss Emily* articles were easy, if frivolous and boring, and Lori had been delighted to be able to pay her rent and have money to live.

But then Fast had returned to England last year and Parker had seemed almost demented with hatred for the man. Increasingly, Lori had needed to set aside her moral reservations and pursue stories that made her more than a little uncomfortable.

She was not so foolish as to think that Parker would keep her on just for her *Miss Emily* columns. No, her job with *The Mercury* was over. And good riddance.

She had a little bit of money saved up; she could last a few weeks.

You can always pawn some of the jewels Fast gave you.

Lori scowled at the thought and picked up the first paper from on top of the pile—amusingly, it was David's paper. Fast took only *The Times, World Examiner,* and *The Gazette.* Not for him rags like *The Mercury.*

She poured herself a cup of coffee and settled in to read.

Half an hour later she was working her way through *The Gazette* when a name leapt off the page.

Is it true that the ethereal Miss D____ P____ the undisputed Diamond of the Season has fallen to the recently returned King of the Rakes? My sources at Lady M________'s country estate say the two lovebirds were spotted frequently during the weeklong escape from the London heat.

Also attending the festivity was the recently out of mourning E____ of M_____ who has been making his intentions toward Miss P___ clear all Season.

What a fascinating week that must have been, my dearest readers!

A little bird whispered in my ear that Lord M____ is out of the running. If you are unwilling to take my word, then you can ask the bride-to-be's father. The renowned industrialist Mr. B_____ P_____, announced his daughter's betrothal at a dinner party held at his town house immediately after the house party, at which the happy couple reportedly danced not one, but an unprecedented three sets at the impromptu ball.

The King of the Rakes has, after more than two decades, abdicated his throne for matrimonial bliss. Will he, dear Reader, become the King of the Husbands? Only time will tell…

She swallowed as she stared at the page. Gossip was one thing—as *Miss Emily* she knew better than anyone how to stretch the slightest rumor into a column of newsprint—but Bryok Pascoe announcing his daughter's betrothal at a dinner—with Fast evidently in attendance—could only mean one thing.

Fast was engaged to marry Demelza Pascoe.

Lori painstakingly refolded the newspaper, as if by making it appear perfect and unopened, she could somehow unread the dreadful news.

Fast had said he loved her while he was, all along, betrothed to another woman?

Hysterical laughter bubbled up inside her. It could not be happening!

It was the same nightmare all over again.

Truly, would Lori never learn? How could she have believed that the heir to a marquessate would want her for anything other than a temporary pleasure?

She *was* a tart. And a very stupid, gullible one, at that.

How could she have believed that a man who'd broken hearts for almost as long as Lori had been alive would give his heart to a scruffy ink-stained wretch?

You could sell the story about Fast, his brother, and Lord Moreland to Parker…

Lori flinched away from the repulsive suggestion.

Just because Lord Severn is a manipulative, immoral garden slug of a man does not mean that I must sink to the same level!

How comforting your principles will be now that you are without employment.

Lori squeezed her eyes shut, as if that would somehow stop the horrible thoughts.

It only made it worse.

She barely made it to the basin before vomiting the food eaten less than an hour before.

Good God. How had this happened to her yet again?

Chapter 29

Fast seethed as he paced back and forth in the small, cramped room, infuriated that he'd spent the last five hours stuck in this blasted inn instead of in bed with Lorelei's warm, sweet body spread alongside him.

But he'd had no choice in the matter because Bevil had finally responded to the letter Gregg had sent him. He agreed to exchange Ellie Jensen for Albert's signed confession, and the meeting was to take place at this out-of-the-way inn.

Fast had arrived early, with a *confession*—not the real one of course, but one prepared by Gregg—in his coat pocket. But the appointed time had come and gone hours ago, and the earl had never arrived. Fast hadn't wanted to leave, just in case the other man had been delayed by the wretched rains or his horse had thrown a shoe. There were a dozen reasons why Bevil might have—

The door to his room swung open and Gregg entered. "I received another message."

Fast snatched the paper from him and read the brief contents:

You disobeyed my last instructions and allowed your men to loiter with you. I will give you one last chance. Go <u>*alone*</u> *to the Crown and Thistle and await further instructions. If you are not there by nine o'clock the girl will die. You are under constant observation, if I find out your men are following you, the girl will die. If you disobey me in any way, the girl will die.*

Fast crumpled up the message and swore. "Moreland has somebody watching me—he knew that I wasn't alone. He wants me to go to the *Crown and Thistle* where there will be further instructions.

"The *Crown and Thistle*? Isn't that on the Great North Road?"

"Yes, and I need to be there by nine."

"You'll need to hurry if you're to make that."

Fast nodded.

"We'll follow, but we'll stay at least a half mile—"

"No. Nobody follows me."

"That is madness, Severn. You must let us—"

"I said *no*."

"I hope you know that you're walking into a trap."

"Probably. But I'm not entirely defenseless." He could see Gregg wasn't convinced. "I won't condemn an innocent young woman to death as well."

"She's probably already dead, Fast. I just can't see Moreland keeping her alive."

The other man hadn't called him by his nickname since they'd set foot on English soil last year. It was a sign of his agitation that he did so now.

"She very well might be, but I can't take the risk." he said quietly.

"Christ, but you're a stubborn bastard!"

Fast grinned. "Thank you old friend. Now, I must get going." He narrowed his eyes. "Nobody is to follow me, Gregg."

"I don't like it, but I'll do as you say. I took the liberty of bringing Cnut, my lord. He's rested and ready and waiting for you below."

Fast smiled his first genuine smile in hours. "If any horse can get me there, it's Cnut. Take the others back to The King's Purse."

Gregg nodded. "Any word for Miss Fontenot?"

Fast grimaced, recalling what he'd told Lorelei about having dinner with her tonight. At the time, he'd had no idea that Moreland would drag this business out for almost twenty-four hours. By God tonight would be the end of it!

"Tell her I'm sorry about tonight—about missing dinner and our…talk." And he was sorry about that. Regardless of what happened in the next few hours at least he'd finally be able to tell her the truth about Moreland and the whole bloody mess. Whether it was the last thing he said to her before boarding his ship and leaving England forever, or whether—Fast put the thoughts out of his mind and met Gregg's curious gaze, "Just ask her to be patient for one more day."

"I'll tell her, my lord."

Fast slapped his friend's shoulder and jogged down the rickety steps, his mind already on the journey ahead.

The big roan stallion was pawing the cobbles when Fast arrived in the courtyard, one of the inn grooms holding his bridle and eyeing the huge beast with obvious trepidation. Fast tossed the lad a coin and relieved him of his burden.

He took a road that led him a bit out of his way but would avoid the more heavily trafficked areas. For the next hour, all Fast thought about was getting clear of the city. Not until he was two miles from the *Crown and Thistle* did he give serious consideration to the trap he was riding into.

Fast had one pistol—one built especially to fit in his boot—and five knives, more than he'd worn since his early years at sea.

He wasn't the handiest man with a knife, but he could do some damage before a bullet brought him down.

Fast knew that Moreland would not be satisfied with the letter Gregg had expertly forged. His old friend would certainly try to kill him.

Whatever he had planned, Fast's death had to look so convincingly like an accident that nobody would ever gainsay it.

He smiled unpleasantly when he thought about how surprised Bevil would be to realize that Fast was thinking exactly the same thing.

***

Fast waited for four hours in the *Crown and Thistle* before the message came.

Come to the graveyard behind the abbey. If any of your minions follows you, the girl will die. If you aren't there in two hours, the girl will die.

Fast sighed, threw back his ale, tossed some coins onto the table, and headed out to the stables, glad that Cnut had had a few hours rest because this next journey would be even harder.

The abbey in question was only a few miles from Grandon Castle, which was also the vicinity of Moreland's father's estate. Or at least what was left of it.

Fast, Percy, and Bevil had used the cemetery for any number of antics as young men. Indeed, Fast now recalled that he and Bevil, when they'd been fifteen or so, had taken two village wenches there together once, reveling in the taboo sensation of fucking in another man's presence.

It made him sick to think of it now. Not because he was ashamed of his mild voyeurism, but because he now wondered if Moreland had ever raped a woman just because she'd been one of Fast's lovers.

How could he had been such good friends with a man so rotten inside? Was he rotten, as well? There must be something wrong with him never to have seen Bevil's true nature. As much as he'd like to blame it on youthful ignorance, he simply couldn't forgive himself for being so blind.

And what about Percy? Poor Percy. Fast hated to think of his brother's last moments on earth. Jensen's brother's confession had mentioned how Percy had looked up at the sound of his approach, his expression amiable if rather surprised that it wasn't Bevil.

At what point had Percy recognized one of his own dueling pistols in Albert Jensen's hand? What must he have thought?

Bevil Norman wasn't just a killer, he was sadistic and cruel and cowardly to have sent a man to death without the decency of facing him.

Fast suspected Bevil would do the same to him if he could only be sure that such an act wouldn't leave loose ends that would lead back to him.

Rage swelled inside him and fast ruthlessly shoved it down. Now wasn't the time for anger; men made mistakes when they were angry. Now was the time for cold calculation. Because the man he was facing was easily the coldest and most dangerous that Fast had ever met.

***

With Cnut's help, Fast made it to the old cemetery a half-hour early. He let the horse graze on the verdant grass at the edge of the gravestones while he sat under a tree, trying to keep old memories at bay as the sun disappeared over the horizon.

He was kept waiting two hours before a vaguely familiar man rode up on a piebald mare, bringing the horse to a halt a laughably far distance away, as if Fast might fling himself at a mounted man while he was afoot.

"You were part of my crew," Fast said, suddenly recalling where he'd seen him before. "One of the two men the *Vixen* dropped off in Gran Canaria before returning to London."

It wasn't a question, but the man nodded and smirked. "Sí, Captain."

"I hope you're being well-paid for your betrayal. You know Moreland had your friend Garcia killed, don't you?"

The other man laughed. "*I* had Garcia killed. I told his lordship where to find him. He got greedy and wanted more than his share." He scowled. "He also allowed that bloody confession to fall into your hands."

So, there was Fast's confirmation that the confession was still out in the world somewhere.

"What are you getting out of this now that you have nothing to blackmail Moreland with?" he asked. "How long do you think it will be before he has *you* killed?"

"What I am getting is none of your affair," the other man shot back. "You are to go to the barn where his lordship's father kept the winter grain. He said you would know where it was."

Fast nodded abruptly. "I know the place."

"You have half an hour."

Fast didn't waste his breath telling the man that he'd never make the trip in time. Instead, he caught up Cnut's reins, swung into the saddle, and rode like the devil himself was after him.

His mind stopped spinning, and his thoughts went blessedly calm as he rode the last leg of a journey that had begun more than sixteen years before. He didn't even need to think to guide Cnut toward his destination. The land around him was as familiar to him as the back of his hand, each bend in the road and cluster of trees bringing old memories back to life.

It was just falling dark when Fast turned onto the weedy, overgrown track that led to the big grain barn. There were no horses or carriages in sight, but a dim light emanated from the smaller of the two doors that led into the ancient structure.

He rode Cnut over to the trough before dismounting and pumped in some fresh water. When he turned around, he was confronted by Bevil Norman lounging in the doorway.

"You made it, Fast—with three minutes to spare!" The other man laughed, and the years fell away in a blur and he was, for a fraction of a second, once again a boy. Any minute now Percy would join the two of them and they would be off to do something foolish and reckless.

The vision, as intense as it was, shimmered and shattered like glass. This man had never been his friend; not twenty years ago, and certainly not today.

"Come inside, Fast," Bevil called, stepping back into the building and out of Fast's sight.

He strode toward the door, the hairs lifting off the back of his neck when he crossed the threshold. He skidded to a halt, staring at the wraith-thin, faded woman sitting on a wooden chair not far from the entrance, her hands bound at the wrists and resting on her lap.

"Miss Jensen?" he asked stupidly.

She nodded slightly, her anxious gaze sliding to where Bevil had set up a table with one chair.

Fast knew Ellie Jensen was a good ten years his junior, but she looked two decades older. Haggard and frail and beaten down. She also had a fading bruise on one cheek and her lower lip was swollen.

"Did you do that to her?" he demanded of Bevil.

Rather than look ashamed, the Earl of Moreland merely smirked. "Playing the hero, Fast?"

Fast knew if he opened his mouth at that moment that he'd not be able to stop himself. He also knew that nothing he could say would have any effect on such a man. Besides, it was clear that Moreland enjoyed baiting him; the best thing he could do was deny him the pleasure of snapping at the hook like a starving trout.

A quick survey of the low-ceilinged, dusty room showed it was just the three of them. Of course, there was no telling how many of Moreland's minions might be lurking outside the building or hiding behind a piece of old farm equipment.

"It is only the three of us," Bevil said, reading Fast's thoughts.

Fast took a step toward the other man.

"*Uh uh uh,*" Bevil chided. "You are fine where you are."

Fast smiled. "Why Bevil, are you worried I might hurt you?"

Bevil laughed, and it sounded genuine. "I can't believe you didn't kill me at the countess's house party. I expected you to sneak into my house and kill me in my bed."

"The thought crossed my mind," Fast admitted. Especially since he'd roamed Bevil's estate looking for Ellie on four nights.

The earl's smile curdled. "But you were too busy sniffing after that Pascoe bitch, weren't you? Did you fuck her, Fast?"

"No, but I did warn her about you, Bevil. She'll never marry you. Indeed, I fear you'll have a difficult time finding any young woman to be your wife. At least not any wealthy woman." He smiled.

Bevil's handsome face turned ugly. "You have always underestimated other people's greed for status and connections, Fast. It's because you were born so bloody well-larded you just never could fathom how it is for the rest of us mere mortals who were not so fortunate. Demelza might not want me, but her father doesn't give a damn what she wants. And Bryok Pascoe will be delighted to accept me as his son-in-law once you are out of the way."

Fast was sorely tempted to tell the other man that Demelza would soon be married and beyond Bevil's grasp, as well as her father's. But he kept his mouth shut because if he managed to get himself killed today, he didn't want Bevil to have any information he could use against the poor girl and foil her plans.

When Fast didn't respond to his taunting, Bevil resumed his blathering. "Take my word for it—she will be grateful to marry me. But you will not be around to witness it, will you?"

"Are you going to kill me, Bevil?" He began to reach inside his coat. "I brought the evidence and lived up to my half of the—"

"Stop right there!"

He lifted his hands. "I was just getting the confession. You gave me your word that you would let the woman go if I brought it. And I have. I'll stay here once she is gone, and you and I can settle this between us."

"*I gave you my word*?" Bevil repeated, his expression derisive. "Do you really think I'll help you put a noose around my neck just so I can keep my *word*?" Bevil laughed. "You arrogant fool! How the hell did you survive all those years at sea as stupid as you are? I know you brought a pistol," he said when Fast merely stared. "And probably a knife or two, as well. Take off your overcoat—slowly—and toss it aside. Then do the same with your coat."

"Are you going to strip me naked, Bevil?" Fast asked, amused.

Moreland lifted his pistol. "Do it or I'll shoot you right now."

"No you won't. Then you wouldn't get to gloat," he said. "But I tell you what, Bevil. I will do what you say if you tell me why you killed my brother."

A nasty smile spread across the other man's face. "With pleasure. Now, remove your bloody coats."

Fast reached for the buttons on his overcoat.

"If you had any sense at all, you'd have figured it out years ago," Bevil said, his tone conversational and almost…jaunty. "Percy found out about Louisa. That's why I did *it*."

"Found out what?"

"That Louisa hadn't come to him a maiden." He laughed at whatever he saw on Fast's face—anger, surprise, loathing. "Yes, I had her first. And last, too, as it turned out. If you want to blame someone for Percy's death you should really blame Louisa because it was her fault he had to die. The silly cow *told* Percy that I'd forced her." He shrugged. "What else could I do?"

"How about not rape women to begin with?"

Bevil's eyebrows shot up and he looked surprised. But rather than be ashamed or embarrassed, an expression of smug delight colored his features. "She might not have cared for it that first time. And maybe even the second. But she learned to like it after we were married." He smiled, the expression so slimy that Fast's vision blackened around the edges and he took a step forward.

"No. That is not a good idea, Fast." He lifted the pistol and pointed to a huge anvil a few feet away from Fast. "If you come any closer to me than *that,* I will shoot you. Finish removing your coat."

Fast locked eyes with the other man and the raw animosity he saw rocked him to his core. What had he—or Percy—ever done to earn such hatred?

"Get on with it," Bevil snapped, jerking the gun.

Fast reached for the buttons of his coat. "Tell me how it happened?"

"You've read Jensen's confession. You know how."

"I want to hear it from you."

Bevil shrugged. "Louisa went to Percy after you'd thrashed him, when he was still laid up. I gather she went to beg him for forgiveness and spilled the entire story." He gave a dismissive gesture. "Whatever her reasons, when I went to see Percy, he was waiting for me and in a rage. He was so weak he couldn't even rise from his bed—but he tried. I worried he'd have some sort of relapse then and there, so I begged him to calm down—to wait until he was better, and we could discuss the matter in a civilized fashion." Bevil snorted. "Of course, the moment he could crawl out of bed he demanded that I meet with him."

He laughed, his eyes suddenly vague as he stared into the past. "It could hardly have worked out better. He picked somewhere nice and quiet—and isolated—to meet me. But I never showed up; Albert Jensen did. I'll admit I wanted to lurk in the trees to watch how that went, but I needed to have a nice, secure alibi, didn't I? And my alibi couldn't be *you*, Fast, because I didn't want you to have one. I wanted to plant a seed of doubt in everyone's mind that *you* might have shot him." Bevil chuckled evilly. "Who better to provide my alibi than your grandfather?" He grinned. "He had summoned me to his study to tell me about the letter he received from my taskmaster at the Home Office, Lord Burton. Your grandfather was delighted with how happy old Burty was with my services." His mouth tightened. "As if I should be happy that I'd been reduced to such a plebian role."

Fast had to force his hand to unclench so he could toss his coat aside. "That was a job you had because of Percy. He was devastated when your father lost everything. Percy did all that he could to—"

"I *know* what bloody Percy did," Bevil snarled. "You don't need to tell me that, you dunce! I was always perfectly aware of the many, many, *many* kindnesses your family did for poor little Bevil Norman whose father left him a pauper. As if I was just another charity, no better than a workhouse orphan you tossed crumbs to from your grand buffet." Bevil's chest rose and fell too quickly for a man standing still, and his eyes sparked with fury. He jerked his gun higher, until it was aimed at Fast's face. "Put your hands above your head. I'm going to check you for weapons."

Fast lifted his arms.

"If you so much as twitch I'll kill you," Bevil warned, standing close enough to rest the tip of the pistol in the hollow of Fast's throat while he searched him roughly with his other hand.

He laughed when he found the pistol and then again when he came across the second and third knives. "Bloody hell!" he said when he found the fourth knife. "You came armed for battle. Too bad it won't do you any good. Where is the letter?"

"In the front pocket of my coat."

Still keeping the pistol trained on him, Bevil found the letter and backed away to the table before opening it with one hand, snatching glances at it while keeping his gun on Fast.

After a moment, he nodded. "Thank you, Fast."

"I've lived up to my half of the bargain; let the woman go. She can take my horse."

Bevil lifted the glass chimney off the lantern and held the letter over the flame, darting glances from Fast to the paper as it caught fire and flared. He shook his head, an expression of wonder on his face. "You really did come here alone, didn't you?"

"Yes. Didn't you?"

"Of course I did! But that's hardly the same, is it? Albert Jensen taught me one thing, and that was never to involve anybody else when it comes to killing. For sixteen fucking *years* I've worried his loose lips would come back to haunt me. And it did, didn't it? Well, there won't be any witnesses *this* time. The damned confession is nothing but ashes and so is the only man who could have sworn to the truth of it."

Fast gestured to Ellie. "She can say whatever she wants about you, Bevil, but she will have no proof to support her claim. It would be her word against that of a lord. Let her go. This is about the two of us."

Bevil laughed. "Fool! Of course I can't let her go. Ever." A nasty smile spread across his face. "You're not going anywhere, either. I'm going to kill you both and then set the stage with your corpses. It will be a sad, tawdry story of a depraved lord forcing himself on a defenseless woman. But this time, she'll get the upper hand and shoot him" He cut a sneering glance at Ellie. "And then she will kill herself, too ashamed and afraid to go on." He laughed at the shock and revulsion on Fast's face. "If you weren't such an arrogant blockhead you wouldn't have wandered into what was obviously a trap. But that has ever been the way with you, hasn't it? Women mistake your arrogance for bravery, but it's really just stupidity, isn't it?"

Fast ignored the question. "Did you ever love Louisa, Bevil? Or was it always just a competition to you—wanting to snatch her away because Percy and I loved her?"

Bevil sneered. "Love!" he scoffed, giving Fast his answer with just that one word. "Only an idiot believes in such a fantasy. Louisa was what every other man our age wanted. She was a beautiful heiress. She was the *best* and I made her mine."

"And then you proceeded to make her life hell."

"I made her a bloody *countess*!" Bevil roared. "But that was never good enough for the bitch." His pistol in his hand shook as he suddenly lunged toward Fast, spittle flying from his mouth, his eyes glittering with something that was either madness or rage. "She mourned you and your bloody brother for *years* and I tolerated it."

If Fast was going to act, he'd have no better time than now.

"You made her your broodmare and dissipated her fortune," he goaded. "You are no better than your father. In fact, you are—"

The searing pain in his shoulder and deafening *bang* were simultaneous. Fast lunged toward the other man even as the sharp report rang over and over in his ears.

But Moreland was ready for him. He flung the pistol aside while stumbling backwards, out of reach, and grabbed a pistol from behind him, where it must have been tucked in his waistband. "You stay right where you are!"

Fast froze, every part of him except the fingers of his right hand, which subtly twitched the fifth knife from the sheath strapped to the inside of his wrist.

Bevil gave a hysterical but gloating laugh. "Thought I had just the one pistol, did you? But I was a step ahead of you—just like I have *always* been a step ahead our entire lives." His eyes slid to Fast's shoulder—the one grazed by the bullet—and he blenched at the sight of the blood soaking the shirt. He swallowed convulsively and wrenched his gaze away, looking as if he might vomit. "If you believe that I will—"

Fast gripped the hilt with the tips of his fingers and threw the knife. Time seemed to slow as the small dagger arrowed toward the other man and he stared in morbid satisfaction as the blade struck Bevil at the base of his throat. Before he could celebrate his accuracy, a second *bang* exploded.

Fortunately, this shot wasn't accompanied by any pain.

At least not until Fast took the first step toward Bevil's fallen form and was doubled over by a sudden agonizing pain like a red-hot poker hot in his left side. He barely made it to where Bevil lay bleeding before his knees collapsed. "Bloody fucking hell," he hissed, dropping beside Bevil with a pained grunt. The earl's mouth gaped like a fish, but no words came out. Based on his ragged, gurgling breaths, the knife in his throat must have severed his vocal cords as well as his airway.

"This is too damned easy for you, you piece of filth," Fast snarled, glancing around the barn for some way to make the bastard suffer before he died too quickly and cheated him.

His gaze settled on the anvil, and he smiled. "That'll do," he muttered. But when he tried to stand, he couldn't—the second wound had robbed his body of strength.

But he could still crawl, by God!

He grabbed Bevil by his hair and dragged him inch by painful inch. His vision grew blurrier by the second and he began to fear he'd lose consciousness before he could achieve his task.

Suddenly, his burden was much lighter; so much lighter that he stumbled forward on his knees. He glanced back and saw that Ellie Jenson had one of Bevil's arms and was dragging him, her bound hands gripping Bevil's wrist.

"Where to?" she asked breathlessly.

"Anvil," he muttered.

His head was spinning by the time he reached the huge lump of iron. When he turned to Bevil his heart lurched at the other man's parchment pale face and closed eyes. For a moment he feared death had cheated him.

But then Moreland's eyelids flickered open, he fixed Fast with a glassy-eyed stare, and his lips formed the word, *mercy*.

Rather than elicit the reaction Bevil intended, the plea revivified Fast's flagging fury and the sound that tore from his chest was pure animal. "Mercy? You can ask God for that," he raged. "There will be none here on earth." He spared a glance for Ellie. "Go now if you don't want to see what I am about to do."

Her dead eyes suddenly flared to life as her gaze bored into Bevil's limp form. "It is *my* family he destroyed—not just yours."

Fast had no energy left to argue. So, he nodded and turned back to Bevil.

And then he wrapped his hands around his neck.

Chapter 30

Escaping The King's Purse was almost disappointingly easy. There were no guards by her door and none at the bottom of the servant stairs.

Indeed, the entire house had seemed almost eerily empty.

Fearing that Fast might come to Freddie's house searching for her, Lori decided to seek refuge with her friend Serena, who'd not long ago married the wealthy industrialist, Gareth Lockheart. The couple maintained a London residence even though they were rarely in the city.

The Lockhearts's housekeeper, Mrs. Poole, recognized Lori immediately. "Naturally I remember you, Miss Fontenot. Mrs. Lockheart has standing instructions that a room be kept ready and waiting for any of her friends who choose to visit." She took Lori's valise and cloak. "Are you hungry? It wouldn't take but a quarter of an hour to have something for you. Nothing fancy, mind, but something good and filling."

"No, thank you, Mrs. Poole, although that is very kind. Just some hot water so that I might have a wash, and perhaps some tea. But don't let me interrupt your dinner, afterward is fine."

"Bless you, child," the old housekeeper said with an amused chuckle, "Poole and I finish with our meal before the sun even begins to go down. Let me take you up to the blue room and get you settled in and then I'll have your water and a tray sent up."

Lori loved the old couple who ran Serena's London house, but right now she just wanted to be alone.

Fortunately, Mrs. Poole—accustomed to Gareth Lockheart, one of the most taciturn people Lori had ever met—was used to serving people who had no desire to chatter, and soon left Lori alone in the comfortable suite of rooms.

Once she'd had a wash and drank three cups of tea, she felt more human, but no less miserable.

The night seemed interminable, and she tossed and turned in the comfortable bed, alternately fearing that Fast would find her or that he'd not even bother looking.

By the following morning, she decided that she had behaved far too dramatically not going home.

The truth was that Lord Stand Fast Severn didn't care that she had gone. Indeed, he was probably overjoyed to be spared the irritation of having to tell her about his betrothal to Miss Pascoe and ask her to leave.

And so, after she had broken her fast, Lori took her leave of the kindly Mr. and Mrs. Poole and went home.

It was something of a shock when she opened the door to the parlor and Freddie smiled up at her. "Oh, you're back," she said, looking not at all surprised to see her.

That was when Lori remembered that she had supposedly written to her friend and that Freddie had no clue that Lori had spent the last two weeks in a brothel.

Before she could compose her face, Freddie was on her feet, heading toward her with outstretched hands. "Lori? Whatever is the matter?"

Without any warning—either to herself or to Freddie—Lori burst into tears for the second time in less than a week.

Freddie took her in her arms and gently comforted her while the storm raged. Once her calm friend had soothed Lori to the point of hiccupping and sniffing rather than wailing and sobbing, Freddie stood and crossed the room to pull the servant cord before rejoining Lori on the settee.

"I will order some tea," Freddie explained.

Lori nodded.

"Feeling better?"

"Yes. Thank you for listening to my sniveling."

"That is what friends are for. You can tell me *why* you had to snivel once we have tea. I suspect we will need it."

Lori gave a watery chuckle. "As always, you are right. I will need to fortify myself before I commence my confession. In the meantime, why don't you tell me what has happened while I've been gone."

Freddie was in the middle of describing the most recent scandal—two well-known widows who'd actually come to blows over the same man—when the door opened, and Mrs. Brinkley entered carrying a tea tray.

The housekeeper laughed when she saw their startled faces. "I saw you when you came in, Miss Lorelei. I knew what you'd need before her ladyship even rang."

"Oh, Mrs. Brinkley!" Lori said, yet again choked up. "You two are both so good to me. You're going to make me start blubbering all over again."

Freddie patted her shoulder and said, "You cry as much as you want. Everyone needs a good blubber on occasion."

It was so like Fast's words from the other night that her eyes prickled dangerously.

Once the housekeeper had departed and they each had a cup, Lori begged Freddie to join her in splitting a cake.

"I know you are still out of sorts when you can't even eat a whole one," Freddie chided, dabbing her lips delicately after a bite of the decadent cream cake. "Now. Tell me what happened."

Lori tried to organize her thoughts—as if she were pitching the idea for a story to David—but the moment she opened her mouth, it all came pouring out in a rush.

Not just everything that had happened these last two weeks, but even her mortifying history with Lord Dorian.

She ended her tale of woe with the article in today's newspaper.

"Is it true about Lord Severn's betrothal to Miss Pascoe, Freddie?" Lori asked. 'Or could I have misunderstood the announcement?"

"I'm sorry, Lori, but I'm afraid it is the truth. That wretched Mr. Pascoe approached me again. He offered me so much money to plan the wedding breakfast that I couldn't turn him down." She saw Lori's look of horror. "Of course, now that I know about you and his lordship, I shall cry off and tell Pascoe—"

"*No,* you most certainly will not!" Lori interrupted. "That will do nothing for me and will only ruin your reputation. Please," she added when her friend opened her mouth to argue.

Freddie finally sighed but nodded. "Very well."

"When are they to marry?"

"In three weeks', time. As soon as the banns have been read."

Any hope that Lori had been clinging to disintegrated. "Three weeks," she repeated hollowly.

"Lori, darling?"

"Yes?" Lori said, barely able to squeeze the word out.

"Am I wrong in thinking that *you* would like to marry Lord Severn?"

Lori bit her lip, struggling to get control of her emotions, which were rioting like a flock of chickens being savaged by a fox.

"I love him, Freddie," she said, her voice breaking. "Even now that I know what a vile, duplicitous rat he is." Thankfully, she didn't dissolve into tears again. "I—I'm ashamed to say that I would have abandoned all my so-called principles in a heartbeat for him." She gave a bitter laugh.

"Oh, Lori. I am *so* sorry. I used to envy you for your position on marriage. It seemed so—"

"Safe?" Lori guessed.

Freddie nodded.

"I suppose I thought so, too. It turns out that there is no safety. At least not if a woman wants to live in the world and not in a cave out in the middle of a swamp."

Freddie smiled sadly. "What will you do now?"

"I'll finish my new book and then try to sell it."

"Please tell me you will continue living here while you do. You don't need to leave because you're not working for that dreadful Parker. You have always believed that *I* am doing a favor for *you*, but the reverse is also true. A single woman living alone is prey to—" She broke off and bit her lip, a scowl suddenly marring her ice queen façade. "That man who works for Lord Severn—"

"Has Mr. Gregg been bothering you?" Lori demanded.

A delicate flush spread across Freddie's cheeks like a pink mist. "Well, bothering is rather *harsh*. But he does seem, er…"

"Interested in you?"

Freddie nodded.

"Has he been inappropriate or—"

"No, no. Nothing like that." Freddie gave a dismissive wave of her hand. "In any case," she said, before Lori could delve further. "I really wish you would stay."

"Oh, Freddie. I just can't be here right now—at least not for the next three weeks."

Freddie knew what she meant without Lori having to put it into words. "Why don't you go and visit Portia? Or I know Annis would love to see you."

Both Portia and Annis were dear friends from their teaching days. Both women had often invited Lori to visit. But…well, right now she didn't want to be with friends. She wanted to be alone in a cave, where she could lick her wounds. That wasn't possible, but she would look for the next best thing.

Lori smiled at Freddie. "Now would be a terrible time to visit. Portia is caught up with the twins and Annis is all but a newlywed. So is Miles," she said before her friend could suggest him.

But Freddie wasn't beaten, yet.

"I have been thinking of taking a place in Brighton this summer, Lori. Perhaps you might go down there and investigate what is available in advance?"

Lori laughed. "I will *not* allow you to put yourself into debt leasing a house in Brighton just to save my pride. I am going to visit my brother. It has been ages. The girls will all be unrecognizable." Indeed, it grieved her greatly how much of her nieces' childhoods she'd already missed out on thanks to her avoidance of scaly men such as Lord Dorian and Daniel Fenton.

"Is that wise, darling? I know you were most unhappy there. And now, after you've told me the reason you fled Moorcross…Well, I cannot blame you for avoiding the place for so long. Are you sure you—"

"I need to face my demons. I can't run every time I make a foolish decision." She gave a bark of unamused laughter. "There will soon be no place left for me in Britain if I do that. Besides, you need to—to plan this wedding. And also finish launching the twins."

"Oh, did I neglect to mention they have both accepted offers?"

"Freddie! Congratulations."

Freddie smiled wearily. "I hope they are happy. Rose accepted Viscount Dorset—who is a kind, sweet boy. But poor Lily is marrying Baron Sterling."

"Lord! Sterling must be forty."

"Try one-and-fifty."

Lori hissed. "That should be illegal."

"Her fond papa is not forcing her. Lily wants the marriage, the social-climbing little minx."

"Well, it must be a weight off your mind to have them both off your hands. Will you manage their weddings?"

"No, that I will *not* do." She waved her hand. "But I don't want to talk about the twins. When will you go, Lori?"

"Tomorrow."

"Why so soon?"

Lori shrugged. "There is nothing to keep me here."

"What about Parker? Can you just leave without giving him any notice—not that the wretched man deserves the courtesy."

"Oh! I forgot to tell you that part. I went to see him directly after leaving The King's Purse"—she felt her face heat at saying the brothel's name but ignored it— "and I stopped at *The Mercury* offices this morning, and both times the door was locked and there was nobody there, not even his secretary. Indeed, the man seems to have disappeared into thin air." With her manuscript, but Lori didn't bother mentioning that.

"Shouldn't you at least stay until you can speak to him and retrieve your manuscript?"

"I would like it back, but I had the sense to make a copy of it—a tedious process I now am grateful for—after talking to Mr. Keats." She paused and then added the real reason she wanted to be gone so quickly, "I don't want to be here if Lord Severn should come looking for me."

And worse, she didn't want to be there if Severn didn't come.

***

As much as Lori dreaded going back to Moorcross, she was thrilled to see her family again.

All of them—her brother Jeremy, his wife Sarah, and their five daughters, from fifteen to four—were waiting at the coaching inn to greet her when she arrived on the stage.

There was squealing and weeping and laughing and Lori floated back to the vicarage on a cloud of family love and affection.

Lori's first three days at the vicarage were pure heaven, and she spent every minute getting reacquainted with her family. She had only ever seen young Gwendolyn, her brother's youngest child, at her christening almost five years before. Of all her brother's daughters Gwen looked most like Jeremy and Lori. She had the same dark, wiry hair and green eyes while her other nieces were the very image of their pretty auburn-haired, blue-eyed mother.

Not until the fifth day did the outside world come crashing back in, when her brother brought a copy of the *World Examiner* home.

"Sir Matthew remembered how much you enjoyed reading the newspapers and sent this along after my visit today."

Few people could afford a subscription to a newspaper, so passing the copies from person to person was common. Sir Matthew, a kind man, also had the misfortune to be Daniel Fenton's father.

Lori glanced at the well-thumbed newspaper as if it were a fresh turd. "How kind of him."

Jeremy laughed. "You needn't wrinkle your nose. I know it's not your precious *Times*, but it's better than nothing, *hmm*?"

"Yes, of course," she muttered.

Lori held off opening the *World Examiner* for a record two days. That meant she'd not read any news from London for a *week*. An unprecedented dry spell from news these past seven years.

"You are picking up that newspaper as if you wished you had tongs," Sarah teased.

It was a Saturday evening and the family had retired to what Sarah called the *Great Room*, a name that was more wishful thinking than accurate.

Lori smiled tightly and turned immediately to the back section.

Jeremy—who was watching her rather than working on his sermon, which is what he was supposed to be doing—chuckled. "I wouldn't have believed it if I'd not seen it with my own eyes."

"What?" she rudely demanded.

"Is this really my sister turning to the society section of a newspaper?"

She scowled at him. "Shouldn't you be busy working on words to inspire the masses tomorrow morning rather than scrutinizing my reading habits?"

"Touchy," he murmured, but slid his reading spectacles back down and returned to his labors.

Georgie, her second youngest niece, popped up beside Lori's chair. "Will you play a game of Spillikins, Auntie Lori?"

Lori smiled. "I'd love to. You play Clara, first, and I'll play the winner."

Once everyone was occupied, Lori took a deep breath and marched through the various snippets of nauseating gossip, not breathing normally until she'd gone all the way through to the end.

Thankfully, there was nothing at all about Miss Pascoe or Fast. Indeed, it seemed to be an especially dull week for gossip. Lori could only assume that was because the Season was winding down.

She sighed and tossed the paper aside, feeling a great deal like a soldier who had just dodged a bullet.

But that Sunday, Lori had to face not only one bullet, but a veritable barrage.

Lord Dorian, his wife, and three perfect children had recently arrived to visit Dorian's mother and father—the Earl and Countess of Seton. Of course he wasn't the only unwanted face from her past; there was also Daniel Fenton, who still lived with his parents.

Jeremy had insisted that Lori stand beside him while he'd greeted his flock. "They are all eager to see you," he said, using guilt to get her to comply.

Dorian had merely nodded loftily at her while he'd ushered his family past on his way out of the church.

But Daniel had obviously relished an opportunity to talk to her. "I heard you've been here almost a week, Lori. Where have you been hiding?" His lips curled into an unpleasant smirk.

Before she could answer Jeremy narrowed his eyes at the younger man. "It has been a long time since my sister's last visit, and we have been selfishly keeping her to ourselves."

Daniel met what Lori thought of as Jeremy's *fire and brimstone* gaze and his smile dimmed. "Yes, yes, of course you are," he muttered, stepping out of the way to allow his father—who really was a dear old man—to greet her.

"What a delight to see you again, Lorelei," Sir Matthew gushed, his bright blue eyes sparkling with good humor. "I do hope you will accompany the vicar the next time he comes to call so we can have one of those lively conversations we used to enjoy. I have missed your newfangled opinions about female suffrage, my dear."

Lori bit her tongue rather than point out that most of the arguments she'd posed had been around for years. "I would like that, Sir Matthew," she lied.

"I'll send over a few newspapers this afternoon so you can enjoy a Sunday treat, what?"

"Thank you, sir. That is very kind."

"There, that wasn't so bad, was it?" Jeremy murmured as the last of his flock wandered back to their individual pastures.

Not as bad as having sand rubbed in my eyes.

"No, not bad at all."

"I can't say that I liked the way Daniel Fenton was leering at you. That is one young man I cannot like. And today he was looking even slimier than usual."

Lori laughed. "How un-vickarish of you, Jer!"

Jeremy pulled a face. "That observation should stay between the two of us," he murmured, and then said more forcefully, "It is wonderful to have you back, Lori. I have missed you more than you can know."

Sir Matthew continued to send over newspapers and Lori—against her better judgement—continued to read them. They were filled with stories that were almost uniformly bland and boring, except for one shocking piece of news regarding Lord Moreland's death.

Evidently, the earl had died in a fire, but his death had gone unnoticed for some time. His lordship's servants in London had believed he'd gone up to Yorkshire to his estate, while his Yorkshire staff believed he was in London.

It transpired that he was at neither place. Instead, his lordship had paid a rare visit to one of his minor holdings. He had been inspecting a barn of some sort and must have been overwhelmed by smoke when a fire started.

It was fortunate that his signet ring had been found in the rubble or his death might have remained a mystery.

Lori felt sorry for anyone who suffered such a miserable end, but if there was one person who deserved it, it would be Moreland, the serial rapist.

She imagined that Fast would be relieved to learn the man was dead.

As for Fast himself, she had not read a word. And not for a lack of looking, either. Indeed, she'd scoured every newspaper the squire sent over and had even purchased one of her own at exorbitant expense in the village. Nowhere did she see the announcement of his marriage to Miss Pascoe.

That was odd as the banns would have been read the requisite three weeks and Mr. Pascoe had clearly been eager to secure his quarry.

Lori was tempted to write to Freddie, not just to ask about the wedding, but because she had not heard from her friend since the first week of her stay. Freddie's only letter had been brief in the extreme. It had also been carefully crafted, clearly composed with the intention of making no mention of *the wedding*. It was passing strange that that had been Freddie's only letter as she was usually a diligent correspondent.

If Lori didn't receive a letter in tomorrow's post—which would mark more than three and a half weeks in the country—she'd swallow her pride and write to ask Freddie for details of Fast's wedding.

As if thinking about the post had summoned it, her brother opened the door to the small sunroom where Lori was in the habit of writing most mornings.

"This is for you," he said, handing her a letter and eying her curiously.

Lori understood why when she saw who the sender was: W.H. Newcastle & Sons.

She made a mortifying gulping sound as she stared at the copperplate writing on the envelope, which shook in her trembling hand.

"That's a very respected publisher, is it not?" Jeremy asked.

Lori nodded dumbly. She was amazed that David had actually sent her manuscript to W.H. Newcastle—for that is the only reason she'd have a letter from them because Lori had been far to cowardly to approach such a prestigious publishing house.

"Aren't you going to open it?"

She shook her head.

Jeremy laughed and sat down beside her. "I don't think I've ever seen you quite so terrified, Loribell."

She looked up at the old nickname. "I can't open it, Jer." She thrust the envelope at him. "Will you read it? And if it is dreadful… Well, if it is dreadful, don't say anything. Just burn it."

He took the letter without speaking, his eyes moving quickly over the sheet, his expression giving nothing away before he looked up and said, "May I read it to you?"

Lori was finding it impossible to speak, so she jerked out a nod.

"Dear Miss Fontenot,

I am writing in regard to the manuscript titled, Briarly. *I apologize that it has taken me so long to respond. I received your book several weeks ago but was unexpectedly called out of the City before I could draft this letter to you. I'm pleased to inform you that I began reading on a Monday afternoon and did not stop until sometime early Tuesday morning—"*

Lori shrieked.

Jeremy looked up. "Lori?"

"Keep reading," she barked.

Her brother grinned. *"It is my pleasure to offer you a contract for the publication of* Briarly, *which we would likely release in three volumes. We can offer you £150, the terms to be discussed in more detail if you deign to accept.*

I understand that you've been employed by David Parker at The Mercury *and therefore will understand if he already made arrangements for your manuscript before he closed his paper and left the country.*

In any event, I look forward to hearing from you, should you be interested in our offer.

Respectfully,

W. H. Newcastle"

Jeremy finished reading and looked up. "Well? Isn't this a matter for celebration?"

Lori shook her head, and his eyebrows shot up.

"Whyever not?" he demanded.

"No, I didn't mean it's not cause for celebration," she clarified. "I was shaking my head because I can't believe David Parker left the country—and why has there been no mention in any of the newspapers I have read of him closing *The Mercury*? And if David didn't give *Briarly* to Newcastle, then who *did* give it to him?"

"I don't know. But does it really matter at this point?" He grinned. "You've received an extremely respectable offer to publish your book."

Lori could hear the words, but she couldn't quite believe them.

Jeremy put a hand over hers. "I suppose this means you will be leaving us soon, doesn't it? I *do* hope you won't stay away so long before your next visit?"

She heard the sadness in his voice, and it penetrated the fog of shock surrounding her. Lori smiled at her brother, squeezing his hand. "No. I will never stay away so long again."

"Why did you stay away, Lori?" He chewed his lip, the gesture so familiar it gave her a sharp pang. "Something happened to you here, didn't it?" His mouth turned down at the corners. "Something with Lord Dorian—or Daniel Fenton?"

"It was a long time ago."

His hand tightened painfully. "Did either of them—"

"No, Jeremy. It was nothing like that. Really," she assured him when he continued to look skeptical. "I left because I'd outgrown Moorcross and it was time to stretch my wings. I needed to go away from here and seek my fortune."

His jaw worked for a moment, and she feared he might pursue the issue. But he must have sensed her reluctance, so he smiled and said, "So, then. When are you leaving us?"

"I'll stay until your next service and then leave on the following Monday. There's no—"

The door to the parlor flew opened and Sarah stood on the threshold, her cheeks flushed and her eyes sparkling.

Jeremy shot to his feet. "Is something wrong, Sarah? The girls—"

"No, no, the girls are all fine," she said, her gaze fixed on Lori. "I'm sorry to interrupt, but there is a visitor for you."

"A visitor?" Lori and Jeremy said at the same time.

"It is Lord Stand Fast Severn," Sarah said in an unnaturally high and squeaky voice. She looked from Lori to Jeremy and back again, as if she were struggling with something, and then she burst out in a gleeful voice, "The King of the Rakes is at this very moment in my very own sitting room!"

Chapter 31

"Viscount Severn is here to see *Lori?*" Jeremy repeated before Lori could respond.

Sarah nodded vigorously. "Yes." She stuck out her hand and Lori saw there was a card in her palm.

Jeremy turned to Lori, his eyes bulging. "Good Lord, Lori! You know *Severn?*"

Lori was startled by her brother's use of the Lord's name and met his shocked gaze with a guilty shrug. "Yes."

His eyebrows lowered and she could see that there would be questions—many of them.

But not now.

Lori lurched to her feet. "I will go speak to him."

"But Lori!"

She stopped and turned at Sarah's raised voice. "Yes?"

"Er, don't you want to tidy your hair?"

Lori glanced in the small mirror beside the door and scowled at her reflection. She had a tendency to pluck at her hair absently when she wrote. She looked like she'd come away the loser in a wrestling match with a hedge.

"No, it is fine."

Her sister-in-law gasped. "Surely you want to change your gown!"

Lori glanced down at herself, as if she'd forgotten what she was wearing. "No, Sarah; Severn can see me as I am."

"But you are wearing your oldest dress, and it has cherry juice splatters all over it from helping me make jam and—" she broke off when her husband set a hand on her shoulder.

"Sarah, let her be."

Lori cut Jeremy a quick, grateful look and then strode resolutely down the short hallway.

Only when she reached the staircase and had a moment to herself did she slump against the handrail and exhale the breath she'd been holding.

What in the world was he doing there? And after all this time!

She struggled to calm her breathing.

Had he brought his *wife* with him? Surely Sarah would have mentioned that. Or possibly not, given how starstruck her sister-in-law had appeared just now.

Lori shoved down her nervousness but kept her anger. He had some nerve showing his face after what he'd done to her.

The murmur of Jeremy and Sarah's voices behind her interrupted her rapidly snowballing anger. It would have been nice to have a few more minutes to collect her thoughts, but that was not to be, so Lori steeled herself and resumed walking even though her legs felt like jelly.

When she reached what Sarah called the *sitting room*—really a glorified parlor—she took yet another deep breath and flung open the door. "I can't imagine what *you*—" Lori broke off at the sight that met her eyes.

Gwen, her youngest niece, was perched on Fast's knee and he was holding the girl's favorite book in his hands.

Fast smiled up at her, his expression one of rueful amusement. "Hello, Lorelei."

She stared at him blankly for a moment before turning to her niece. "What are you doing in here, Gwennie?" Lori knew that Sarah didn't allow the children to come into the sitting room unless she accompanied them.

The little charmer smiled winsomely up at Lori, her huge green eyes blinking innocently. "Wode Sevone is weeding Miss Fwuffington to me, Auntie Woahwee."

"Is he, now?" she asked, her gaze moving from her niece to Fast, who was trying to assume an expression as innocently charming as the tiny girl on his knee and doing an annoyingly fine job of it.

Gwen nodded enthusiastically, her black curls bouncing.

"It's time for big people to talk now, Gwen." Lori fixed Fast with an evil stare. "But *Wode Sevone* will read to you after you have your tea—as many times as you like, in fact. You should run along now as I have it on good authority that there will be cherry scones with cherry jam for—"

"Chawees!" Gwen shrieked, causing Fast, whose ear was not far from her mouth, to jolt and recoil in pain.

Forgetting all about the book, Gwen scrambled from Fast's lap—inadvertently jabbing him somewhere sensitive, if the *ooofing* sound he made was anything to go by.

Lori held the door open wider for the little girl. "Walk, Gwen. No skipping in the house!" she called after her niece.

When Gwen disappeared around the corner, still skipping, Lori shut the door before turning back to Fast, who'd stood now that he didn't have Gwen on his knee. She crossed her arms and leaned back against the door, scowling. "What are you doing here?"

He held up the book—*Miss Henny Fluffington Goes to Market*, whose cover had a large, speckled hen wearing a fancy bonnet and carrying a reticule over one wing——and asked, "You wrote this?"

"Don't avoid my question, my lord."

He lowered the book—which Lori had indeed written and illustrated and then had bound and printed for her eldest niece years before—and said, "Won't you sit?"

"I'm happy right where I am. But don't stand on my account."

Instead of sitting, he prowled toward her.

"That's close enough," she said, not trusting herself to be any nearer to him. "I will repeat myself for the third time: what do you want?"

"You."

Lori ignored the leaping sensation in her chest. "It is too late for that."

"I'm not married."

She sneered. "Came to her senses, did she?"

"I never planned to marry Miss Pascoe."

"Oh. I see. So… was it she who tricked you? Or perhaps it was her father?"

He sighed. "Won't you please sit? I have a lot to say, and I'd like to take my time and get it right."

"Fine," she snapped. "I'll sit here." She dropped into the chair nearest the door. "You sit over there." She pointed to the settee when he would have taken the chair next to her.

He sat without any demur. "I wish you'd not left The King's Purse and disappeared that day."

"Oddly enough I didn't want to wait for you to come back once I'd read about your betrothal in the newspaper."

He looked hurt, rather than angry. "It's too bad you didn't wait, because then you might have learned the truth, Lorelei."

"Which is?"

"Demelza and I never planned to marry. The only reason I agreed to the betrothal was to help her."

Lori crossed her arms and stared.

He sighed. "She is in love with another man—a clerk in her father's counting house. But her father wanted a peer for a son-in-law and refused to approve the marriage. Moreland had already asked Pascoe for permission to court her; if I didn't help her, her father would have applied unpleasant pressure on her to marry the earl. We—Demelza and I—decided to fake a betrothal just long enough to distract her father. Ever since she confessed her love for his employee, he had kept her imprisoned. She was sure that he would relax his guard if he believed that she'd fallen into line with his wishes." He paused and gave her a questioning look.

"Go on, I'm still here."

"I gave her money, because she had none even though she is a great heiress, and Gregg helped her sneak away when she was supposed to be getting fitted for her trousseau. He took her to where her lover—who is now her husband—waited for her, and the two took off to Scotland. When Pascoe was forced to admit that his daughter had absconded, I shamed the truth out of him—that she had only agreed to marry me because he had forced her." He gave a tiny but smug smile. "I wish you could have seen me, Lorelei. I was quite impressive in my rage. I told him he should be ashamed for trying to auction off his daughter when he knew that she was in love with another man. I ranted about how I would be humiliated if the truth were known. Finally, once my anger began to cool, I said I would spare her—and Pascoe himself—any embarrassment and admit that the betrothal had ended amicably. But I only agreed to do so on one condition. I told him he had to forgive his daughter as I didn't want to be the cause of a family breach, and I babbled a great deal of claptrap about how I'd been embroiled in a fracas with my own grandfather for two decades." He cut her a sheepish look. "And I also promised to put his name up for membership at one of the clubs I belong to. I suspect it was really that last thing that persuaded him to forgive her."

Hope had been fluttering wildly in her chest for at least a minute, but she brutally quashed it. "You expect me to believe that story?"

"Demelza said you'd probably not believe a word of it, so she gave me this." He reached into his coat and took out a folded sheet of paper, which he held out to her.

Lori snatched it from his fingers and unfolded it.

It was brief:

Dear Miss Fontenot,

I would like to apologize for any trouble my deception caused you. You have been kindness itself to me on the few occasions we've met this past Season, and I'd hate to think I hurt you by any of my actions. When Lord Severn told me at the Countess of Mansfield's house party that he had no intention of offering marriage to me—that he had already given his heart to you—I felt terrible about using him as my means of escape. But he insisted you would understand completely. Neither of us expected my father to make that announcement at his dinner party. In fact, Lord Severn had asked Papa to keep the matter in strictest confidence until he spoke to the Marquess of Grandon about the betrothal—which he never would have done, of course. But my father is a law unto himself and contrived that awkward announcement, making sure it was announced in the newspapers.

Lord Severn told me how you'd read of the betrothal and I can't imagine how hurt and horrified you must have been! I cannot apologize enough. If I had not begged his lordship to keep our agreement in complete secrecy—for I knew my father had his spies everywhere—then he might have confided the truth in you and you would not have been hurt. Please forgive me and know that Lord Severn has only ever been a gentleman, friend, and savior to me.

Regards,

Demelza Lions, née Pascoe

Lori carefully refolded the letter, her emotions churning.

She felt movement and looked up to find that Fast had taken the chair next to her.

He scooted it closer and took her hand. "Am I forgiven?"

"Why did you wait so long to come here and tell me this?"

He snorted. "Not out of choice, I assure you. It's… well, yet another long, convoluted story."

She pulled her hand from his and crossed her arms again. "I'm listening."

***

Lorelei hadn't yet forgiven him yet, but she was rapidly thawing.

"Before I answer your question about why it took so long, let me go back in time to last year—just after I left here on my final voyage as the *Vixen's* captain."

She nodded.

"I was in a small port town in Venezuela when I encountered a mutineer from the *Sea Ranger*."

"You have told me this before—remember? Although you didn't say how many mutineers. You picked up only one?"

"I did. And…this will sound astounding, but I knew the man." He then told her, as simply as possible, about finding Joe Jensen and then discovering he was the brother of the man who'd killed Percy.

"That is an incredible coincidence. My God, Fast! I am astonished that you didn't kill him on the spot when you found out."

Fast looked away from her. "I… wasn't kind to him."

"I don't think anyone could blame you for that. If somebody admitted to me that a member of their family had killed Jeremy… well, I would want my pound of flesh, even if the messenger was innocent."

"I was insane with rage, but Gregg had the sense to restrain me until I could come back to my senses. You see, Jensen's brother—Albert—had acted at the direction of another man and did so under duress."

"What do you mean? Did somebody give him money to do it? Who?

"Jensen said his brother wasn't paid to kill Percy, but that he did it because somebody threatened to destroy his family—specifically Jensen's two sisters and his mother—if he didn't comply."

"Good Lord!"

"Jensen said he would only tell me the real killer's identity after I'd done something for him. He said he had a signed confession that his brother had written years ago—an insurance policy against the man who made him do the murder, in case he tried to hurt either Albert or his family. As things transpired, the real murderer didn't wait for Albert Jensen to talk."

"He had him murdered, too?" Lorelei guessed.

"Close enough. He had both Albert *and* Joseph press-ganged. The last thing the killer said to them was that if they ever uttered his name to anyone their two sisters and mother would pay for their indiscretion."

"What a nasty, nasty character."

"Yes. Especially since he punished the three women, regardless."

She swallowed. "I'm almost afraid to ask. What did he do?"

"It's awful, Lorelei. Too awful for your ears."

She gave him an exasperated look. "I work, er, *worked* for a newspaper, Fast."

He held up his hands. "Fine, fine. He sold the girls to a bawd who runs several of the worst establishments in London. The mother he sold to a workhouse."

She bit her lip, her eyes becoming glassy.

"To make a long, horrible story shorter, Albert sickened and died less than a year later. Joe knew he couldn't go home—not with the murderer's threat still clear in his mind—and he resigned himself to never seeing his family again. And then Pigot took over as captain. And you know how that turned out."

"The poor man," Lorelei murmured.

"That is not even the worst of it. Jensen had consumption and was dying by the time I picked him up. He had tried to send word to his mother using a mate's name—so as not to alert the killer, if he were still watching Jensen's family—but the letter was undeliverable. And then of course the crew mutinied, and he had no chance of getting back to England and looking for them."

"So you told him you would find them?"

"Yes, in exchange for the confession and his own testimony, although I doubted he'd survive that long. I thought it would be consumption that killed him, but I was wrong."

"What do you mean?"

Fast sighed. "Everything might have gone along as planned if not for three men on the crew who overheard the conversation with Jensen and decided to stick their hands in. They must have killed him while trying to get the confession from him—although I believe Joe took one of the men with him as only two came to England." He shrugged. "I will never know what truly happened to poor Joe. But I do know that the men found the confession because they used it to extort money from the killer."

She shook her head. "This is just so… incredible that I don't even know what to say. How did you ever unravel it all?"

He gave her a wry smile. "I think you might have been the key to that."

"Me? But…how?"

"You were poking into matters that led you in the direction of the killer."

She blinked. "So…then you were *not* exaggerating when you said I was in danger?"

"No, darling. I was most certainly *not.*" A familiar wave of nausea assaulted him, just as it did every time he thought about how close he had come to losing her. "The brute who grabbed you in the alley that night was a bloke named Carey, and he worked for the killer and—"

"*Was* named?" she broke in. "Is he…dead?"

"Yes, he was murdered later that same night."

Lorelei reached for Fast's hand and he clutched it tightly. "I'm sorry I ever doubted you, Fast."

He raised her hand to his lips and kissed it. "I went back and forth about telling you the truth, Lorelei. I just—"

"I understand why you didn't," she said, her words surprising him. She gave a wry laugh. "I would have kept digging, Fast. I know that about myself." She paused, and said, "You mentioned somebody had stolen the confession. Does that mean you never found out who killed your brother?"

"No. I found out who it was through his henchman, Carey. It was Bevil Norman, the Earl of Moreland."

Her eyes threatened to bulge out of her head. "*What*? That—that cannot be true!"

"It is."

"But…*why*?"

"Because Percy had found out what Bevil did to Louisa."

She gasped. "You mean—"

"I mean that he did the same thing to her that he did to Martha and the other women," Fast said.

It took a moment before she could seem to force any words out. "I read that Moreland died in a fire. He didn't, did he? You never brought any of this before the authorities, did you?"

"How could I?" he asked, ignoring her first question. "I didn't have the confession, and I didn't have Joe Jensen. I had nothing. And then there was the fact that Bevil was holding Jensen's younger sister hostage and threatened to kill her if I refused to meet him—alone. Jensen never got the chance to hand over the confession, but he *did* set me on the path to finding the killer. I owed it to him to save his sister if I could."

"So you met a murderer…alone?"

"Yes," he said, smiling at her thunderstruck expression. "And that meeting was why I wasn't back in time to wake up with you that morning. Or have dinner with you."

Her face screwed into an expression of confusion. "But…I don't understand. This all happened almost a month ago?"

"Yes."

She huffed. "Tell me about this meeting. *All* of it."

Ten minutes later, Lorelei shook her head at him. "That was quite a risk you took meeting him at that remote place. He might have just shot you before you even entered the barn."

"I knew he wouldn't. Moreland was too smug—too arrogant. He'd gotten away with murder for too long and wanted to crow about it to somebody. To me. Besides," he added wryly, "he believed that I'd stolen Demelza from right under his nose at that wretched house party. He wanted the chance to tell me how much pleasure he'd take in snatching her back once he'd killed me." Fast's hands flexed, his anger rising. "He took great pleasure in telling me how he'd made Louisa's life hell."

He looked up from his unappetizing thoughts to find Lorelei in front of him. She nudged aside his knees and perched on his lap before sliding her arms around his neck. "I'm so sorry, Fast. So terribly sorry."

He drew her soft, comforting body closer. "I should have never left her to him, Lorelei. I only wish she had told me! If I'd known then what he had done to her—" he broke off and shook his head. "I should have guessed."

"Why? You couldn't have known about Moreland and how evil he was and the things he'd done."

"Is that really true?" Fast asked, the question as much for himself as her. "Or did I willfully ignore the signs of his sickness? It is something I will revisit for the rest of my life. Bevil Norman was the closest to pure evil I've ever encountered," Fast admitted. "And it disturbs me more than I can say that he was ever my friend."

"You can't blame yourself, Fast. A man like that was adept at hiding behind his mask. Why would any right-thinking person ever suspect what he was?"

He kissed her and then tightened his arm around her, wincing when her elbow nudged his side.

"What is it, Fast?" Her eyes narrowed. Are you hurt?"

"It's nothing serious, love, just a little graze from the first bullet."

***

"He *shot* you?" Lori squawked. "Wait! The *first* bullet? Just how many bullets were there? And why did you leave this out of the story you just told me?"

Fast winced. "Not so loud in my ear, darling. And yes, Lorelei, he shot me. That's usually how bullets do their damage."

"Quit being so cavalier and tell me what happened."

"Moreland paused too long to gloat, and while he was prosing on at me like a villain from a gothic novel, I threw a knife at him and—"

"He let you have knives?"

He gave her a pained look. "He didn't *let* me. He searched me and found the pistols and other knives, but he—"

"A pistol *and* knives? How many knives did you have?"

"Darling?"

"Yes?"

"If you would stop interrupting, then I could finish telling you the story."

"Oh. Sorry." She pursed her lips to illustrate her silence.

"He searched me but neglected to find a small knife I had strapped to the inside of my wrist and—"

"A wrist knife? How did you—Oh, sorry," she blurted again. "I'll be quiet. I promise," she added when he cocked his eyebrow in that odiously attractive way he had.

"I was a privateer in my former life, sweetheart. Er, you knew that, didn't you?" he asked, his tone more than a little arch.

Lori clucked her tongue. "Now, now, don't be testy."

"Of course not, dear."

She laughed at his martyrish expression. "I really will be quiet now."

"There isn't much more to tell." He shrugged and then grimaced. "Ow."

"Poor darling," Lori murmured. "Where does it hurt?"

He pointed to his shoulder and Lori kissed the expensive superfine of his coat.

"*Mmm,*" he said, smiling at her with heavy-lidded eyes. "That feels better already. Perhaps you might do that to all my injuries. But with my clothes off. Yours, too."

"*All* your injuries! How many times did you get shot?"

He sighed. "You are focusing on the wrong part of what I just said, sweetheart."

"Fast," she said in a warning tone. "How many times?"

"Just twice."

"Just. Twice." Lori had to take a deep breath and hold it to calm herself before she could say, "Explain."

"It's not a pretty story, Lorelei."

"When will you understand that I am a newspaperwoman and accustomed to dealing with unsavory subjects?"

"Fine," he said in a flat voice. "If you must have it, I brought him down with the knife and then I beat his head against an anvil until he was no longer breathing. And then I set the building on fire, with his body inside it."

Lori's lips parted and she mouthed the word *Oh.*

"You are shocked."

It wasn't a question, but she nodded. "Yes." After a moment she felt compelled to add, "But I cannot say that I am sorry. Moreland deserved it. Not just for what he'd done in the past, but for what he probably would have kept doing."

"I agree."

"You still haven't said why it took so long to come to me?" she reminded him.

"Because I had to see to the Jensen girl, which took a lot longer than I thought."

"You mean Moreland hadn't killed her?"

"Oh, did I forget to mention that she was there in the barn when I arrived?"

Lori rolled her eyes. "You are the worst storyteller *ever*."

Predictably, he laughed. But his expression quickly turned grim. "Yes, she was there—tied up. Bevil was going to stage our bodies after he'd killed us. He said he'd make it look as if I'd raped her and that she'd somehow got her hands on a gun and shot me and then killed herself."

Lori felt ill. "That—that *villain*! What happened with Miss Jensen?"

"First, she helped staunch my wounds. Then we set the barn on fire and watched it burn. Once I'd recovered a bit she rode for help. Afterward, I helped her collect her children—whom Moreland had sold—and brought all three of them to a nice cottage on my grandfather's estate, where they are recuperating nicely. And *no*, I'm not going to tell you about the dreadful hell hole that bought the little girls. Suffice it to say you will read about the place in the newspapers sometime in the coming weeks."

"Were the children—"

"They were fine, but it was a close thing. After Ellie was safely settled, I had to deal with Demelza's situation. After *that* was satisfactorily managed, I came looking for you." He gave her a tight smile. "As for why it took so long to find you? Well, my darling, you never told me your brother had a different surname than you."

She winced. "Oh. Did I not mention that my mother was my father's second wife?"

His expression was withering. "No. And I searched all over hell and gone for a Reverend Fontenot."

"Why didn't you just ask Freddie?"

"She was gone when I went to call on her."

"Gone?" Lori repeated blankly. "Gone where?

"I thought she was just *not at home* to me, but that harsh-faced servant of hers managed to convince me otherwise."

"Oh, Mrs. Brinkley?"

"I believe that was her name."

"Did she say where Freddie went?"

"I got the distinct impression that she did not know where. Only that her mistress had packed her bags and gone on a journey."

"How… singular." And concerning. Freddy had never taken a trip anywhere in all the years Lori had known her.

"I thought the word *inconvenient* was more fitting," Fast corrected.

"So then what?"

"I finally had to go back to Parker's office."

"Oh."

"Yes, *oh.*" He smiled grimly. "Don't worry, Parker wasn't there. At least not that time. It was his harried clerk who I wanted to see in any case. He was only too happy to allow me to ransack his files for your information."

Lori frowned. "Wait. You went *back*? And what do you mean by *that time*?"

**

Fast eyed the love of his life with no small amount of concern, not quite sure how she would take this next part.

"I want you to promise me something, Lorelei."

"What?" she asked, suspicion glittering in her eyes.

"Promise me you won't be angry at me."

"How can I possibly promise that?"

"Just say it."

She gave him a look of profound feminine exasperation. "Fine. I won't be angry."

"The first time I went to Parker was the same day I returned to London from the house party."

"You *what*?"

"Don't get angry," he reminded her.

"What did you do, Fast?"

"I told him you wouldn't be working for him anymore and—"

"You *what*?"

"You've already said that, sweetheart."

She glared.

Fast resumed his story. "I told him how he'd put your life at risk. I demanded to know what hold he had over you"—he winced at her shriek but went on— "when he refused to be cooperative, I had to… persuade him."

She stood and would have walked away if he hadn't caught her arm and yanked her back onto his knee. "You aren't allowed to leave," he told her sternly, hoping to cow her into submission with his *lordly* frown.

It didn't work.

"Just what did you do?" she demanded, thoroughly uncowed.

Why lie? "I beat him until he confessed."

"You *beat* him?" she shouted, and then, "Wait. Until he confessed to what?"

"That he had passed *Briarly* off to publishers as his own book."

"*What?*"

He flinched and hissed through clenched teeth, "Sweetheart, you are three inches from my ear."

"Who—how—" This time when Lorelei jumped up off his lap, Fast let her go.

She paced back and forth across the small room. "I'm too angry to speak right now," she said, "You go on."

"Parker sold your book to Anthony Hayes over at Hayes and Sons. Once got that information out of him I went over and, er, convinced Hayes that it was in his best interest to give me back the manuscript."

Her lips parted and her eyes went wide. "How did you do that?"

"I just told him the truth—that you'd written it."

"And—and he just believed you?"

Fast snorted. "What do you think?"

"Please tell me you didn't beat him, too?"

"No."

She heaved a sigh.

"At least not much."

"Fast!"

"What?" he asked, spreading out his hands. "How else was I supposed to retrieve your stolen property and get him to break his contract with that scoundrel Parker?"

"If you beat every single publisher in London, how will I ever do business there again?"

"I didn't have to beat W.H. Newcastle. At least not when the man finally had a chance to read it."

She gasped. "It was *you* who gave it to him?"

"It sure as hell wasn't Parker." He reached out and caught her hand, pulling her lush bottom back onto his thigh. "Why didn't you come to me for help—rather than that scaly bastard Parker?" He claimed her mouth fiercely before she could offer up paltry excuses—such as she hadn't known Fast back then—and savagely kissed her, all the worry and anxiety of the past weeks pouring out of him.

And all the love, as well.

When he decided to let her breathe again, he released her. "So," he said, taking an immoderate amount of pleasure from her flushed face, dazed eyes, and swollen lips. "Is that explanation good enough for where I've been, why I've been gone so long, and why you will forgive me and marry me?"

Her lashes fluttered and her green eyes—so like those of her enchanting little niece—widened in shock. "Marry? But—"

He laid a finger over her lush lips. "If you utter any of that claptrap about not believing in marriage, I'll drag you back to The King's Purse and lock you up in the Queen's Chambers. I'll keep you there and use each and every one of those implements on the wall on your body until you beg me to marry you."

"Fast!"

He was pleased to note that she blushed prettily and appeared titillated, rather than appalled, by his erotic threat. *Hmmm,* that was interesting. His little authoress was adventurous, was she? Fast could joyfully accommodate her curiosity.

"Well?" he demanded when she continued to stare dazedly. "Will you allow your brother to marry us tomorrow morning? Or must I carry out my threat?"

"But the banns haven't been read."

He patted his pocket. "I came prepared with a special license."

"But…what about your grandfather? Everyone in London knows how high in the instep he is. He will never agree to you marrying me."

"It was only thanks to my grandfather's assistance that the Archbishop was persuaded to issue a special license to a reformed rake such as myself."

She goggled. "You mean he doesn't mind that you aren't marrying a pedigreed peeress or an heiress?"

Fast didn't tell her that the old man had minded a great deal. Nor did he tell her how loudly and passionately the two of them had discussed the matter. And he certainly didn't mention that it had taken almost one entire week out of the last three and a half to finally persuade the marquess to see the light.

Instead, he smiled and said, "He is so grateful that I'm staying in England and have consented to wed that he said I could marry his char woman if she agreed to bear him a grandson." That was the truth, as far as it went.

Fast knew the old man's reservations would disappear after a few hours in Lorelei's company. A few days, at most.

She laughed. "How flattering."

Fast kissed her. "And don't think I'm asking you to be my wife only so I can breed heirs on you, Lorelei."

Her lips parted in that distracting way she had.

Fast smirked. "Although I certainly plan to *practice* breeding you often and vigorously."

She raised her hands to her pink cheeks. "You also plan to keep me in a perpetual blush."

"I do," he agreed. "But as to the matter of children, I will make every effort not to put a baby in your belly until and *if* you are ready for it." He gave her a faint smile. "I think you know I'm more than delighted to take and give pleasure in a variety of other ways."

"What if I never want to have a baby?" she asked quietly, no longer smiling.

"Then we will do our best to make sure you don't fall pregnant." He tilted his head. "You really don't want children?"

"No, I want them. Very much, in fact. I just want to make sure that isn't the reason you are marrying me."

Fast couldn't help feeling relieved at her words—at least the first part. As for the second…

"I can't believe you would think I'd only marry you for heirs, Lorelei."

She stroked a soothing hand over his chest. "I don't. I just want everything to be… clear. I've seen too much misery when there are no children—or if there are girls, and no heir. I want to know that you will not be terribly disappointed if I cannot have children. Or if I only give you daughters."

"I would adore having a daughter with you. Especially if she looks like you." He sighed and laced their fingers together. "I don't think I made my feelings entirely clear, Lorelei. I will be forty years old in a few months, so I have not been in any hurry to marry. I want a family for my own pleasure and happiness, not to secure a title I care very little about. The fact that my marriage will please my grandfather is just a happy bonus."

"*Hmmm*. Forty," she said, eying him speculatively.

"What? Is that too old for you, you little shrew? How old are you by the way?" He cast his gaze ceilingward and said, "Please say you are at least twenty."

"I am five-and-twenty," she retorted. "Is that too young for you?"

He grinned at her taunting. "For your information, you are perfect for me. You are perfect, full stop." He raised her hand to his mouth and nibbled on her finger, regarding her hungrily from beneath his lashes. "Every single part of you is perfect."

Her cheeks blossomed with color. "You can't resist an opportunity to make me blush."

"No. I cannot."

She snorted and shook her head. "You *are* a rake. I can't imagine how devastating you were when your powers were in full bloom."

"I like to think I've just become better with age."

She laughed.

Fast kissed her thoroughly, until she was breathless with something other than laughter. "Witch," he muttered. "You have enchanted me thoroughly."

His brazen little newspaperwoman shyly lowered her gaze. When she looked up again, she said, "What did your grandfather say about you marrying a newspaper woman?"

Fast hesitated, and then admitted, "I did not raise that subject with him. I told him what little I knew of your family connections. And I mentioned you lived with Lady Sedgewick."

She pulled her hands away from him and the joy drained from her face. "So, in other words, you utterly concealed who I am."

"My grandfather is almost ninety years of age, Lorelei. He is the product of another time and set in his ways. He would not approve of your aspirations to be a novelist, and he emphatically would not approve of me marrying a newspaper woman. *However*"—Fast raised his voice to be heard over her scoffing—"*however*, there is no reason that he *should* know of your ambitions, is there? At least not immediately."

"What about the book contract you all but negotiated for me, Fast?"

He was genuinely surprised by her question. "What about it?"

"Do you expect me to just refute the offer if I agree to marry you?"

"Of course not!"

"Then how will your grandfather not find out about me?"

Fast frowned. "Surely you did not mean to publish your books under your own name?"

***

Lori wanted to retort *of course* she'd meant to claim credit for her novel. But it would have been a lie. She had always known she would need to employ a *nom de plume.* If she didn't, she would feel constrained in her writing, fearing that she would put something into print that would shame her brother and his family.

So why did it annoy her so much that Fast might expect the same consideration for his family?

Because you are scared. Here is the thing you wanted and thought you could never have—marriage to this magnificent man—and you are scared that you are transgressing your own principles.

Was that true? Was that all she really cared about? The preservation of her *principles?*

"Lorelei? What are you thinking? Don't hide from me. *Talk* to me."

Lori began to rise up from his lap, but Fast tightened his grip on her fingers and slid his other arm around her waist to keep her on his knee.

"Not so fast, Lorelei. I have no objection to my wife writing books, but—"

"But you would not allow the woman you marry to work for a newspaper?" she couldn't help retorting.

"Under no circumstance would I allow my wife to plunge heedlessly into danger, as you have been accustomed to doing. But that doesn't mean we can't come up with a mutually acceptable compromise."

"As long as you get what *you* want."

"Precisely." He chuckled. "Quit squirming to get away," he chided.

"I won't be told what to do by some man!"

"I won't be *some man*. I will be your husband."

"That doesn't—*mmmff*"

Fast kissed her until she stopped trying to escape, until she reached for him, her fingers sliding into the silky heat of his hair. Before she knew it, she was moaning and pressing herself against him, taking control of their kiss, *reveling* in finally being joined to him when she'd feared for almost a month that he was going to marry another.

It was Fast who pulled away, his eyes heavy lidded. "Lord, but I've missed that."

Lori shook off her erotic torpor. "Just because I allowed you to kiss me does not mean I agree to abide by your commands."

He sighed. "Is working for a newspaper what you really want, Lorelei? Because I recall you saying that you only took the job with Parker so you could afford to do what you truly love, and that is write novels."

Why had she ever told him that?

"Well?" he prodded.

"It is true that I want to work on my novel *now*, but what about if I decide to do something else later? What then, Fast? Are you going to forbid me to do as I wish?"

"I want us both to get what we want, Lorelei," he said, holding her gaze. "We will work together to make sure we are both happy. I promise you that."

"You can say that now, but once we're married—"

"Once we are married you are my property under the law," he finished for her.

She swore she heard the clanging of a cell door.

He lightly caressed her jaw. "I cannot change what the law says, Lorelei. But I can give you my word that I will always love, cherish, and protect you—without trampling your rights and desires in the process." He gave her a rueful look. "Unfortunately, you're going to have to take my word for that because I can't change the law for you, no matter how unjust I think it is."

"And you will accept no arrangement other than marriage?"

"If you're asking whether I will stop seeing you if you refuse to marry me, then the answer is *no.* But if you're asking if I think that sneaking into each other's dwellings of an evening would satisfy me for long? The answer is also *no.* I want you in my life. Not just as a lover, but as a companion, a wife, a mate, and a mother to my children."

Lori stared at him, both her stomach and her mind churning.

You are arguing with a man who is offering you more than you ever dared to dream you could have! He knows about you and Dorian, and he does not care. You don't want to write foolish gossip columns or crawl around the docks in the dark to investigate stories, you want to write novels! And yet you continue to argue.

"What is it, sweetheart?"

Lori inhaled deeply and met his gaze. "You expect concessions of me, Fast—well, I have one for you."

"If it is within my power to give it, I will do so."

"Most men of your class keep a mistress—or go to places like The King's Purse to satisfy their carnal urges. I could not live with that. It would destroy me if you were unfaithful."

"I am not like my father, Lorelei. I have always vowed to myself that if I ever married, I would be a faithful husband. Have I had a lot of lovers in my life? Yes, many. Certainly enough to know when I've found a woman who is special and singular and worthy of my fidelity."

"But you fell out of love once before," she couldn't help saying. "What if it happens again?"

He hesitated, looking torn, before finally saying, "There are no guarantees when it comes to love, Lorelei—at least none that I know about. All I can tell you is that I love you with my whole heart. And I honestly do not believe that I have *ever* felt so deeply for anyone else." He smiled. "I am well and truly caught and grateful to be so. I have never met anyone like you. You entice, please, challenge, infuriate, and entrance me. I love you, Lorelei. And I hate the thought of living without you."

Lori's face blazed at his declaration.

Tell him you love him, too! Tell him!

But she couldn't make herself say the words. Instead, she nuzzled her face between his neck and shoulder and softly asked, "Are you sure about this, Fast? Truly sure?"

"I'm sure, darling. Truly sure."

She squeezed her eyes shut. *You love him. You know a lifetime with him is what you want.*

She sighed, squirmed a bit, and then pressed her lips to the tender skin just below his jaw, kissing and tasting him.

He groaned and pushed himself away, until she was forced to meet his gaze. "Stop tormenting me, you temptress. Will you marry me? Or do I have to carry out my diabolical scheme to make you surrender by seducing you into submission?"

Her body's reaction to his words shocked her—although why it should at this point, was beyond her.

Stricken with a shyness that was foreign to her, she lowered her eyes before saying, "If I say *yes*, can we still go back to the Queen's Chambers so you can *seduce me into submission* with all those *implements*?"

Fast gave a shout of triumph that Lori suspected could be heard throughout the entire vicarage and pulled her close to kiss her soundly.

"That is one promise I cannot wait to keep, my adorable darling!"

Chapter 32

Both Jeremy and Sarah were delighted by the prospect of marrying Lori and Fast in their village church.

Sarah, not unnaturally, wanted Lori to wait for at least a week so that all their friends in the neighborhood could attend. Fortunately, Fast stepped in while Lori was scrambling for an answer that wouldn't spell out just *why* she had no interest in inviting all their neighborhood *friends*. He explained that the reason for the small ceremony, as well as the haste, was because of his grandfather's uncertain health.

That was enough to make Sarah relinquish her dream of a large wedding, but she still remained attached to the notion of hosting a big wedding breakfast.

This time it was Lori who spoke up. "Right now, there is only conjecture in the village about Fast's identity, Sarah. But the minute anyone knows he is here for certain, he shall be a target for nosy newspapermen and gossips. It is terribly important that the Marquess not learn of his grandson's marriage in a scandal sheet."

"Of course, it shall be just as you wish," Sarah agreed, and then laughed. "To be honest, I am delighted that you are marrying at all," she added, cutting Fast an arch look. "You should know this is all something of a miracle to Jeremy and me, my lord; Lori has always been a staunch opponent of marriage for women."

Fast smiled. "I do know that. I count myself extremely fortunate to have convinced her to change her mind."

Dinner that evening was a relaxed and lively affair. It was clear to Lori that both her brother and sister-in-law were thrilled by the match, regardless of what either of them might have read in various newspapers about his raking past. If Lori accepted Fast, that was good enough for her family.

After the meal Fast and Lori were able to snatch a few minutes alone in the garden.

"Are you sure such a modest wedding will be acceptable to your grandfather?" Lori asked, more than a little concerned that he was engaging in a tiny wedding for her sake alone.

"It would have been his preference to have a large affair at St. George's," Fast admitted. "But, in truth, he is so delighted that I am marrying that the size and grandeur of the ceremony is no longer as important as it once might have been."

"You believe he means that? That he is not only saying it to please you?"

He chuckled. "You will have to meet the marquess before you understand why I find that question so amusing. It is not what he would prefer, Lorelei, but he *did* assist me in procuring the special license. We will not have to face recrimination on that score when you meet him." He turned to her, tilting her chin until she faced him. "Are *you* sure you don't wish for a larger ceremony? At least one that includes all your teacher friends?"

Lori had been thinking about that. "I would prefer to have a party later to celebrate our marriage. Perhaps next year, when most of them have already said they will be coming to town."

"That can be easily done." He smiled and kissed her lightly before asking. "So…shall we marry tomorrow, then?"

Lori felt a grin take possession of her face. "We shall."

And so it was that Lori and Fast were married the following day in a tiny ceremony with only Jeremy, Sarah, and all five of Lori's nieces in attendance.

The brief sacrament passed in a hazy blur and Lori felt like an observer for most of it, watching from outside herself in amazement as she spoke the vows she had never believed would pass her lips.

She was getting married. She would be a wife and have a husband.

You will be Fast's chattel, just another of his many possessions, for the rest of your life.

The thought did not strike fear into her as it had in the past. She loved him and living without him had felt empty and…incomplete.

Marriage would be an adjustment, but being with him would be worth it.

And so when Fast leaned toward her at the end of the ritual to deliver a brief kiss it felt surprisingly natural for Lori to meet his delighted—and slightly smug—smile with an answering smile of her own.

A few hours later the four of them were relaxing in the sitting room after the tiny wedding breakfast.

Sarah's father and mother—Sir Nigel Smith and Lady Smith—lived only a half-hour's drive away and had sent their carriage to collect the five girls. Jeremy and Sarah would shortly join their daughters, giving Lori and Fast some privacy on their wedding night.

Tomorrow, Lori and Fast would leave for Grandon Castle, where Fast's grandfather was awaiting them.

It was all happening so fast that it was difficult for Lori to believe it was real—that the gorgeous, clever, fascinating man sitting beside her was her husband.

"I do wish you could both stay more than just one night," Sarah said, breaking into her thoughts.

"I am eager to meet my new grandfather," Lori said, sparing Fast from having to answer. Sarah was a dear but could be persistent on some matters and this wasn't the first time she'd mentioned them extending their visit.

"We will come back for another visit whenever you invite us," Fast assured his new sister-in-law.

Sarah opened her mouth—probably to extend an invitation right then and there—but Jeremy stood and held his hand out to his wife. "Come, my dear. We had better be off if we want to get to your parents' house by dinner."

It took another quarter of an hour to talk Sarah toward the door and into the waiting carriage.

As Lori waved them on their way, she said through her smiling teeth, "Thank you for being so patient with her."

The carriage disappeared around the corner and Fast turned to her. "It took no effort at all to be kind to her, Lorelei. Sarah is a wonderful woman who loves you very much." Fast offered her his arm and led her back inside the house. "I don't suppose we could go to bed now?" he whispered in her ear as they walked past Mrs. Gerber, the housekeeper, and Betsy, the maid of all work, both of whom appeared to be busy doing nothing in particular, having obviously positioned themselves for another look at Fast.

Lori laughed. "No! I'd never be able to look Mrs. Gerber in the eyes again."

He heaved a sigh of regret. "Well, then how about some exercise to help digest our enormous wedding breakfast?"

Sarah had indeed out done herself, especially on such short notice.

"I would love a walk," Lori admitted.

"Go fetch your hat and cloak and you can show me where you used to wander and gain inspiration for your writing."

A short time later they were both hatted and gloved and heading out through the vicarage gate.

"Where are you taking me?" he asked as Lori's feet naturally turned in the direction of her favorite walk.

"There is a small wilderness near a lake—although it is in truth more of a pond—and some lovely old growth trees."

They strolled in companionable silence before Lori said something that had been weighing on her mind since Fast's arrival.

"I know it is not precisely on the way, but I would like to stop in London to check on Freddie before we head to Grandon Castle."

"Of course we have time to do that. Are you really so worried about her?"

"Freddie never goes anywhere, so this is sudden trip is extremely unusual."

"But the two of you have friends all over, don't you—the other teachers—maybe she went to visit one of them?"

"Maybe."

"You sound doubtful."

"It just isn't like her. It sounds like she left not long after I did, but she never mentioned taking a trip anywhere."

"We shall certainly check on her so that we can put your mind at ease. We can stay a few nights at Severn House, and you can go speak to W.H. Newcastle and sign your contract. Or did you forget about that in the excitement of the wedding?"

"No, I have most certainly *not* forgotten."

"I thought as much. A mere husband cannot hold a candle to a book contract," Fast said with exaggerated self-pity.

"Well, to be fair, I have been seeking a book contract for years. Now a *husband,* on the other hand…"

He clutched his heart. "*Ooof!*"

Lori laughed. "Poor, poor Severn." She paused a moment. "You, er, want to stay at Severn House?" she asked, not sure how to raise the subject on her mind.

"Why not?"

"Won't it have been closed up for the summer if your grandfather has gone?"

"There will still be plenty of servants in residence to see to our needs."

"Yes, of course."

They walked in silence as she squirmed and tried to come up with a subtle way to remind him about his threat about the Queen's Chambers.

The sound of a low masculine laugh made her turn. "Why are you snickering in that odious way?"

He grinned. "Because it is both amusing, and charming, to watch you try to conceive of a subtle way to say that you want to go back to the brothel and do unspeakably naughty things with me."

She bumped him with her shoulder, but it was like bumping a warm brick wall and he didn't budge. "I was not thinking that!"

"Were so."

Lori laughed. "Oh, very well. So, I am curious. Is that really so dreadful?"

He stopped, turned to her, and slid his arms around her. "It's not dreadful at all. It's delightful. Wonderful. Lovely. Kiss me."

"Here?"

"Yes. Here."

Lori looked about, but they were alone except for the birds, insects, and summer sunshine. She slid her arms around his neck and stood up on her toes while pulling him lower.

His mouth was hot and tasted of good black tea with a hint of sugar.

Lori relaxed into his arms, pressing her breasts against his chest, earning an approving growl. He tilted his head and opened wider so she could explore him. When she paused to catch her breath, he was smiling down at her, a hungry glitter in his eyes.

"I cannot wait to get you back to the Queen's Chambers," he said in a husky voice.

"Oh? Why is that?"

"If I told you, it would spoil all the fun." He lightly ran his fingers up her side, from her waist to her ribs.

Lori shrieked and jerked away. "Don't!"

His lips curved into a truly evil smile and his eyes widened. "What is this? Is my new wife *ticklish*?" He reached for her again, but Lori darted away.

"Where do you think you are going?" he demanded. "Your lord and master wishes to tickle you, it is your duty to submit like an obedient, proper"—he lunged like a blur and almost caught her.

Lori bolted, laughing as she plunged off the trail into a thicket, purposely heading toward an area she knew would be too low for him to easily follow.

"Come back here this instant, Lorelei!"

She laughed.

The sound of muttered threats and breaking branches came from behind her.

"You'll never catch me!" she taunted breathlessly, and then shoved her way through a narrow gap where two hedges met.

Once she was on the other side, she hurriedly looked around for somewhere to hide so that she could leap out and pounce on him when he came through. But a sound pulled her attention away from the hedge and trees; Lori had to bite her tongue to keep from cursing when she saw the four riders, immediately recognizing the first two as Dorian and Daniel. The other men were strangers.

They must have noticed her before she'd seen them because Dorian had led his horse off the path and the other three had followed.

Lori had seen Dorian in church, of course, but this was the first time she'd been so close to him in over seven years. He was just as handsome as ever and his full shapely lips pulled into a smirk that told her he was remembering other times they'd encountered each other in these very same woods.

"Well, well, well, look who we have here!" he said, his grin insufferable. "Daniel claimed that you never left the vicarage unless you were with your brother or sister-in-law. And yet here you are, alone. It is almost as if you were looking for me." He leered down at her.

"You flatter yourself, my lord," Lori retorted coolly.

Dorian laughed. "I see your tongue is as sharp as ever."

"I have looked for you in these woods every day, Lori," Daniel piped up behind Dorian, the hateful glitter in his eyes telling her that he had neither forgotten nor forgiven the scratches she'd given him all those years ago.

Lori did not justify his comment with a response.

Dorian gave an ugly laugh. "You appear to have forgotten that it was *me* Lori was so fond of, Dan. Naturally she could not resist seeking me out—as was always the case."

Before Lori could open her mouth, Fast's voice came from behind her. "What is this?" he demanded, needing to employ brute force to shove his big body through the narrow gap in the thicket.

Lori immediately went toward him.

"Who the devil are you?" Dorian demanded as Fast broke free of the last branch and strode toward them, leaving a trail of leaves and twigs in his wake.

Before Fast could answer, not that he looked like that was his intention, one of the two men Lori didn't know quickly brought his horse closer.

"Lord Severn! How grand to see you, sir," the younger man shouted in obvious delight, scrambling off his horse in such haste that he fell to one knee, and then quickly popped up again like a jack-in-the-box and bowed low in Fast's direction.

"Who is your rude friend, Rawley?" Fast asked, his piercing gaze fixed on Dorian.

Dorian's eyes had widened when the other man used Fast's title, his mind visibly racing to make sense of this new development. Lori recognized the very instant when he came to the most repellent conclusion and chuckled. "So, Lori, up to your old tricks, are you? I guess you decided to add another title to your collection." His gaze flicked dismissively over Fast and his sneer deepened. "A little long in the tooth, isn't he?"

"I say, Dor!" Lord Rawley exclaimed in an appalled, overly loud voice that made the horses restless. "That's not quite—"

"Get off your horse." Fast did not raise his voice, but his menacing tone was enough to raise goosepimples on Lori's skin.

Dorian frowned. "What did you just—"

"Get. Off," Fast growled, closing the distance between himself and the other man in a few long strides.

Dorian laughed. "I'll do no such—*aaarrrgh*!"

Fast moved with the lightening-fast speed that Lori had seen him display on more than one occasion and grabbed Dorian's horse by the bridle with one hand while his other hand closed around the younger man's booted ankle, and—in a show of brute strength that was both awe-inspiring and arousing—he yanked Dorian out of his saddle.

The horse reared and whinnied, and chaos erupted. For a few moments there seemed to be a dozen horses and men as the other men struggled to keep their mounts from bolting.

But even in the midst of the pandemonium, Fast did not release his grip on Dorian, who was frantically clawing at his saddle.

"Move back, Lorelei! *Now*!" Fast barked, shaking Lori from her stunned gaping.

She didn't hesitate to obey. Not only was it safer away from the flailing man and rearing horse, but it provided her with an excellent view of Dorian hitting the path hard enough to send up a puff of dirt.

He yelped piteously as Fast grabbed the back of his clawhammer coat and dragged him to his feet. Before Dorian could catch his breath, Fast caught him by the throat and pinned against a nearby tree.

He easily held the thrashing peer. "Choose your second, *boy*, and I'll meet you—"

"No duels!" Lori shouted. "You promised me, Fast," she reminded him, scrambling toward her husband and grabbing the arm that wasn't holding Dorian in a death grip.

Fast glanced down at her, his expression shifting from murderous to baffled annoyance. "Surely I did not say—"

"You promised, me," she repeated, the words barely able to get past the lump in her throat.

He must have tightened his grip on Dorian's neck because the younger man gave a strangled yelp, his limbs spasming.

"Fast, *please.* He is not worth it," Lori begged quietly.

Her husband's chest swelled as he inhaled and then held his breath a moment before exhaling in a noisy rush. "Fine," he snapped, and then turned back to Dorian. "I promised *my wife* that I wouldn't engage in any duels."

Hope leapt in Dorian's bulging, watering eyes.

Fast crushed it immediately by taking a step closer and saying through bared teeth, "That means I will just have to kill you here and now."

"No killing either!" Lori yelled, yanking on his arm as if to pull him away. Naturally he did not yield so much as an inch.

"I don't recall promising that," he shot back.

"Please, Fast… it is—it is my wedding day."

Finally, after what felt like years, he grumbled and released Dorian, who slid to the ground for the second time in less than five minutes, holding his throat and coughing.

"No killing. *Today*," Fast amended. He looked as if he was going to turn around but then suddenly lunged for the other man. "But maybe *you* would like to challenge *me* to a duel? I didn't promise not to *accept* a challenge."

Dorian cowered away, muttering something too soft for Lori to hear.

"What's that you say?" Fast demanded, grabbing him around the neck again and jerking him to a sitting position. "Speak up!"

Dorian's voice was squeaky, but loud, "I'm terribly sorry for my behavior, my lady!"

My lady?

It took Lori a second to realize that was her. Lori smiled. *She* was Lady Severn.

She slid a hand around her husband's bulging biceps and said, "Please, Fast. I want to go back to the vicarage."

He hesitated only a second, and then leaned close to Dorian, who tried to flinch away but only managed to bang his head against the tree in the process. The low rumble of Fast's voice filled the silence for a few seconds and then he barked, "Understood?"

"Yes, my lord!" Dorian shrieked.

Fast grunted and then released him.

Lori experienced an almost crushing feeling of exultation when Dorian fell to the dirt like a broken doll. Was it petty to enjoy the moment? Yes, but she didn't care. It reminded her of that day all those years ago when *she* had been at his feet. Dorian should be grateful that she had stopped Fast from killing him.

As for Daniel…

When Lori looked up from Dorian, she saw that the squire's son had slunk away while her attention had been riveted elsewhere. She felt a mild pang of regret that he did not get his comeuppance but then recalled Fast did not know that he had physically attacked her all those years ago. If he had known, she feared she would not have been able to stop him from killing Daniel.

"My love?" Fast held out his arm and she lightly set her trembling hand on his sleeve.

There wasn't so much as a peep as he led her away from the silently staring men.

Not until they were out of the woods and the vicarage was in sight did the excitement of the last few minutes hit her.

A flush swept her entire body—as if her clothes had been set on fire—and she began to shake, her teeth clacking audibly. For a second, she feared she might faint from sheer, overwhelming emotion.

"Lorelei?" Fast asked in a gentle voice that was all the more powerful when contrasted with his menacing tone of only moments before. "Is aught amiss, love?"

With all the strength she could muster she launched herself at her husband, wrapping her arms around his neck and legs around his waist, and not caring if her skirt was hiked to her thighs.

"What's this, sweetheart? Not that I'm not delighted to have you in my arms," he said, sliding both hands beneath her bottom to lift her a bit higher. He pulled his head back just enough that he could meet her gaze. His brow was furrowed with concern and his pale eyes blazed like magnificent sapphires in the sun.

"It's—that was—" It felt like her tongue was made from lead. She swallowed and tried again, "I l-l-love you so much, Fast!" Her voice was so raw that it didn't even sound like her. A confusing medley of love and amazement and gratitude roiled inside her. She had never wanted anyone to rescue her before—not her parents or her brother or her friends—but what Fast had just done, and the way it had made her feel so cherished—felt…exquisite. For the first time in her life, Lori desperately wished that there was an even stronger word than *love.*

"Ah, sweetheart," Fast murmured, pulling her close. "That's what I've been longing to hear. I love you, too, Lorelei. More than you can imagine."

Chapter 33

Despite Lorelei's protests—which were interspersed with frequent, breathy sobs—Fast carried his weeping wife the rest of the way to the vicarage.

The whole time, her words echoed in his ears: *I love you so much, Fast*!

While he could have wished that she hadn't been weeping and distraught when she'd finally decided to declare her feelings for him, he understood that the tears were from an excess of emotion—the strain of the prior weeks—and not directed at him personally.

In any event, they had the vicarage to themselves for the next twelve-or-so hours and it would be Fast's particular pleasure to help ease her tension in every way imaginable. And he had an *excellent* imagination.

Smiling at the thought, he shouted for Mrs. Gerber the moment he opened the door to the foyer. The woman came scurrying into the small entry hall so quickly that he suspected she couldn't have been far away. "Yes, my lord?"

"Have hot water sent up to the bridal chamber. You might as well have the girl bring up the cold supper Mrs. Simpson said you'd prepared."

"You want supper *now,* sir?" Mrs. Gerber's wide eyes swiveled from Fast to the window, as if to assure herself it was still daytime.

"Yes, send it up *now.* Her ladyship and I don't want to be disturbed for the rest of the day. And night." Fast gave the fussy servant a hard look, hoping that she took his meaning, which was that she and the maid should make themselves scarce.

"Won't Miss Lori—er, my lady—need help with her gown?"

"I'll see to that," he assured her, amused by the faint gasp that slipped out of her.

She dropped a hurried curtsey. "Very good, my lord." Her curious gaze slid to Lori, who'd wrapped her arms around Fast's neck and tucked her face into the ruins of his cravat.

"We'll want that water right away."

The woman gave a startled jolt. "Yes, my lord!" And she hurried off in the direction of the kitchen.

"That was cruel," Lori murmured as Fast carried her up the stairs. "She just wanted to get a good look at The King of the Rakes."

He smiled, relieved to hear the teasing note in her voice. "Too bad all she got to see was The Most Perfect Husband in Britain, instead."

Lorelei laughed.

"I don't know why you're laughing," he scolded as he reached the landing and strode toward the room he knew belonged to the master and mistress of the house, but which they had kindly vacated for tonight. "Open the door, love," he said once he'd stopped.

She fumbled for the handle and once they were inside, he hooked his foot around the door and pushed it shut before laying her gently down on the big four poster bed.

She caught his wrist and brought his palm to her face, the look in her eyes one he'd never seen before: almost worshipful. "Thank you for avenging me, Fast."

He scoffed but kissed her palm before saying. "You should have let me shoot him. Or run him through with a sword."

"But then you'd have had to run from England."

"At the very least you should have allowed me to beat him a little."

"I think nearly choking him to death sufficed."

"*Hmmm*," he hummed, the noise doubtful. And then he licked the spot he'd just kissed.

She giggled.

Fast paused his licking, his eyebrows almost to his hairline. "Did you just—"

"If you tell anyone I giggled, I shall write the most odious story about you and sell it to the scandal sheets."

He laughed, and then slid her index finger into his mouth.

Her mouth opened but only a soft, "*urgh*" came out as he sucked.

"Oh, Fast…that is so…"

He removed her finger with a damp sucking *pop*. "So?" he prodded, moving to her middle finger.

"So very, very naughty." She groaned as he suggestively stroked her finger with his tongue, letting her know what he was going to be doing to some other part of her body very soon.

It was his turn to groan—unhappily—when somebody knocked on the door to the adjoining sitting room.

He reluctantly released her finger. "I'll go and deal with that. While I do, I want you to strip."

Fast strode from the room while she was still struggling for a response. He shut the door behind him before letting the servants in.

"I'll take that," he said to the housekeeper, who had a ewer of hot water. "You can set the rest on the table," he told the maid.

Once they'd deposited the cold supper, he bade them both a firm *good night* and shut and locked the door behind them before turning and striding toward the bedchamber. He'd seen the mulish look in his beautiful wife's eyes. She wouldn't have obeyed him about taking off her clothes.

That was fine; he'd enjoy stripping them off her himself.

He flung open the door and then stopped in midstride, gaping like a yokel at the sight that met his eyes.

It was his new wife lying utterly and completely naked on the bed. She'd assumed a modest pose—one leg crossed over the other to cover her sex and one arm draped across her breasts.

As he stared a flush crept up her body. She was…entrancing.

Her throat flexed as she swallowed. "Er, Fast?"

"*Hmmm*?" he asked, setting down the water so clumsily it almost fell off the table.

"You're staring."

"I am," he agreed, yanking off his cravat and tossing it aside before going to work on his coat and waistcoat.

"You have a strange look on your face," she said, her own expression nervous.

"Strange?" he repeated, shrugging off both his coats at once and throwing them off to the side without looking.

She laughed at his deliberately careless gesture—which had been his intention—some of the tension draining from her face. "Your valet isn't here to tidy up after you, you know."

He grunted, not taking his gaze from her luscious body as he toed off his Hessians in a rough way that would have Bixby scolding him, kicking them off to join all the other clothing strewn across the floor.

He shed his pantaloons and drawers on the way to the bed only pausing to bend and push down his stockings. When he stood, he was naked.

Her smile had disappeared, replaced by a hungry look that made his already hard prick throb even harder.

Fast gripped the base of his shaft and slowly pumped himself, reveling in the heat in her darkened gaze. "You like watching me stroke myself, don't you?"

She nodded, her big eyes huge.

"I'd give you a proper show if I didn't think I'd shame myself in less than a minute," he said, reluctantly releasing himself and climbing onto the bed. "Oh, no you don't! Where do you think you're going?" he growled when she tried to scramble to the other side of the bed. "I want you right here."

Here was beneath him and he straddled her hips. She'd moved both her hands to cover her breasts, so he caught them easily and then held them above her head with one hand.

"Fast!" She squirmed beneath his greedy gaze.

"God, you're beautiful," he murmured, drinking in the sight of her full, firm breasts and their large pink nipples. "It embarrasses you that I'm staring, doesn't it?"

She pursed her lips and her eyes—which had been fixed on his mouth—jumped up to meet his. "No."

Fast laughed. "Liar."

"You enjoy making me blush and squirm, don't you?" she accused, doing both to perfection as she hastily looked away.

"I love it," he admitted. "Especially when you are naked. Eyes on me, Lorelei."

She obeyed immediately and her lips parted, either in surprise at her own behavior or because his commands aroused her. Or maybe both.

"I'm going to release your wrists, but I want you to lay your hands above your head and keep them there. Understood?"

Fast loved watching the struggle that took place within her, the independent bluestocking at war with the sensual young woman, the former fighting to bring the latter to heel.

What she needed was a bit of taunting to make the struggle even more entertaining…

"You like submitting to my commands, don't you?"

She exhaled shakily—which caused her lovely breasts to tremble in an entrancing fashion. "I don't know what is wrong with me." Her eyelids lowered until her eyelashes were fanned against her cheeks. "But I do like it, Fast."

"Look at me, Lorelei."

She raised her gaze slowly, something that looked like mortification flickering across her face.

"You have nothing to be ashamed of, love. You can obey me in the bedchamber and still be a strong, intelligent woman. What we do in private is our concern and ours alone. I love having you at my command. And I love that it arouses you. All too often the women of our class are told to stifle their urges and fantasies while their husbands are encouraged to look outside of the marriage bed to satisfy their sexual appetites." Holding her gaze, he leaned low enough to take a nipple between his teeth, nipping and tugging the sensitive bud until she hissed, her eyelids fluttering and her back arching. Fast was pleased to note that for all her squirming her hands remained in place.

He released the tightly puckered bud and gave it a gentle kiss before saying, "I want you to be my sexual slave in the bedchamber, Lorelei." He moved to the other nipple. "And I want to be yours, as well." He smiled when her breathing quickened. "You would like that, wouldn't you? Making me kneel before you. Making me obey your every command and beg for my release?"

A shiver wracked her, but her voice was coolly defiant when she retorted, "I believe I might."

Fast gave a triumphant laugh. "I imagine you will be a deliciously cruel mistress."

She bit her lip but could not retrain her scandalized laughter. "You are absurd!"

He grinned, pleased that she felt relaxed enough to laugh and jest with him. "I am, darling. And I am all yours. Now, keep your eyes on me." He moved back a foot and then gently nudged her clenched legs apart before kneeling between them. He firmly caressed the long taut muscles of her thighs, sliding a hand up and up. "I like it when you watch me, Lorelei." His questing finger traced the seam of her sweet, pouty lips.

She gasped and raised her hips when he parted her folds and circled her slick, engorged nub.

"This is what good girls get, Lorelei." Her nostrils flared at his patronizing words, but the way she spread her legs wider without his urging told him how much she liked it.

"You're so wet and eager," he breathed, increasing the pressure of his caress.

She tensed and made soft whimpering sounds, her hips pulsing by the time he slid a finger deep inside her.

"What a beautiful cunt you have," he praised,

A broken moan tore from her lips at his crude compliment and she shuddered.

His naughty wife loved his vulgar tongue and Fast did not hold back. "You're so tight," he whispered, watching his finger slide in and out of her body, rapt. "I have been dreaming about fucking you for weeks." Fast smiled at her sharp gasp and the sudden clenching of her inner muscles and eased a second finger in alongside the first, the sight of her body stretching to accommodate him excruciatingly arousing. "Good God! I wish you could see yourself, sweetheart." He circled her bud, his touch purposely too light to bring her to climax.

A whimper of frustration slipped from her mouth, and she bucked her sex against his fingers. "Fast…*please.*"

"As you wish," he said.

And then he gave her what she needed.

"That's right," he murmured as she cried out and came apart. "Come for me, darling."

***

Lori decided that making love to her husband was her new favorite pastime.

Not only was Fast skilled and generous, but he said the most wonderfully naughty things Lori had ever heard.

And then there was the way he seemed to see right to the core of her—to those uncomfortably erotic thoughts she'd always kept locked away. Somehow, he had not only found the key, but he made no bones about unlocking the door and exploring her every hidden desire and secret fantasy.

It might not be entirely comfortable, but already she could see theirs would be a much richer marriage for his erotic prying.

"Are you sleeping my beautiful lover?"

Lori forced her heavy eyelids up and smiled up at her new husband, who was once again on his knees, stroking himself as he gazed down at her.

Her eyes opened wider. "I am awake now."

He chuckled. "I love the way you look at me."

"And I love you."

His hand stopped moving and *his* eyes widened.

"What?" she taunted, "did you think I had misspoken earlier?"

"No, not at all. I just didn't expect to hear it again without some, er, provocation."

She snorted. "I don't need to stop you from killing a man to tell you I love you, Fast. I've felt it for a while—since you first confessed your feelings for me. I was just too…"

"Cautious?"

She gave him a wry look. "I was going to say *cowardly*. But thank you." Her gaze dropped to that most fascinating part of him. His hand hadn't moved again, and he'd lost some of his tumescence while they'd talked. Lori cut him a shy glance. "May I touch you?"

"You never need to ask. I am yours to do with as you please."

He said the most intoxicating things! Lori had always thought herself articulate, but he disarmed her with his direct honesty.

He groaned when she wrapped her fingers around his shaft, his big body swaying toward her as she caressed the impossibly silky and rapidly hardening length of him. The small slit produced a fascinating bead of liquid that was mute evidence of his desire for her.

Being with Fast was so different from the dry, furtive, and painful couplings she'd had with Dorian that there was no comparison.

"What is it, darling? You are giving my cock the most accusatory look."

Her face heated at the word *cock*, which was ridiculous given that she currently had her hand wrapped around it. "That's what you prefer to call it…*cock*?"

He shrugged, his hips pushing against her hand which made her realize she'd stopped stroking. "Cock, prick, jack, Adam's dagger, Sir John, shaft of delight—any of those will do and all are more interesting than *penis* in my opinion."

"*Sir John*?" Lori laughed so hard her eyes teared up. "Those cannot be terms that are actually in use."

"Indeed, they are—I would never jest about such an important matter. Surely, you've heard such terminology in your dealings with newspapermen? I'd always understood them to be an earthy lot."

"I don't know what you think my days and nights were composed of, but I scarcely associated with any other journalists."

"Ah, so your education in this area is my responsibility then." He rubbed his hands together with exaggerated glee. "I cannot wait to teach you all I know."

"There are *more* terms?"

"Ramrod, nature's delight, stallion—"

"*Stallion*?" She choked on a laugh, but then recalled that she still held his, er, *Sir John* in her fist and resumed her pumping.

Fast gave an appreciative purr and then said. "Tighter."

She firmed her grip. "Like this?"

"A bit more—*ahhh*, perfect," he sighed when she complied.

"Are you sure that doesn't hurt?" she asked doubtfully.

"Quite sure," he said, his voice rough, his lids drooping low over his eyes. "Oh, yes. Just like that."

"Could I make you, er, e-ejaculate this way?" Lori asked, disgusted that she couldn't spit out the word without stumbling over it.

"There is no doubt in my mind—and rather speedily, too, I'm afraid." He set a hand on hers and Lori stilled her erotic labor. "I am very close," he explained at her questioning look. "I want to be inside you."

Lori swallowed. "Yes…I want that, too."

He lowered to one elbow, positioned himself at her entrance, and then flexed his hips enough that the hot blunt crown bumped against her.

"Rather like a battering ram at a castle gate," Lori murmured.

Fast shook with laughter and pushed until just the fat tip was inside her.

They both gave hisses of pleasure.

"Fast?"

"Yes, darling?" he asked in a tight voice.

"You don't have to withdraw."

His brow furrowed. "If I don't withdraw, then—"

"Then the chances are greater that I shall conceive," she finished for him. "I know that."

"I am in no hurry to start a family, Lorelei."

"Neither am I. But I no longer fear becoming pregnant, either," Lori said, wanting him to understand just how earthshaking her change of heart was. "I have always loved and wanted children, but I've spent the last seven years telling myself that no man would want to marry a woman with my tattered reputation. And now, quite suddenly, I've discovered that isn't true. Indeed, I've fallen in love with a man who has not only accepted me—mistakes and all—but is my champion."

He growled. "I cannot believe how much you've suffered because of that lout, Lorelei. You should have let me beat him when I had my hands on him. Who is his father?" he demanded, the question startling her.

"He is the Earl of Seton's heir. Why?"

Fast's eyes narrowed and his gaze turned distant, as if he were plotting.

"You cannot challenge his father to a duel or kill him either," she added quickly.

He barked a laugh, the menacing expression draining from his handsome face.

Lori stroked his back. "I do not want to think about him, Fast. I just wanted you to know that with you, everything is different. And…and I am excited to have your child."

"I know exactly how you feel, darling."

"Truly?"

"Truly. Just remember that it doesn't always happen immediately—sometimes it may take years."

"I believe either alternative would be fine… with you."

"I love you, sweetheart," he said, and then flexed his hips, slowly breaching her. He cocked his head and paused. "You are holding your breath. Am I hurting you?"

"No, not at all. It's just that…er, you are bigger than I remember."

"You say the nicest things, sweetheart." His hips fell into a rhythm of slow, deep thrusts. "*Mmm,* such a tight, wet little pussy." He propped himself on one elbow and reached between them. "Let me see if I can make you even wetter, love."

Lori shivered as he unerringly located the source of her pleasure and commenced to drive her mad.

It did not take long to reach her climax, and Lori was distantly aware that her shouts had to be audible down in the kitchen but couldn't bring herself to care. Each time her inner muscles flexed, the blissful sensation was intensified by having something big and hard filling her.

"Feeling good?" he asked a few moments later, once she had floated back down to earth.

"*Mm-hmm.*"

He kissed her as his hips—which had stilled during her climax—resumed their steady pumping, slow at first, but gradually picking up the pace, each thrust deeper and harder than the last.

Lori groaned when he changed the angle, causing a subtle, delicious friction in exactly the right place

His skin slicked with his exertions and his breathing roughened, but the pounding rhythm of his hips did not falter.

Lori gave herself up to the primal sensation of being so utterly possessed, so completely owned. Within moments, her body was yet again speeding toward the brink, each savage pump ratcheting the need inside her tighter and tighter and—

"You need it harder, don't you, my little temptress?" Fast demanded in a breathless voice. The question made Lori aware that she had bent her knees and was digging her heels into the bed to meet his thrusts.

When she didn't answer, he…*stopped.* "Don't you, Lorelei?" he repeated, his lips curved into a cruel, sensual smile.

She lifted her hips, grinding against him and trying to regain that glorious momentum.

"Beg for your orgasm, Lorelei."

Lori's entire body stiffened. "Wh-what?"

"Beg and I'll give you what you want, my beautiful lover. What you need." His smile grew larger, and she knew it was because her body had—yet again—betrayed her by tightening in response to his erotic mockery.

"You—you—" She lost sight of what she'd been going to say when he slammed in hard enough that she saw white spangles.

She whimpered when he yet again went motionless.

"Eyes on me, Lorelei."

She forced her eyes open and looked into bottomless black pools.

"Beg," he whispered, flexing his thick shaft inside her, the feeling somehow more wicked than his powerful thrusting had been. "Say it. Say *Fast, please give me an orgasm.* When you do, I'll give you everything you need and more."

"I hate you," she hissed.

"I'm waiting," he taunted, moving his hips so subtly it was torture.

Lori gritted her teeth. "Please, Fast—just—just—make me *orgasm,* damn you!"

His hips were in motion before the last word left her mouth and it took scarcely a dozen strokes before she came apart. Unlike the last time, he didn't stop during her climax, but intensified his thrusting, as relentless and pitiless as the surf pounding the shore.

A scant moment later he drove himself deep and shuddered, his shaft swelling inside her as he flooded her with heat. "I love you, Lorelei," he rasped in a wrecked voice, his big body convulsing over and over, the spasms lessening into jerks and then twitches.

Finally, all the tension drained away and his body went heavy and limp. "All mine," he mumbled, the words almost unintelligible, as if it had taken every last bit of effort to utter them.

Lori was reveling in the sensation of being surrounded by hard, hot male when Fast began to lift up on his elbows. "Don't go." She wrapped her arms around his broad back and held him tightly against her, not wanting him to leave just yet.

"But I'm crushing you."

"I like it."

He resisted for only a second and then relaxed with a groan that spoke of bone deep satisfaction. "*Mmmm.* Just a few minutes." The last word was more of a yawn.

Lori smiled as his breathing gradually slowed. Even in her post coital daze she was aware that tonight had been a first for him, that she was the only woman in the world Fast had ever wanted to fill with new life.

The thought brought unexpected tears to her eyes—happy ones—that he'd waited so long. For her.

She pressed her face against the damp skin of his throat, inhaling his heady scent. "I love you, Stand Fast Severn."

Her new husband's answer was a soft snore.

Lori laughed and held him tighter.

The End

Epilogue

London
The King's Purse

Fast cleared his throat and looked up at Lori with an amused, but pained expression. "Er, darling… it's a bit chilly in here. If you wouldn't mind?"

Lori shook herself. "Oh! I beg your pardon," she said, and then quickly, but reluctantly, pulled the wicked black leather counterpane up over his magnificent body, debating whether she could leave his chest and nipples exposed. Just a little bit—enough for her to—

He laughed and her head whipped up. "What is so amusing?"

"When I hinted that I was cold, I wasn't asking you to cover me with a blanket."

"Then—"

"I want your naked body, sweetheart," he said, lifting his hips off the bed—at least as much as he could with both his wrists and ankles bound—his long, thick shaft creating an erotic ridge beneath the leather.

Lori couldn't tear her eyes from the sight, her sex clenching so hard she could feel an orgasm lurking not too far away. How remarkably wonderful was that? Just looking at his covered body was enough to—

"*Loreleiiiii.*"

Again, she looked up. "What?"

He pushed out his lower lip, obviously trying to look pitiful. "That dressing gown is lovely, darling, but won't you remove it, pull this damned counterpane off, and *fuck me* as if you want to *destroy* me?"

Lori's eyes threatened to roll back in their sockets at his words. With her pulse pounding in her ears, she swallowed and reached for the edge of the black leather bedding and then *slowly* pulled it back, peeling Fast's body like a luscious, exotic fruit.

His penis—or cock as he preferred to call it—sprang up with a mute exuberance that startled a laugh out of her.

Fast growled and jerked against the manacles that kept him stretched out and immobile. Every muscle in his big body rippled and flexed. It was…entrancing.

"So, you find my predicament amusing, do you?" he asked.

"Yes."

He snorted. "Witch." He yanked harder on the chains restraining his wrists. "If I had known how you were going to just stand there and torture me rather than—" The words withered on his tongue when she pulled the sash on her new green silk dressing gown and then let it fall to the ground.

Fast's hips bucked up off the bed, a thin stream of clear liquid stranding from the fat crown to his ridged abdomen. "Please," he begged.

She wanted to stare at him for hours—he was utterly mesmerizing—but she wanted to feel him inside her even more, so she clambered up onto the high mattress with more enthusiasm than grace and straddled his hips.

"Yes, that's a good gir—*mercy!*" he yelped when Lori gave his *shaft of delight* a swat.

"You will get what I give you and be grateful for it." Lori said, stroking him hard—but only once—and earning a hiss and shudder.

"Yes. Yes yes yes yes I will," he murmured, aroused rather than chastised, his hips pumping in time with his chanting.

She laughed.

"You are a cruel mistress."

"You love it."

"I do," he said without hesitation.

He was so beautiful—there was no other word for it.

He raised his hips again when she merely gazed down on him, her sex still inches from his thrusting organ. His expression turned adorably petulant. "Lover, are you just going to look all night?"

"I might." Lori enjoyed having such a fine, powerful male animal at her mercy, but—in truth—she was every bit as wet and aroused as he was and so she took his pulsing shaft in her hand and fitted him at her entrance before sinking down with agonizing slowness.

Fast made a noise that sounded as if he were being murdered and Lori was briefly grateful that neither Rufus nor Gregg was posted outside the door.

"Ride me!" Fast barked the moment he was fully hilted.

Lori considered punishing him for his willful behavior, but she wanted him too much. So she dropped her hands to his bulging biceps and used him to steady herself before rolling her hips.

"God yes!"

She couldn't help the laugh that slipped from her mouth at his crazed shout, and her sinuous rhythm—which she'd been quite proud of—faltered.

"You evil, evil hussy," he moaned when she stopped.

"Poor darling," she crooned, smirking at his outraged look. "Is this what you want?" She rocked her hips again, this time not stopping when he moaned his approval.

Lori rode him in such a way that each stroke offered perfect friction, and it did not take long to stimulate herself toward the edge. "Come with me," she said in a breathless voice when she felt him struggle to control his climax.

Fast's hips jerked with the force of his orgasm and together they spiraled into bliss.

***

Fast's orgasm—which he'd been throttling for a good half hour—exploded only a few seconds after Lorelei surrendered to ecstasy. Her hips stuttered and stilled, but her inner muscles carried him over the edge, her tight sheath milking him until he had nothing left to give.

"Oh," she murmured a few minutes later, her body slumped over his, the hard thudding of her heart pounding against his chest.

Fast flexed his softening cock one last time, earning a soft grunt. "Before you fall asleep you need to remove these bloody things." He rattled his chains. "I want to hold you."

She grumbled but heaved herself up and crawled up his body, dragging her belly and then her mons into over his face in the process. Fast laughed and caught the skin just above her thatch of curls with his teeth as she fumbled with the manacles.

"Fast!" she squawked when he bit her.

He released her and licked the reddened skin, using his newly freed hand to pull her closer and tongued her navel.

She shook with laughter as she released his other hand and then tried to wiggle free. "Let me get your ankles."

He reluctantly let her go.

Once she had liberated him, she stretched out alongside him. "I must look a fright," she said, shoving her hair from her eyes.

"You look beautiful," he said, carding his fingers into the wild tangle and gently stroking it off her forehead.

"So do you," she said, mirroring his actions. "It has become quite long—past your shoulders."

"Shall I cut it short?"

"No," she said instantly. "I like it long. It looks…rakish."

He laughed. "I should certainly cut it as I am no longer a rake."

"You are *my* rake."

He leaned in and claimed a kiss. "Such sweet words out of my evil wife! Who would have expected it? So, did you enjoy having me at your mercy?"

She cocked her head and looked thoughtful. "I enjoyed the novelty of it, but I would rather your hands be free. You are so skilled with them."

"I'm glad to hear it. I like to have the use of my hands, too. I think tonight, after dinner, I will tie *you* to the bed." He relished the heat that flared in her eyes.

"And will you beat me with one of those?" She pointed to an especially vicious looking cat o' nine tails.

"I should do after you were just so cruel and naughty to me." He smiled when her lips parted in shock. "In all seriousness, sweetheart, I would never do anything you did not like."

"Would you like it?"

"Would I like using it on you or having it used on me?"

"Oh," she said, nonplussed. "I never even thought about doing that to you."

He chuckled. "Good, because I do not enjoy pain, nor do I derive sexual satisfaction from causing it."

"I do not think I would like it, either," she said after a moment.

Fast kissed the tip of her nose. "I hope you will always make me aware of your likes and dislikes, Lorelei. You needn't feel shy about anything that arouses you. Or anything you think might arouse me." He slid a hand around her head and caressed the taut cords at the base of her neck. "I want to drive you wild with pleasure."

"I want to do the same."

"Finally, something we can agree on."

She laughed. "Surely there must be more than one thing?"

"There is—we both love your book."

***

Lori was so pleased by his words that she was flustered. "I—I didn't want to ask if you liked it," she admitted after a moment. She had given Fast her copy of *Briarly* to read a few days before. "I didn't even know if you had read it."

He tucked a lock of hair behind her ear. "I read it while you were out seeing to your various errands, and when I was supposed to be sorting through my mountain of unanswered correspondence. I had planned to take a peek, but—as Mr. Newcastle said—I could not stop reading once I'd started. You are a brilliant writer, Lorelei."

Lori had to blink rapidly to hold back her tears.

"No weeping," he chided gently.

"Not even happy tears?"

"Well, perhaps a few."

"If you didn't finish your work, does that mean we will stay longer?"

"Perhaps a day or two, if you do not object."

"That would be perfect. I have some questions for Mrs. Marlowe and a few of the others." She hesitated, and then said, "I would also like to see Freddie again."

"Are you hoping she will tell you more about her trip to Brighton?"

"I'm not sure I believe that she went to Brighton."

Fast's eyebrows rose. "Where do you think she went?"

"I don't know. I just—well, I just wish that she didn't keep me at arm's length. I wish I knew more about her past and what she wants for the future. I would just like to know her better. It wasn't until Mr. Gregg asked me so many questions about her that I realized how self-absorbed I've been."

"Gregg asked you about her?"

"Yes." She frowned. "Do you know why he is so interested in her?"

"I don't."

"But you knew he was?"

Fast hesitated. "I did notice that he seemed interested, and I tried to explain that Lady Sedgewick was not the sort of woman who would accept a man like him."

Lori frowned.

"Am I wrong?" he asked.

"That's just the thing: I don't know what sort of man she likes. Or if she likes any sort at all. I wish I knew more about what her marriage was like."

"Sometimes people need to confide in you in their own time, Lorelei. I've known Gregg for sixteen years and I still know nothing of his past. To be honest, I did not tell him about mine until the matter was forced by Joe Jensen arriving in my life." Fast shrugged. "All you can do is be her friend and let her choose the time."

Lori nodded unhappily. "I know. It's just—well, I'm so happy now that I want her to be, too."

"That is a generous impulse, my love. Do you think she would accept an invitation to stay with us at Grandon?"

Lori blinked. "Oh. I'd not thought of that. But don't you think it would be a bad time to invite her?"

"Are you worried my grandfather will not like guests?"

"Well…yes."

"Grandon will be your home, too, Lorelei. My grandfather is not an ogre, you know. Our part of the castle is a house unto itself. You must invite whoever you like, whenever you like. I would only ask for a week or two before we entertain." He hesitated, and then said, "You'd mentioned having a wedding celebration here in London next Season?"

Lori nodded.

"What about having it at Grandon sometime in the next few months?"

"What an excellent idea! Is there enough room? Could we invite everyone?"

Fast chuckled. "There are dozens and dozens of guestrooms."

She grabbed his hand and kissed his palm. "I would adore that—and we could have Jeremy, Sarah, and the girls, too?"

"Of course. I believe I still owe Miss Gwendolyn several hours of reading Miss Fluffington."

Lori gazed wonderingly at the opposite wall, not seeing sexual implements, but a houseful of her loved ones. "We could have a real house party?"

"As opposed to a fake house party, you mean?"

Lori ignored his teasing, her mind already racing.

Fast kissed her. "Yes, my love. We can have a house party of our own—many of them."

She laughed out of sheer giddiness, threw her arms around him, and covered his surprised face with kisses. Already her mind was brimming with excitement at the thought of getting all her friends and family together in her new home.

She would pick a time carefully—so that *all* the teachers from the Stefani Academy for Young Ladies could be together.

Lori could hardly wait…

The End

Dearest Reader:

I hope you enjoyed Fast's and Lori's love story, my final book of 2024! This book was on the back burner for an entire year as I was supposed to have published it LAST December but a nasty bout of Covid laid me low for about two months.

Anyhow, a bit of background on the story…

Lori has popped up in earlier books, but just a little bit here and there, so the only thing I knew about her was that she was…*scrappy* and opinionated.

As for Fast? Well, I was happily writing along on DANCING WITH LOVE when Fast shoved his way into the betrothal ball in that story.

So, that's how this bluestocking and rake story began. And what could be better than a rake with a Puritan name?!

Let's talk about Mr. Gregg…Sheesh! Where the hell did he come from? Yet another character horning in on a book and demanding his turn in the spotlight. Yeah, and he'll get it, too. *Heh, heh.*

I can promise you will be seeing more of him in the final book in the series, THE ETIQUETTE OF LOVE.

But let's talk about this story a bit before I discuss the series concept, and how it came about…

Would Lori really have written a book about a brothel during this era (and found a publisher for it)? Writing about the sex trade wasn't unheard of. *Fanny Hill* came out more than fifty years before the Regency period and features a prostitute's journey, although it was written for titillation rather than education. Of course, the publishers of the book were arrested and the book has been banned FOR CENTURIES believe it or not—the most recent case involving it was 1966.

So, all that sounds like something Lori would definitely enjoy!

The Temple of the Muses, the bookstore I mention early in the book, was a real place and authors really did cruise the stacks to make literary connections.

I used an actual mutiny—the *Hermione* (1782)—in the story but changed the date and name of the ship. The captain was Hugh Pigot and 85 men really died from flogging on his watch.

Stand Fast and Perseverance were Puritan names I stumbled upon while researching New England ages ago and I've always been enchanted by them.

This series has been a long journey, and it isn't finished yet!

The first book—THE MUSIC OF LOVE—was initially titled DANGEROUS MOONLIGHT and was a solo book. It won so many awards when I sent it out to various contests that my agent at the time said, "Can you make this a series?" Because the heroine in that book owned a school for girls the logical choice was to feature the former teachers in subsequent books.

It has been an odd experience writing only one book on the series every year. I won't do it again! It is just too long between books for me to remember all the details I've woven into prior books.

Anyhow, the only character left is Freddie. I have to admit that I feel like she is an old friend as I've visited her every Christmas for five years, lol.

THE ETIQUETTE OF LOVE is on my publishing schedule for the end of January 2025, but it is likely that I will have to push the date back. I apologize to those who have pre-ordered. My brain has been more frazzled than I anticipated these past few months, and I have fallen behind.

As you might have guessed from the epilogue in this book, the background in ETIQUETTE is a house party! I love house party romances and especially ones in which I can bring together so many of my favorite characters.

After ETIQUETTE is KATHRYN, book 6 in THE BELLAMY SISTERS. I'm very excited about her story! I haven't put the last 2 books in that series up for pre-order as I'm vacillating about the order of the stories. Doddy first? Or Lucy? (yes, she's only a sister by marriage, but I have some fun times in mind for her!)

As always, I appreciate you supporting my work! I love hearing from readers and you can always drop me an email at: minerva@minervaspencer.com. I do have a presence on a few social media sites, but—I'll be honest—I feel like Facebook and IG do their best to hide comments in multiple places. I frequently discover messages from readers months afterward and then feel like a toad for not having responded. Also, FB has become so fraught with scammers that I get dozens of spam/bot messages on my author page every day, so messages are apt to get buried. All that is to say that email is best.

I wish you a peaceful and joyous holiday season.

Let's hope 2025 is full of lots of great books!

Xo

Minerva

Who are Minerva Spencer & S.M. LaViolette?

Here is Minerva/S.M. with Mr. Spencer and Lucille (on my lap) trying to wrangle Eva and Winston for a Christmas photo.

Minerva is S.M.'s pen name (that's short for Shantal Marie) S.M. has been a criminal prosecutor, college history teacher, B&B operator, dock worker, ice cream manufacturer, reader for the blind, motel maid, and bounty hunter. Okay, so the part about being a bounty hunter is a lie. S.M. does, however, know how to hypnotize a Dungeness crab, sew her own Regency Era clothing, knit a frog hat, juggle, rebuild a 1959 American Rambler, and gain control of Asia (and hold on to it) in the game of RISK.

S.M. lives with her very own romance hero in the mountains of Northern New Mexico. When she isn't scribbling away on a new story she is playing with her poultry, knitting, beading, sewing, doing one of a dozen crafts, or playing board games with her husband.

S.M. Loves hearing from readers so shoot her an email at:

minerva@minervaspencer.com

Read more about S.M. at: www.MinervaSpencer.com

Follow 'us' on Bookbub:

Minerva's BookBub

S.M.'s Bookbub

On Goodreads